CROSSROADS

The Last Plague

Meja Mwangi

D1524979

HM BOOKS

Published in USA by HM Books
A division of HM Productions Intl.
Columbus - Ohio

First Edition 2008

ISBN 978-1491270721

Cover design by Bonsalles

Contact: info@ hmproductionsinternational.com
www.mejamwangi.com
HM BOOKS

For Mwari wa Njoya, she who had all the answers.

Chapter One

Mzee Musa stepped off the veranda, walked heavily to the middle of the road and stood there scowling at the street. The street was empty but for the solitary old man playing draughts by himself at one of the tables on the veranda, and an old beggar sleeping inside the old phone booth.

Musa coughed and spat hard. The sound of the phlegm landing on the dust woke up the beggar.

"You, old man," he called out. "Give me money."

Musa, ignoring him, took off his prayer turban and scratched his head as he surveyed the street. He had just finished his morning prayer and was in a sad and angry mood. Finally, convinced that nothing had changed in Crossroads since his last inspection half an hour earlier, he slouched back to his veranda and approached the lone player.

Uncle Mark heard him approach, weighed down by sadness and sighing heavily, and continued his one-man game. He heard Musa stop behind him, sighing and sighing again, and let him simmer for a dignified minute before looking up to ask, "How now, old bull?"

"I don't know," said Musa. "I don't know anymore."

"Know what?"

"What?"

"Shall we play?"

"Play?" he asked, disturbingly distracted.

"Draughts?" said Uncle Mark.

"I don't know."

He felt the table with his fingers, as if looking for faults, sighed and said, "I don't know anymore. I should close down. "Go away from here."

"At your age?" Uncle Mark chuckled. "Where would you go?"

"Away," he said. "I don't know anymore."

That part of their morning over, Uncle Mark resumed his game, glancing now and then at Musa's face. Sometimes he could play by himself for hours while Musa watched and brooded.

"How do you do it?" Musa asked him.

1

"Do what?"

"Play by yourself?"

"I pretend I'm two people."

"You cheat yourself," Musa concluded.

"That too," Uncle Mark agreed, smiling his old, bemused smile. "You see, hands have no eyes, so I can move one here under the table, like this, while the other makes a move, like this, and then ... it's all up here, all in the mind."

Musa shook his head, taking it all too seriously, and turned to stare at Crossroads. He was certain of only one thing - Crossroads would drive them all insane before they died of despair. He started feeling the table again, pressing it and kneading it.

"I shall die from sadness."

"That at least would be different," Uncle Mark said, hanging onto the table, to stop him carrying it off into the teahouse. "But it's highly unlikely."

In one of his many lives Musa had been a mason. Crossroads' crumbling architecture was a testimony to his craftsmanship, his determination and his inventiveness. He could truthfully say that he had built most of Crossroads with his own hands, from the teahouse to the Highlife Lodge, from the collapsed petrol station to the derelict post office. Musa had built them all. Now the sight of overgrown buildings, crumbling and falling to ruin, made him feel like weeping.

Was this all that a man's life was about? Was it all that an honest man's labour, his blood and sweat amounted to? Did it all finally add up to rotting beams and broken masonry? Was there no more meaning to life than this? Was there a greater injustice than to live to see one's work mangled and rendered useless by time?

It hurt to see his labour of love, for most people had failed to pay him for it, crumbled to dust. It was more than a man should have to bear. It made him angry.

Uncle Mark watched his fingers dig into the table, squeezing and throttling, as the rage swirled up inside him. Hanging onto the table, Uncle Mark tried to calm him saying, quietly, "There, there now, old bull, don't let us start on that business now."

When he was upset, Musa picked up things and carried them from one place to another for no reason other than that he had to do something. Most of the time he moved the furniture about, arranging and rearranging it optimistically on the veranda hoping it would draw back the customers. By ten o'clock, he would be moving chairs and tables in and out, and in and out, and arranging and rearranging them in all sorts of patterns. By three o'clock he would have bags under his eyes from exhaustion.

Uncle Mark again invited him to a game of draughts. He grunted and shook his head, but he sat down, all the same, and watched Uncle Mark play.

"I shall close down," he said.

Uncle Mark let out a tired old chuckle. He had heard it before, too many times before, and he was certain that Musa would never leave. Like himself, Musa had nowhere to go. He was a Crossroads man. Crossroads men were never happy anywhere else. Like other men, he had left and come back. He knew he was now doomed to live out his life in Crossroads. They would both live in Crossroads forever, unless death intervened.

"Light the fire," he suggested. "Someone will see smoke and come to investigate."

The waiting was wearing him down too.

"Someone will stop by today," he added, trying to sound optimistic himself. "I feel it in my bones."

Musa grunted, sighed again and again. Finally he rose, yawned and slouched off back to his kitchen, where he proceeded to vent his anger on the charcoal brazier, shaking it so violently it shed rust and rivets, and sent a cloud of ashes and charcoal dust drifting out to the veranda, where Uncle Mark sat worrying for the both of them. He heard the racket that Musa made, smelt the ashes and realised it was going to be another long day.

"Something must give," he thought, glancing at the point on the highway where one heart-broken road crossed another.

A group of distraught travellers were huddled together at the old bus stop waiting for a bus to take them away from Crossroads. They had had enough of Crossroads. Their luggage, comprising mostly of sadness and bagged-up despair, said it all.

"Something must change," said Uncle Mark, watching them.

Crossroads was dying. Any old fool could see that.

Uncle Mark was the first to announce the imminent end of Crossroads. He had prophesied it one sunny day, when he felt it approach, thundering down the roads like a runaway locomotive, crashing down everything that lay in its path. He had seen it churn the clouds and felt it shake the earth, and watched in awe as it turned everything upside down; buffeting communities and shattering hopes and dreams, crushing minds and spirits and leaving behind only emptiness and despair.

He had seen it first in a vision, seen it before it hit them, and warned everyone about it, but no one who heard him had understood. Aids had not reared its head in Crossroads yet and not enough residents had been to the places he had been or witnessed the things he had seen. The nearest railway line they ever heard of was hundreds of miles away at Zoa. They had no idea how much havoc a runaway plague could wrack.

Uncle Mark preferred to be thought of as a retired survivor, though it was not clear what he had survived. As far as Crossroads was aware, he had not been to the first war or to the second war. He had not been to the other wars either, but they knew him to be neither a coward nor a fool. The old people were ambivalent about him and called him *kibogoyo*, the wise fool. Women admired him and they, in turn, referred to him as *mzee kijana*, the young, old man. Young people, those who respected him and hoped to grow up to have his style and charisma, called him *ka guy*, the small guy. Others tried to convince everyone that he was really *wa Guka*, a legendary bank robber and the most wanted criminal in the land. That would explain his clothing and his spending habits.

That he had money was not in dispute. As to how much money he had, how he had made it and where he kept it, since there were no banks in Crossroads, no one had any idea. His real worth was as much a puzzle as were his age and his purpose. Much of his past, and most of his present, were perennial topics wherever idlers met to trade gossip.

Whatever he had done in the past, before he stopped doing most things, had left Uncle Mark trim, almost thin, and too fit for his age. It had also left him grey from his hair to his eyebrows, from his moustache down to his hairy arms and chest. But, though he was Crossroads born and bred, there was little that was Crossroads about him. His features were nomadic; some said accusingly, his stature that of a highland peasant and his unhurried gait that of a coastal fisherman. When he laughed his old laugh, which happened often, his body heaved and shook and his eyes danced and he was amusing to see. His language and manners were something else. He was the most sophisticated old man Crossroads had ever known. Women liked him while men hated him, for no specific reason, and children had to stare for a while before deciding he was harmless.

4

Whether they loved him, hated him or suspected him, everyone respected Uncle Mark's opinion. They did not, however, know what to do with him, so most ignored him leaving him to do whatever it was that he wanted to do with his life.

Every morning at seven, he left his ten by ten lodgings at the back of Musa's Teahouse dressed in his dapper suit, shoes and hat, and took his seat on the veranda of the teahouse. The teahouse was just a stone's throw from the old highway, the ragged trail that distraught truckers had renamed the *Hell Run*. He ordered a cup of tea and settled down to watch a town die.

Dying was not new to Crossroads. The place had died before, many times before. One time it had died completely when the new highway shunned it, choosing instead to wander among indifferent strangers, miles away over the hills, among communities that had no cars, no bicycles and no donkey carts, confounded nomads who had no idea at all what on earth to do with their new highway. When rumours got back reporting that the nomads dried their hides and skins on the new highway, heart-broken Crossroads simply died from the outrage. Then more rumours, this time of a gold find somewhere to the north, had revived the old town only to see her die again when the gold turned out to be fools' gold. She had risen and died and risen and died again many times after that; so many times that she had become too good at dying.

But this time it was for good, anyone could see that. This was the one death that not even Crossroads could return from. Only a miracle could raise her from this death, such a miracle was unthinkable among the people of Crossroads. And, because no one would listen to him, Uncle Mark had stopped talking about it. Now he sat alone on the veranda of Musa's Teahouse, playing by himself to kill the time, and waited for Crossroads to finally give up the ghost. It made him angry too.

It angered him to see the town of his youth die such an unnecessary death. Most of the lodgings and the shops and the bars had closed down, moved elsewhere or died in anticipation of death. The post office, the last hope of deliverance, had died too and was entombed in rusty, old iron sheets and weathered chipboard. Only the phone booth remained, like a weary sentinel, keeping vigil over the dead street. The old beggar had claimed it for himself and made it his home.

Uncle Mark watched him emerge from his cocoon-like wrapping of plastic, stretch, yawn and get ready to go to work.

5

"You!" the old beggar called across the road.

Uncle Mark decided not to notice him.

"You, old man!" he yelled, out, refusing to be ignored.

Uncle Mark went on with his game.

"I'm talking to you, Uncle."

"What do you want?" Uncle Mark asked, giving in.

"Give me money."

"Why?"

"I have no money."

"Neither do I."

"Then buy me tea."

"Why me? Why always me?"

"I have no money," said the beggar.

"Go to work."

The beggar leaned back on the phone booth and appeared to doze off.

At the far end of the once lively street, the petrol station lay broken and vandalised. The Mobil Pegasus, once a sign of hope, hovered uncertainly in the air, leaning precariously over the empty street. Two white minarets, all that was left of the old mosque, jutted out of the ruins of the old town, two skeletal fingers pointing skywards in a chilling gesture.

"There," the fingers seemed to say, "there is your judgement."

But Uncle Mark did not care much for judgement today. He had slept poorly and his stomach had grumbled all night from Musa's cooking. In all the years he had lived alone, he had never found it necessary to cook for himself. Recently, however, he had started to wonder if it had not, after all, been a big mistake to believe that cooking was for women and cooks.

The sound of the traffic on the highway, a few hundred metres away, rose and fell intermittently as vehicles passed by unheeded, like the bearers of old news, and Uncle Mark passed time pushing bottle tops on the black and white squares painted on the table.

"Something will have to give," he said, speaking as to the empty street. "Not even death can go on forever. Something must give in the end."

As he uttered these words, the nine o'clock bus arrived from Biri Biri piled high with market goods and passengers. When it pulled away from the bus stop a moment later, the crowd of refugees was gone, leaving three arriving passengers. One of them was a well-dressed young woman, the other two a despairing old couple. Their combined baggage consisted of two huge cartons and a coffin.

Uncle Mark sat up to watch with renewed interest as the young woman took one of the boxes on her head and started across the road.

"Musa," he called out. "She is back."

Musa yelled back something angry, and unintelligible, and went on berating his pots and pans.

As far as Uncle Mark knew, Musa had never married. His work had been his life. The teahouse was his current wife, its contents his children, and he treated them as he would have treated the family he never had. He loved them when he was happy and hated them when he was sad. He sang to them when he was in an exuberant mood, sang them old songs that no one sang anymore, and promised them things. He promised them new dishcloths, promised them new aromatic detergents from Sokoni and softer, gentler scouring pads. But, when he was angry, he swore at the tables and kicked the crockery, hurled kitchen knives at the charcoal brazier and beat up the pans with the ladles. Then he apologised to everything and explained to them why he was in a foul mood. His world was falling apart. He was alone in the world and had no one to turn to. He begged their understanding and promised not to be so angry.

The business of apologising to crockery worried Uncle Mark more than the outbursts.

"Musa?" he called again, as the woman approached.

There was total silence in the kitchen.

The woman came on, her movements firm and graceful in spite of the load on her head, a strong, earthy woman oblivious of the excitement her gait stirred.

"You, auntie," the beggar called out to her. "Give me money."

She crossed the road to the teahouse, paused on the veranda and looked for a place to leave her carton. When their eyes met, Uncle Mark tipped his hat at her. She ignored him and walked into the teahouse to reappear, almost immediately, without the box. Barely glancing at him, she strode back to the bus stop.

Musa emerged from the kitchen, his face streaked with soot and charcoal dust.

"What?" he demanded.

"There," Uncle Mark said, pointing.

Musa followed the finger to the woman walking away to the bus stop, walking at an easy and unhurried pace, but covering the distance with admirable speed. She stepped aside to let the old couple pass, walking slowly down the street with the coffin on their heads.

"Who are they?" Musa wondered.

There was a time he had known, by name and by clan, everyone who passed by his teahouse.

"Are they from here?" he asked himself.

Uncle Mark did not know the old people either. The times had indeed changed. Even the beggar knew better than to ask for alms from people carrying a coffin.

Only Musa had not changed with the times. He refused to be changed by anything, and expected to know everyone who passed by his teahouse, dead or alive. He stepped out onto the street and confronted the old people.

"Greetings," he said to them.

They stopped, startled. People did not intrude in the grief of others with unnecessary greetings. But, finding their way blocked by a morose stranger, they had no choice but to respond.

"Greetings," they said.

They were old and grey, Musa now realised, all gnarled and dried out. They stood, with their pine coffin on their grey heads, and waited for Musa to speak again. Himself lost for words, he turned to Uncle Mark.

Uncle Mark obliged him by rising and taking off his hat. Musa started to take off his cap and discovered he had left it on the kitchen table. He scratched his head instead and made some sorrowful noises deep down in his throat.

"Who are you?" he asked the old people.

The man replied that they were just two old souls with sorrow in their hearts and a load of grief on their heads. Musa scratched his chin thoughtfully. That was not what he wanted to know.

"Who is in the box?" he wanted to know.

"Our son, Thomas," the old woman replied.

Which did not tell Musa what he needed to know either. He scratched his chin and asked, "What happened to him?"

"He died," the old man said, his voice steeped in bitterness.

"Great sadness," Musa said to him.

He did not know what else to say to comfort them. Again, he turned to Uncle Mark. Uncle Mark was busy flicking invisible dust from his hat with his finger.

"He was a big man," the old woman volunteered.

"An important man," added the old man, his voice heavy with anger.

"A Government man," said the old woman, in reproach to his anger. "Thomas was a Government man."

"But he died," affirmed the old man. "Our son, Thomas, died."

Musa scratched his chin again and, again, tried to understand what they were talking about. Why were they telling him all these things, the things he had not asked them, instead of the thing that he wanted to know?

"What killed him?" he had to ask them. "What ate your son Thomas?"

The old woman shook her head. What did it matter? She wondered. Thomas had been her only son. And now he was dead.

"Did Aids kill your Thomas?" Musa asked her.

Thomas had not believed in plagues, the old man revealed, his voice drenched in indignation. Thomas had not believed in anything.

"That is what ate him," he said bitterly.

"Great sadness," Musa mumbled, and again turned to Uncle Mark.

Uncle Mark cleared his throat.

"Why do you bury him alone?" he asked the old couple.

"Who is there to bury him with?" said the old man. "The rogue had no wife or children. He lived alone, all alone like a wild bull."

"Have you no other children?"

"Aids ate them all up," said the old woman.

"Such sadness," Musa groaned with deeply felt sympathy. "Such great sadness."

He stepped aside to let the old people pass, and they carried their grief down the street, with the woman sobbing while the man fumed and ordered her to be quiet.

Chapter Two

Uncle Mark donned his hat. Musa looked despondently up the street as the woman walked back from the bus stop carrying a carton on her head. When she got to where he stood, Musa sighed forlornly.

"Greetings," he said.

On a normal day, she would have scoffed at the gesture and had a mouthful to say in response. Now she simply passed them and carried her carton into the teahouse. They followed her inside.

"What do you have there?" Musa asked, watching her drop the second carton next to the first one.

"Work."

She had a pleasant voice, but she wore her grief like a dark shawl.

They watched her rip the cartons open, watched sort the contents, shifting them from box to box and tossing them in and out with punitive fury.

"Do they really use all these pills?" Uncle Mark asked, trying to tempt her out of her dark mood.

"Ask them," she said tersely.

She was breathing heavily and sweating a little too, and it drove Musa mad. Uncle Mark watched Musa suffer and worried. He wished there was a way he could tell Musa the truth, that he did not stand a chance of ever being Janet's husband.

"So many condoms," Musa marvelled. "Who uses all these things?"

"Men," she told him.

"How?" he asked, genuinely.

"Read," she said, thrusting a box in his hands.

Musa stared at the box. He examined it, turning it in his hands, and decided it did not look like anything.

"You know the old bull can't read," Uncle Mark reminded her. "Maybe you should show him how."

"Show him what?" she turned on him. "What does he need to know about condoms for?"

"Musa is not as old as you think."

He stopped himself suddenly; afraid he had carried the tease a little too far. Janet, however, was not in the least flustered. Taking a condom from the box, she handed it to him.

"Show him yourself," she told him.

Uncle Mark, finding himself thus outmanoeuvred, laughed merrily and said to Musa, "What do you say, old bull?"

"I want her to show me," Musa said, taking the whole thing a little too seriously.

"There!" Uncle Mark handed back the condom. "The old bull has spoken."

"Old bull, indeed!" She dropped it back in the box. "Don't you ever know when it's over?"

"When what is over?" Musa asked her.

On a normal day, her laughter would have split the air like thunder. She did not mind being teased by the old men. She knew it was their way of letting her know that they were on her side. But this was not a normal day, as was becoming evidently clear.

Now Mzee Musa scratched his head thoughtfully and asked her, "Would you like a cup of tea?"

"No."

"What about *mandazi*?" he tried.

"No."

"Not even on the house?" Uncle Mark offered.

Musa turned on him sharply.

"On me then," he said quickly. "What about on me?"

"Not on your life," she told him.

They were at a loss with what to do with her, how else to cheer her up. They watched her finish with her cartons.

"I'll fetch them later," she said to Musa.

"You did not ask me if you could leave them here," he observed.

"Didn't I?" She asked walking out of the teahouse.

They followed her outside.

"What is eating her now?" Musa wondered, as they watched her cross the road.

"Auntie," the beggar tried again. "Give me money."

She disregarded him and walked back to the crossing, stepping as purposefully as ever.

Musa hated to see her in such a mood. He was happy when she came to the teahouse, even when she stopped by just to taunt him and to use the place for her own convenience. She brought with her warmth and vivaciousness that were sadly lacking in the old place. He had never told anyone, not even Uncle Mark his friend and confidant, but Janet was the sole reason he was still in Crossroads.

"A woman should not live alone," he observed quietly.

"She does not live alone," Uncle Mark reminded.

"She needs a man," Musa said, his voice heavy with longing.

"Janet needs a man?" Uncle Mark guffawed. "Like a fish needs a bicycle."

Musa looked up startled.

"What for does a fish need a bicycle?"

"I have often wondered about that myself," said Uncle Mark. "I have heard so much foolishness in my time it amazes me too. But don't let it trouble you, old bull. Don't let it worry you at all."

Musa was not worried about fish with bicycles. He was worried about Janet. He watched her cross the highway, on her way to a home where no man waited for her, sighed and sighed again, deep sighs that rose from his soul.

"I can't live here anymore," he said. "I shall leave this place."

Uncle Mark laughed that tired old chuckle that said he had heard it all too many times before. He too had on occasion considered joining the exodus away from Crossroads, abandoning her to her woeful fate. He had no land, no wife and no children to tie him to the place. There was nothing and no one at all, to bind him to this life of sorrow. But he could not leave Crossroads. He did not expect Musa to ever be able to leave either, but if, by a terrible turn of fate, Musa did leave Crossroads, Uncle Mark would have to pack up and leave too.

"Make some tea," he said. "I could do with a cup myself."

Mzee Musa sighed and considered it. He had woken up the brazier and he had made a fire. It would not do to let the charcoal go to waste. He turned and stalked off to the kitchen.

Uncle Mark glanced at his watch. It was old and solid, with real chrome and real leather, and it did not have a piece of plastic in it. It was a work of art made like the men of old - tough and indestructible. A true symbol of strength and reliability; conceived back when men had time to create beautiful things, by men who understood time and had the intention to conquer it. Men who made watches that would outlast time itself. There would never be another watch like his.

He had had the watch for most of his life. Together, they had survived everything fate could throw his way. From violent mugging in the cities to mangling road accidents on the highways; from raging bush fires down in the Serengeti, where he had once prospected for rubies, to roaring flash floods up in the northern frontiers, where he had panned for gold. Like the owner, the old watch had grown a little slow and a little weary of life. But it had learned to live with that too, like the owner. Time hardly counted in Crossroads, anyway, except on Tuesdays, when the *Far Traveller* came by with his week-old newspapers.

The *Far Traveller* was always on time. Uncle Mark could not understand this, since the old driver did not have a watch. No one worried about what time they got wherever they were going, anyway, and half a day either way meant nothing to inveterate *Far Travellers*.

At ten minutes past ten, Uncle Mark rose from his table, adjusted his hat on his head, brushed his moustache with his finger and, straightening his tie, started for the bus stop.

The bus stop was deserted, as it was every Tuesday morning when the *Far Traveller* passed through Crossroads. It was an express service from Makutano to Kakuma, deep in the northern deserts. And, because it was a once a week service, with no scheduled stopovers anywhere along the way, only Uncle Mark was there to meet the *Far Traveller* when it arrived.

It arrived ten minutes after Uncle Mark, hot and dusty from charging down the old Hell Run, and pulled up in a cloud of dust. Captain Speed, a fellow traveller, from the days Uncle Mark had places to go and reasons to go there, leaned out of the driver's window and handed Uncle Mark a bundle of old newspapers.

"Here you are, old man," he said. "A week old as you ordered."

"And here's your money, old man," Uncle Mark gave it to him. "Half the price, as we agreed."

The Captain put the money in his pocket. That done, they socialised. They did not talk much but they understood each other well, respected each other and conducted their business with dignified forthrightness.

"Let me take you somewhere today, old man," the Captain offered.

"I have no wish to go somewhere today," Uncle Mark told him.

The Captain nodded and asked, "Did you ever find Harar?"

"Harar?" Uncle Mark was a little lost. Then he remembered and laughed, "Oh, that Harar? Harar was with me all along. As were all those other places that I tried to reach. As you know, old man, the world is round."

"So you will never travel again?" the Captain asked, a little worried.

Uncle Mark laughed again, that wise old laugh of his, and said, "That is a possibility I always dread."

Now he did his travelling in his mind, he informed the Captain. And in the old newspapers that the Captain brought him from the world out there. And when he got the burning itch to rise and go somewhere far, he cured it by narrating to Musa of the many incredible places he had been to and of the many and wondrous and impossible things he had done there.

And when he tired of reading old news and telling tall tales to the mesmerized teahouse keeper, he played draughts. And when he tired of draughts, he read and reread the papers. Sometimes he read them out to Musa and sometimes Musa read the pictures for himself and asked for the stories, if he liked the pictures.

He was sitting on the veranda perusing the new batch of old papers when Musa emerged from the teahouse, looking distraught and in dire need of encouragement and sat down opposite him. He let out an old sigh, heavy with despair.

"What now, old bull?" Uncle Mark asked him.

"Nothing," he sighed.

Uncle Mark folded his papers and offered a game of draughts. Musa declined and Uncle Mark offered to read the newspapers to him, instead.

According to *The People* newspaper, a terrible earthquake had wiped out an entire village in Honduras and killed six thousand people.

"Imagine that!" Uncle Mark said. "Six thousand men, women and children, old and young, all gone, just like ..."

"Where is Honduras?" Musa asked.

"Quite faraway," Uncle Mark told him.

Closer to home, an overloaded ferry had capsized in Lake Nyanza and drowned all the six hundred people on board.

"What is a ferry?" Musa asked agitated.

"You have never seen a ferry?" Uncle Mark asked. "A ferry is a big, big boat-like thing that goes on water. Like ... like a bus on water."

Talking of which, even closer home, a bus plying the Hell Run between Sokoni and Maili Kumi, via Crossroads, had broken its kingpin and plunged into the murky Black River, drowning all the sixty people on board.

"What is kingpin?" Musa wanted to know.

"Kingpin?" Uncle Mark thought. "A kingpin is ... a thing that buses have."

He saw how he was confounding, and distressing, his old friend and stopped. He perused the paper, looking for scandalous features and photographs of women with curvaceous bodies for Musa to marvel at. He found only disasters and calamities.

One report stated that *wa Guka*, the country's most famous bank robber, had eluded the police again and robbed three banks and shot dead three policemen, before heading north from Pwani.

No one knew the notorious criminal's real name. No one, not even the police gunmen looking to shoot him dead, knew what he looked like. The photographs they had retrieved from his wives showed four different men and baffled the wives as much as they baffled the police. *wa Guka* had never been reported to be wearing any disguise during his bank raids, yet he had eluded capture for so long that his many admirers believed he would never be caught.

"What do you think, old bull?" Uncle Mark asked.

Musa was not an admirer. The fate of gangsters and policemen did not interest him in the least. Uncle Mark put the newspaper aside and wondered what to do next. He wondered if he should go back to bed or visit one of his widow friends. Musa did not care either way. His day was ruined before it had begun. All his days seemed that way.

Another bus stopped at the crossroads to disgorge another load of coffins and their bearers. Musa watched the coffin bearers pick up their burdens and take them home.

"Don't despair, old bull," Uncle Mark said to him. "Even this will pass away. All things must come to an end."

"When?" he demanded.

"When?" Uncle Mark chortled. "When all the gourds of wrath have been emptied and the calabashes put out to dry."

"When?"

"When the wine of calamities has been drunk to the full," Uncle Mark told him. When all those who have to die have died and the gnawing of tongues and gnashing of teeth has stopped. When the cursing and swearing have ceased and the mourners have gone home. When all the burial places are full, then it will cease."

Musa regarded him with consternation.

"This is the time of tribulations," Uncle Mark revealed, announcing it in the lofty manner of a zealous, barefoot, market preacher from the Crossroads of old. "The time of moaning and groaning; the time of squirming and thrashing about in endless torment. The time of relentless and unmitigated grief, exactly as was promised by the prophets of old."

Musa was staring at him, mouth hanging open like a hyena with a bone stuck in his throat. On normal days, Musa barely understood half the things Uncle Mark articulated. Today, Uncle Mark was not making any kind of sense at all.

"These are but the birth pangs of the Apocalypse," Uncle Mark informed. "The dawn of our seasons of agony."

Musa rose quietly and fled back to his kitchen.

The land laboured under the enormity of its grief.

Along the dusty highways, hearses of every nature and description groaned under the weight of their grief. Battered lorries and pick-up trucks and buses, heavily laden with coffins and mourners and hung with red ribbons, chugged along, creaking and complaining and steaming at the radiators; their overburdened engines about to give up and die themselves.

And along the country roads and the footpaths and the cattle trails that snaked across the highway like living things, and divided and entangled the land in a troubled spider's web, ox-wagons and donkey carts, loaded with coffins and hung with red flags, dutifully delivered their cold burdens to the gaping holes that awaited them in every village and in every hamlet and in every homestead all over Crossroads.

There were burial mounds everywhere one turned; large, brooding things, darkly vibrant with death, and there was hardly a single homestead in Crossroads that did not host one, or two or three or more, of these terrible reminders of the futility of man. And where there was one today, tomorrow there would be two. Two became four and four became eight. They grew, they

16

multiplied and they mutated. They turned into monsters; hungry beasts with insatiable craving for human life.

They grew and grew and spread until there was no room left for them to expand. Then they spilt over the burial plots and the farm boundaries and reached out to eat up more homesteads and their homesteaders. They consumed the homesteaders, chewing them up and spitting them into the graves, till the last member of the family had been buried; hastily thrown into the yawning graves by fearful neighbours and, just as quickly, covered with the earth. Only then did the ferocious mounds, their number complete, cease. Then grass and weeds grew over them all, obscuring the wreaths, the headstones and the crosses and every single reminder of who lay beneath the earth, and everything returned to bush.

In time, the walls and the fences crumbled too and the sheepfolds and cattle pens rotted away and broke down, and the livestock strayed and were hunted down and devoured by wild animals and stray dogs. Then the deserted homesteads were taken over by the rats, the snakes and the ghosts, and a deathly veil of silence fell over the broken granaries and the empty cattle enclosures, and it was terrible to hear.

Like the mounds, the black homesteads themselves grew too and encircled and devoured everything in their path and threatened to take over the entire earth. Everywhere one cast a woeful eye, there was a dark homestead, dead or in the throes of death. Dark brooding places where the human spirit had suffered its final, devastating blow and despair had triumphed.

The living lived in awe of these places, and hurried past them with averted eyes and were afraid to awaken the ancient curses and angry spirits that had vanquished their former occupants; the relentless reaper who knew no mercy and harvested the ripe and the green alike and consigned them to his earthen granaries.

The women dressed in mourning, wailed and tore at their hair and buried their men folk. But in time they too died and were buried by their grieving children. And when the children too died, one by one, they buried one another, until the last of them had died. Then the neighbours came, gathered fearfully at dusk, to bury whatever the stray dogs and the wild animals had not eaten up.

The homesteads were left dark like graves, shrouded in death and gloomy desolation and issuing their threat of death, and their assurance of more death, like deadly fumes from a putrid swamp.

17

People avoided them like an affliction and talked of them only in whispers. But, when they could no longer bear to live with the fear, the boys crept out in the night and torched the abandoned houses and scattered the vermin that infested them back into the bush; along with the old demons and the angry spirits and their ancient burdens that were said to bind them to the place.

These ancient entities then went on to waylay unwary and ignorant people and to follow them home and to lay their homesteads to waste also, and it seemed there was no cure to it.

But it was to this Crossroads, to this land of death and despair, that everyone returned when they died, or when they thought that they were about to die.

Chapter Three

The bus that brought Frank Fundi back to Crossroads disgorged him at the bus stop one hot and dusty afternoon; spat him out by the roadside like a bitter seed, and sped away shuddering with the awe of the place.

He stood still, eyes closed, and held his breath, until the dust raised by the fleeing bus had settled. Then he picked up his cardboard suitcase from the ditch, where the conductor had dumped it and dusted it. It was a simple and ordinary case, and it contained all his worldly possessions; three dog-eared books, tomes of modern veterinary medicine, two changes of clothes and a spare pair of shoes. That was all that Frank Fundi brought back to Crossroads after many years of absence.

He was twenty-seven years old, long-faced and stoop-shouldered, from the terrible burdens he had had to carry. A great deal had happened to him during that time, and he had grown older and wiser and harder and many things besides, but that was as it should have been. No one returned the same person that they were when they left home.

As he crossed the old highway into town, he realised that Crossroads had changed too. The joyous town of his youth had aged, and done so badly. The walls had caved in, the roofs had collapsed and the streets were lined with piles of rubble from countless dead buildings; mountains of crushed masonry and heaps upon heaps of decomposing dreams. Crossroads lay still and despondent like a disease-ravaged animal, hopeless and despairing, an affliction-ridden creature whose resistance to infections had finally and decisively collapsed.

While crows watched from the broken rooftops, dust chased plastic bags down the dead street and an old hen scratched in the dust outside the teahouse. Dark smoke issued reluctantly from the leaning chimney on Musa's Teahouse. It was the only sign of habitation. From afar came the faint throb of a funeral drum.

As Frank Fundi made his way down the road to the only building that appeared alive, the old hen saw him and ran into the teahouse, terrified.

"You, Bro," hailed the beggar. "Give me money."

19

Uncle Mark looked out of the window and saw the stranger stop, startled by the beggar's greeting.

The stranger reached into his pocket and gave the beggar a handful of coins. The beggar glanced at the money and observed that it was not enough to buy him a cup of tea. The stranger gave him a few more coins and remarked that it was more than he could afford.

"Where is everybody?" Uncle Mark heard him ask.

"Everybody?" asked the beggar.

"The people," the stranger said. "Where are they?"

"Funerals," the beggar answered. "That is where they all are."

"All of them?" the stranger asked.

"All of them?" the beggar's laughter woke up the street. "I don't know about all of them. But they must be there too, for they are not here."

Frank picked up his suitcase, without another word, and crossed to the teahouse.

The teahouse was exactly as he remembered it; the interior was taken up by the long tables and the rough benches, but the glass counter that once displayed *mandazi* and home made cakes was now empty and covered with dust. And the place was deserted. In the old days, the teahouse had throbbed with life, men relaxing after a hard day's work, playing draughts, laughing and telling long tales that no one believed. Frank remembered killing many an idle afternoon here, playing with the old men, arguing politics and drinking buckets of Musa's unpredictable tea.

Only one old man remained now, sitting exactly as Frank remembered him, in his incongruous suit and hat, and it seemed he had not moved at all in the years Frank had been away.

"Musa," the old man called out to the kitchen, when Frank entered. "What did I tell you? You have a sorry-looking one now."

"What does he want?" Mzee Musa shouted back.

"You'd think he would be the first out with the welcome dance," Uncle Mark said, with a happy chortle. "But don't mind him, he'll be here in a moment. Sit down."

Frank placed his suitcase on the bench and sat down beside it.

"What does he want?" Musa called again from the kitchen.

"Tell him," Uncle Mark said to Frank.

Frank looked at the old menu painted high up on the wall. It was now streaked with soot.

"What has he got?" he asked.

"What have you got?" Uncle Mark called out to the kitchen.

"What does he want?" Musa asked, impatiently.

Frank raised his voice and called, "Musa."

"What?" Musa called back.

"Do you have *masala* tea?" he asked.

There followed an ancient and uncertain silence. Uncle Mark laughed quietly and said, "You don't want to ask Musa such old questions now; this is a new place, with new furniture and all."

"Musa," he called out to the back. "How about some tea. And make it fast, before we change our minds and go somewhere else."

"There," he said to Frank. "That ought to hurry him up a little."

Then he laughed again, a dusty old cackle with no mirth at all, and observed, "This is not his day at all."

"Did he ever have a good day?" Frank wondered.

"Oh, yes, indeed," said Uncle Mark. "Three months ago, a bus-load of Americans ate here. They were lost, I believe, and could not count, and paid Musa more money than he could count himself. And only last month, a traveller came in to ask for directions and stayed to have some tea. So, you see, it's not all dark and gloom here. Still we do miss the old days, when the place was so full of customers that Musa could toss some out. Those were the days, indeed."

He fiddled with the bottle tops. Frank watched him lay them down, half facing up, the other half facing down.

"Last I heard," the old man said with a chuckle, "you were on your way to America to further your education. Isn't that what they said in those old days? Going away to further your education."

"I never went," Frank said.

Uncle Mark paused, waited for the story to begin.

"It's a long story," Frank said to him.

He finished laying down the tops and motioned Frank to make his move.

"Let's see if you gained anything from your roaming," he said to him.

Frank moved. He had no hope of winning. He had not played draughts in ages. No one, it seemed, played the game outside Mzee Musa's teahouse. Uncle Mark, on the other hand, had had a lifetime of experience. Ever since retiring from whatever, and deciding he had no desire to be a peasant, he had done nothing but play draughts at the teahouse.

Frank watched him make his moves and tried to remember how he had countered those moves.

"You've lost much weight," Uncle Mark observed.

Frank nodded. He had lost all joy too, and most of hope, and he was a sad and wretched man.

"How long are you back for?" Uncle Mark asked.

As he thought of an appropriate answer, Mzee Musa came out with a huge, black kettle and two tea glasses. He uttered a gruff greeting and poured the tea and was about to withdraw to the kitchen when he registered Frank's presence.

"Son of Mateo," he said to him. "So you have come back at last."

"I have," Frank replied.

"When did you finish school?"

"I did not," Frank said.

"Why?" Musa wanted to know.

"It's a long story," he told him.

Mzee Musa placed the kettle on the table, crossed his arms, and waited for the story to begin. Time was something Musa had a lot of.

Frank was about to start narrating the story of his life when Janet rode up, in a whirlwind of noise and motion, and interrupted the proceedings. She had a huge, man-sized bicycle, with a full crossbar and a carrier cage in front. Men had laughed at her when she first received it from the ministry, and expressed their awe and wonder at how foolish a ministry could be, to expect a woman to ride on a man's bicycle. Then they had called her shameless when, instead of sending the abomination back to the Government at once as expected, she had simply mounted it and ridden it, just as a man would have done. In time, many had come to accept it as inevitable, and to admit to themselves, albeit grudgingly, that there was not much that a man could do that a woman could not do too.

There was nothing womanly in the way Janet rode her bicycle or the way she hopped off, before it had fully stopped, and leaned it on the wall of the teahouse, under the very sign that prohibited it.

"You!" Musa called out at once. "Don't you read?"

He knew at once it was her from the way she arrived, in full force like an army of Amazons, the way the earth shook under her footsteps and the way her aura preceded her by a moment before she stamped into the place.

"Greetings," Uncle Mark called out cheerfully. "Your boy has already picked up the other carton."

She ignored him too. All of Crossroads knew that she had a pathological aversion to lecherous, old bullocks and men who lived alone without women. Men who had no purpose in life, other than to lead a quiet life while their world broke to pieces about them. She loathed and detested the whole perverted herd of them.

"Greetings," Frank called out to her.

She had come expecting to find the old men alone and she stopped suddenly on seeing him.

"What are you doing here?" she asked him.

"I'm back," he told her. "How and why is a long story and you are in a hurry."

"She is always in a hurry," Musa complained. "She is always in a hurry."

Janet ignored him and went after her carton. Frank rose to help her carry it outside and the old men exchanged worried glances. In all the years they had been in Crossroads, and in all the numerous occasions that she had left her wares at the teahouse, it had never occurred to either of them that Janet might need any assistance from any man to do anything, least of all to carry her cartons to her bicycle. She had never asked for their help, or in any way indicated that she needed any, and they had never offered it, and they had all happily coexisted, under the wise, old adage that stipulated that no elephant was ever too weak to carry its own tusks. Now they watched with amazement, as Frank helped her carry the carton, and wondered what sort of a dimwit he had turned out to be.

"How are your people?" they heard her ask him, as she secured the carton on her bicycle.

"I haven't seen them yet," they heard him tell her.

"Walk with me then," they heard her say to him. "You can tell me what happened to you on our way home."

Frank hurriedly paid for the tea and said goodbye to the startled old men; and he could not understand their sudden silence as he took his suitcase and walked with Janet out of Crossroads and along the overgrown cattle trails that led to the farmlands west of the old highway.

"Why have you come back?" Janet asked him.

"This is my home," he said.

The landscape was exactly as he remembered it. Vast and green and throbbing with expectation. Women worked hunchback in their fields as before, and children grazed their sheep by the roadside, but many of the farms were wild and overgrown and frightening to look at. An eerie silence hovered over the whole land, but the hills were grey, exactly as he remembered them, and the sky was blue and sprinkled with fluffy clouds that spoke of many more sunny days, and it felt good to be home.

"Don't let the season fool you," Janet warned, watching him take gluttonous breaths of the fresh country air. "The land may be green and the crops may thrive, but the people are dying and the land with them."

"People die everywhere," he reminded.

"But no one dies like here," she said to him.

No one could perish like in Crossroads, she informed. Grave digging had replaced hoeing and, where once they had dug holes and planted yam and cassava, now they planted people. Their own people, young and old, men and women and children. Planted them deep in the ground without hope of ever harvesting anything but more sorrow.

From the distance came the thud-thud of a funeral drum, rising and falling as the wind blew it over the hills and down the valleys.

They walked on in uncomfortable silence, a silence heavily pregnant with harrowing questions and distressing answers. A woman saw them pass by her field and ran to the fence to talk to Janet.

"Janet, have you got those things?" she asked.

"What things?" Janet asked her. "Condoms?"

"The other things," she said. "The *dawas*."

Her arms were covered with wet soil to the elbows and she was sweating from the heat. Frank held the bicycle while Janet rummaged in the carton for a packet of pills. Meanwhile, the woman looked Frank up and down and wondered if she knew him.

"He is the son of Mateo," Janet told her.

"I knew I had seen you before," the woman said to Frank. "You can't remember me, I was very small in those days. Even

Janet was ahead of me in school. But she doesn't grow old, does she? You see how young she looks, like a girl. Because she has no husband to wear her out."

Her full and vigorous laugh echoed across the fields, and Janet smiled and assured her that looks had as much to do with the number of children a woman had as with the nature of the man she had for a husband.

"You know men too well," the woman said to her. "That is why you are always unhappy."

They left the woman to her labours and pushed on.

"It's true she was behind us in school," Janet confirmed. "A fresh and lively young thing, full of dreams."

Now she was just another old and bitter woman, with numerous mouths to feed, eking a living out of an unforgiving land.

Janet's own bitterness was hard to conceal as they walked for a moment in uncomfortable silence, along overgrown trails bordering abandoned fields and overgrown broad bean hedges. From up ahead came the sound of drums. It was not the dark thud-thud and thud of a funeral drum but the frenzied rhythm of ritual drums.

They were walking along the side of a gentle hill. Across the valley were numerous overgrown homesteads, dark and still structures, monuments to the death and despair that had taken root in Crossroads.

"See that one over there?" Janet pointed to an old ruin, partly hidden in the trees, which was all that was left of a once grand estate, now overwhelmed by weed and bush and slowly choking to death on bougainvillaea that had gone mad from neglect.

"A rich man lived there," she said to Frank.

The garden bristled with gravestones, an entire clan having perished there in that big house. No one had survived to tend to the graves.

"And over there," she pointed to another hill. "The same thing happened there."

Only one very old woman remained to care for her grandchildren.

"And over there ... and there and there."

Frank's heart was weighed down by her sorrow, a cold sadness that grew heavier with every dead homestead they passed.

The grief grew until it was like a drum beating inside his head and he started to sweat.

They ran into the drummers round a bend in the road, where the road narrowed into the bridge. There was no room to stand aside and let the drummers through. Janet and Frank stopped in the middle of the road to let the drummers and accompanying dancers stream past them. The circumcision party was led by a wild-eyed man, in a leopard skin cape and ostrich feathered headgear. He stopped abruptly on seeing Janet.

"Is that you, my sister?" he asked her.

She barely heard him over the drums.

"Who is this hungry man?" he asked of Frank.

Janet smiled and said to Frank, "You remember Kata Kataa?"

Kata Kataa was an herbalist, diviner, fortune-teller and, some said, medicine man. He was also the only surviving traditional circumciser in Crossroads. Many feared him, including some who claimed to be free from traditional beliefs and superstitions.

"I don't remember this one," he said, scrutinizing Frank suspiciously. "Is he from here?"

"Frank Fundi," she said. "The son of Mateo."

"The one who went to America?"

"The same one."

Kata had been the chief guest at Frank's *harambee* party. He had spoken loudly and eloquently to let everyone know that he had sold three goats and a calf to send Frank to America. In the traditional spirit of *harambee,* everyone had contributed something towards Frank's further education, but none as generously as Kata.

"I gave a lot of money," he reminded Frank. "When did you return?"

"He didn't go," Janet informed.

"Why not?" he asked Frank. "Why didn't you go to school?"

"It is a long story," Frank said.

"Come to my house and tell me there," said Kata. "We have not had a cow doctor here since you left us. Has she told you my brother died?"

"Solomon, the preacher," Janet said to Frank.

Solomon had been an assistant to Pastor Bart for many years. Then he had defected to Makutano to set up his own church there and died there.

"He just died," said Kata. "My brother just died. "Come to my house to see to my cows and we shall talk."

He had been circumcising boys over that hill there and now he was going to the next hill. Tomorrow he would be somewhere else making men out of boys. By the end of the season, not a single boy would be left uncircumcised. He signalled to the drummers. The drums came to life and the procession throbbed down the road.

"Now he inherits his brother's wife," Janet said bitterly. "He could not be happier."

Frank did not understand the bitterness in her voice. They came to a fork in the road. Janet's home was a few hundred yards to the right, her roof visible over a hedge.

"Come in for some tea," she said to him.

"Another time," he told her.

He was still a mile or so from home and he had to let his people know that he was back.

"Go well then," she said.

She pushed her bicycle away and he watched her go. Had she perhaps realised the reason for his returning? He worried about it all the way home.

Chapter Four

Janet Juma's compound comprised of a three-bedroom house, a grain store and a chicken house. It was simple and clean, and it had none of the clatter of chicken, goat and cow enclosures that crowded Crossroads' homesteads.

A short distance from the house, in a partly overgrown field, was Janet's old house, one that her missing husband had built for her. The roof had caved in, and the doors and windows had been taken down and used for the new house. The old ruin was a source of constant pain and regret for Janet, and many a time she had thought of demolishing it or burning it to the ground. However, she lacked the courage and the strength to make the final break with her past. Deep in her heart, deep down there where old ghosts dwelt, there also lingered the last traces of hope and the unreasonable expectation that her husband Broker would one day come home, as mysteriously as he had left, and pick up the pieces of their life together from where he had dropped them.

She stood in her yard, lost between contemplating the old ruin and organising her inventory of the condoms and pills, when Big Youth arrived. He was a big youth, a little too big for his age, and he was quick and almost too resourceful. Orphaned by cholera at the age of five, he had been brought up by his grandmother and taught to fend for himself from an early age. His real name was Jacob, but everyone called him Big Youth. He stopped by Janet's house from time to time on his way to and from school to help her with her chores.

"You will be late for school," she worried.

"I'll run," he promised.

She showed him what to do. All he had to do was to empty some cartons and fill up others. It was a simple task that he had performed numerous times before. Then she forgot about him and returned to her worries, sighing and clucking her tongue.

"What is it?" Big Youth asked her.

"Nothing," she said opening another carton for him to work on.

She moved slowly and tiredly like some of the people he had seen lining up at the old hospital before it closed down. She stopped to listen. He listened with her and, when the wind changed directions, heard wailing and the dry thud-thud of a distant drum.

"Just a funeral," he said to her.

She resumed her work and he continued to worry about her. She had a quiet anger, which sometimes erupted in a verbal tirade to which no one, not even her closest friend was immune. Watching her, he wondered what had happened. She looked up and caught him staring at her.

"Our teacher died too," he reported.

"You told me," she said curtly.

"Not that one," he said. "Another one."

His school had lost three teachers and some students. Everyone was afraid to die but did not know what to do about it.

"I'll go away from here," he said. "I will go far, faraway from here."

"And leave your grandmother?" Janet wondered.

"I'll take her with me."

"Take her where?"

For all his size and his resourcefulness, Big Youth was as simple as the rest. He had never been out of Crossroads and, like most youths, thought paradise was at the other end of the highway.

"You'll not get a job," Janet said to him.

"I am too tired of sadness."

"So are we all," she told him. "The whole people are tired of funerals."

She looked up suddenly, as a woman came rushing through the gate.

"I can't stay," she said to Janet. "I come for those things?"

"Greetings," Janet said to her. "Greetings first, Hanna."

"Greetings," she laughed. "I forgot I have not seen you today. Where have you been?"

Hanna Habari lived three plots down the road from Janet. She visited often, bearing some gossip and a good laugh. They said her laugh could light a gloomy day; a clean and honest laughter of someone who found most things hysterical. But Hanna was also always in a hurry, rushed by her many children, and by the crops in her *shamba* and a husband who was impossible.

"He doesn't give up and the last one is just learning to stand," she complained often to Janet.

"Make him wait?"

"Make him?" she laughed her genuinely amused laugh. "This is why I like coming here, Janet, you make me laugh. Did your husband ask you whether you wanted a baby?"

"He never thanked me for any of them," Janet said.

"He just keeps them coming," said Hanna. "The only time he'll worry about their numbers is when there is a dowry to be paid."

Then she noticed Big Youth and her demeanour changed.

"What are you doing here?" she asked harshly.

"He helps me with the boxes," Janet said, handing her a box of pills.

"Give me more," Hanna said. "I don't want to be like Naaman's wife. Do you know she is expecting again? Her last is still crawling, her husband has gone off to find a job and she is alone with the children in her big house. Janet, you don't know how lucky you are to be without a man. I don't know what God had in mind when he made men."

"Someone to build houses," Big Youth volunteered.

"How many have you built?" she asked him, tersely.

"I'm not married," he said.

"Then be silent, when women are talking," she ordered him. "Men are just there to make women sick."

"And to drive buses," he said.

"You must shut your mouth now," she said, irritated. "I did not come here to talk to you."

Then she noticed that Janet's thoughts were drifting.

"You are sad again," she said to her.

"Just tired," said Janet.

"Where is Grandmother? To whom is she marrying you today? I hear that the new Police Chief is not even married. You know Janet, if I was you I'd do something with my life."

"Do what?"

"Stop sitting here worrying and … I'll tell you when I'm not in a hurry. Stay well now."

"Go well," said Janet.

"Go to school," Hanna said to Big Youth. "You will grow up to be useless like your father."

She was hardly out of the gate when Grandmother came through the gap in the fence that separated her compound from Janet's. She walked slightly bent, weighed down by age and by the fatigue of life. She was leaning heavily on a bamboo cane and holding on to the hand of little Jeremiah, an orphan boy she had inherited from a neighbour.

Big Youth greeted them heartily. The boy smiled back, but Grandmother ignored him as she cast her old eyes here and there in search of unhappiness. Finally, she found it in the dust in the yard, and scowled at Janet.

"Whose footprints are these?" she asked, pointing with her cane.

"Mine," said Big Youth.

"You don't wear shoes," she said harshly.

"Oh, those?" laughed Big Youth. "Those are Hanna Habari's shoeprints."

"These are a man's footprints," said Grandmother. "I heard a man's voice here last night."

"You must have been dreaming again, Grandmother," Janet said to her. "No one came here last night. No one visits me at night."

Grandmother grunted and cast her eyes about.

"Why is he here?" she asked of Big Youth.

"I'm always here," he said, with a grin.

"Don't show me your rotten teeth," she said, raising her cane to strike.

Big Youth jumped back out of the way.

"Would you like some tea?" Janet asked her.

Grandmother continued her inspection of the yard, touching this and touching that and tapping things with her cane. She poked it into a carton of condoms and stirred, clucking her tongue with disapproval as she did so. She looked inside Janet's doorway and shook her head again.

Janet let her see for herself that there was no man in the house, before speaking to her again.

"I want to talk to you about Julia," she said.

"Talk about yourself," Grandmother said, sullenly. "You don't have a man of your own. What are you doing about it?"

Janet, deciding not get angry, asked her again, "Would you like some tea?"

She had not come to have tea, she announced. She had come to talk about Janet.

"Would you like to sit down?" Janet asked her.

Grandmother turned on Big Youth instead and demanded, "Have you no home to go to?"

31

"He is on his way to school," Janet told her. "Would you like to sit down?"

She had not come to sit down, she said.

"Why have you come?" Janet asked.

But the old woman could not get Big Youth out of her mind.

"You will be late for school," she said to him.

"I have time," he said, smiling irritatingly.

"You don't."

"Ask Janet."

"Why do you want your sister to be like you?" she asked Janet.

"Her husband is dead," Janet reminded.

"Why do you want her to abandon his family?"

"I don't want her to abandon them," Janet said to her. "But her brother-in-law died from the plague."

"I knew," said Big Youth.

"You knew that?" even Janet was surprised. "How?"

"How?" demanded Grandmother.

"Faru's brother also died from Aids," Big Youth informed them. "And that other man from the Chief's place, the one who beats his wife on Sunday, he too died. And the man with the donkey cart, he has Aids."

"You know too much," said Grandmother, silencing him with a wave of her cane. She had slept badly and dreamt terrifying dreams, she confessed to Janet, as she brooded and mumbled to herself. She was angry about most things in Crossroads, but today she was most angry with God. How could God just sit and watch as the plague, dwarfed everything, made living impossible and mocked life? How many people would have to perish before God did something about it?

"God has nothing to do with it," Janet told her.

"Why doesn't He stop it then?" she asked, indignant.

"Because we refuse to see," Janet informed her. "It's easier to believe the plague is witchcraft than to see it for what it is, a disease."

"A disease that doesn't fear medicine?"

"A disease that doesn't fear anyone."

Grandmother grumbled unhappily and said that she had not come to talk about the plague. She had come to talk about other things, more important things. She resumed her mumbling and tapping at things with her stick.

"I have seen plagues," she said.

32

She had survived famines and disease epidemics. She had been knocked down by earthquakes and swept away by floods. She had seen death, lived through sad times and was not afraid.

"I'm tired of worrying about you and the children," she said. "You must get married."

"Again?"

"A real man," she said. "Someone who can take care of you and your children. A real man."

"In Crossroads?" Janet scoffed.

"Crossroads is full of men," Grandmother told her.

"Men who can't take care of themselves, let alone their women," Janet reminded.

Even Grandmother agreed with her on this sometimes. She had once, in a moment of clarity, observed how unfair it was of God to have given her Crossroads, a land of men with large beer stomachs and bloated egos. She belonged in the land beyond the hills, where men killed lions with their bare hands to protect their women. That was where all women belonged.

But such moments of defeated rationality were rare for Grandmother. Most days she was bitter and contradictory, even going as far as to argue that a half a man was better than no man at all, as long as he stayed home where he belonged. It was up to their women to make lion-eaters out of rat-eaters. Thus, it was up to Janet to find herself a man, no matter how puny, and make a giant of him.

But Janet was not ready for any more of that. She had wasted a near lifetime trying to make a man out of a rogue buffalo and had no wish to repeat the experience. Never again would she lie awake at night worrying about a man.

Grandmother grumbled. Men liked Janet, and even Chief Chupa liked her and he was the richest man in Crossroads. Janet reminded her that the Chief had three wives and children to look after. He had more than enough to worry about.

Grandmother refused to accept defeat and looked about for something to vent her anger.

"You go to school," she barked at Big Youth. The things she had come to say were not for his ears.

Big Youth smiled and stayed.

"You can't go on living like this," she said to Janet. "I will not allow it."

Janet tried to appease her by explaining that she was contented and did not need a man to complete her happiness. She was still trying when Frank arrived, looking as unhappy as the old woman, and walked to the middle of the yard.

"What do you want?" Grandmother asked him.

Frank stopped, so startled by her hostility that he was lost for words. She scrutinised him from head to toe and turned to Janet.

"Do you know this one?"

"You know him too," Janet said to her. "He is the son of Mateo."

"The son of Mateo?"

"The one who went away."

Grandmother squinted at Frank.

"When did he come back?" she asked Janet.

"He did not go," Janet informed her.

"He didn't go?" she had finally found something real to be angry about. "We gave a lot of money. Why didn't he go?"

"It's a long story," said Frank.

"We sacrificed for you," she railed at him. "What happened to all the money we contributed?"

"I'll give it back," he said to her. "I'll give it all back."

That did not make her happier.

"Mateo was a good man," she grumbled. "Your father was an honest man."

He was an honest man too, Frank said to her, and he would pay back the money as soon as he could. But it was not the money that made her unhappy. It was the realisation that nothing was certain anymore, that no one could be relied on anymore. It made her angry.

"You go to school," she ordered Big Youth. "You will end up useless like your uncles."

"Which uncles?" Big Youth asked, genuinely startled for he had no uncles.

"The chicken thieves who don't let women sleep in peace at night," she said to him. "Don't tell me you don't know who they are, maybe you are one of them. Come, Jeremiah, give me your hand."

The boy took her hand. Janet and Frank watched them go, the old woman complaining how nothing was the same anymore.

"She wants Janet to marry the Chief," Big Youth said to Frank.

"Go to school," Janet suddenly said, tossing his bag at him.

"We have not finished."

"We'll never finish," she said to him. "Go to school."

Big Youth picked up his bag and headed for the gate and Janet turned to Frank.

"You don't look so happy yourself," she told him. "Sit down and have some tea."

He sat on the stool vacated by Big Youth and she poured him the tea Grandmother had turned down. He had a lot to be happy about, he confessed. His people had all but fled, when he showed up at home, believing him to be a ghost of himself. Someone had informed them that he had died of the plague and been buried in a mass grave in Harare. It had taken him half the night to convince them that he had never been to Harare and had never been dead.

"The place was full of children," he said to Janet.

They slept in the empty grain store and in the empty goat-house and on the beds and under the beds and anywhere where there was space to lie down to sleep. His mother had inherited them from neighbours and relatives who had died, and from parents who were too ill to care for their children. Frank had spent the night sitting by the fireplace, the only space not occupied by a sleeping child. Now he was on his way to his aunt's house to see if she could put him up for a few days.

"Your aunt collects orphans too," Janet informed him. "You don't know what you have come home to."

"It is good to be home again," he said to her.

He had not been called the son of Mateo since his school days. He had been school captain, games captain and the student most expected to succeed.

"The girls had eyes for you," Janet reminded him. "But you were always in your books."

He had decided to study hard and become a doctor. He came from a long line of school dropouts and had had to study hard to pass his examinations. He had gone on to become the first veterinary doctor from Crossroads.

"You didn't talk to me at school," he reminded Janet.

"Your father was a preacher," she reminded him.

"And yours was an Imam."

But, religious differences aside, her mother would have skinned her if she had caught her talking to boys. Then Frank had left for University and Broker had stepped up, respecting neither religion nor family, married her and estranged her from her parents. Janet's parents had left Crossroads shortly after that to escape the stigma, mourning the fact that she who had lacked nothing in life had given herself to a non-believer and a rogue whom everyone knew would come to nothing.

But all that was in the past now, along with juvenile dreams and old wishes, and all the things one could do nothing about.

"Will you stay long?" she asked him.

"I want to set up business here," he said.

"We have not had a vet here for a long time."

The last one, a Government man from Pwani, had left Crossroads at night convinced the place was haunted. He had lived at the teahouse for a while. People would sometimes keep the coffins at the teahouse overnight, when they arrived too late in the day to get to their final destination.

"I think that is what got our doctor," Janet said.

Musa did not allow coffins at his lodgings anymore, but so many people had died that it was easy to believe in spirits.

"Thanks for the tea," Frank said, rising. "I'll go see if Musa has a room for me."

He arrived at the teahouse at midday, when the sun was at its hottest and the streets shimmered from the heat. He stopped by the post office to rest his arm and once again was astonished at what had happened to Crossroads. He was exhausted from hauling his luggage through the farm roads and was pouring with sweat.

"*Ndugu*," the old beggar hailed him. "Give me money, brother."

"I gave you yesterday," Frank reminded him.

"Give me again," the beggar said.

In Pwani, and in other places Frank had visited, beggars operated in gangs and, like illegal toll collectors, confronted passers-by to extort money from them using threats. One could fight back, and risk injury, or pay up and move on. However, this was Crossroads.

"I have no money," he said to the beggar.

"No money?" the beggar was flabbergasted. "Then what are you doing here?"

Frank picked up his case and crossed to the teahouse. Uncle Mark was alone at the draughts table staring at the board and talking to his imaginary opponent.

"I got you now, old bull," he was saying. "Crown that and let's see who is the fool."

He looked up, when Frank's shadow fell on the board, and said cheerfully, "Greetings!"

"I'm back," said Frank.

"So I see," he said, regarding the suitcase with curiosity. "Sit down and play me a game. Musa is at prayer."

"Musa prays?" Frank asked surprised.

"He is a religious man now," Uncle Mark said, rearranging the bottle tops.

After Maalim Juma left for Pwani, and the old mosque collapsed from neglect, Mzee Musa had taken it upon himself to keep Islam alive in Crossroads. Like most inhabitants, his faith was the only weapon he could wield against the *majinis*, the evil spirits and the ghosts that roamed the town at night, crying for blood.

He found Uncle Mark telling Frank how those who feared the plague turned religious and accused those who did not fear it of immorality. Without a word to Frank, Musa sat down and moved the piece he was about to move. Then he turned to Frank and, assuming him to be a hungry traveller, asked him, "What do you want?"

"A room," Frank said.

"What for?" Musa asked, moving another piece.

"To let," Frank told him. "To live in."

"Don't you have a home?"

The short exchange took place while Musa played and Frank watched. Now Musa looked up and told him how much the room would cost. In Pwani, where life generally cost a lot more than it was worth, Frank had stayed in better lodgings and paid less.

"Why so expensive?" he asked.

Musa looked up again, his hand poised over a piece he was about to lose to his opponent.

"Expensive?" he asked, looking surprised. "You want cheap? Cheap is that way, down that road, at a place they call Highlife. I don't care if they have breakfast but I have heard that they have women and bedbugs and they drink alcohol too. Here I give you morning tea and you pay for the *mandazi* and hot water."

He turned his attention back to his game, leaving Frank unsettled. Frank watched him make a move that would cost him the game and gained a little satisfaction from it.

"I'd like a room," he said.

"How many?" Musa asked, his mind on the game.

"One."

"Cash in advance," Musa said.

"Insurance," Uncle Mark explained, "in case you die at night or otherwise depart without letting us know."

He chuckled at the expression on Frank's face and added, "You will be surprised at how many lodgers we have caught sneaking out in the dead of the night."

"It better be a good room," Frank said, unhappily.

"All my rooms are good," Musa informed him. "Tell him, old bull."

Uncle Mark laughed and, with one swoop, cleared the board.

"There," he laughed. "The game is finished. Go show him his room."

Musa stared at the board. Then he rose, seething with rage, and Frank quietly took out his wallet.

"I should have charged you double," Musa said, carefully counting the money.

When he was satisfied it was all there, he put it in his pocket.

"No alcohol permitted," he said to Frank.

"I don't drink," Frank told him.

"And no women."

"I don't know any women."

Musa regarded him suspiciously.

"Do you smoke?"

"No."

"Do you eat pork?"

Uncle Mark burst out laughing and said, "Now, now, old bull, you know there are no pigs left in Crossroads."

Musa nodded uncertainly, turned and stalked off through the kitchen door in a foul mood.

"Sit," Uncle Mark said to Frank. "Sit down and give me a game while Musa thinks about you. He doesn't trust anyone who has travelled beyond Biri Biri."

He rearranged the board, smiling quietly to himself.

"The last time I gave money to send a favoured youth to America," he now said to Frank, "the clever boy went away and bought himself a tour bus and was never heard of again. Your move?"

Frank moved.

"Years later, I met him at a place called Loyengalani with a bus-load of tourists. Your move."

Frank moved and began to wonder where the story was going.

"The young rogue did not remember me," Uncle Mark said with a chuckle. "But he was fat and well dressed, and his American tourists seemed happy with him, so it may be that he was not such a bad boy, after all. Your move."

Frank moved.

"So," the old bull finally asked him. "What did you buy for yourself?"

"Nothing," said Frank.

"Nothing?" marvelled Uncle Mark. "Not even a small wife?"

"Not even a bicycle."

Uncle Mark paused to look at him, reading him from his dusty shoes to the weary suitcase by his side.

"You know what?" he nodded. "I'm tempted to believe you. In fact, I believe you."

Then he moved his piece.

"So, tell me," he said. "What did you do with *our* money?"

"Many things," Frank admitted.

Some of them were part of the original plan, others born of necessity. He could not begin to tell all of them now.

"But you will get your money back," he promised.

"All of it?"

"All of it."

"Good," Uncle Mark looked amused. "I'm sure there are some who will need their money back, but I am more interested in what happened. Why you have come back."

"I want to settle down," Frank said.

"Here?"

"I'd like to set up business here."

Uncle Mark laughed, again that tired old laugh of one who had heard it before.

"Another boarding house, no doubt," he said.

"A store," said Frank. "Animal medicine."

"Animal medicine?" Uncle Mark nodded. "Not entirely a foolish idea."

"I thought about it for a long time."

"Did you think who would buy your medicines?"

"The same people who did before."

"Do they still live? Do they have money?"

"We'll see," Frank said.

"That we shall," said Uncle Mark moving his king. "Your move."

Frank was cornered. Sidetracked by the old man's questioning, he had played himself into a losing situation and there was no easy way out of it.

"Who owns the kiosk across the road?" He asked, to distract his opponent.

"The thing without a roof?" Uncle Mark did not even look up. "Who knows? Who cares? The whole place is empty, as you can see, and no one remembers who owned what. Just move into any of the ruins and wait to see who complains. Musa! Give us some tea here. Your move."

Frank moved.

Chapter Five

Julia was in a hurry. She was always in a hurry whenever she came to visit and Janet suspected her sister evaded her for the same reason other people did - to avoid hearing the truth.

"Sit down and have some tea," Janet said to her.

"I can't stay," Julia said.

She had people helping with the harvest, and her husband, Kata, was expecting visitors.

"I was about to come see you myself," Janet pressed her into sitting down and poured her a cup of tea from the kettle that resided by the fireplace and was always hot.

"About your husband," she got straight to the point. "You can't let him take Solomon's wife."

"Janet," Julia asked, the cup was halfway to her lips, "Is that what you wanted to talk to me about?"

"Solomon died from the plague," Janet informed her.

The silence that followed was unsettling. Julia considered several angry options, among them giving back the cup of tea and walking away.

"You know that Kata must care for his brother's family," she said finally. "That is the custom."

"A dangerous custom," Janet told her. "It must be stopped."

"By me?"

"By all of us," said Janet.

"I'm a married woman," Julia said, after a moment's consideration. "I'm not like some people who have no one to tell them what to do."

"Listen to me," Janet said to her. "I just want to help."

She was deep into informing Julia of her rights and her obligations, when Grandmother arrived leaning on Jeremiah and asked to be told what the noise was all about.

There was no noise, Janet informed her, only a friendly talk between sisters.

"Have you told her?" Grandmother asked Julia, "Tell her what I told you."

Julia shook her head firmly. This was not what she had come here for, she said. She had things to do and no time to argue.

"I don't want to be involved in your quarrel," she said.

"Tell her," Grandmother ordered.

Julia watched as Jeremiah, temporarily released from his duties, amused himself by tossing Janet's beans at her chickens.

"I can't stop Kata doing anything," she said to Janet. "You know he is a traditional man."

"You can't change our tradition," Grandmother added.

"I don't want to change your customs," Janet told them. "The plague will do that for you. The plague will change more than tradition, unless it was stopped."

"Stopped by her?" Grandmother asked.

"By all of us," Janet said.

"All of us?" Julia asked astonished.

"I'll not sit and watch you die," Janet told her. "I'll not let you leave me her children to worry about. You must leave Kata now."

"*Hauui*," wailed Grandmother. "What are you telling your sister? You know she can't leave her husband."

"She can," Janet said. "Come live with us."

Grandmother was beyond despair. What was this world coming to? What sort of advice was that to give to a sister?

"Do you want her to live alone without a man like you?" she asked Janet.

"Kata's brother died from Aids," Janet said to her. "Do you understand what that means?"

"It means that his wife has no one to care for her," Grandmother replied.

"Kata will die from the plague," Janet turned to Julia. "Who will look after you?"

"If it's God's will, then we all shall die."

"You don't understand anything?" Janet said to her. "If he takcs his brother's wife for his own, he will die. There's no doubt about that. Then you, Julia, will die too."

"So now you know when people will die," Grandmother said. "You think you know everything?"

"I'm tired of you telling me what to do," Julia said, defiantly.

"I worry about you."

"You are not my mother."

"I'm your sister. I must worry about you."

"Monika is more of a sister to me," Julia said rising. "We have husbands. We are not prostitutes."

Then she stormed out leaving behind a charged silence, an anguish-filled stillness.

"She doesn't mean that," Grandmother's voice was heavy with sadness.

"I know," said Janet.

"She is not like that," Grandmother said. "She is not like that at all."

"No," Janet agreed. "She is not like that."

But the hurt was deep and hard to ignore.

"Everyone is changed," observed the old woman. "Sisters now fight over nothing and no one has a kind word for the other. What happened?"

"The plague," Janet informed. "The plague has changed us all."

"A common enemy is supposed to unite us," Grandmother said talking to herself. "To bring us together. But not so this plague. The plague destroys everything, eats up relations and severs family bonds."

The plague exploded faith and trust, and caused despair. The plague was the greatest confounder Crossroads had ever known. And, because few understood it, the fear it caused was great and destructive. Wives feared husbands and husbands suspected wives. Families talked witchcraft and pointed fingers at one another until, it seemed, there was no purpose to life anymore.

"She will die," Janet observed, quietly. "Stubbornness will kill my only sister."

Grandmother heaved a weary sigh.

"She is a grown woman," she said. "She can look after herself."

"She cannot," said Janet. "You know that too."

Ever since they were children, Julia had looked up to someone else for direction. Most often it had been to Janet that she had turned, when life confounded her. Now she looked only to her husband.

"We can't ask her to leave her husband," the old woman said. "He must take his brother's wife."

Janet picked a stool, forgot what she wanted to do with it and set it down again.

"You are angry again," Grandmother observed.

"I'm not," she said.

"I know when you are angry."

"My sister just called me a prostitute," Janet reminded.

"You know she did not mean it," Grandmother told her. "Julia would never say a thing like that if she meant it. Stop blaming her for your sadness. You are always unhappy these days. You need a man to look after you."

"Manhood doesn't make man," Janet reminded. "You told me that yourself, when I wanted to leave Broker. Then he left me."

"I will tell you something else," Grandmother said, forcefully. "Old lions must learn to eat grass."

"I'm not an animal," Janet yelled.

"Broker is dead," said Grandmother. "And you are growing old."

Broker had been gone more than ten years, and the Chief was alive and able to take care of Janet and her children.

"He has lots of land," reminded Grandmother.

"I don't want his land."

"He is not a bad man," Grandmother said. "He got you your job?"

"No one else wanted it," Janet reminded her.

Grandmother herself had tried to persuade Janet against taking the job. She had said only a shameless woman would take such a job; telling people not to have babies.

"He'll get you another job," she promised. "One that you like."

"I like my job," Janet said.

"He can make your work easy," Grandmother insisted.

"Easy?" Janet had to laugh the mirthless dry laugh that Grandmother called an old widow's laugh. "Only the Government can make my work easy."

"The Chief can make them give you another job," Grandmother said.

"Is that what he told you?" Janet asked her. "What else did he promise you?"

"I want to see you happy before I die," said the old woman. "I dreamt ..."

"I would be happier if you stopped dreaming for me. A husband is not a priority right now and ... why don't you dream for Julia instead? Dream her a better husband."

"Leave Kata alone," Grandmother said, irritated. "Think about yourself and your children. Do you want them to grow up with nothing, without even a father? Only a selfish woman would want that."

Then, having said most of what she had come to say, she hobbled away to her gate, leaning heavier on her cane than she had when she arrived. Jeremiah ran after her, expecting her to give him her hand. She did not.

"I must not despair," Janet said aloud. "I must not give up."

She did not despair and, by the time she had finished sorting her beans, she had a plan.

Chapter Six

She caught up with Frank halfway down the old main street. It was a hot and dusty day and he was sweating heavily. She was sweating a bit too after cycling from her house.

"I want to see you," she said.

Her scent disrupted his concentration. It reminded him of things better off forgotten. However, he was flattered that she had sought him out and he told her so as they walked back up the street. Most of the buildings were beyond repair, and those that could be repaired needed money that Frank did not have.

"It must be cheap," he said to her. "That is the only way I can keep the prices affordable."

His plans did not interest her much, but she let him talk on and nodded and made appropriate noises and waited for him to finish. She had thought about her plan for the whole night. Now she was impatient to get on with it, but she had to have his undivided attention.

She watched him contemplate the vandalised kiosk next to the old post office. The walls were broken and crumbling, the roof rusty and caved in. The door and the windows, and the vegetable racks, were gone and the interior was overgrown with grass. She saw him nod.

"Might you know the owner?" he asked her.

"Maybe," she told him.

"Is he reasonable?" he asked.

"She is," she answered.

"Cheap?" he said.

A strange smile came to her face.

"That is up to you," she said.

"You can arrange it?" he asked excited.

Something about her smile bothered him. There was little joy and no mirth in it at all. Frank had lived in Pwani too long to believe in charity. In Pwani, where he had spent some considerable time, the first thing they taught their children was to never lick an empty hand.

"Come with me," she said.

He abandoned his search and followed her across the street to the teahouse. Uncle Mark was sitting at the draughts table, plotting new moves to baffle Musa with, when saw them come, one strutting and the other slouching, and wondered what was going on. Raising his voice, he called out to the kitchen.

"Musa, you have two now."

Then he greeted Janet and asked how she was. She disregarded him completely and led Frank to a corner table, as faraway from him as possible. Musa came out with a teakettle and two glasses and served them tea. He was getting ready for his prayers and had his turban on his head.

"Anything else?" he asked them.

"*Mandazi*," Janet said. "Fresh ones, not the ones you sell to everyone."

Musa went for the *mandazi*.

"*Daktari,*" Uncle Mark called out to Frank. "The condom army never won any victory I heard of."

Frank smiled and Janet ignored Uncle Mark.

"We can't let Kata take his brother's wife," she said, launching into the purpose of her visit. "We can't let it happen."

Frank decided to disregard the *we*, for the moment, and asked her, "What does your sister say about it?"

Julia had not had a point of view since she was a baby crawling on the dust of her mother's yard. So it was up to Janet to have all the say.

"How do I come in?" he asked her.

"We must stop him," she said.

She had been to the hospital in Sokoni and talked to the doctors and the nurses who had attended him. The lengths to which they had gone to explain to her the exact cause of death had told her more than words could say.

Frank was quiet, thinking of a friendly way to disappoint her. She watched him think. He thought until she could not stand it anymore.

"Speak," she said. "Will you help me or not?"

"This is serious," he said lamely. "It is not just about you and your sister. It's about a man and his wife and his social responsibilities."

"Monika is not his wife."

"Is that her name?"

"What does it matter?" her voice rose. "Will you help me stop them or not?"

"I must think," Frank said to her.

"Think," she crossed her arms.

"I need more time than that."

"More time for what?" she snatched her bag from the table and rose abruptly. "To find an excuse for not helping me?"

She rose abruptly and rummaged in her bag.

"You are all the same," she dumped the money on the table, as Mzee Musa came back with a plate of *mandazi*.

"There is your money," she said to him.

"What about these?" he asked, confused.

"Take them back."

"They are fresh, as you ordered."

"Take them back," she told him.

"I don't return food to the kitchen," Musa said. "You know that."

"Then eat them yourself," she turned and stormed out.

Musa, totally baffled, stood with the money in one hand and the plate of *mandazi* in the other, and watched her leave. Then he turned to Frank and demanded to know what he had done to make her so disagreeable.

"Nothing," said Frank. "Ask the old man."

"I warned you," Uncle Mark said, laughing quietly. "You can't say I didn't warn you."

Frank crossed the veranda to join him at the draughts table.

"I didn't commit myself," he said.

"But you will," laughed Uncle Mark. "Oh yes, you will."

Musa counted the money, found it to be just enough for the tea they had consumed, and followed Frank to Uncle Mark's table. Placing the plate of *mandazi* on the table in front of him, he demanded to know who would pay for it.

"We didn't eat any," Frank said.

"I don't return food to the kitchen."

"Then follow her and make her pay for it," Frank suggested.

Musa unwound the turban from his head, folded it neatly and placed it on the table. Realising that he was readying for unreasonable violence, Uncle Mark picked *mandazi* from the plate and ate it, saying, "There, now we have eaten it. You give Musa his money."

"I didn't order it," said Frank.

48

"Just give him his money," Uncle Mark said. "You don't want bloodshed so early in the morning."

Frank took out the money and handed it to Musa. Musa counted it twice, picked up the rest of the *mandazi* and his turban and left them

"In the old days, Musa would fetch his machete," said Uncle Mark. "Some things never change but, thank God, some things do change. Your move?"

Frank picked the piece closest to his hand and moved it without much thought.

"So?" Uncle Mark asked him. "What does she want with you?"

"We didn't get to that part," said Frank.

Uncle Mark laughed and said, "There are men in this town who would give their gourds to be wanted by Janet."

"Why?" Frank wondered.

"You have not found out?"

"Found what out?"

"Janet is no ordinary woman," the old man laughed.

"That I know."

"Men walk in the bush to avoid her," said Uncle Mark. "She doesn't approve of men beating their wives. To her, men are a stampede of warthogs with no idea how to please a woman. She said that. And, according to her, amorous aardvarks and drunken donkeys are more competent than Crossroads men. She said that too, our Janet did."

Janet had a lot to say about Crossroads men, and to them, and she did it with as much restraint as an angry bush fire.

"Crossroads men have been known to say things about her too," added Uncle Mark.

Some said she was a creature from mad women's hell, an angry spirit sent back to torment Crossroads men. And that was not all. When they drunk too much, they told everyone who would listen, including confused children, that Janet was not a woman but a eunuch from Pwani masquerading as a woman. That, they said, was why her husband had run off with another woman. What she needed now, they said with drunken fervour, was an ox trainer, someone to whip her back to womanhood.

"She needs a man," Musa confirmed, returning from his prayers. "To put her in her place."

"Fortunately for us all," Uncle Mark said with his quiet laugh, "Such a man does not exist here in Crossroads. Broker was the only real man for her."

Broker was notorious, as a bully and a rogue, long before Janet met him. Then he had landed a job at her father's petrol station and declared his love for her. Barely sixteen at the time, she married him, against all good counsel, and condemned herself to life in Crossroads.

"Maalim was very upset about it," Uncle Mark said. "He harboured great designs for his daughter. He never forgave her."

"He was a good man," Musa said. "A religious man."

"He knew the scoundrel was up to no good," Uncle Mark agreed. "Anyone could see it, anyone but Janet."

Wildly independent, Broker had started by changing her religion. Then Julia, her only sister had followed Janet into the new religion and married a man old enough to be her father. Then, as if that was not enough to break the old Imam's health, Broker had stolen his money and run off with a girl from Highlife Lodge. Maalim had disowned his daughters, wound up his businesses and left Crossroads. Thus had yet another man, a good and God-fearing man, been ruined by the wiles of women, Musa observed.

"She wants to stop Kata from taking his brother's wife," Frank confessed.

"How?" Musa asked.

Frank had no idea. He had not liked the way she had stared him in the eye and dared him to be something he was not, and the way she had smiled at him, as though she knew he would pay whatever price she put on her friendship.

"I would love to see you try," Uncle Mark said.

"Kata killed a man, " Musa warned. "Slit his throat from ear to ear like a pig."

He emphasized the action by passing his open hand across his own throat like a knife.

"The man was an infidel," he explained. His tone implied it was all right to do away with heathens.

"Kata is a madman," Uncle Mark added. "How mad? You will find out when you start meddling in his business. Janet is not all there either, if you ask me. I don't see why she needs you, as she is capable of tackling the entire Kata clan by herself."

After Broker's departure, she had taken over his responsibilities at the petrol station to prove to her father that she was as good an issue as any son he could have sired. She had pumped petrol, scrubbed floors, kept books and stopped just short of overhauling diesel engines. Her determination had failed to impress her father, but it had inspired others to name her *Mama Chuma*, the woman of steel.

Frank heard Uncle Mark talk about her, shrugged and concentrated on not losing the game. But Uncle Mark had set him up well, in the course of telling him all he did not want to know about Janet, and his defeat was just a matter of moments.

As they rearranged the tops for another game, Janet came back up the street loaded with shopping. The old beggar greeted her with his usual, "Give me money."

"Give you money?" she asked him. "Are you a man?"

The beggar fled to his booth terrified. The men at the teahouse exchanged worried glances, as they watched her cross the street, with a purposeful gait that shook the ground driving Musa to desperation. Without a word to them, she loaded her bags on her bicycle. She had left it leaning on the wall of the teahouse as usual.

Frank said, rising abruptly.

"I'll be back."

"Careful now," Uncle Mark said, loudly for Janet to hear. "Don't let the skirt fool you."

Frank laughed nervously, as he walked out to offer to hold the bicycle for her. She informed him she could manage on her own.

He stood redundantly by watching her manage. He tried not to look at the men he knew were watching through the window and, he suspected, laughing at him.

"May I walk with you?" he asked, when she finished loading her bicycle and pushed off.

When she didn't respond, he fell in step with her. He waited until they were out of sight, and earshot, of the teahouse before trying to talk to her again.

"I would really like to help you," he said.

"Then do so," she told him. "Talk to Kata."

"I can't do that," he said, his resolve reinforced by the old men's talk. "It's not that simple."

"Simple?" she asked. "All I'm asking you is to talk to him, not wrestle with him. How hard can that be?"

"Why me?" he asked her, trying to sound reasonable. "Why not the old bulls."

51

"Those old bulls?" she tossed her hand in the direction of the teahouse. "Don't make me laugh."

"They are decent old men."

"Then go be decent with them and stop following me like a homeless ..."

Realising that this was the wrong moment to be defending old rogues, he said quickly, "Your sister should not have married him, in the first place. Kata is old enough to be her father."

"You tell him that," Janet said.

"He's old enough to be my father too."

"Now you want to hide behind taboo," she said.

"Your brother-in-law is not a nice man," he tried again. "I've heard that he has killed a man already."

"Two men," Janet corrected.

"Two men?"

"They tried to kill him," she said. "So now you are afraid of him too, is that it?"

"What is the matter with you,?" he asked her. "Why are you so set on destroying him."

"Me?" she asked. "Destroy him? You are just as ignorant as the rest. Education has done nothing for you."

She mounted her bicycle and, before he could think of an appropriate response, rode away. He watched her go, until she turned out of sight, then walked back to the teahouse. The old men saw him return dragging his feet and wondered.

"I told her I can't," he said unasked.

"And?" they asked.

"She went away."

The old men exchanged knowing glances. They knew her better. Like a family curse, Janet never went away. They returned to their game. Frank remained standing, looking out of the window at the empty street near despair. He had been back just a few days and already antagonised the one person he wanted to like him.

"I need an axe," he said, suddenly.

"Under the counter," said Uncle Mark.

Everyone knew that was where Musa kept his axe, just in case a desperate thug thought he was easy to rob.

"Do you have a hammer too?" Frank asked him.

"Hammer?" the old men asked, alarmed.

"I must do something, or I'll go mad and leave."

They considered it, found it a reasonable alternative and shrugged.

"In the kitchen," they said together.

"Under the long table with the *matumbo*," added Musa.

A few moments later, Frank crossed the road to the old kiosk and went to work. He chopped and hammered, grunting and talking to himself, until the old men abandoned their game and rushed to enquire what on earth was going on. What was he was doing? Did he have any idea whose property he was destroying?

He replied that he did he not know and he did not care. He would battle the devil rather than go mad waiting for something to happen. The old men returned to their game and moved it on the veranda to watch while they played.

"She has him now," Uncle Mark concluded.

"How?" asked Musa.

"The thing belonged to her father, did it not?"

"So?"

"She has got him exactly where she wants him."

"Where," Musa asked.

"Where she has got him now," Uncle Mark said.

She would make use of him like no man had ever been made use of in Crossroads.

"I don't see how," Musa admitted, his mind on the game.

But Frank more than saw how, when, after days of toiling and sweating at it, after he had hammered in most of the nails and his fingers, Janet showed up. He had painted the kiosk and named it FRANK'S ANIMAL CLINIC and was ready to stock it with merchandise. Then she turned up with two policemen and slapped a giant padlock on the door.

Frank was away all day in Sokoni, purchasing his first stock. He arrived back in Crossroads late in the evening, loaded with cartons of things, to find the kiosk padlocked.

"What happened?" he asked the old men.

"Janet," Musa reported. "The kiosk belongs to her father."

"And you let me do all that work?" Frank was furious. "You watched me spend so much time and money and you couldn't tell me?"

"We didn't want to slow you down," said Uncle Mark.

"That was mean," Frank raged.

"We knew you and her would come to an understanding," Uncle Mark told him.

53

Which they did, the very following day, an understanding in which she did all the talking and he did all the nodding.

"When I said you could have it for nothing," Janet scolded, as they trudged to Kata's house, "I didn't mean you should steal it."

"I didn't steal it."

"Did you have the owner's permission?"

"You didn't tell me it was yours!"

He was still furious after a whole night of thinking it over.

"I meant we could make a deal."

"Which we have," he said to her. "So let's do what I have to do and get it over with. I only have to talk to him, right?"

"Right."

"What he does after that is up to him, right?"

"Right."

They walked the rest of the way to her brother-in-law's house in a charged silence, arriving along an overgrown footpath that was in desperate need of attention. There were several children playing in the yard. It was a large compound comprising of six dwellings, two of which were abandoned and crumbling. A pot of porridge bubbled on a three-stone fireplace outside one of the houses.

The children swarmed Janet wanting to know what she had brought for them. Their mother was away at the market, they told her, but their father and their little mother were at the cattle enclosure.

"I'll go talk to him," Frank said to Janet.

"I'll come with you."

"I better talk to him alone, man to man."

"Tell him everything," she said.

Frank made his way to the back of the huts. There was a family burial plot with several graves, one of them recent, right behind the house. Beyond the burial place was the cattle enclosure, large enough for several herds, and a smaller one for the goats Kata received for his services.

Kata was by the cattle enclosure, just as the children had said, with a woman Frank did not remember and a cow whose calf they had just helped deliver. He was shirtless, his trouser legs rolled up to his knees.

"*Daktari,*" he hailed, cheerfully. "You come too late already. I have done the job myself with the help of this woman."

His late brother's wife was younger than him. She shook hands and said she remembered Frank.

"But you don't remember me," she said to him.

She put on a brave face, though she was still in mourning.

"The animals are not here, Daktari," Kata said to him. "I'll send a boy to fetch them."

"There's no need for that," Frank said to him. "It's you I want to see."

Kata, looking puzzled, left the woman tending to the calf and led him away to the family graves.

"This is where I buried my brother Solomon," he said. "We can talk here."

Frank hesitated. It was not the best place for what he had come to do, which was to malign the dead man, a man who had never done him any harm.

"Solomon was a good man," he said to cushion the impact. "I'm sorry about his death."

"So are we," Kata said. "Although he was a preacher, Solomon was a good brother. But no one cried the day we buried him. We are all dead to grief."

Frank nodded. Then, with the grave of Pastor Solomon at his feet, he unveiled the reason he had come to see Kata, making it clear it was all Janet's idea that he talk to him about it.

"She tells me you want to marry his widow," he added.

"It is customary to shoulder your brother's burdens," Kata agreed.

Frank searched for words to keep the conversation cordial.

"How is she?" he asked.

"As you see her," Kata said to him. "Do you think she can survive on her own?"

Frank doubted it. She was bending over the newborn calf coaxing it to its feet. Thin and emaciated, she was not much different from numerous Crossroads women who, it seemed, were born to suffer and die without experienced any joy in their lives.

Frank realised he had taken on more than he had bargained for. He had come imagining to do battle with an Amazon, a giant man-eater of Janet's proportions, only to encounter an ordinary, countrywoman, as much in need of support as the one he had come to support.

"Are you not afraid of dying?" he asked Kata, desperate to conclude his risky mission, and go back to Crossroads and relative sanity. "Janet says ..."

"Janet is a woman, *Daktari*," Kata interjected. "We are men. I am not afraid of anything."

"So you know your brother died of the plague?"

"Who said that? Janet? She told you that?"

"Everyone knows," Frank said, trying to play it down.

"*Daktari*," Kata shook his head, "people were dying before the plague came to Crossroads. Witchcraft, cholera, malaria and other diseases were all here before the plague came. But a man can't die anymore without hearing he died from the plague."

"Which is the truth for most deaths," Frank said. "I know these things too."

"What things?"

"The plague," Frank said, cautiously.

"Why do you keep talking to me about the plague?" Kata now wondered. "What about all the other ailments?"

"Like cholera? The plague travels easily among too, especially people who are close. People who dip their horns in the same gourd die of the same poison."

Kata's eyes narrowed, thoughtfully. Then his face turned ugly, blood vessels swelling up on his forehead.

"So!" he bellowed.

"I'm trying to help," Frank said, taking a step back.

"Help whom?" the second bellow knocked the calf to its knees.

"Janet," Frank said. "It was all her idea. But she means no harm."

"So this is why you have come?" Kata raged. "To insult me in my house?"

"I'm only trying to ... "

By then, Frank had no idea what he was trying to do, apart from pleasing Janet. Kata went berserk, tearing down a fence post and wielding it at him. Frank fled.

Janet was serving porridge to Kata's children, and worrying about the silence from the back of the houses, when the first angry howl reached her. It was as sudden as a thunderclap. Just the one crash of fury then nothing. Resisting the urge to rush in that direction, she continued serving the children. The second bellow was followed by the sight of Frank running for his life, with Kata hard on his heels. She remained calm as she finished dishing out the porridge. She was about to pick up her bag and follow in the direction they had taken, when Kata returned, sweating profusely and breathing hard. He was so angry the veins stood out on his face and neck. He could hardly speak for the fury in him.

"I'll kill him," he raved. "If he sets foot here again, I'll kill him."

He whacked the pole on the ground breaking it in two. Janet kept her distance, afraid he would hit her with it.

"You tell him ...," he gasped for breath. "You tell him I'll kill him."

Then he turned and stormed away, back to the back of the house, leaving her more than a little shaken.

She found Frank half way to her house, sitting by the path staring at the scratches he had suffered during his flight through the bush.

"Is that what you call man to man?" she asked him.

"He's an animal," he informed her. "You knew that, when you sent me to be killed by him."

"I have offered to come with you," she reminded.

"Why wouldn't you come alone?" he said to her. "You are his sister-in-law. He would not lay a finger on his sister-in-law."

She had hoped Kata would take it better, when the message came from a man. She had believed Frank could do it best, being a respected doctor.

"I'll take him to court," she said.

"What crime has he committed?" he asked her. "Mind your business and leave your sister to mind her own."

She snorted angrily and tried to walk past him.

"Are you serious about saving your sister?" he asked, barring her way. "Get her rat poison."

"Get out of my way."

"Let her serve it in his food."

She pushed past him, angry and implacable.

"It's the only way," he yelled after her. "I'll even get it for you."

She stopped and looked back, took a deep breath thrusting her chest out in the most arrogant manner she could master and laughed the haughty laugh that reduced insolent Crossroads men to idiots.

He had been away from Crossroads for so long he had forgotten about it. Instead of squirming and crawling into hiding, his face lit up.

"You ... " she said, choking on her indignation. "You, small man."

Then she stormed away, leaving him to decide whether to follow her or go back to the teahouse and lie to the old men about what had happened.

Chapter Seven

Frank watched and wondered, as dozens of people made their way down the road to the old market square. They came in twos and threes, and in small groups talking loudly about what they expected to see happen.

Uncle Mark emerged from the teahouse, looking incongruous in a white suit and hat he claimed to have acquired in Abyssinia, and stepped into the middle of the busy street. He looked first one way and then the other. People eddied round him, ignoring him completely, and flowed on down the street. Setting his hat squarely on his head, he started after the crowd.

"Coming?" he asked Frank, as he passed by the kiosk.

"No," Frank said.

Janet had not invited him. He was content to be unimportant in her feud with Crossroads.

"You are not curious?" Uncle Mark asked him.

"Only about the outcome."

"I can tell you what that will be," Uncle Mark said, with a sad smile. "But then I'd spoil your suspense for you."

"I can wait," Frank settled deeper in his chair. "I can wait."

Uncle Mark walked away, unhurried and unconcerned about the people rushing around him. The market square was alive with noise and movement. The proceedings had begun, the crowd pushing and shoving, to get a view of the people at the centre of the action. All of Crossroads administration was there, from village elders to Government officers and community representatives.

Janet, Kata and his two wives were facing the Council of Elders, among them Chief Chupa, when Uncle Mark arrived.

"You are family," the Chief admonished them. "Why couldn't you settle this at home?"

"Ask her," said Kata.

"They would not listen," Janet said.

"This woman is bad," Kata said. "She is against everything I do."

"I'm not," Janet informed. "My only concern is my sister."

"She is his wife," the Chief reminded.

"He wants his brother's wife as well," Janet told him.

"A man must take care of his dead brother's wife," said the Chief.

"Does he have to marry her?"

"It is his right."

"It is wrong."

"Wrong?" asked Kata. "It is our way."

Janet, disregarding him, turned to the elders.

"You all know what will happen next," she pleaded. "She will have children, then she will die. My sister too could die. I can't allow that to happen."

"Who are you to allow me?" Kata asked her. "This is an insult to our ways, our traditions and our manhood."

Chief Chupa turned to the elders, but they too did not know what to do about Janet. That they had been summoned and the *baraza* convened was a great affront. Some had tried to dissuade the Chief from convening the *baraza*. He turned to Kata.

"Is it true?" he asked him.

"Is what true?" Kata asked, startled.

"What she says?"

"I'm a man," said Kata. "I don't fear her."

The Chief knew what was expected of him, how he must rule. The woman had to be put in her place. She was notorious for resisting authority, and for her insisting on having the last word. Her way of life was a threat to traditional values. She had to be cut to size and stuffed in her gourd, but they too did not know how to do it painlessly. They hang their heads and left it to Chief Chupa to do the necessary.

Then Uncle Mark spoke.

"May I speak?" he asked them.

They had not seen him approach, else measures would have been taken to keep him at bay. Now he was among them and they did not know what to do.

"Let me speak," he said, respectfully.

They stared at him. He was not a part of what was happening and had never been part of any of Crossroads' traditional processes. His thoughts and opinions, like his clothes, were alien and as welcome as a swarm of dung flies. They looked at one another and wondered what to do. It was Kata who finally, and impatiently, allowed him to speak.

60

"Speak," he said aloud, when it was clear no one else would. "In communal gathering, even the dumb must be allowed to speak. Speak and be hanged for it, for we have many goats to skin today."

"I thank you," said Uncle Mark. "You, truly, are a traditional man. But we are all traditional men here."

He saw the look on Janet's face and added, "And women."

The elders grumbled. They did not take kindly to being lumped together with women and they said so loudly. He let them grumble until they looked foolish and stopped.

"He who forsakes his traditions is a slave," he reminded them. "A fool can make an important contribution."

He waited to be contradicted. No one dared. He was the only man in Crossroads who had neither land nor property, neither wife nor family to bother with. His mind was his property and Crossroads was his family. He was everybody's son, father, brother, grandfather or uncle. No one came to him for assistance and went away unsatisfied. He set about satisfying them by telling them what they knew to be true but refused to hear.

"Our customs are older than the hills," he reminded. "Like many old things, some are tired and not very useful today. Some of them are blunt or awkward to wield and have outlived their purpose. But, unlike old ploughs and broken machetes, we cannot abandon our traditions and go buy us new ones. That is why we tend to them like family heirlooms, polishing and shining them and repairing them, wherever possible. We examine them for their usefulness and correct and modify them, and adapt them to our changing needs. And those we find of no use any more, those that have outlived purpose or are out of their time, we discard them without exception. Otherwise they will make us appear depraved or detestable in the eyes of others."

The gathering moved restlessly. What on earth was he talking about now? They asked themselves. On whose side was he?

He did not leave them to wonder for long.

"The woman is right," he said, finally coming to the point. "To inherit the wife of a man who dies from the plague is not just foolish - it is the height of madness. There, now, I have told you."

The gathering was silent. Chief Chupa cleared his throat but said nothing. Only Kata Kataa dared speak out.

"Solomon did not die from the plague," he told them. "My brother died from witchcraft."

"As always," someone said.

61

Kata lunged at him, grabbed him by the throat and started to throttle him. It took three men to ply his fingers from the man's throat. More people joined in the commotion, causing confusion and chaos. Insults were exchanged and blows traded. And, as Janet sadly watched, the *baraza* broke up in disarray, having achieved nothing for her or for her sister. Julia and Kata's sister-in-law were already leaving.

"Julia," she called after her.

They ignored her and were soon lost in the crowd.

Uncle Mark stood in the midst of the melee, watching the chaos surge and swirl around him, and wondered if he could hold himself responsible for it. A rush of exhilaration rushed through his veins, as he watched fists fly, saw heads rock and blood spill. He had started a few brawls in his youth and treasured the memories. Finally, when it was clear he was now considered so old that no one would hit him, he adjusted his hat on his head and regretfully walked away, slowly and thoughtfully, back to the teahouse.

"What happened?" Frank asked him.

"We lost," he said.

"What about Janet?"

"Janet?" he had forgotten all about the woman.

A smile now appeared on his lips.

"Don't worry about Janet," he said. "Janet can take care of her sister. But she may have to kill Kata to do so."

He saw a shadow of concern cross Frank's face and thought, 'she has him too.' While he wondered how to ease Frank's hunger for good news about Janet, people came by, bruised and bloodied, talking of the riot as the most exciting event in recent memory. They stopped to admire Frank's merchandise and to wonder at his courage for opening a shop in Crossroads when others were closing down. But they all had no money to buy and left as they had come.

"Come play a game with me," Uncle Mark said to him, when his admirers had left. "I'll tell you about Crossroads."

Frank considered his proposal, found it acceptable and followed him to the teahouse.

Chapter Eight

Janet asked the old woman to sit down and gave her a cup of tea.

"Don't you have any cocoa?" Grandmother asked.

Cocoa was for Janet's children, for her friends and for people who made her happy. Today, her grandmother was at the bottom of the list.

She had found Janet in the midst of an impromptu stocktaking, something she had decided on just to keep her mind busy and her hands from breaking something in anger.

"She is his wife," Grandmother said of Julia. "Bought and paid for."

It depressed Janet more. They had had this discussion often. She could not remember a time when she was not sad about Julia.

Grandmother tried to draw her out by talking about this and that, and by steering clear of Kata, but there was little else to talk about. The riot in the market place, which Kata had started and which everyone now blamed on Janet, was now part of Crossroads legends. It was told and retold all over Crossroads with great exaggeration.

After rambling on for a while about children and about loneliness and death, Grandmother embarked on a lesson about men and women, and about marriage. Janet let her ramble on. When she finally finished her tea and rose to go, having talked herself to exhaustion, Janet was no happier than when Grandmother had arrived.

"You are hard to please," Grandmother observed. "No wonder your husband ran away."

Janet swallowed her pain and anger, and watched her pick up her stick and make for the gate to her compound. When she was gone, Janet thought of taking her bicycle and going out to work, hoping that talking to other people might make her feel better. But she was so weary with sadness that no amount of work could get rid of her grief. Nothing could lift her spirits today, not even the sight of Frank striding to her compound with a big smile and a brown paper bag.

"Greetings," he called out cheerfully. "I've brought you something good."

She looked in the bag and discovered two, shapeless loaves.

"Bread?" she wondered.

"Musa baked it especially for you," he informed her.

"Why bread?" she asked. "Hasn't he got enough trouble with *mandazi?*"

"He's in an expansive mood today," said Frank. "It is quite edible, as you will see."

"He never ceases to amaze," she said shaking her head.

"I suggested cake, but he said he was the cook. So bread it is."

"Thanks," she told him.

He stepped closer, looked up in her face and tried to elicit a smile.

"I heard about the case," he said.

She waited for him to go on. His jeans were spotted with paint, and he smelled of turpentine.

"What did you hear?" she had to ask.

"That it ended up being your trial," he said, looking for somewhere to sit. He settled on the stool vacated by Grandmother and realised the teakettle was hot. She offered him a cup of tea.

"How is that business?" he asked, indicating the cartons of condoms by the door.

"How is yours?" she asked him.

"Good."

"Good?"

"They promise to pay."

"*That* good," she said, unimpressed.

"It's a beginning," he said. "Now that they owe me, they will pay."

She smiled a sad, little smile, for she knew Crossroads better, and asked him, "When?"

"When they get the money."

"Exactly how father went out of business," she informed. "Trust and hope."

"What else is there?"

"And what happens when you run out of supplies? What then?"

"It will not come to that."

"You don't know Crossroads," she said. "You don't know this place."

64

"Why do you stay?" he asked her.

She often asked herself the question. She could move out and follow her parents down to Pwani. She could go somewhere else to start a new life for her and her children. Simply run away, as everyone who could did, and give herself a second chance.

She shook her head to clear it and asked, "Was there anything you wanted?"

"Just to cheer you up," he said. "But, as you are so busy, I can come back another time."

"Fine," she said.

"I have a lot to do myself," he went on, talking to himself for he could see she was not listening. "Would you believe there were no painters in Crossroads? Not a single one. Where did they go?"

She did not answer. He knew where they had all gone. They were down in the ground, where Crossroads' best and most able-bodied were headed. Down where their education and their craft were of no use to anyone at all, and most of them so young they had no time to use any skills they might have learned.

"What about Big Youth?" she asked him.

"He tried to sell me condoms," Frank informed her. "He'll make a brave salesman or a bad crook. His nervousness was telling."

"He knows the condoms are not for sale," Janet revealed. "He'll have them accusing me of selling Government property. I could lose my job for that."

She had three children to support and a grandmother who would never tire of telling her how much she needed a man.

"Broker was all the man I needed," she said. "See what he did to me."

Now what she wanted was to be left alone. Some peace of mind and a sense of reality.

"Another reality than this one?"

This was not reality, she informed him, but a dream, a nightmare. She wanted to wake up among people who cared about life and one another. She wanted to wake up yesterday, long ago when death and sorrow were not so familiar. She wished ... she wished ...

Frank heard her out, weighed down by her sadness, and reflected on his own loss. Some of her wishes were his own, but most were for things that even believers did not hope for anymore - things such as equality, justice, food in everyone's stomach and an end to human suffering and despair. Such things as were not guaranteed anywhere on earth anymore.

"You are right," he said, when she had stopped wishing. "You need a strong dose of reality. Unfortunately, I'm an animal doctor and I know of no other reality than this."

"You have no wishes?" she asked him. "No impossible wishes?"

"Just simple everyday wishes like - I wish I never came back to Crossroads."

"You don't have to wish that," she said. "You can leave. Just pack up and go."

Crossroads did it all the time. Men left in droves, running away from their nightmares and horrors of their own making. Women had to persevere alone, to manage life and keep the home fires burning. To live, suffer and die alone.

Frank nodded. He had come determined to agree with her on everything she said.

"How do you do it?" he asked her. "How do you overcome it?"

"We can't overcome it," she said. "No one can overcome death, but a death that is not your own is easy to survive."

Women were unbreakable rocks, forged to bear the burdens of life and death, from the cradle to the grave. There was not a single affliction in life that did not affect a woman in one way or the other, yet they were not allowed to despair.

"You know why?" she asked Frank. "Because I'm a woman and a mother."

So she had to persevere, in the knowledge that she was not alone, and count her blessings, one by one and over and over, until they seemed so many they overshadowed her problems.

"Pain and sorrow diminish in significance where hope is in abundance," she said. "That is how we overcome."

"You have no regrets?" he asked her.

"Everyone has some regrets," she said. "There's always something to be sorry for. Something you did or failed to do, something you have or have not got. Many things. If only I had done this instead of that. If only I didn't have a stomach to remind me of all this pain. If only I had fewer children, fewer mouths to feed and fewer lives to care for. If I had been born there, instead of here."

"Married a doctor?"

"Married a man," she said.

"If only I had stayed?" he asked hopefully.

She finally laughed, not the cold laughter that devastated small men's egos and left them running for cover, but a fully radiant laugh.

"Did you ever wish that?" he asked, startled.

"It's hard to know what one really wishes."

"I wished for you," he said suddenly, surprising her. "When I stood on a bridge considering whether life was worth living, I thought of you."

But, by then, it was too late for anything but regrets.

She too had fallen in dark despair more than once, she now admitted. When Broker left her, she too had seriously considered ending it all with everything from rat poison to drowning. But, she had realised, ending it all could not kill her anger.

"Then there were the children and Grandmother," she said.

Grandmother had thrown away the poisons and hidden ropes and machetes and anything that might be used to commit suicide. Then she had stayed awake to watch over her and to plead for the children. When she saw her children now, running home from school full of life, she was glad she had endured.

"To make sure my daughter doesn't suffer the same fate as I did."

Frank laughed suddenly and said, "Am I mistaken, or have I cheered you up a little?"

She laughed along with him.

Chapter Nine

Crossroads Church of God was not built, as a stranger might have expected, in the centre of Crossroads itself. It was miles away surrounded by farmland and wooded hills that rose into the skies and were lost in mist and fog most of July.

It was a small country church, with wooden walls and a broken roof, and whose door and windows had been broken and vandalised by Crossroads' heathens. Despite its poverty and desecration, the church stood in unassailable dignity behind a low cedar fence secured by a wooden gate through which only believers were permitted to pass. The rest had to stand in the sun outside the perimeter fence and wait for the Pastor to minister to their needs.

It was the funeral hour.

A line of caskets stretched for some distance along the perimeter fence to the gate. The pallbearers, mostly barefoot and raggedly dressed, stood wretchedly by their coffins while the Pastor did his for to their dead relatives.

Pastor Batoromeo was nearly blind with age and looked like a bird of prey in his robes as he conducted the funeral services. Many of those he prayed for were complete strangers and people of indeterminable spiritual affiliations. He did not know what to say about them or how to pray for them. Instead, he said a quick prayer for their souls, asking God to reward them for whatever good they might have done while alive and to forgive them whatever wrong they might have done. Then he blessed each coffin as they were rushed past in single file, and sprinkled a handful of soil saying in a weary voice, "Ashes to ashes and dust to dust."

And the coffin-bearers intoned, "Amen."

Then they went off to bury their dead.

As one casket was taken away for burial, another one was brought forward and the ritual repeated. The plague had forced this distressing ritual on the Pastor, Janet revealed as she and Frank watched from a distance. With so many funerals taking place daily, the Pastor could not attend them all. The dead came to him, or rather by his gate, on their way to their place of interment. The

Pastor was aware that most of them died from Aids, a disease of sinners. However, as a man of God, he could not refuse to bury anyone who claimed to be Christian. They queued by his gate and he did for them what he could.

When the last of the coffins had been carried away for burial, Janet and Frank approached the gate.

"Is that you Jane?" Pastor asked finally noticing them.

"Janet," said Janet.

The Pastor apologised and explained that his mind was on the roof of his church, which was full of holes and the short rains were nearly here. Then he noticed Frank.

"Has your husband finally come home?" he asked her.

"This is Frank Fundi," she told him. "The son of Mateo."

The Pastor shook hands with Frank.

"Your father was a good man," he said. "You are the boy who went to be a doctor, aren't you?"

"I am," Frank admitted.

"Have you brought a cure for the plague?" he asked him. "People are dying like animals here and there is nothing we can do to stop them."

"The plague is everywhere, Pastor," Frank said.

"Will they find a cure?" the Pastor wondered.

"God knows."

The Pastor patted him on the shoulder, then turned to Janet.

"Is everything all right?" he asked her. "No one has died, I hope?"

"No one has died," she assured him.

"The old woman is well?"

"She is well," Janet informed.

"Your children are well?"

"They are all well," she said. "I come about Kata, my brother-in-law."

"Your brother-in-law is an evil man," said the Pastor.

"He wants to marry his brother's wife," Janet informed.

"*Hau!*" the old Pastor exclaimed.

"His brother died from the plague," she added.

"*Hau!*" said the old Pastor. "Is there no end to this badness?"

"Not unless we put an end to it," Janet told him. "Will you help me?"

"How?" asked the Pastor. "Your brother-in-law is a heathen. He worships goats and spirits. You know he does not believe in hell; he told me so himself. He will perish in the eternal fire."

"I think of my sister."

"She married the scoundrel," the Pastor reminded. "She must seek salvation herself. No one can help her now. God helps only those who help themselves."

"And the weak of mind?" she asked him. "What of the fools? What does God say of them?"

"They must bear their own crosses," he said. "They too must seek forgiveness."

Then he gave them a sermon, and lots of Biblical wisdom to take with them back to Crossroads, but in the end they left no more helped than they had arrived.

"That was your great idea?" Janet admonished, as they trekked back to Crossroads.

Frank was in a stupor; he had not realised how hard it would be to talk to Crossroads. Now it was back to Janet and her unorthodox methods. She would have to find a way that worked.

Crossroads was in its continuous-dying state. The beggar lay asleep inside the phone booth and not a soul stirred on the decaying street.

At the teahouse, the old men read the latest old newspapers to arrive on the *Far Traveller*. The papers were scattered on the table, in no particular order, as Musa shuffled the pages in search of entertaining pictures.

"Hear this," Uncle Mark said, reading out to him. "The notorious bank robber, *wa Guka* has robbed a bank in Sokoni and escaped in the direction of Crossroads. A specialised police team has been dispatched to track him down."

"How much did he steal?" Musa wanted to know.

"It does not say," Uncle Mark answered.

Musa grumbled. He could do with a wealthy customer, for a change. All he had now were two dubious customers who would not leave, but pleaded poverty whenever he tried to raise the rent.

"There is a reward on his head too," Uncle Mark informed. "Would you like to know how much it is?"

Musa did not want to know. He was reading the picture of a barely dressed woman in the centre pages of the mid-week Nation. He wondered how any woman could have such long hair and such long legs that went all the way to her neck. There were other things

70

about her that were more amazing and impossible to contemplate, but he dared not discuss them with his companion for fear of being thought decadent. So he stared at the picture until the woman appeared to sway towards him, and he blinked and moved back, startled, and the picture stopped dancing. He wondered out loud in which land the bewitching creature lived.

"In this land," Uncle Mark replied, reading his mind.

"Here?" Musa was astonished.

Uncle Mark laughed his bemused laugh and said, "I believe so."

"In this land?" Musa asked.

"In this very country," Uncle Mark affirmed.

"Is that possible?" Musa wondered.

"It is completely possible," Uncle Mark assured him.

"*Hau!*" the old man was astounded. "I did not know that such a thing was possible."

"Everything is possible," said Uncle Mark. "But you have to travel a little to believe it."

"*Hau!*"

"*Hau,* indeed," agreed Uncle Mark.

Musa turned the pages and read on. But he kept going back to the same page and staring at the picture in disbelief.

"Impossible," he concluded finally and threw the paper on the table.

But, in no time at all, he was leafing through the paper again and muttering to himself that he had never, in all his life, imagined so voluptuous a creature, not even in a picture. This was the height of a disturbing, new discovery.

"Where did you go when you left Crossroads?" Uncle Mark wondered.

"To Biri Biri," he said.

A whole twenty kilometres down the road; where he had, no doubt, learned to cook the Biri Biri omelettes, among other culinary atrocities.

"Then I went to Sokoni," he added.

Another twenty-five kilometres in the opposite direction; where he had learned never to trust another human being ever. Then he had come back to Crossroads, turned the butchery into a teahouse and determined never to leave home again. But now, looking at that picture, the picture of a totally impossible thing that

71

was also possible, added a new purpose to his desire to quit Crossroads for good.

"Had you travelled but a little farther," Uncle Mark told him.

"You would have encountered wonders you would never believe."

The world out there was full of marvels, Uncle Mark assured him. A world where things that were not at all conceivable happened all the time.

"*Hau!*"

"*Hau!*" echoed Uncle Mark.

He wondered if he should take Musa down to Makutano one of these fine days and introduce him to the indigenous hedonism that was to be found there, and a little of the earthy voluptuousness, that he had encountered there. But then, he thought, Musa might like the life of untamed indulgence too much and decide never to return to Crossroads. It was not a good thought at all.

Finally, Musa pushed the papers aside, rose, stretched and yawned, then walked outside to stand in the middle of the street looking up and down the way. There was nothing to see there, except the beggar dozing at his station, and Frank keeping vigil outside his animal clinic and a dauntless wind that blew dust and paper through the ruins. Frank waved. Musa waved back.

A funeral procession turned the farthest corner and came slowly down the road, shimmering in the mirage that flooded the upper end of the street. The coffin was carried effortlessly on the shoulders of two old men and was followed by a woman and her five children, walking slowly and wearily, their feet shuffling silently in the hot dust, their spirits weighed down by their grief. Then, suddenly, as happened often in the presence of death, the world stopped. The wind died out leaving the pallbearers' feet shuffling soundlessly on the ground. It was suddenly stifling hot.

The eerie stillness woke the beggar, and brought Uncle Mark out of the teahouse to join Musa in watching the funeral party approach. When the cortege finally reached the teahouse, Uncle Mark took off his hat and Mzee Musa bowed his head. "Who is in the box?" he wondered out loud. "Ask them," Uncle Mark suggested.

Musa raised his voice and called out to the coffin bearers, "Who is in the box?"

"Big Shoe, the cobbler," answered the grief stricken woman. "My husband, my only man and the father of all my children."

"Great sadness," said Musa.

Like most people in Crossroads, he had known the cobbler all his life and known him to be an honest and God-fearing man.

"What ate him," he asked, his heart heavy with dread. "The plague?"

"The plague could not kill my man," said the cobbler's wife. "His brothers were jealous of him and they bewitched him till he died."

"Great sadness," said Musa.

"Great woe," said the woman, full of bitterness. "Now I must bury him with sadness and rear his children all by myself. Such is the fate of woman."

Musa had no response to that.

The procession moved on and the old men stood and watched it till it turned out of sight. Only then did Crossroads stir again; the wind resuming its constant and aimless agitation of dust, paper and smells, and the old men going back to their newspapers. The beggar, after serious consideration, went back to sleep and Frank considered taking a nap.

Then Janet descended on him, arriving in a hot and furious cloud and skidding to a stop inches from running him over with her bicycle.

"Greetings," he said startled.

"You must come with me," she was highly excited.

"Why?" he asked her. "Why must I come with you?"

"I'll tell you on the way," she told him. "But we must hurry."

"Hurry where?" he asked her.

"I will show you," she said urgently. "There is no time to lose."

For a fleeting moment, Frank considered refusing to go with her before she had told him where they were going. Then the musky, sweaty odour hit him again and he started to lock up the store.

"We must rush," she told him. "Kata is about to condemn some boys to certain death."

Frank stopped in his tracks.

"We must stop him," she urged.

"We?" Frank worried.

"You and I," she said.

73

The memory of their last encounter with Kata was still fresh in Frank's mind. He immediately reversed his movement and started to re-open the kiosk.

"I can't come with you," he said decidedly. "Not back to Kata's house. Not this time, not ever again. The man tried to kill me once."

"He did not," she said incensed. "You did not face up to him, that was the problem. You are a gutless coward. That is what is wrong with you; you are just like the rest of them."

"I'm a man, like the rest of them," he pleaded with her. "Just trying to live my life in peace. What do you want from me? Why do you drag me into your family affairs?"

"I can't do this by myself," she said to him.

"Then don't do it at all," he told her. "Let Kata and his women be. Didn't you learn anything from your ill-advised suit against them? You cannot win against tradition. These things are not new at all. They were here before we were born and they will be here long after we are dead. Why must you stir up everyone and turn everything upside down?"

For once, Janet was speechless.

"You," she started angrily. "You ..."

She could not get it out of her bosom. She turned hopped on her bicycle and rode away.

Frank watched her go and felt sorry for her, and sad and angry with her. He knew what she was doing to be right, but he also knew it to be wrong and impossible. His heart was torn between common sense and his true feelings for her. But he did not have to think long about it. He locked up the shop again and started after her.

"*Daktari,*" Uncle Mark called from the veranda of the teahouse, from where he had witnessed the whole episode. "What is happening now?"

"Trouble," Frank said. "Nothing but trouble."

"Remember what I told you," Uncle Mark advised.

He remembered it well. Janet was the biggest trouble in Crossroads, since the North-South Highway abandoned Crossroads to her ignominious fate. As a friend or as a foe, Janet was a liability to anyone who had anything to do with her.

Frank rushed after her, but she was already out of sight, lost in the overgrown pathways that were all that was left of the old country ways.

The homestead swarmed with people. Men, women and children, all in a good festive mood. The air was hot and stuffy, thick with dust and wood smoke, and the odours of many bodies rose as a haze over them.

Women cooked and sang at one end of the compound. The boys were lined up naked, in a highly charged circle of men at the other end; each one of them supported and braced by two men, both of whom were well fortified with roasted goat and sorghum wine. One of the men held the boy from behind, in a vice-like grip, to stop him flinching, or making any movements that might be construed as a sign of cowardice and disgrace them all. The other man's job was to constantly whisper encouragement to the boy. Those already circumcised stood back, their jaws clenched against the pain and blood oozing down their thighs, and prayed for the ceremony to end quickly so they could go to groan in private.

Kata Kataa, his hands awash with their blood, pranced from one boy to the next and, knife flashing, did his job with gleeful ardour. Behind him skittered an equally delirious assistant with the soot-blackened calabash into which Kata dumped the fruit of his gruesome harvest.

There were many wild and colourful stories told, as to what the pair did with their harvest, but the stories were too banal to bear repeating.

The circumcision party had worked itself into frenzy when Janet arrived. Wasting no time on subtleties, she charged purposefully through the crowd to the heart of the thing and, planting herself defiantly between Kata and the boys, ordered him to cease the primitive activity at once.

Big Youth was among the naked boys awaiting their rendezvous with Kata's knife and, on beholding Janet position herself between them and Kata, he promptly covered himself with his hands and looked for a place to hide.

Everyone and everything abruptly stopped. Silence fell over the compound. The women, who were nowhere near the cause of the disruption, stopped too and searched for the source of the sudden interruption. There followed a moment of absolute silence, during which Kata's face turned all shades of horror and incomprehension. Women were taboo inside the inner circle, where the boys were circumcised and Janet had no business being there at all.

75

The protests, when they came, were harsh and numerous. They came rolling in from every quarter, in a furious cascade of curses and insults and calls for her chastisement. Janet stood her ground and, like an unwavering warrior, braved them all.

"Woman," Kata was astounded. "Have you not a single hair of shame left anywhere on your body? Isn't anything at all in this world sacred to you?"

"Sacred?" Janet fumed. "Have you any idea what you are doing to these boys?"

"I'm making men out of them," he said sincerely. "And you, what are you doing here?"

"I'm here to thwart you," she said, just as directly. "I'm here to stop you making dead men out of healthy boys. To stop you killing them all with this so-called initiation."

Kata had had two calabashes of sorghum wine, and was in a mellow, semi-reasonable frame of mind, and he did not know what to do with her. So he went on doing what he knew best - cutting off foreskins and dumping them in the calabash.

Janet turned to the boys, most of who were covering their nakedness with their hands, and told them they would all die.

"If one of you has the plague," she said ominously. "You will all get it and die."

They were big boys and they knew a fact or two about the plague, but no one, it seemed, had told them they could catch it through this vital ritual. They were all suddenly uneasy about it. Those already circumcised were greatly alarmed. The rest, Big Youth among them, were extremely uncomfortable and looked for a honourable way out of it.

"Stay!" Kata ordered them, harshly. "Will you now let a lunatic spoil our ceremony? Shall we give up our customs because this woman does not approve of them?"

"No," answered the gathering of old men, with drunken conviction.

"Then take her away from here," he ordered.

Few of them were drunk enough to consider laying a hand on the *Kondom Woman*. Such a thing had never, to anyone's knowledge, been attempted before. But Kata's assistant, happy on sorghum wine, and not quite aware of who she was, set the calabash of foreskins down and prepared to tackle Janet. His peers, all sane old men with a healthy respect for Janet's reputation, gasped with horror. He was a puny, old thing, like them, a shrivelled old thing that had never been anything but a foreskin-minder all his life. Janet towered head and shoulders over him in stature, as well as in ferocity, and her reputation as a man-eater was awesome. The crowd marvelled at the foreskin-keeper's folly and moved back to make room for his slaughter.

Then, just as the old man was about to make the mistake of his life by taking Janet in a drunken headlock, a roving cat discovered the calabash, and all hell broke loose. Everyone forgot all about the great encounter and went after the feline, landing with a thunderous crush over the confounded creature. The cat fled in terror and the calabash was instantly obliterated by the mass of bodies. When order was eventually restored, and the foreskins recovered, another calabash was brought out and the recovered treasure carefully counted. But, as no one had kept count, the exercise was soon abandoned and all present agree that they had recovered every single one of them, give or take a few.

Frank arrived at the homestead during the recount, half dead from exhaustion, and took his place by Janet's side. Kata's dismay at seeing him was monumental.

"What is the matter with you, *Daktari?*" Kata asked. "What is the matter with you two?"

Frank was wondering the same thing himself. Until Janet, he had never endangered his life for any cause. He had made it through college without once being clobbered by the riot police, who raided the universities from time to time to teach discipline to the students. He did not believe Janet's was a cause to die for either, but he knew for certain now that what he was doing could cause his death. However, he braved it all and stood by Janet's side, ready for whatever fate had in store for him.

"What shall I do with you?" Kata asked them both.

"Cut them too," Big Youth joked.

"Are they not cut?" the assistant asked, dead serious.

"I don't remember cutting you, *Daktari,*" Kata said to Frank.

"I was before your time," said Frank.

"I don't believe you," said the assistant.

"Show them, *Daktari,*" Big Youth suggested, carrying the joke too far.

"Quiet!" Janet ordered him.

Big Youth ducked out of her sight.

"Cut him, anyway" suggested the calabash holder, reaching for Frank.

Frank leaped back. Janet moved between them and dared Kata to circumcise her first. The gathering gasped in horror. The female circumciser was a different animal altogether, a shadowy creature existing on the periphery of society, a toothless hag who was also the official village witch, and the first person they lynched when the urge to do away with witches was upon them, and it was the height of denigration for a man of Kata's stature to be equated with the circumciser of women.

"Take her from here," he ordered his assistants. "Bring *Daktari* here. We shall make him a man too."

They shoved Janet aside and went after Frank. He fought back, dodging and ducking with every blow and looking for a way out of it. They mobbed him and tried to undress him. Fear turned to panic. He broke free and bolted, taking off through the fields with a mob of youths, some of them stark naked, in hot pursuit. The ceremony degenerated into anarchy and chaos and, with it, died Kata's chance of earning six months livelihood for his growing number of wives and children.

Kata was staring into space, his body raked by violent convulsions and foam issuing from the corners of his mouth. The calabash carrier saw this and fled in terror.

Uncle Mark had followed Frank from Crossroads, to prevent him from doing something fatal, and now suddenly appeared by Janet's side. Janet had never been so grateful to see him. The mob that was swaying to and fro, gathering courage to tackle her, hesitated.

"What is it about you women?" he asked her sadly. "What is it about you women that makes men do such foolish things?"

"Have they caught him?" was all she could think to ask.

"Not yet," he told her. "But, have no doubt, they will."

"Will they hurt him?" she asked.

"Almost certainly," he told her.

"Can't you do something?" she asked him.

"Do what?" Uncle Mark laughed that old and irritating laugh. "You should not have dragged him into this affair, in the first place."

"I did not drag him," she said. "He followed me here."

"You should not be here yourself," he said to her. "This is no place for a woman and you know that. Come now, I will walk you out of here."

78

They left the milling crowd and made their way to the gate. The mob was seething and bubbling and still very angry with her, but no one dared stop them leaving. As they turned onto the old boundary road that led from Crossroads to Janet's home, she said, "I had to do something."

"Something so inconsiderate as to deny your own brother-in-law his livelihood," Uncle Mark observed, nodding wisely.

"Hunger can't justify murder," she said, the old defiance creeping back in her voice.

Uncle Mark regarded her hard, yet fragile, face and shook his head in pity. She was not only prone to confrontational politics but appeared totally convinced of its necessity. She would never find peace until all injustices were wiped out from Crossroads. There was more to the woman than he cared to find out, he thought to himself. At that moment, he felt for her exactly as he would have felt towards the daughter he never had.

He shook his head again in sympathy. Janet was fated to live out her life at war.

The boys had chased Frank a lot farther than even they had expected. Having gone that far, and afraid to return to the uncertainty of Kata's knife and probable consequences, some of them did not return.

Frank's hid in a bush and lay gasping for breath. He heard the hue and cry approach his hiding place and heard it pause uncertainly. He shrank into the bush, now quite terrified of what might happen to him next. Then, suddenly, a big face obscured the sky over his hiding place.

Daktari," Big Youth asked, grinning at him. "Are you all right?"

Frank nodded, too breathless to speak.

"Stay down," Big Youth said withdrawing.

"This way," Frank heard him shout at the pursuers. "He went this way."

The chase party swept by Frank's hiding place and went after Big Youth. Frank lay still and listened until the commotion had died away in the distance. Only then did he realise he was surrounded by thorns and that most of them were buried in his body and starting to itch like mad. He stretched out on the ground, too tired to care, and closed his eyes.

Moments later, he was woken up by stealthy movements approaching through the bush. He sat up alarmed and prepared to flee.

"*Daktari?*" Big Youth called.

"Over here," Frank called back.

"You can come out now," Big Youth said.

Frank crawled out of hiding and began to scratch.

"You must wash in donkey's milk," Big Youth advised. "To stop the itching."

"Donkey's milk?" Frank looked up alarmed. "Where on earth do I get donkey's milk?"

"Only then will the itching go away," Big Youth said.

He was pouring with sweat.

"*Daktari,*" he said, laughing heartily. "They would have cut you today."

"Thanks to you," Frank reminded.

"I was only joking," Big Youth said. "But you better go back to Crossroads now. They will be coming back this way soon, and they believe they must castrate you today."

"What about Janet?" Frank asked.

"Kata will kill you, if you go back there," Big Youth told him. "Come, I will show you the shortest way to Crossroads."

"We must find Janet," Frank insisted. "I must know what happened to her."

"Nothing, I'm telling you," Big Youth said impatiently. "Janet's at home counting her condoms."

He led Frank through the bush, away from the roads and the cattle trails and from wherever there was danger of meeting the boys.

"Everyone is angry with you today," Big Youth informed. "You have spoilt a very important day."

"And you?" Frank asked him. "Aren't you angry with me too? It was your big day too."

"It was," agreed Big Youth. "Until Janet arrived. But I'm happy she came. I don't want to die from the plague."

They arrived at her house, hot and tired from their cross-country hike, to find Janet engaged in a fierce argument with Grandmother.

"I have been told what you have done," Grandmother said to Frank, her voice heavy with disapproval.

"What have I done?" He was completely taken aback by her fury.

"You know what you have done, son of Mateo," she said ominously. "Your father must turn in his grave."

"But what have I done?"

"Forget Grandmother," Janet said to him. "Did they hurt you?"

"What have I done?" he asked Grandmother.

"I said forget her!" Janet ordered him. "Did they catch you?"

"We could not catch him," Big Youth reported. "We chased him all over the place but we could not catch him. *Daktari* runs like a gazelle."

Frank flopped onto a stool and started scratching in earnest. He was full of swellings and bloody spots where the thorns had pricked him and the itching was terrible. He would never forget this day as long as he lived, and that was a fact.

"Today I ran like a coward," he told them.

Grandmother remarked that such was the fate of foolhardy men; men who insisted on poking their manhood in other men's homes and into other men's affairs. Frank assured her that he would never do such a foolish thing again, and meant it, but Grandmother did not believe him.

Chapter Ten

Frank was at his clinic in Crossroads when Kata and the gang finally caught up with him.

It was another dead Crossroads afternoon and the beggar was asleep by his phone booth, his stomach grumbling at the smell of food emanating from Musa's kitchen. Uncle Mark sat at his favourite table in the teahouse keeping vigil over the empty street, and wondering if he should go call on his widows, as he had no one with whom to play draughts. Musa was in the kitchen concocting the evening meal. Frank had decided to devote the day to business and now sat dozing outside the clinic, hoping someone would come along and buy the drugs before they expired.

He did not see them come. Weeks had passed since the circumcision fiasco and Frank considered the matter over and forgotten. He heard a thunderous roar and the next thing he knew the animal clinic was surrounded by a mob of youths brandishing machetes and clubs. They milled around, hurling curses and insults at him and threatening to circumcise him and hang him out on the nearest telephone pole to dry. Frank fled into his kiosk and locked himself inside.

The mob tossed about tumultuously, banged on the walls of the clinic with their clubs and chopped at the air with their machetes and threatened to set the place alight unless he came out to be circumcised. Finally, when they had thoroughly frightened him, Kata gave the order and they stormed away, amid wild chanting and warlike circumcision dances.

Frank had never been so frightened before and he waited a long time before venturing out of hiding. Uncle Mark had rushed out of the teahouse when the mob arrived, but had been prevented from reaching Frank by the frenzied youths.

"Did they hurt you?" he asked.

Frank shook his head. He too was amazed that they had not hurt him.

"I told you the woman was trouble," Uncle Mark told him.

"She needs help," Frank said.

"Help to do what?" wondered Uncle Mark. "To disrupt the community and to cause havoc and chaos?"

Frank shook his head and wondered too.

"You don't know Janet," Uncle Mark laughed. "The only help she needs from anyone is to get out of Crossroads. That is the best you can do for her - take her out of here."

"Janet will never leave," Frank had deduced that much from the conversations he had had with her. "Janet will be the last person to leave Crossroads."

Uncle Mark nodded in agreement.

"What I don't understand is why everyone hates her," Frank said.

"The woman has made it her calling to haunt our collective conscience forever," the old man told him. "We don't like that."

Since he had been back, Frank had not found one person who liked Janet unreservedly. Even Big Youth, who loved her most, admitted to living in awe of her.

"Everyone likes Janet," Uncle Mark now said to Frank. "It may appear to you as though we make her life miserable, but only Janet makes Janet's life difficult. You see, she refuses to accept that we cannot change. That we are set in our old ways and we do not want to change them."

The Government had hired Janet to educate Crossroads, to enhance the quality of the lives of the people there and to try and change Crossroads' outlook on life. The Government had given her condoms and pills to dish out, free of charge, in order to save the community from poverty and death. And what had Crossroads done to Janet? Crossroads had derided her and laughed at her and dismissed her crusade as a vulgar and foreign imposition and an exercise in futility. Crossroads had said many shameful things about Janet and dumped her reputation in the latrine; along with the birth control pills and the condoms that no one used.

"We have chosen death over change," Uncle Mark added. "And that is something she will not accept."

To deliver the point home, a funeral procession wailed down the deserted street towards them, shrouded in gloom and dark despair. It was composed of one man, his one wife and their six children, all of them choking with grief and too sorrowful to shed tears. The parents were the pallbearers, carrying the feather-light coffin effortlessly on their heads while the children followed behind, shuffling their bare feet in the hot dust and sobbing silently.

Uncle Mark took his hat off and Mzee Musa emerged from the teahouse to call out to the coffin bearers to ask who was in the coffin.

"My daughter, Nerita," said the sorrowing woman.

"She died," said the man.

"Great sadness," said Musa.

He was dressed in a grimy net vest and his face and hands were covered with flour and the fresh dough of the *mandazi* he had been making when the pall of silence drew him hither.

"What ate her?" he asked them.

"Nothing," said the father.

"She was a good girl," added the mother. "My Nerita was a good girl."

"Just out of University and not even married," said the father. "She was not a harlot."

"She was a good girl," affirmed the mother.

"Great sadness," Musa said.

He scratched his stomach unhappily and the procession went on its way to have their brief ceremony at the church gate and to bury their beloved Nerita. Then Musa noticed Uncle Mark with Frank and crossed the road to the clinic.

"I must leave this awful place," he announced.

Business was bad and he was weary of funerals. It was not fun to be alive in Crossroads anymore. He made this announcement with the usual seriousness and it was received with the usual scepticism.

"You will get used to it," Uncle Mark said, as always.

There was a time when he too had thought of leaving Crossroads. Way back before they closed the post office and effectively marooned him in the land of death. It was exactly as if someone had locked him in and thrown away the key. Without postal and telephone communications, he could not tell whether the people he wanted to run away to were themselves alive or dead. So he had stayed and grown used to it all.

It fascinated him to be witness to the death of a community, the extinction of an entire people. And nothing, it seemed, could be done to stop it. Though she tried, it seemed that Janet and her condoms were doomed to failure. New devices, and more dynamic strategies, would have to be found to deal with the problem.

Uncle Mark had a few theories of his own, but none of them was in the least acceptable in this land of total men. He had thought of them after reading an article in the newspapers.

"What about the women?" Musa had asked. "Would you squeeze them too?"

"That would be quite a task," Uncle Mark had admitted.

Mzee Musa had mulled over it for weeks before finally asking, "Do you think it would work?"

"Highly unlikely," Uncle Mark had to admit. "Crossroads would find a way of continuing as before."

And that had been the end of that bright idea. But it was a thought and, like many such desperately inane thoughts, it would remain a possibility until men found a workable option.

"I shall pack up and leave this place," Musa now said.

He said it with the same conviction he had when he predicted that, one day, Janet would be his wife. It was an expression of bold optimism, rather than of hope, and the others accepted it as such.

"Before you go," Uncle Mark said to him. "Give us two glasses of tea."

"And some *mandazi*," added Frank, feeling suddenly famished.

Musa waddled back to the teahouse, shaking his dumbfounded head and muttering to himself. Nothing made any sense to him anymore.

"How about a game?" Uncle Mark said to Frank.

Frank locked up the clinic and they followed Musa to the teahouse.

Pastor Bat's Parish Committee was composed of a motley group of old men and women; a self-satisfied group to whom the crumbling old church house was their only refuge, a private ground where only the chosen and the privileged had a right to be.

They listened to Janet and Frank unfold what they thought was a brilliant idea; a grand plan to turn Crossroads from an abode of despair into a place of hope. From a garden of death to a spring of life. A place where joy reigned and people came to live, not to die. A house where children laughed; not a hovel where babies cried all day. Janet talked herself hoarse detailing her plan to return Crossroads to paradise on earth.

When the Parish Committee had heard it all, they nodded wisely and asked to be allowed to confer.

Janet and Frank waited while their plan was discussed in detail. It was turned upside down and examined for leaks and for booby traps. They heard it praised for the wrong reasons and they heard it attacked for the wrong reasons. Finally, when everyone had had their say, several times over, and it appeared that they would never stop, Pastor Bat stood to speak. He announced that church finance was the next item on the agenda and they had no time to waste on private matters.

"My views are well known," he said to one and all. "This church belongs to the people. Therefore, it is up to the people, through the Committee, of which I am only the chairman, to decide on the matter. We must put it to the vote. All those in favour of turning this hallowed ground into a playground for sin raise your hands."

Not a single hand went up. He turned to Janet and said to her kindly, "There is no more to be said."

"But, Pastor ..." she tried.

"We have important matters to discuss," he told her.

"More important than the fate of orphans?" Janet asked him.

"You are being unreasonable now," he tried to usher them out of the meeting place.

"Is this not a Christian place?" Frank asked, suddenly fed up with it all.

He had not come willingly and he was more than a little angry at being dragged halfway across Crossroads to talk to a mountain of impotency.

"Is this a house of God or a house of finance?" he asked the startled Committee. "The Christian without sin is one who takes care of widows and orphans. Isn't that what the Book says?"

He paused, more startled by his own outburst than the Committee was. But it had worked. Pastor Bat hesitated and the Committee sat up to listen. Seeing that he had captured their attention, Janet motioned Frank to continue.

"You all know me," he said to the Committee. "I'm one of you, Crossroads born and bred. I was a member of this church long before the plague was heard of. Back when Crossroads was a place where neighbour buried neighbour and orphans could look up to the community for sustenance. Now orphans bury their parents by themselves while the righteous gather in the house of God to discuss church finance."

The Committee was stunned.

"Who are we?" he asked them. "What have we become? You know, as well as everyone else, that not only the sinners die from the plague. Some of you have lost your loved ones to the plague. Would you say that they died because they were sinners? How long will you barricade yourselves inside this holy place while the world dies outside?"

The old men squirmed in their seats, cleared their throats, and looked everywhere but at Frank.

Janet took the opportunity to restate her case. There were over twenty orphans crammed in old Mateo's home. As everyone present was aware, old Mateo was dead and his wife was too old to care for the children. There were numerous such cases of helpless, old people living alone with orphaned children all over Crossroads. If all the orphans living in dead or dying homesteads could be brought to the church compound, then the whole community could share in the responsibility of looking after them and ease the old people's burdens.

The Committee nodded uncomfortably and turned to Pastor Bat for guidance. The Pastor was the only one of the Committee who lived on the church grounds and he knew what the proposal, if accepted, would mean for him. It would mean a total and thorough invasion of his privacy and his dignity. He would have to be grandfather to all the orphans and, knowing Crossroads, he would end up having to care for the orphans all by himself. He lingered over his decision but for a very brief moment.

"There is no easy way to Calvary," he said resolutely. "The vote is cast; let everyone carry his own cross. There is no more to be said."

As they trekked back to Crossroads, in humiliated silence, Frank made several resolutions of his own. One of them was to resist any attempt to involve him in any more of Janet's crusades. They took too much from the soul.

That night, he had the nightmare.

He saw again the endless vista of graveyards and burial mounds; the forest of gravestones that stretched farther than the eye could see. He saw the dead rise from their graves, and dance about, dressed in nothing but their caskets. He saw them swap coffins and graves in an endless carnival of decomposing cadavers and rattling skeletons. He beheld Death dancing on the graves of the dead, and round the tombstones, chanting incantations. Then the vast cemetery turned to a garden of death and the gravestones swayed in the wind like wheat that was ready for the harvest.

And, in the eerie stillness, Frank heard the cries of the dead and the anguish of the damned, and thought he heard the tombstones sing.

He woke up drenched in sweat. He lay in his bed, his heart pounding and gasping for air and waited for the shaking to stop. Then he rose and went outside to relieve himself, and discovered that it was full moon and there were uncountable stars in the sky, and that he was still alive.

Next door, Uncle Mark was having nightmares of his own and talking loudly in his sleep. Across the yard, Mzee Musa was dreaming about Janet and breathing like an old bull engaged in mortal combat.

Frank returned to his bed and plunged into a different and more horrific version of his nightmare. In this one, he saw and was petrified to recognize the face of Death. He was tall and powerful and his face was hard and the eyes glowed and were too bright to stare at. And Frank saw himself trotting behind Death with the souls that he harvested dangling from a stick over his left shoulder.

The cocks were crowing, and the sky over the hills was reddening with the approach of dawn, when the raiders came marching down the street. There were thirty of them, dark shadows in large overcoats, and they were armed with machetes and clubs.

Only the old beggar saw them, from his phone booth in the uncertain light of dawn, and he wet himself from fright. He shrank back into the dark of the phone booth and watched fearfully as they stormed Frank's clinic and set about demolishing it. He covered his ears from the awful din they made as they smashed wood and metal and scattered cartons and their contents all over the street. The noise they made was terrible and it was inconceivable that no one else heard it, not at the teahouse and not from anywhere else in Crossroads. The raiders were thorough and quick and, when they were done, they disappeared back into the twilight, just as fast as they had come.

The beggar waited until they were safely out of sight before crawling out of his hiding place and rushing to the teahouse. The door was locked and everything quiet within. Not wishing to arouse Musa's ire by knocking on the door, he sat on the step and waited. He waited until Musa opened up, and was engaged in his early morning prayer on the floor of the teahouse, then sneaked through to the back of the teahouse to rouse Frank.

The lodging rooms were arranged in two rows on either side of the yard, with the doors numbered one to twenty. At the far end of the yard, next to the back entrance, were the toilet and the bathroom. The beggar had never been this far before, and was amazed at how big the place was, and he had no idea where to look for Frank.

"*Daktari?*" he called knocking on the nearest door.

There was no reply. He knocked harder and yelled, "*Daktari!*"

"Number six!" an angry voice barked from within.

The beggar was at a loss. He knew the voice to be that of the old man. He also deduced that the voice was angry, but he had not understood what it had said. He was about to knock again, and be damned, when Frank opened the door to his room and was startled to see who was looking for him at such an hour.

"Come," the beggar said urgently.

"Come where?" Frank asked.

But the beggar was off, hopping about and missing his step in his excitement. Sensing that something extraordinary was about to happen, Frank dressed quickly and followed the beggar through the teahouse. Musa was prostrating himself in prayer and did not see them pass.

The beggar stood on the veranda of the teahouse pointing across the street to where Frank's clinic used to be. It was fairly light by now and there was no doubt about it - the clinic had disappeared. In its place was an enormous pile of rabble and rubbish.

"Many men," the beggar explained.

Then he rushed across the road to the scattered debris and, while Frank watched stunned, set about looting the merchandise. Smashed up wood and torn up cartons were everywhere.

Musa came out moments later to stand next to Frank and wonder what on earth had happened to his kiosk. Frank shook his head and they watched the beggar sift through the wreckage and pop tablets and things into his mouth. Some of them were bitter and he spat them out immediately. Others he chewed on with relish.

"You!" Musa bellowed at him. "Get away from there."

The beggar ignored him and continued hunting for things to eat. He found a bottle of sheep de-worming syrup and joyfully gulped it down. Frank was in shock, trying to comprehend it himself, and he was too distressed to stop.

"What happened here?" Uncle Mark asked, turning up suddenly beside them.

They had not heard him come, so engrossed were they in Frank's tragedy. Now Frank shook his head despondently and Musa answered for him.

"Kata," he said.

Uncle Mark nodded too, as if that made a lot of sense, and made helpless sounds of sympathy. Then he led the move across the road to join the beggar in sifting through the debris and picking up broken bits of this and that; looking for anything that could be salvaged. It was a hopeless endeavour. Bottles were scattered out of their cartons and thousands of unlabelled tablets were strewn everywhere with no way of telling what they were or where they had come from.

Frank soon tired of it, found his stool intact and sat down. Presently, Musa gave up the search too and announced he was going to light the brazier and make them all a nice cup of tea. Uncle Mark also tired of looking for nothing in particular and said he was going back to bed.

Frank sat and thought and watched the beggar pick things and put them in his mouth. Finally, when he had thought himself into madness, he rose and strode resolutely to the teahouse.

Chapter Eleven

The sun was rising over the distant hills when Frank shut the door of his room, for the last time he thought, and carried his battered suitcase across the yard and out of the back entrance.

Uncle Mark had gone back to bed, and was snoring loudly, and Musa was in the kitchen battling the brazier. Frank had no wish to see any of them again ever. He had paid his rent, three months in advance, and Uncle Mark had already told him *"I told you so"* in as many words, and Frank had no reason to wait for others to tell him the same distressing thing too.

He was at the bus stop before Crossroads was fully awake and only the milkmen and the market women were about. Other runaways and quitters joined him a little later; people who, like him had no intention of ever returning. Then came a few ordinary people, market women and men going for their weekly market at Sokoni. And then, just as Frank was starting to feel confident of a clean getaway, Janet turned up, a huge carton of condoms and pills on her head, and there was nowhere to hide from her.

"Where are you going so early in the morning?" she asked him.

"Away," he told her.

"Away?" she did not get it. "Away where?"

"Away from here," he said.

He had had it up to here, he explained. He had suffered his final and devastating blow. He was through with Crossroads. He told her about the clinic, how it was no more, how it was ruined beyond repair and the merchandise trampled in the dust. How everything was gone. Everything he had worked so long and strived so hard to achieve. All gone. So he was leaving Crossroads and there was nothing she or anyone else could say or do to change his mind.

"I should never have come back here," he said. "It was all a terrible mistake, thinking that I could start all over again."

Janet was crushed. She had hoped, sincerely hoped, that Frank was here to stay with her and to fight with her for all the things they believed in. With him, she had glimpsed the light at the end of the darkness. She had started to believe that together they could make a difference.

"I shall not try to stop you," she now said. "I thought you would be the last person to run away from us. I believed you, when you said that two could change a whole world."

"You believed me?" he was angry with himself too. "How could you believe me? I was new here and had no idea what I was talking about. No one can change a people who had rather die than change."

"But people are people," she said to him. "You said that yourself. And people can change. People do change."

"There are no people here," his voice was filled with bitterness. "Only zombies and corpses. The don't matters and the don't cares. You are living in a festering cemetery. Do you hear me?"

"I hear you," she said, quietly, determined to stay calm and composed.

She heard him all right. She heard him loud and clear, and she understood every word he said. But she did not agree with him; she dared not agree with him at all. She had decided long ago that she would live out her life in Crossroads; and she would never accept anything that contradicted that belief, or questioned the wisdom of her decision, or tried to sway her determination in any way. But one thing was clear, here and now. She needed Frank. She needed Frank in a way she had never thought she would ever need a man again.

The *Blue Runner* arrived moments later, groaning and creaking under the weight of its terrible cargo. It was a rugged, old shuttle bus that served the communities living in the interior of the country, faraway from the new highway and its traffic police. It had no road licence, no passenger insurance and no spare wheel. It had no comfort of any kind and its job was to take passengers to places along the new highway so that they could board real buses to real places. *Blue Runner* was overloaded, overworked and stuffy, but it was a familiar, old thing inside which people knew one another by name.

Janet pushed and shoved and created space for both of them next to the driver. As the bus pulled out and got under way, she turned to Frank.

"So now you too have decided to run away like a coward?" she said to him.

Those who heard her, the driver included, turned to see the coward who was running away.

"Yes," Frank said bravely, and hoped it would end there. "I have decided to leave, like everyone else."

"What about the children?" she asked him. "Have you thought about the children?"

The passengers were suddenly curious to see this gutless coward who would abandon his children. The driver was about to stop the bus and order Frank back to the children.

"I have no children," Frank told him.

Then he turned to Janet and demanded, "What are you talking about?"

"I'm talking about the orphans," she said to him. "The orphans we were to find a home for. The ones we vowed to save from Aids."

"You vowed," he told her. "I did not vow to do anything for anyone. They will be saved by their mothers."

"Why their mothers?" Janet was definitely on the warpath now. "Why always the women? What do men do?"

"Don't ask me," he said, for once hating her. "Ask them. I'm only one man."

"Let them tell us," said a woman, from the interior of the bus. "What do they ever do?"

The men kept quite still and out of it. Frank knew it was the height of folly to argue with Janet. The driver knew it too, for he finally smiled at Frank and shook his head in sympathy. The rest of the male passengers stared out of the windows, determined to have nothing to do with the matter.

But Janet was not nearly done telling them.

Men were the most selfish creatures on earth, she told them. Men gave up on their communities, turned their backs on their women leaving them to give birth and to nurture their offspring alone.

That was why Janet, a woman, soldiered on alone. Ignoring the derision and the snide remarks that men made about her, expecting no gratitude from anyone and getting none. Alone, always alone. Alone against the preachers of intolerance and division, alone against the administrators of ignorance and apathy, alone against traditional intractability and obstinacy. Always alone.

Frank, thankfully, withdrew into male anonymity and let Janet rave on. She held the bus captive with her stinging words for the rest of the journey. There was little that was new in the things she said. Frank had heard them all before, and not all of them from Janet.

Everyone in Crossroads knew Janet's life story and of her numerous confrontations with the authorities. She was a mother at sixteen and a deserted wife at nineteen. She was pushing pills and condoms to the scandalised Crossroads community before she was twenty-two years old. Everyone also knew that she had three children, all of them Broker's, and that since Broker's departure she had had numerous decent, and indecent, proposals from all manner of men in Crossroads. From preachers to lechers, from wealthy bullocks to draught oxen, from deranged old rakes to delirious young boys; she had an attraction for men that bordered on witchcraft. Men were known to have gone mad for her love and done some terrible things without ever having spoken a word to her. And, as a long time confidant of women and girls in Crossroads, she had enough reasons to despise every man and boy in Crossroads.

By the look on their faces, there was not a single woman in the bus who would not have gladly given up her mission in life to join Janet in hers. The men, on the other hand, could not wait to arrive where they were going and flee from her presence.

"You are a man," she said to Frank, just as he was starting to believe she had forgotten about him. "You are bigger and stronger and more educated and know more things than I will ever know. People listen to you when you talk and they do not laugh at you and call you a shameless prostitute. Why do you run away?"

"You cannot understand," he said to her.

"Because I'm a woman?"

"Because it is bigger than any of us," he told her. "And it's all crammed in here, in my head and in my heart, where you cannot see it. My spirit has taken all the beating it can withstand."

"I see," she said.

Then she clammed up and did not utter another word until they arrived in Sokoni.

"Where will you go?" she asked him.

"I don't know," he said, truthfully.

This far he had thought only of leaving Crossroads, getting away from the apathy, and from the humiliation he had suffered so drastically at the hands of her brother-in-law. He had not thought at all of what he would do after he got away.

The passengers disembarked. Their luggage was off-loaded and the bus started loading up for the return journey.

Frank picked up his suitcase. He paused to watch Janet struggle to lift her carton on to her head. When he was certain that she would not succeed on her own, he offered to help. They carried the carton from the bus stop to the market place. The place was full of people and merchandise and it took them some time to find a free space for her to set up shop. Then she thanked him for his help and wished him well on his flight.

"Goodbye," he offered his hand.

She took it in a hard clasp that sent a surge of excitement throughout his body. They had not shaken hands since his arrival, eons ago, and the feel of her big, fleshy hand round his calloused and bony one, swallowing it completely, almost devouring it, was overwhelming. The sensation lasted a fraction of a moment, but his hand, when she let it go, floated away and his body was hot and tingling all over.

"Go well," she turned to her business.

She was finished with him.

He watched her unpack her wares, trying so hard to ignore him. It aroused in him a concomitant brew of emotions that was hard to ignore. He wanted to embrace her and to shake her violently, to scream at her and to smother her with affection. He wanted to be in her arms, to crush her in his own arms, to feel her warmth and to give her his strength and to wallow in her uniquely overpowering odour.

She looked up and was surprised to find him still there and staring at her with glazed eyes.

"Well?" she asked.

He stirred and said, "Stay well."

"Go well," she said again. "I wish you well."

"No, I wish you well," he said to her. "You are the one who has set herself an impossible task."

"Impossible?" she smiled, disdainfully. "You don't know me. You don't know me at all."

She wrenched at the carton. It was glued tight and would not yield to her angry fingers. She fought it, wrestled with it and ripped at it with her tough, thick nails. But she was too enraged, and her fingers too slippery with sweat, to get a good grip on it. He watched and waited until he was certain she was not about to succeed.

"Let me help," he said.

"Go catch your bus," she told him.

"Why are you so angry?" he asked her, trying to control his own rage. "Why are you always angry?"

He was angry with himself, for what he was about to do, and at her for not stopping him. And he was incensed at everyone for forcing him to make such a desperate move.

"Let me help," he pleaded with her. "There's no one waiting for me at the end of the road. Why are you trying to get rid of me?"

"Me?" she laughed, the rustic laugh that was offensive and, sometimes, defensive too. "Get rid of you? Have you forgotten who is running away from it all? Have you forgotten who has had it up to here with the apathy and the misery that have nothing to do with you? Why do you try to make me feel guilty about it now? I did not ask you to come back, from wherever you were, and I did not ask you to go away. These were your own decisions. They were not sensible decisions, but they were your own decisions, concerning your own life, and you can do whatever you want with them."

It was no use arguing with her.

A market woman caught Janet's attention and beckoned her aside. While they consulted in private, Frank opened the carton with his pocket knife. He took two collapsible posters from the carton and unfolded them. He was leaning them on the carton when Janet and the woman returned.

"How many boxes did I give you last time?" Janet was asking her.

"Three," she said. "But now we are ten in my group and we need more boxes. You must come talk to our new members too."

Janet rummaged in the carton and gave a box of pills to Frank to open.

An old woman, who knew Janet from when she was a girl, passed by and wondered, in good humour, at how she was still telling women not to have babies, when people were dying like rats.

"What is the purpose of having them today to bury them tomorrow?" Janet asked her.

"Giving birth is a woman's fate," the old woman said. "It is inevitable and, like death, it is God's way."

Janet disagreed with her vehemently. It was not God's plan that people be too many, too poor and too sickly. God did not create people in his image to breed like rabbits, to live like rats or to die like animals.

"We must have children by choice," she said to her. "Have them, not because we are women, but because we want children."

The old woman laughed a long and healthy laugh that was full of energy.

"Go tell it to the men," she said to Janet. "Try telling it to the men."

She had given birth to twelve children herself; at a time when choice was unthinkable. All her children were now parents themselves and she had nothing to regret in them.

The market woman revealed that the women in her group used the pills secretly because their men would murder them if they knew that they were trying not to have babies.

The old woman laughed and went on her way. Other women came and took her place, some to listen to what Janet had to say and others to expound on personal beliefs. Still there were those who came to heckle and to ridicule her.

Frank found himself lost in the midst of market women, listening to arguments he had heard so many times before that he now knew them by heart. Men, total men, gave the gathering a wide berth and went about their business, shaking their heads and boasting how they were glad they had married real women and fathered real women, not shameless rabble-rousers like Janet.

Presently, Janet ran out of pills and had to fetch more from the District Health Office. Frank went with her to carry the cartons. When they were back in the market place, with the women swarming around them again, she touched his arm, affectionately he thought, and told him she was glad he was there with her.

"Now they dare not laugh so loud," she told him.

"I can't stay long," he said, quickly.

"Don't worry," she laughed at his discomfiture. "I'll release you as soon as we are finished with this lot."

Release? Her choice of words was worrying. But he had little time to despair. The crowd changed and shifted and was augmented by a gang of truant boys, who had never seen a condom before, and their dogs. They hung out at the periphery of the crowd, hoping for a glimpse of the *thing* they dared not mention by name.

Sometime at the mid-morning, an irate elder came back with the Chief and two henchmen. The henchmen were armed with heavy clubs and came ready to disperse the women and to arrest Janet and Frank for corrupting the morals of children.

"What children?" Janet asked them.

The urchins and the dogs had scampered at the sight of the Chief and his bullies. On realising there were no children about, except for the babies on their mothers' backs, the elder changed his song and accused Janet of inciting women not to have babies.

Janet defended herself vigorously. She reminded the Chief that he was a Government employee, just like her, and that it was Government policy to fight the plague and to encourage women to have fewer children.

The Chief considered her words, while his henchmen waited for orders to disperse the gathering. The only reason he did not give the order was Frank. Who was he? What was he doing there with the women?

While the Chief pondered these questions, the women started to disperse. Janet would soon be without her audience unless she did something fast.

"Say something," she said to Frank.

"Say what?" he asked, confounded.

"Anything," she told him. "We are in it together."

They were not in anything together, Frank told himself, but this was not the time to argue about it. He cleared his throat and said the first thing that came to his mind.

"Only man gives birth *ovyo-ovyo*," he said loudly. "Without reason."

The Chief gaped. His henchmen gaped too. They knew very well that men did not give birth in Sokoni. Frank saw the total lack of comprehension on their faces and attempted to explain himself.

"I mean man and woman," he said to them.

The women heard woman mentioned and stopped their outward drift. They paused to wonder what the man was on about.

"I mean without a plan," he told them. "You, women, must know what I mean."

They had not a clue. They waited for more details.

"Explain," Janet whispered.

"What I mean is ..." he told them all. "Man is the only creature that makes babies out of season. I mean ... man is more intelligent than other creatures. Wouldn't you expect man to decide when to have children?"

"And how many to have," Janet added.

The Chief turned to his henchmen to ask, "And who is this fool?"

They had no idea.

"He is not from here," one of them ventured.

The Chief addressed Frank, for the first time, and asked him who he was and what he was doing in Sokoni.

"He is a doctor," Janet answered.

"A doctor?" puzzled the henchmen. "From whose hospital?"

"Animal doctor," Frank told them.

Then he turned to Janet and asked her, "What am I doing here?"

She ignored his question and said to the Chief, "He is from Crossroads."

"From Crossroads?" puzzled the henchmen.

Until now, they had believed they knew all the little there was to know about Crossroads.

"You have no doctor in Crossroads," they informed her. "We have no doctor here and we are bigger and more important than you are."

"We do now," she said to them. "His name is Doctor Fundi."

The Chief and his men were confounded. The henchmen wondered out aloud for all dissidents to hear, if they should clobber Frank as well. The Chief ordered them to desist.

"So you are a doctor?" he said to Frank. "My wife is sick. Can you treat her?"

"He can," Janet answered for him. "As soon as we are through here."

And, having thus secured herself official leave to continue inciting the women not to have too many babies, Janet returned to her interrupted business.

"I am a veterinary doctor," Frank tried to explain to the Chief.

"My goats are sick too," said the Chief. "The woman knows my house, she will show you the way."

Then he led his men away, leaving the crowd baffled, and the elder who had summoned him seething with rage. The women

99

came back and Frank soon found himself answering all sorts of medical questions, never mind he was an animal doctor, and revelling in his newly found respect.

"We make a great team together," Janet said, when the women had finally dispersed. "Come, I'll buy you something to eat."

He helped her pack her things, all the time wondering what to do next, and followed her to a teahouse where she bought him lunch. With the carton of condoms on the table beside them, and his suitcase under it, Frank had the uneasy feeling he had lost the fight for freedom. Janet, on the other hand, was charged with excitement as she told him how it would be.

It would not be easy at all to talk to men about condoms. Few men would admit they made babies by lying down with their wives and even fewer women wished to hear it from Janet. She had had to teach herself courage, to do away with the old fears and the embarrassment and to address the issues face to face, to look women in the eye and tell them the truth; that each time they slept with their husbands, they stood a good chance of getting pregnant; that babies did not come from God, as they would have everyone believe, but were made by men and women, through one very specific act. That was the way it was and no amount of self-deceit could change it. It was heart breaking to realise how many women were resigned to having babies as often as they came.

"Our hope is in the youth," she said to Frank. "We must capture them before they start to produce babies."

But Frank had no time to capture anyone. He had no time at all to devote to causes.

"No one has time," Janet said impatiently. "We must find time. We must make time, if we are to make anything at all in this world."

"You don't understand," he said to her. "I'm dying."

"I understand," she told him. "We are all dying."

"I don't mean that," he said to her.

"I know what you mean," she told him. "I know very well what you mean. No one returns to Crossroads, except to die."

Frank was deflated. He had jumped off a cliff and discovered he had been on the ground all along. He was suddenly all hollow and empty inside and did not know what to say. The moment he had dreaded, ever since resolving to return to Crossroads, had come and gone and he was still alive.

100

"I never told anyone," he confessed.

"Crossroads is Crossroads," she told him. "It used to be that a woman could not have indigestion without hearing that she was pregnant again. Now a person cannot grow thin without hearing that she has the plague. You can rest assured that everyone else knows too."

The relief was exhausting. If everyone knew, then there was no fear of discovery and he could now die in peace.

"Live in hope," Janet told him. "Live with a purpose and finish the work we have started."

He could help save a few lives too, she told him. The youth would listen to him because he was one of them, an educated one at that, and a doctor; someone to look up to. The greatest dishonour, she said, would be in retreating into self-pitying obscurity, in sneaking off to die alone in silent anonymity, like a wounded animal. Not to speak out now would be the gravest sin.

Chapter Twelve

The school house was a long building, constructed of grey stone and corrugated iron sheets. The roof had originally been painted green, but it was now patchy and brown from the rust and from years of neglect. The school had not seen a coat of paint in years. The walls were rough and most of the windows were now gaping holes. But it was a sturdy structure, for it was built in the old days, the days when community spirit could move mountains; the days before avarice and self-interest turned a whole people into unprincipled monsters, predators that preyed on their own kith and kin.

A tattered national flag flew on a rotting pole in front of the parade ground. The crooked pole itself stood on about a square yard of cactus flower garden, the only space that had not as yet been taken over by grass and weeds. And it was by this accidental garden that Head Faru met Janet and Frank. He had no time to waste and he asked them to state their business, as quickly and as briefly as possible.

They did just that.

They had been doing it for weeks now and were quite good at talking to hostile school heads with no time for them. In less than a moment, they had told him what they wanted.

"I can't let you do that," he said immediately.

His name was Frederick Faustian Faru and no one, not even other Headmasters, dared call him Fred.

"I run a good school here," he told them. "A decent and well-respected school. My children do not know of such things as you are now telling me about."

"Quite right," Janet said reasonably. "That is why we must teach them now. Teach the children ourselves before they learn from other children and learn the wrong things."

Head Faru was silent. He knew Janet and he liked and respected her. He knew Frank too and he thought highly of him. But he was an experienced teacher too and was used to weighing his thoughts before making a decision.

"How shall I explain it to the Ministry?" he asked them. "How do I tell the PTA why I let you teach their children such things?"

"We teach them how not to die from the plague," Frank said.

"I can't let you teach that here."

"Where else can we teach it, if not in a school?" Janet asked him.

"Not in this school," he said.

"Every school head says the same thing," she told him. "We thought you might be more understanding."

"This is not my school alone," the said. "You must talk to the Ministry. You must talk to the School Board too and you must talk to the chairman also, and to the parents. I have a class now. Don't come back here without proper authorization."

With that, the meeting was ended. He went back to his class and Frank and Janet were left stranded by the flagpole.

"What now?" Frank wondered, as they made their way out of the school gate.

"We do as he says," Janet said, unperturbed. "We go talk to the Chairman of the Parish Committee."

They found Pastor Bat eating a harried lunch, somewhere between the baptisms and the funerals. He had just baptised the grandson of the first man he was going to bury after lunch and he was not in a good mood at all. He had baptised and married nearly everyone in Crossroads. Now, it seemed, he would have to bury them all too and he was not happy about it at all. In truth, he was downright angry about it.

"You do the talking," Janet whispered to Frank.

The Pastor let Frank speak.

When Frank had said his piece, the old man heaved a sigh, took off his glasses and rubbed at his old eyes saying, gravely, "Son of Mateo, you know very well that children should not do those things that you talk about."

"I do," nodded Frank.

"Not before marriage," the Pastor said.

"But they do," said Frank.

"They must be stopped," the Pastor said calmly. "They must wait until they are married."

"That is what we want to tell them," Frank continued nodding agreeably. "But there are those who will not wait. What shall we do about those?"

"You must stop them at once," the Pastor ordered. "You know that it is immoral and sinful. You must stop them."

"That is what we want to do," Frank told him.

"You must tell them that it is wrong," said the Pastor. "Bring them to church too. I'll tell them myself and get them back on the right path. Bring their parents as well and I will teach them how to do their duty."

His ten children were all grown up and respectfully married people. All of them were well-educated people with responsible jobs and a bright future. He had brought them up properly. As all parents should.

"Parenting is not the issue," Frank tried to say.

People were dying in droves, in spite of good parenting. People of all ages, men and women of all social status, were dying every day. Plagues had never been respecters of human life, but this plague had outdone them all. A whole community was about to be wiped off the face of the earth and it did not care.

The Pastor heard him out, with his eyes closed, his lunch forgotten on the table before him, but nodding now and then to show that he was awake. Finally, when Frank had talked himself dry, he opened his eyes, glanced at his watch, and announced it was time to go bury his old friend.

They left the Pastor's house no better off than when they had arrived.

As they trekked through the afternoon heat to their next appointment, Frank realised his nightmare was coming true. The fields would soon be as thick with corpses as they once were with millet.

Chapter Thirteen

It was Janet who suggested that they hang the posters in the schools and in the beer halls and in the dispensaries, and anywhere else that people congregated for whatever purpose. But it was Frank who first thought of using the youth volunteers to post the notices around Crossroads.

The boys from the high schools thought it way below their dignity to carry such posters. Their school heads agreed, and Janet and Frank were ejected from every school they visited. They were about to call the whole thing off, when they had their first bit of good luck.

They were six miles from Crossroads, having walked the whole day, from school to school and across the farmlands, when they met a group of Polytechnic students walking home from school. The students were just as loud and boisterous as the high school boys, but their training was practical in nature and they were more outgoing and less inhibited.

One of them asked for balloons to decorate his birthday party. Janet understood very well that he would do what he wanted to do with or without the condoms.

"Does anyone else have a birthday?" she asked the other boys.

They laughed and said they did not need such things. There was no Aids in Crossroads, one of them declared. Diseases came with the outsiders and people from other places. The plague came with the truckers and with the *Far Traveller*s who stayed overnight in the lodging houses in Crossroads. As long as one did not have any dealings with the truckers and the foreigners, one did not need any balloons.

His name was Sikarame, a notorious Crossroads scoundrel, a teenage debaucher of disturbing proportions who, everybody believed, was destined to die an exceptionally nasty death, at the hands of irate fathers whose daughters he seduced and made pregnant.

Janet did not argue with him. She reminded him that the disease was already in Crossroads, and in abundance. It did not matter anymore that one had never travelled at all, that one had never had any dealings with foreigners. The plague did not discriminate, and it killed the innocent and the foolish just as dead as it killed the prostitutes and the perverts.

"Rubbish," he scoffed.

He knew everything about Aids. It was all a lie hatched up by the preachers and the teachers to keep the youth from enjoying their youth.

"Where did you read?" Janet wondered.

"In a magazine," he declared.

It worried and saddened Janet, who expected such nonsense only from stubborn old bulls, men past their time and resentful of it, not from such a young man. He was destined to grow up to be a disturbed, old bullock, like his father was, if he lived that long.

"Didn't your sister die from Aids?" one youth said to another.

"She did not."

"But she did."

"So what, if she did?" said a friend of the dead girl. "Is it any business of yours?"

"So don't lie to us that there is no the plague in Crossroads," the youth said.

"We all must die," Sikarame told them all. "The important thing is to enjoy your life and to go in style. To live fast and die young and leave a good-looking corpse."

"Have you ever seen a corpse that had died from the plague?" Janet asked him.

He had not, he admitted. But some of the others had, and they assured him there was nothing good-looking about it.

"You know your problem?" Frank said to Sikarame. "Too much ignorance masquerading as high knowledge. You watch out."

He unrolled one of the posters he was carrying and showed it to them. It read: This Land is Dying from Ignorance.

"I was once as stubborn as you are," Frank said to Sikarame. "Nothing could touch me, not even reason. But now I know better. You too will learn."

They gathered round him and wanted to see the rest of the posters.

"We want to hang them all over Crossroads," Janet told them.

Below the various bold headings, the messages the posters carried were simple and direct. They reminded everyone that there was no cure for Aids and exhorted them to lead clean and decent lives; to refrain from bad behaviour and to protect themselves from the plague.

The youths laughed at the posters. They were too simple and silly. They talked about them and argued about them. By the time they reached Crossroads, Frank had convinced several of them to join the poster campaign.

It was agreed that Janet would provide the boys with the ink and the paper. Big Youth would show them what to do, and how to do it. They went away happy and excited to be part of something new and daring.

Janet and Frank went home happy too, completely unaware of the monster they had raised.

A few days later, Crossroads woke up to the most bizarre sight.

The land was covered with posters. Hundreds of posters hung from every tree, every door and every wall in Crossroads. Any surface that could support a sheet of paper had a poster stuck to it. Some of the posters were simple and comprehensible notices: Warning! Beware of Aids.

But most of them were blatantly incomprehensible works of art, bearing crude and outrageously explicit illustrations.

The boys had done a thorough job of it too. And, because they suspected their activity to be somewhat illegal, they had done it all in one pitch-dark night. As a result, many of the posters were back to front, upside down and at every imaginable angle.

"Still," Janet laughed a little, when she heard about it. "It's the thought that counts."

But Crossroads was not amused. Nor was Frank, when he came to realise the extent of the damage the boys had caused.

"Wait till dark," Big Youth said unperturbed. "I'll make the boys go back and correct their mistakes."

Which they did.

But that was not the end of the matter.

Frank was having a quiet game of draughts, with the old men at the teahouse, when the first of the repercussions hit.

Uncle Mark was about to defeat Mzee Musa for the third straight game, when Waziri wa Siri, the most disagreeable man in Crossroads, stormed into the teahouse. He had never, to anyone's recollection, set foot in the teahouse before and they were all more than startled to see him stride in. They watched, mouths agape, as he huffed up to the draughts table and dumped the handful of posters he had ripped off the walls of his lodging house on top of the game in progress.

"What is this?" he demanded of everyone present. "Someone tell me what this is all about?"

Only Frank had any idea what it was all about, and he decided to keep it to himself. Musa regarded the posters, with unreasonable disgust, like a pile of used toilet paper, and wondered what they were doing on his table.

"Read them," said the angry man.

Waziri wa Siri had been a powerful Government Minister and, thereby, acquired wealth and power beyond any mortal man's fantasy. But since his ouster from Parliament, by a man neither as rich nor half as big as himself, Waziri had retired to Crossroads, from where he rose every now and then to take on anyone who threatened his reputation as the most disagreeable man around.

"Read them," he ordered Musa. "I want you to tell me what they say!"

"Me?" Musa was more than puzzled.

Only a fool would ask Musa to read anything. The whole world knew he could not read and he had never pretended that he could.

"You!" Waziri was pointing at Frank. "You read!"

"Why me?" Frank asked.

"You started it all," Waziri said to him. "It is all your doing."

Frank turned to the old men, expecting a bit of teahouse solidarity, but got none. They had no idea what was going on and, moreover, they had no wish to argue with someone who had once bragged that he had enough money to buy the whole of Crossroads, and all its occupants, and do whatever he wished with them. A man who had once shamelessly declared his vote and that of his wife to be worth more than those of all his poor and illiterate constituents put together; a man who had once declared his God mightier than the God of the poor and worthless electorate; a man who was so notorious for making such outrageous outbursts in Parliament that he was legend; a man whom his own family had disowned for, as his old father put it, speaking through his anus. The man who now stood over them with balled fists breathing like a buffalo about to cause some mayhem.

"Waziri is very unhappy," Uncle Mark observed, quietly. "Nephew, you are the one that went to school. You read the silly things for him, before he does something foolish."

There was no way out of it. Frank picked up the posters and unrolled them. Then he read them out, one by one and with great exaggeration, like Chief Chupa making great proclamations.

"Read it louder," Uncle Mark suggested, laying out the board for another game with Musa. "Read it louder, so we can all hear it and bear witness."

"This one here says, "Crossroads is Dying," Frank told them.

"We know that," Uncle Mark said nodding as he moved his turn. "We bury the dead everyday."

To Musa he said, "Your turn."

Musa glared down on the board, determined not to lose this game.

"And this one says," Frank cleared his throat significantly. "Crossroads is dying from ignorance."

"We know that too," said Uncle Mark. "Anything new?"

The word ignorance was spelt in a startling new way, but Frank did not bother them with that.

"Aids Kills," he read on.

"Anything new?" Uncle Mark asked looking up. "Is there anything in any of those papers that we do not know already?"

Frank shrugged.

"Where did you find them?" Uncle Mark asked Waziri.

"On the walls of my hotel," he said.

The hotel in question was an old boarding house on the edge of town, once popular with long distance truckers. Only low-down drunkards and people of the lowest moral character went there now. Waziri had found the posters plastered all over the walls.

"I did not put them there," Frank said truthfully.

He had not been anywhere near the place since his return.

"We had no trouble in Crossroads until you came back," Waziri said to him. "Why don't you go back where you came from and die there?"

There was silence at the table.

"We know all about you," Waziri added.

Musa turned to Frank, regarded him quizzically and wondered. Frank went on shuffling the posters, discovering numerous spelling errors, and refused to get angry or be discouraged.

"Can we get back to our game?" Uncle Mark said to Musa.

Musa was staring out of the window at a funeral procession approaching down the empty street. It was a small procession, much, much smaller than usual, even by Crossroads standards. The pallbearers and the mourners were all children, and none of them was older than thirteen. The coffin was small and narrow, made out of light plywood, and it was carried so effortlessly by four of the children that it was hard to believe it contained the remains of their once mighty and formidable mother. But they carried it with courage and dignity and not even the youngest among them shed any tears.

They walked slowly and silently down the street, past the broken houses and the ruined businesses, past the post office and the teahouse, and across the old highway to rendezvous with other funeral processions outside Pastor Bat's church for the burial service.

When the procession had gone past the teahouse, and the old men could breath again, Uncle Mark stirred and said, "No one can say that it does not kill."

"That what does not kill?" Waziri asked completely lost.

"Whatever killed her," Uncle Mark said. "No one can say it does not kill."

But Aids did not just kill, no; that would have been too merciful. It deprived the body of its resistance to invasion by disease and destroyed all of the body's natural ammunition. Thus cruelly disarmed, the body fell prey to all sorts of terrible maladies, from internal ulcers to suppurating body sores; afflictions that defied all forms of cure as they ate up the flesh and softened the bones, lapped up the blood and sapped the body all of its vital energy, leaving nothing but a hulking shell, so light and so feeble it could not support the spirit.

That was what Uncle Mark had surmised from his observed experience with the plague that was killing Crossroads. The last funeral he had attended, the family of the dead man had had to weight the coffin down with rocks to prevent it from blowing away in the wind.

"It is really not my business," he now said to the angry man. "It is not my business at all, but I don't think it is such a bad idea to tell people about a monster that is about to eat them up."

Waziri regarded them all with renewed contempt.

110

"The authorities will hear about this," he promised, picking up his posters.

Then he stormed out and went to the authorities.

Chapter Fourteen

Crossroads was desperate for the little traffic that strayed off the new North-South highway. Serious business had fled to new towns along the new highway, where people appeared more likely to go on living, and farming was dying as fast as the people in Crossroads. More pertinently, the Chief was part owner of a lodging house in Crossroads and he knew just how bad business was. His official car was rotting outside his house for lack of spares and money had never been this scarce for as far back as he could remember. This was not the time for irresponsible talk of incurable diseases and death.

No one understood Waziri's problem better than Chief Chupa.

"Don't worry," he said to the worried Waziri. "I will get to the bottom of this. I'll personally punish whoever is responsible for it."

He would have the culprit bundled off to the cells, as quickly as possible, have him charged with economic sabotage and have him put away forever. But first he had to find the culprit.

"The son of Mateo," Waziri was convinced of it. "He is the one."

"The son of Mateo is our animal doctor," the Chief said, uncertainly. "We must think of someone else."

However, he could not think and was reduced to going round questioning anyone he suspected could read and write. It was an enormous task. He had never before suspected there were so many literate people in Crossroads. Undeterred, he stuck the rolled up posters under his arm, hopped on his bicycle and rode to all the schools in Crossroads. On the way there, he stopped anyone he came across and asked them if they, or anyone they knew, had written the posters.

"If only my boys could spell this much," said Teacher Paulo, the head of the village Polytechnic. "If only they could have done it."

The Chief was unable to comprehend this wish and quietly folded the evidence and headed for the high school across the ridge. As he pushed his bicycle up the hill in the late afternoon heat, it occurred to him that this was not the job for an obese, old chief but one for a menial henchman, way down the ladder of importance. But his henchmen were busy too riding all over Crossroads tearing down and destroying all the posters they came across. It also did occur to the Chief that, apart from what Waziri had told him, he had no idea what the evidence under his arm actually said.

Head Faru studied the posters longer than the grave Polytechnic Head had done.

"*Eggnolance?*" he read bewildered. "Who wrote this?"

"That is what I have come to find out," the Chief confessed.

"You think that, maybe, one of my boys did it?" Head Faru asked him.

"Maybe," said the Chief. "I am trying to find him out."

"Here, in my school?" Head Faru was outraged. "If there was a boy here who could not spell *ignorance*, I would cane him until he spelt it backwards. What do you want with someone like that?"

"I want to arrest him," said the Chief.

"Arrest him quickly," said the Headmaster. "And bring him here to be whipped and taught to spell."

The Chief, who himself could not spell *ignorance*, nodded vaguely and asked the Headmaster if he thought the son of Mateo could have done it.

"The son of Mateo?" Faru was thoughtful. "Fundi was one of my best students. He has been abroad."

"He has not," the Chief confided. "He never went at all."

"He never went?"

"That is what I have heard."

"He never went abroad?" Faru was again outraged. "How come he did not tell me?"

He was the only person in Crossroads who did not know it by now. He was an old teacher, respected by parents and feared by students and teachers alike. No one ever told him anything he did not ask to know; especially not about the many wild rumours that passed for knowledge in Crossroads.

The Chief was the only person who did not live in awe of Head Faru. They had gone to school together; read the same books together. Then the Chief had dropped out in despair, barely able to read and not even certain how to spell *ignorance,* and had gone on to prove to old Crossroads cynics that education had no relevance at all in the acquisition of wealth and power.

113

"Fundi did not go abroad," he said again thoughtfully and hopped on his bike. "I don't know why, but I will get to the bottom of it."

He called on every school in Crossroads and he got the same story everywhere he went; half the schools could not spell *ignorance*, and the other half could not misspell it.

At last, completely lost for direction, the Chief went to the police.

"Someone was here to complain about this matter too," said the Inspector. "A big fat man about your size. I told him to go bring us the culprit. We shall charge him right away and send him to jail. We cannot have people going around spreading fear and despondency. Just show him to us and we'll do the rest."

"I don't have him," the Chief said.

"What about suspects?" asked the Inspector.

"I don't have any," the Chief confessed.

"You must show us a suspect," the Inspector told him. "Point him out and leave the rest to us."

They would extract a confession, charge him right away and send him to prison. The Law had its ways of dealing with troublesome suspects.

They came for Frank at dawn. Four hefty men, armed with sticks and guns, who did not speak any language he understood. They tore down the door of his room, hustled him out of the back of the teahouse and bundled him into the boot of the police car for the bumpy drive to the police station at Sokoni. He was half-dead with cold by the time they got him there.

Only the old beggar witnessed the brutal arrest. He was suffering the lingering effects of the overdose of the sheep deworming medicine he had looted from Frank's clinic, and was returning from the bushes at the back of the post office, after a phenomenal bout of earth-shaking diarrhoea, when the raiders brought Frank out of the teahouse. They were kicking him, and punching him; knocking him about without mercy, and when the beggar saw it he was terrified and he scampered to hide in the bushes at the back of the post office. Much later, when the sun had well risen and there was no more fear of the dark, he crawled out of his hiding place and ventured to the teahouse to tell Uncle Mark what he had seen.

114

"They held him like this," he said, demonstrating the vicious headlocks and body holds that the men had used on Frank as they forced him into the boot of their car. "Then they kicked his manhood like this and like this and they threw him in their car."

Uncle Mark listened patiently, until the beggar had finished his excited narrative, then laughed and sent him to Janet.

"She got him into it," he said to Musa. "Let her now get him out of it."

"What about my door?" Musa asked, sullenly. "They broke down my door."

"We could try asking Janet to pay for it," he said, with a quiet laugh.

Musa was not amused. Nor was Janet, when she heard of it.

She stormed the police station at noon, just as Inspector Iddi was about to go out for his roast goat. He looked up startled as the inflamed woman dumped the bundle containing Frank's clothing on the table, and demanded to know on what charge he had been arrested.

He was not used to anyone, least of all a woman, demanding anything from him. He regarded the angry woman with a mixture of annoyance and astonishment.

"Are you his wife?" he asked her.

"No," she said.

"Are you his girlfriend, perhaps?" he asked her.

"No," she told him.

"His sister, maybe?" he was now intrigued.

"No," she said.

He scratched his chin and asked her, "Are you, by any chance, his mother?"

"What does it matter what I am to him?" Janet said, raising her voice. "Where is he? What have you done with him? Why are you holding him? I want to see him, at once. I demand to see him now."

The Inspector was fascinated by this woman who had no fear of him. Was it possible she had never heard of him? Never heard of Inspector Iddi, the terror of Sokoni? Impossible! Everyone in Crossroads knew of him. Every woman in the land, and lots of men too, were terrified of him. Many women would have married him, just to be safe from him, but he had his full complement of wives, as laid down in the Koran. But this woman bothered him. She was the first woman in this region who had ever stared him in the eye and talked to him about human rights. Was her impudence, perhaps, derived from knowledge of somebody or something he did not know? Possible. He decided, there and then, to tread carefully. In the Civil Service, fortunes were often made, and just as often lost, through such irrational and apparently insignificant confrontations.

"Sergeant Matumbo!" he called to the outer office. "Bring the Crossroads' suspect here."

Frank was dragged out of the cell in his underwear, exactly as they had brought him, dishevelled and thoroughly demoralised. They had not started to work on him yet, but the cold and dark cell, crammed with smelly drunks and ugly ruffians, had done its job. Another two nights in cell, thought the Inspector, and the suspect would have emerged ready to confess to being the devil himself.

"Have they hurt you?" Janet asked, handing Frank his clothes.

They had not, he reported, pulling on his trousers. He was swollen where they had kicked him outside the teahouse, but he could not tell her about that.

"Why did you arrest him?" she asked the Inspector. "On what charges?"

"Charges?" the Inspector smiled, a little amused by her innocence. "Now you want to know about charges? Let's see now - how about, just for starters, being a vagrant of no fixed abode? Seedy lodging houses do not qualify as fixed abode in our books. He was also found in possession of obscene materials, condom, posters and things, with the intention of corrupting the morals of minors."

"Which minors?" she asked him.

"We have witnesses," the Inspector told her.

"Witnesses to what?" Janet said. "We don't corrupt minors."

"We?" the Inspector looked puzzled.

"And just in case you think that you can abuse me also," she revealed. "I'll have you know that I'm a Government officer, like yourself, and I discharge my duties, as directed by my superiors, without fear or favour."

Superiors? he wondered. Exactly where was she coming from?

"Everything we do is cleared from the top," Janet confirmed.

The Inspector nodded thoughtfully and asked, "What exactly do you do?"

"We are educators," she told him.

"Educators?"

"Teachers," she told him.

"What do you teach?"

"We teach Family Life," she said.

"Family Life education," he said, thoughtfully. "I have heard about that. You teach children not to have children!"

"What is bad about it?" Janet asked him.

"Teaching children not to have children?" he shook his head, amused. "There is everything wrong with it."

"How would you like your child to come home from school pregnant?" Janet asked him.

"Not at all," he said seriously. "In fact, I think I'd shoot the head teacher and whoever else was responsible for it. However, that is not possible as all my children are boys."

"Do they know about Aids?" she asked him.

"They are only boys," he told her. "Too young to know of such things."

Suddenly eager to change the subject, he turned to Frank and regarded him with predatory eyes. He was famous for extracting difficult, sometimes impossible, confessions from the most unlikely of suspects.

"What do you have to say for yourself?" he asked Frank.

"I have no idea why I'm here," Frank said.

"You heard the charges," the Inspector said to him.

"All of them false," Frank said. "They are all false and you know they are."

Inspector Iddi glanced at his watch. They were eating into his lunchtime and he did not like that. He sighed wearily and wondered what to do with the pair.

"Is it true you are an animal doctor?" he asked Frank.

"He is," Janet confirmed.

The Inspector wondered what veterinary medicine had to do with sex education, what cows had to do with condoms, but he did not ask.

"Can you cure a sick cow?" he asked, instead.

"He can," Janet confirmed.

The Inspector thought. He had recently bought a milk cow, to mow the grass around his house, and around the station, but the animal was not doing too well. The Sergeant, who had two of his own engaged in the same venture, had diagnosed *dagana*. But the

117

Inspector was not sure and wondered if Frank could pass by his house on his way home and have a look at the animal? Frank would be glad to oblige, Janet reported eagerly.

That settled, the Inspector relaxed.

"It has been recommended that I deport you from Crossroads," he said to Frank.

"Recommended by whom?" Janet asked.

"It doesn't matter," he said to her.

"Under what authority?" she asked him.

"Authority?" he laughed, amused by her boldness. "We can find authority. Believe me, we can find authority to do anything we want."

"You can't do that," she protested. "It's against the law."

"I know about the law," he said, laughing. "But those rich people don't know anything about the law; in fact, they don't know anything about anything at all. They believe that they can buy anyone they want on this earth and get away with it, and they are right. Do you think I like to be here, in this God-forsaken place? A rich man had me shipped here from Pwani, because I refused to arrest his mother over a land dispute. Can you imagine that? He wanted his own mother arrested and locked up, so that she would not interfere with his plans to cheat his brothers out of their inheritance. Imagine that! Until then, I thought that such a thing could not be done in any God-fearing country. Now some rich people here are unhappy about this condom business, and what it is doing to their businesses, and they want it stopped at once. I realise that you two must do your job, but then so must I. I, therefore, must order you to cease at once or, at the very least, tone it down a little."

"Tone it down?" asked Frank.

"How?" asked Janet.

"I have no idea," he admitted. "That is up to you."

The Sergeant stuck his head in the doorway to remind him that the roasted goat meat was getting cold.

"Bring the *Daktari* his things," the Inspector ordered.

"The suspect has no things," the Sergeant reported.

They had brought him as they had found him, in his underwear. The Inspector cleared his throat, uncomfortably, and said to Janet, "Can I trust you to do as requested?"

"To tone down?" she was disgusted.

"To modify?" said the Inspector.

118

"How?" asked Frank.

"I don't know," Inspector Iddi admitted. "Perhaps, by being less direct?"

"Less direct?" Janet was on the verge of, once again, being rude. "How do you indirectly tell a young girl that her very first sexual experience may cost her life?"

"That is up to you," said the Inspector.

"Up to me?" cried Janet. "Why up to me?"

"You are the teachers," he told her. "When we grew up, we did not have this, so called, sex education. Yet we knew what was what and what went where and why it was so. What you people call making love nowadays was something that animals did, not people. We didn't have such things as pills and condoms, and still teenage pregnancies were unheard of. Children did not get babies, in those days, and we grew up to be respectable individuals and good parents."

"You did not have Aids then," Janet pointed out.

"We did not have the plague then," agreed the Inspector. "And you know why we did not have the plague then? Because we lived clean lives, upright lives and respectable lives."

"Those were different times," Janet said to him.

"What is so different now?" asked the Inspector. "We are the same people we were and children are still children. Why must everything now be suddenly so urgent, so explicit?"

"Today's children are way ahead of your time," Janet told him. "They are discovering things at an age when you did not know anything. As we sit here arguing, youths all over the place are discovering it or thinking about it. By the end of the day, some of them will be carrying babies or Aids or both. One of them may be your son."

Up until now, the Inspector had been a calm and reasonable person. Now he exploded to his feet and bellowed, "Out!"

Frank did not stop to wear his shoes until they were safely out of the gates of the police station.

They arrived back in Crossroads, a tired and subdued pair.

"Come home with me," Janet offered, when the dust raised by the *Blue Runner* had settled. "I will make you something to eat that will lift your spirits."

But Frank did not want to eat. He wanted to be alone, to think his life over again. He did not like the direction it had taken, or any of the things that were happening to him. He did not like being locked up in smelly police cells and, right now, he did not like Janet very much either.

Back at the teahouse, he took a thorough shower and scrubbed himself raw in a bid to cleanse himself of the filth and the experience. Then he went to bed and slept for the rest of the afternoon and the night too.

It was Uncle Mark who woke him up the following day, banging on the door and asking him to declare if he was dead or alive. He was alive, he declared.

"Alive enough for a small game?" asked the old man.

Frank thought.

"What time is it?" he asked.

It was nearly the funeral hour.

Frank was silent, thinking. Sooner or later he would have to get out of bed and face the old men and the day, whatever was left of it.

"Give me a minute," he said to Uncle Mark.

They spent the rest of the day at the draughts table, but Uncle Mark's attempts to coax information out of Frank came to naught.

"Did they beat you up?" Uncle Mark was finally obliged to ask.

"Not at the station," Frank said. "Not in the body."

But his spirit had taken a thorough bashing. He had never in his life committed a crime, or even imagined himself locked up in dungeons with thieves and drunkards and other social misfits.

Uncle Mark laughed and said, "In the old days they would beat you half to death before locking you up in dark, water-logged cells and abandoning you there for a while. Sometimes they would remember to feed you on bread and water and sometimes they would not. Then they would let you out, after about a lifetime in the dark, and ask if you had anything at all to tell them. One usually had a whole lot to tell them."

"Thanks for informing Janet," Frank said. "But for her, I would be rotting in the cells."

"But for her, you would not have landed in the cells, in the first place," Uncle Mark reminded.

Frank suddenly looked up. The old men were sitting very still, waiting for him to admit to his folly and promise to reform. There was no doubt that they were unhappy at what had happened to him. But they were also angry with him, he could see that. What Frank could not see, however, was that they were weary of waiting for him to come to his senses and return to the security of the male fold.

"You hate her," he observed quietly.

"You don't hate her?" Musa asked him.

"No," he said.

Uncle Mark laughed and asked him, "After all she has done to you?"

"I can't hate Janet," he said, honestly.

The old men exchanged dismayed looks. The boy, their boy, was definitely beyond rescue. They returned to their game. Uncle Mark moved a piece, looked up, and regarded Frank with intense curiosity.

"I'm angry at her," Frank admitted. "I'm angry at her for all that has gone wrong with my life."

Because of her, he had lost his life's savings. Because of her, he had spent a night in police cells, like a criminal. He had all but ended up destitute, because of her. All because of her. But no, he did not hate Janet.

"Do you love her?" Musa asked him.

"What sort of a question is that to ask?" he asked them.

"An interesting question," said Uncle Mark.

According to his long experience abroad, in places where men were not too total to reveal their true emotions, love and hate were the two faces of a dichotomous monster.

"We love what we can't hate," he said to Frank. "And we hate what we can't love."

Musa was staring at him, his mouth wide open in utter consternation. He smiled kindly at Musa and said to him, "Don't worry, old bull, the boy has read enough books to know what I have said."

There was not a man in Crossroads who did not love Janet. And there was not a man in Crossroads who did not hate Janet. Some loved, or hated her more than others, but they all had their mixed emotions about Janet. In her, they beheld one or the other of the most problematic women in their lives. Some saw their mothers in her, others saw their daughters; some saw their wives, while others saw their lovers in her. The accumulators and the disintegrators of their lives, all rolled in one. But no matter which woman they saw in Janet, they just could not be dispassionate about Janet.

"Fortunately," Uncle Mark laughed his wise old laugh, "Most of us love her. We pretend to detest her so we can retain our potential to love her."

Musa threw up his arms in despair; trying to understand Uncle Mark was like trying to beat him at draughts - impossible.

Frank too was a little fed up with all this talk about Janet. He was certain that he did not hate her; but he held her in some awe, and he hated that. He was not certain that he did not love her, and he hated that too. It was true he felt a sweet ache in his groin, whenever he thought about her, a pain he could not get used to and yet did not want to be rid of. But he could not go as far as calling it love.

Uncle Mark regarded him for a long moment before, suddenly, bursting into gales of hale laughter.

Chapter Fifteen

Janet was with Big Youth when Frank called to see her. The yard was littered with empty cartons and paint tins, and painted posters were hung everywhere to dry.

"Would you like some tea?" she asked him, as he flopped into a chair by the doorway.

"Let me catch my breath," he said to her. "Then I'll decide what I want."

He had started out to take a long walk in the country; to think his life over and to decide what he wanted to do with the rest of it. He had walked all over the hills and across the valleys of Crossroads in search of answers. Then he had allowed his weary legs to carry him where they wanted to go and they had brought him here. Now that he was here, he wondered what he had come here for. He could not articulate, even to himself, what he wanted to say to Janet.

Janet watched him anguish. They were about the same age, but she had always considered him a boy. He was too sensitive and too sympathetic to be lumped together with Crossroads men. But since his arrest, throughout which he had conducted himself with extreme dignity, she had decided that he was a man. He was not a strong man, or a particularly handsome one, but he was a man-man, solid and sincere and very earnest at whatever he did. The sort of man she could have married.

A funeral went past her gate, the mourners beating on a broken drum and wailing dismally. The funeral drum was as weary of the funerals as the people were, and the sound of it was worse than the howling of a soul that was doomed for all eternity.

Frank worried about that too.

"Will this sadness never end?" Janet wondered.

"I don't know," Big Youth answered. "I don't think it will ever end and I don't want to be the next one to die. I must leave this place soon."

"Run away?" she asked him, as always.

"Yes," he said.

"Like a coward?" she asked him.

"Yes," he admitted, unabashed.

"Where will you go?" she asked him.

"Anywhere people don't die so much," he said.

"There is no such place," she told him. "Ask Frank."

"*Daktari?*" Big Youth called. "Is it true, what she says?"

Frank was staring into space, listening to the funeral drum fade away in the distance. He was a thoroughly troubled man.

"Frank has been all over," Janet said to Big Youth. "Tell him, Frank. Tell him there is no place to run to, to hide from Aids."

Frank was out of it, lost in his own troubled world.

"Frank?" she called.

She decided to leave him in peace.

"Don't worry," she said to Big Youth. "Everything must change."

There was a time she too had thought of running away from Crossroads. Then she had been offered the condom job and had realised that Crossroads could be saved, that the plague could be stopped.

"Now I know for certain," she said. "This plague can be stopped. We have to stop it."

"We?" Big Youth asked uncertainly. "You mean just you and me?"

"You and I," she corrected him.

"Just you and I?" he asked doubtfully.

"Who else is there?" she said to him. "The two of us are enough. I can't tell you what a great help you have been to me, Big Youth."

"But I am too young to die," Big Youth said seriously. "I don't want to get used to death and dying."

"Then do yourself a favour," she advised him. "Tell it to all your friends too. Tell them they must stay alive, for you. Tell them to be smart and stop their foolish behaviour. Tell them that condoms are not for fools and cowards."

"That's a good one," Big Youth suddenly brightened up. "*Be Smart, Stay Alive, Use Condoms.*"

"What do you think, Frank?" Janet tried.

Frank was brooding seriously now. He saw everything they did and heard every word they said, but he had no strength at all left in him to be enthusiastic about any of it. He had not eaten for two days now and had walked a long way to get to Janet's house.

"Good work," Janet said to Big Youth. "Write a few more while I prepare some tea. Then we shall go out and post them in Crossroads."

"Again?" Frank suddenly sat up.

"Again," she confirmed.

"You will do it again?" he was incredulous.

"We must replace the ones the Chief destroyed," she told him.

Frank was tempted to believe that what the old men said about her was true, that she was probably a reincarnation of *Wanguru*. The old witch had ridden on men's backs and intimidated Pwani to submission before the coming of the missionaries.

"Are you hungry?" she asked him.

Deciding there was little left to lose by accepting her hospitality, he nodded.

"Big Youth?" she asked.

"I must go home soon," said Big Youth. "My grandmother is cooking sweet potatoes today."

"Finish that lot then," she told him. "Then have some tea with us."

During the tea, which they had in the living room, complete with pancakes and tablecloth, Frank suddenly said, "I'm leaving."

"Leaving?" Janet was genuinely startled.

"For good," he told her.

"Again?" she said wearily. "You can't leave now, when things are starting to look up."

"You call this looking up?" he smiled bitterly. "The only thing looking up here is the grass."

"Just because we have had a few drawbacks is no reason to give up," she said. "We must never give up hope."

"What hope?" he asked her. "When was the last time anyone showed any genuine interest in your condoms? Wake up, woman. There is nothing here for me but troubles."

"Nothing for you?" she sounded disappointed.

"Only problems," he maintained.

Troubles that had little to do with her or her condoms. It was something bigger, something deep inside of him. Something heavy and aching that refused to accept Crossroads' endless process of dying. So he had to leave Crossroads and, this time, it was for real.

"Take me with you," Big Youth begged. "I don't want to live here either."

"No, Big Youth," Frank said. "You don't have to run away like me. You are young and smart. You will survive. Just continue to do as Janet says and you will be all right."

She was staring at the kettle in front of her in a state of shock and dejection.

"I'm sorry," he said to her.

"Sorry for what?" she asked stirring herself back to life. "There's nothing here for you. Nothing here has anything to do with you. You don't belong here and you don't have to live here. You don't owe us a thing. You don't have to be sorry about running away. You are a free man and you can do exactly as you wish."

She put her cup down, rose and bustled off to her bedroom.

"Now what have you done to her?" Big Youth asked Frank.

"Me?" Frank was exasperated. "Have you seen me do anything to her?"

"Can't you be good to her?" Big Youth asked. "Don't you see she loves you?"

"Janet cannot love a man," Frank said a little too bitterly. "She hates men so much she sends me to be butchered by her brother-in-law."

"But she loves you," Big Youth insisted.

"How would you know that, you stupid boy?" Frank asked him.

"I'm not stupid," he said sounding hurt.

"Did Janet tell you that herself?" Frank asked him.

"I see things," he said. "I'm not stupid, you ask her yourself. Janet!"

"Stop this nonsense," Frank ordered.

"Janet!" he called again.

"Stop the nonsense!" Frank said rising to leave. "You are the most foolish boy I have ever met."

Big Youth hung his head, like a beaten dog, and seemed about to fall to pieces. Seeing the hopeless look on his face, Frank thought of something good to say to make amends. Then Hanna stormed into the room, all excited, and they both forgot their present predicament. She was halfway across the room before she noticed them.

"What are you two doing here?" she asked them somewhat irritated. "Can't you two leave Janet alone for a moment?"

"No," Big Youth told her.

"Where is she?" she asked. "Janet!"

Big Youth raised his voice and called out to Janet.

"There's someone to see you."

There was a brief pause before the bedroom door opened and Janet came out, hurriedly composed.

"Have you been crying?" Hanna asked her.

"Who cry?" Big Youth said. "Have you ever seen Janet cry?"

No one, except Grandmother, had ever seen Janet cry.

"It's nothing," she said to Hanna. "What do you want?"

"I want those *things*," Hanna said. "You know which ones I mean."

"What *things*?" asked Big Youth. "Condoms or pills?"

"Am I talking to you?" the woman snapped at him. "Why are you here? Why are these two always after you?"

Janet brushed the question aside, saying, "I gave you a whole box of pills just the other day."

"I finished them," Hanna said.

She was taking them morning and evening, just to be sure.

"You must not do that," Janet warned her. "I told you it's harmful to take more than one a day. You should seriously talk to your husband about using condoms."

Hanna laughed heartily at that and said, "You say that just to hear me laugh, don't you?"

"No," Janet said to her. "I really wish you would."

She had too many children already and her husband had a reputation as an indiscriminate seducer of widows and bar girls. A self-proclaimed absolute man, a real-man of the old order of total men and, in Hanna's own words, a stubborn buffalo. Not even his mother could make him do anything he didn't want to.

"Make him use a condom?" she found the suggestion hilarious in the extreme.

Janet shrugged, took a carton and started to open it. Normally, she would have snapped it open with a single flick of her powerful wrist. But today she was too troubled and her heart was not in it.

"Get me a knife," she said to Big Youth.

Big Youth went for the knife while Hanna took the box and tried to open it. Failing to do so, she handed the box to Frank. He tried, but the binding tape was too hard to break with bare hands. He waited for Big Youth to bring the knife. Meanwhile, Hanna chattered on about men, how difficult and perplexing they

127

were, how right and wrong they were, and how hard it was to do without them.

Big Youth brought the knife and gave it to Frank. He cut the box open, handed it to Janet. Then, feeling somewhat redundant in all this talk about men, he followed Big Youth outside.

"How do you do without a man?" Hanna asked, when they were alone. "Everyone knows men are mad after you."

"I'm not mad after men," Janet told her.

That was the difference between her and many women. True, there had been times, soon after Broker's desertion, and while the sensation was still fresh in her, that she had yearned for his embrace. She had missed his warmth, his rough sweaty nature and the ecstasy that went with it all. There had been times too when she was tested beyond endurance; when every man and lecher had beaten a path to her door, at all hours of the dark, to knock on her door and to ask to be let in for a little talk. Some had brought presents, others only promises; but they had all come bearing implausible tales and ridiculous pledges, having forgotten, all too soon it seemed, that she was not a witless young doe to be enticed and entrapped with empty sweet talk. But she had survived them all, by reminding herself that Broker had come to her in the exact same manner and left her worse off than he had found her.

"What about Frank?" Hanna asked her.

"What about Frank?" she asked.

"He is a handsome one, isn't he?" Hanna said smiling guardedly.

"There's nothing going on between me and Frank," Janet informed her. "Whatever you may have heard about me and Frank is not true. It's not at all possible."

But Hanna saw the forlorn look that was on Janet's face when she talked about Frank, and laughed merrily.

"You like him," she said happily. "You cannot hide it from me, I'm your best friend. Tell me, is he good to you?"

"There's nothing like that going on between me and Frank," Janet said, firmly. "Nothing at all."

"You are a strange woman," she said finally. "You are a very strange, strong woman."

"Strength has nothing at all to do with it," Janet told her.

It was a matter of choice, of decision. When Broker had decided he preferred a common prostitute to her, Janet had decided she wanted to live her own life for herself. It was her own decision and, since then, men had not bothered her at all.

Until Frank Fundi.

But she could not tell Hanna about Frank. So she told her about the other things, the ludicrous things, the absurdities about men that gave women such a good laugh; and about the supposedly upright men, well known Crossroads saints, who crept up to her door at night, to croon to her about how much they adored her, how much they needed her, and to promise her heaven and earth and things that their own wives had never had.

When Hanna left, thoroughly invigorated by the laughter and loaded with enough pills to last her an eternity, Janet had good reason to feel proud. The gloom had lifted and she had forgotten all about Frank's expressed desire to leave Crossroads. She stepped outside and found she had even more reasons to feel good about herself. Frank and Big Youth were up to their elbows in paint, exchanging friendly banter as they went about writing posters.

"*Daktari*," Big Youth was saying to Frank, "How about this one? *Aids Kills You Kabisa.*"

"Keep it simple," Frank told him.

Big Youth did not understand simple, but he tried, anyway, giving it his total concentration. Frank paused to marvel at one of the posters that had come off the walls of Highlife Lodge; part of the original poster blitz that had gone haywire.

"What is the connection between cholera and condom?" he puzzled.

The only connection, Big Youth said without any scruples, were the first letters.

"We got tired of writing the same thing over and over," he explained.

So they had decided to liven up the task by juxtaposing lines and phrases from one poster to the next. Frank had experienced the full horror of the exercise when he had come across a poster that declared, without shame or apology, *Slim Slays, Condom Cures.* The outrage had dragged him back into the condom war.

This is it, Janet thought, watching her two favourite men work. This is an all out war.

"Condoms don't cure anything," Frank was now saying to Big Youth. "Condoms prevent. Condoms only prevent. Let's keep it simple and sane this time, shall we? Something like *Aids Kills. Beware of Aids.*"

"Too boring," said Big Youth.

"This is not art," Frank told him. "Keep it plain and simple and remember to include *condom*. That is the whole purpose of the campaign, isn't it?"

Janet nodded, and watched and wondered.

"How do you spell *circumcision?*" Big Youth asked next.

"What for?" Frank was again, suddenly, on the point of despair. "What has circumcision got to do with what we are doing?"

"It can give you Aids."

"Circumcision in itself is not dangerous," Frank said.

It was the way it was done that was dangerous. The way Kata lined up the boys and slashed his way through them, like a combine harvester.

Big Youth laughed when he remembered the day they had nearly circumcised Frank. He had never seen a fully-grown man run so fast.

"Were you afraid to be cut?" he asked.

"Of course not," Frank said. "I was cut before you were born."

"I'm cut too now," Big Youth confessed. "Do you want to see?"

The look of horror on Janet's face amused him greatly.

"What is the matter with this boy?" Frank was dismayed.

"I'm telling you I am not a boy," Big Youth said emphatically. "I was cut at the hospital in Biri Biri. I was so scared, after you broke up our circumcision party, that I went straight to hospital and had it done there."

So Janet now knew where Big Youth had disappeared to during the weeks he had kept away from her place.

"I'm not stupid," he told them. "I don't want to die from Aids."

"There is another one for you," Janet said to him. *"Be Smart, Use Condoms."*

Big Youth toyed with it for a moment. He decided it had no music to it and tried a few more lines and came up with nothing that pleased him.

"What about this one?" he said finally. "Man plus woman, minus condom, equals baby plus Aids."

It was the sort of thing that only a thoroughly uncomplicated mind like Big Youth's could come up with.

"Say it again," Frank told him.

Big Youth did and, this time, sounded he convinced.

"Let's be serious here," Frank said shaking his head. "How many of your friends understand that many words?"

"I can," said Big Youth.

"You are a smart boy," Janet told him.

"Man," he corrected. "I just told you I'm a man."

"Finish what you have started, man," Janet said to him. "Afterwards you can take this lot out and post them. Everywhere people can see them."

"Everywhere?" he asked, hopefully.

"Except on church doors and school houses," Frank warned. "And no upside down jobs, like the last time."

"That wasn't me," Big Youth said. "That was the stupid polytechnic boys Janet hired."

"They volunteered," Janet corrected him. "I can't employ anyone. They all volunteered."

"This time it is just you and me," Frank said to him. "I'll come checking them myself."

Big Youth gathered the posters and rolled them up.

"I have much homework to do today," he told them. "I shall hang them up tomorrow."

"Whenever you have the time," Janet agreed.

They watched him walk away with pride, a new spring in his walk and a new purpose in his life.

"He likes you," Janet observed.

"He adores you," Frank told her. "You and him are the only real friends I have."

"And the old men at the teahouse," she reminded him.

"Those too," he agreed.

She laid her hand on his shoulder and said, "Would you like to come live here? I have a room to spare and ... people will talk anyway."

The question took him by surprise. For weeks now he had been hoping, searching for a way to get closer to her. He had known she had a room to spare but had not dared ask her to rent it to him. Now he had no idea what to say to it.

He considered. He had read a whole lot about Aids, read of people who lived happily together without infecting each other.

But he had never imagined himself in such a relationship. He gave it very deep thought.

Janet waited. She had thought about it for days; about Frank's uncertainty over his future and his desperation over the living conditions at the teahouse, which she suspected were behind his intermittent desire to quit Crossroads for good. She had given it a very long thought too before making her decision.

The heavy and awkward silence, which enshrouded everything while Frank contemplated his next move, was broken by the sound of a car turning into Janet's gate.

Chapter Sixteen

It was a large, low car, the like of which had not been seen in Crossroads for a long, long time. It was a long and wide monster, black all over, and with silver trimmings and dark tinted windows.

They watched intrigued as the car purred to a stop in the yard, among the cartons and the tins and things. They waited in dry apprehension as the door swung slowly open and the driver stepped out. Then they were lost for words.

They had expected to see an opulent, middle-aged man, robust of character and forceful of nature, in keeping with the status of the vehicle. What they now saw was one emaciated, old creature, of indeterminable age, with a shiny, bony forehead, thinning brown hair, large ears and eyes that were about to disappear back into their cavernous sockets.

"Greetings," he said to them.

"Greetings," they responded.

The stranger's frightful physical appearance was, however, the only thing that was meagre about him. His clothes, like his car, were excessively loud; he wore a cream suit, a red shirt and a wide black tie and his shoes had not yet made acquaintance with the pervasive Crossroads dust. A thick gold watch hung loosely around his bony wrist and his skeletal fingers had gold and silver rings.

While Frank and Janet made these observations, the man reached into the car and took out his walking stick. It was long and shiny, carved from ebony and fitted with an ivory handle; the universal symbol of authority and power that powerful men and insecure politicians carried and which everyone knew had a concealed dagger inside it. Leaning his weight on the stick, the stranger limped to the middle of the yard and stopped. He looked about the place searching for a landmark.

His eyes regarded the many empty cartons and the paint tins that littered the yard, with obvious disapproval, then went from the house to the grain store, to the posters hanging on the walls and the trees. They lingered on everything, absorbing, digesting everything and trying to extract some succour and meaning from everything they saw. Finally, his probing gaze found the crumbling house, partly lost in the bush, and seemed to soften.

Big Youth had met the car down the road and now came running back to see what it meant. He could hardly believe his eyes as he walked round the car, mesmerised. He could not resist the urge to touch it.

"Don't touch," said the stranger.

His voice had a powerful timbre to it, in contrast to his appearance. It was a big voice, a voice full of authority. Big Youth stepped back smiling nervously.

The stranger was staring at the old house and nodding to himself as one who had found the answer to a long-standing puzzle. Then he turned to Frank and asked him, "Who are you?"

"Me?" Frank was caught off balance. "I'm Frank."

"Frank what?" the man asked.

Janet held up her hand at Frank.

"Who are you?" she asked the stranger.

"Who am I?" he seemed amused by the question. "Who am I? You don't know who I am?"

"Who are you?" she repeated, tersely.

"I'm Broker," his eyes danced with mirth. "I'm your man, Broker."

When Janet was twelve or thirteen, Grandmother had taken her to a bearded old woman who had lived behind the old Mosque, and introduced her as Janet's *mutiri* - her instructor; the teacher and guide who would steer her down the difficult road to womanhood. The old sage was long dead now, but, before she died, she and Grandmother had taught Janet everything there was to know about being a woman; from clearing the fields to hoeing and planting, from harvesting to winnowing and grinding. The old women had taught Janet everything there was to know about being a woman, everything except how to deal with the pain. The pain had to be endured.

Janet had experienced a great deal of pain in her life. From the indescribable, bone-grinding pain of childbirth, to the fever of unrequited love; from the agonizing pain of betrayal, to the throbbing ache of a heart about to break, Janet had experienced all manner of hurt. But she had not understood pain in the way the old women had promised it - pain so intense that it made you wish you were dead. Now, as Big Youth came forward mouth agape with amazement to scrutinize the stranger in absolute wonder, Janet finally understood pain.

"You?" Big Youth was saying to the bag of skin and bones that once was Janet's husband, "You are her husband? You? You?"

Broker, a little sobered by the insolence, regarded the barefoot youth with contempt.

"Do I know you?" he asked him.

"No," Big Youth said. "But I have heard a lot about you. Are you really Broker? Are you Janet's husband? Seriously?"

The same question was all over Janet and Frank's faces.

"The one and only," Broker said to them.

"But you look so ... " Janet started to say.

"Finished?" Broker laughed. "No, not quite finished. I may not look like you remember me, but I'm far from finished."

"Far from finished?" marvelled Big Youth.

"What happened to you?" she asked.

"Everything," he said. "Anything and everything that could happen to a man. And then some."

Big Youth was looking from him to the car and back flabbergasted.

"You should have seen me a few months ago," he said. "Belly up to here, buttocks up to there. I had a neck like a hippopotamus, they told me. They called me Kiboko."

"Kiboko?" Big Youth sounded impressed.

Broker smiled tolerantly at him then turned, apparently bothered by the cartons that littered the yard. He tapped at one of the cartons, flipped it open with his cane, and was surprised to find it full of condoms.

"Do you sell condoms?" he asked Janet.

"We give them away," Big Youth answered for her.

"Away? Away how?"

"Away away," said Big Youth.

"For free?"

"For free."

"Why?"

Big Youth started to answer, then realised he was not certain.

"Ask Janet," he said.

Janet was staring past Big Youth to the car, a puzzled look on her face. Big Youth, reading her mind, said, "There is no one else in the car."

"I'm all alone now," Broker nodded at her. "Not a friend left in the world. That's what happens when life kicks you in the … Ask me to sit down."

Janet was wrestling with her pain, with the furies in her heart, the homicidal dragons with poisoned tongues urging her to fetch her machete and bring to pass the planned vengeance that had started the day he walked out on her.

"What happened to the roads?" he asked her. "I have been driving all afternoon looking for this place."

He had lost himself for hours in the maze of cattle trails and rattraps they called roads, he told them.

"Doesn't anyone here care for roads anymore?" he wondered.

"We have no cars to drive on them," Big Youth informed him.

"What about the Government officers?" he asked.

"The Chief rides a bicycle," said Big Youth.

He turned to Janet and asked her, "Where are my children?"

"In school," Big Youth answered.

"And your parents?" Broker asked Janet. "How are they? How is your father?"

"You remember him too?" Janet's head was beginning to ache.

"How could I ever forget him?" he said. "Your father gave me my first real job. The things he taught me I could never have learned from anyone else. Does he still run the petrol station in Crossroads?"

Janet was seething with rage and about to boil over. He noticed it and said, "I would like to repay him for his kindness."

"You repaid him enough," Janet retorted. "When you stole his money and ran off with a bar woman."

"Borrowed," Broker said harshly. "Borrowed, not stole. I had to make a break. You know he would not have given me the money. I did what I had to do, and anyway, I'm here to apologise and to pay him back, tenfold."

And how would he pay back for the other things? She wanted to know that. The broken trust? The desertion? Abandoning the old man's foolish and trusting daughter to bring up his children all by herself? And the heartbreak? How could he ever pay for that?

Broker shook his head and said to Big Youth, "Women have an amazing memory; some things they never forget, others they never remember."

At this point, only Big Youth found the turn of events amusing. He was getting a serious education, watching them fight, and he was grinning from ear to ear and enjoying himself.

"You keep off the car!" Broker barked at him.

Big Youth jumped back and laughed foolishly. The others were standing very still, waiting for something to break.

Broker turned to Janet and said, "I did it for us. You know that. You must believe me, my dear."

"I am not your dear," she said it so coldly it frightened Big Youth.

This was all familiar territory, she was thinking, as she tried hard to suppress the hammering in her head. She had seen it all before; the loud, confident laughter, the inflated affection and the charming, deceitful smile, calculated to beguile. She had experienced them all before, in another world and in another time.

The air was heavy with impending doom. Frank stood it for just as long as he could, shifting his feet uncertainly, then decided it was time to remove himself from the imminent disaster and cleared his throat.

"I must go now," he said.

"Are you still here?" Broker asked annoyed.

"Why must you go?" Janet demanded.

She had no wish to be left alone with this bellicose stranger who claimed to be her husband. There was no telling what would happen next. She remembered well his explosive fury; the battering she had endured in the name of love. She also remembered promising herself, long after he had left and she had got used to her new identity, that, if he ever came back and tried it again, she would kill him. To her great shame, she had exacted that revenge many times in her imagination. Then, when it appeared certain the man would never come back, she had let go of the anger and forgotten all about it.

"You will find this hard to believe," Broker was saying, not very convincingly. "But I left here with the best of intentions. To better myself, to make something of my future with you."

His career as a pump attendant had been on the wane and he could hardly make ends meet. And Janet's father, who had understood and hated Broker from first sight, had warned him never to imagine himself inheriting from the Maalim Juma estate, except through sheer hard work. At the time, Broker had been the entire labour force at the service station. It had not taken him too long to sum up the truth; the truth that he was destined to die from overwork before his father-in-law retired.

"I had to break out of here," he now explained to Janet. "To find a way for the both of us and come back for you and the children. Now I'm back."

"It took you long enough," she said to him.

"Not for lack of trying," he told her. "Believe me, it's a madhouse out there."

He turned to Big Youth and said, with a friendly smile, "You don't know how lucky you are to live here."

Which was something Big Youth could not understand. Lucky people left Crossroads with the early morning bus. Lucky people went off to faraway places, and got themselves big jobs and made their fortunes. Lucky people came back in big cars and built big houses for themselves and for their relations. Really, lucky people did not live in Crossroads.

Big Youth shrugged, smiled and felt very encouraged by Broker's return. There was still hope for him.

Broker turned to Janet and said, "Now, my dear."

"Don't call me that!" she snapped.

"You used to love it," he reminded her.

"That wasn't me," she told him harshly. "That was the foolish village girl you enticed out of school."

"Enticed?" he sounded disappointed.

"And robbed of an education," she said. "Cheated her out of her life."

"Cheated?" he was scandalised.

"And abandoned," she added bitterly. "Without a word of when, why or where you were going."

"You would not have understood," Broker said sombrely. "You never understood anything I said or did."

"Go on and blame me now," she felt the old anger slowly surface. "You who never did or said anything that made sense to anyone. You who never told me one word of truth from the day that I met you."

"Now she calls me a liar," Broker said to Frank.

Frank was resolved to remain out of it. Big Youth, he who had never before witnessed such a cold war, a vicious dispute between man and wife that did not entail clubs and machetes, followed the whole proceedings with mounting interest. He was nodding and shaking his head as the arguments moved him.

"You were a liar to the last," Janet was telling Broker. "Remember what you told me the day you disappeared?"

"Went away," Broker corrected. "The day that I went away."

"The day you deserted me," Janet said. "Do you remember what you said to me?"

"What did I say to you?"

"You don't remember?"

Broker turned to Big Youth and said, with mock weariness, "What did I tell you about women? Some things they even remember too well. And get off my car!"

Big Youth hopped off the car, grinned and decided Broker was someone he could like. Anyone who dressed like that, and drove such a car could not be bad.

"All right," Broker said to Janet. "What did I say to you on the day that I decamped?"

"See you soon, my dear," she said. "That is what you said to me. See you soon my dear."

"Just that?" he sounded a little disappointed. "That was all?"

"That was all you said," she affirmed. "I was washing, remember? See you soon, my dear, you said. I was standing over there."

"I can't remember that far back," he said to her.

"But you remembered your way back here," she reminded.

"No one forgets their way home," he said and tried to sound remorseful.

"I thought you had gone to Crossroads for cigarettes," Janet told him. "Can you imagine how I felt when you did not turn up for lunch, then for dinner, then for breakfast and again for lunch? Can you imagine the pain? I was going insane with worry. I thought you had been arrested or been killed in an accident or something. Then I heard that you had boarded a bus for Pwani with a fat woman from Highlife Lodge. Have you any idea how that hurt?"

"It must have hurt a lot," Broker said regretfully. "I'm sorry."

"Sorry?" Janet finally exploded.

"What else can I say?" he asked her.

"Say?" she cried.

"What would you like me to do?" he asked in earnest. "You say it and I'll do it right now."

"Go away," she said.

"What?" he was incredulous.

"Go away," she repeated. "That is what I want you to do. Get back in your car and leave. That is what I want you to do. That is what you must do."

Broker's swaggering confidence slipped and started to fall to pieces. His jaws bunched up and his smile disappeared. The face hardened and the eyes darkened.

He had not expected this much trouble from Janet, it was true. He had never had trouble dealing with women and had foreseen no serious problems with Janet. Just a brief shouting match, a few tears, some apologies, and it would all be all right again. Now it was clear he had a lot of mending to do. His eyes were no longer humorous.

Before Frank's amazed eyes, Broker transformed from the optimistic persuader to a vile offender. It was obvious he had come expecting an easy victory and a quick reunion.

"I can't go away again," he said firmly. "I can't do that at all. I am here to stay, for good."

Big Youth was nodding encouragement, so strongly did he feel for this charismatic stranger. This was what his father must have been like.

"Not in my life," Janet said to Broker. "You are not back in my life. You will never be back in my life."

This was the point at which she should have gone for the axe and hacked Broker to size, Frank was thinking. But Janet did no such thing. She was not afraid of Broker anymore. She was way past ever being afraid of him again. She was stone cold, dead to his existence, and it frightened him.

"We shall sort this out in a moment," he said to her.

Turning to Frank, he said evenly, "Tell me you did not know she had a husband."

"A husband?" Janet laughed the devastating Crossroads laugh; the scornful, emasculating blast that had men running for cover.

"Simmer down," Broker said, unperturbed.

Frank and Big Youth were aghast. How was that possible? How could Broker be still on his feet, ego intact, after such a venomous fusillade from the heaving bosom of his own wife? Truly, the man was awesome.

"Everyone here knows my husband died ten years ago," Janet said.

"I said, simmer down!" his voice rising. "I'll get back to you in a moment."

She was speechless. He let her simmer for a minute and get used to the fact that he was back in the saddle. He had worked it all out in advance. Within twenty-four hours, she would be eating out of his hand and licking it.

"Now you," he turned to Frank. "Do you know what we do to men who talk to other men's wives?"

Frank had an idea but he shook his head, all the same. Broker grabbed his stick in both hands and snapped the dagger out of its scabbard with such savagery that Big Youth jumped back and cried, "*Woi!*"

It was a long silver sword, thin and sharp and as fast as a snake's tongue, and it glinted in the sun when Broker shook it in the air.

"*Hau! Hau!*" exclaimed Big Youth.

"Then we skin them and hang them out to dry," Broker added.

"*Hau!*" exclaimed Big Youth thoroughly horrified.

He wasn't so sure about this man anymore. Such savagery was new to Crossroads and did not befit a man of his stature.

"I'm not your wife," Janet said to him as calmly as she could. "Can't you understand that? You haven't got a wife here anymore. Why have you come back?"

"To see you," he said evenly.

"To see me?" Janet asked. "Just to see me? You have seen me. I'm still here, where you left me, and I'm not crying and I'm not desperate. Now put away your foolish knife and leave."

"I must see my children too," he said, demonstratively chopping at the air with his sword.

"You cannot see my children," Janet's mind was made up.

"They are my children too," he reminded.

"Not anymore," she said with certain finality. "You can't see my children. Understood? Now leave."

Sensing a dangerous hiatus, Broker turned on Frank.

"Who are you to her?" he asked holding his sword at Frank's throat. "Are you her boyfriend or her lover? Her new husband, perhaps? What are you to her?"

Frank froze, the touch of cold steel at his throat. Men had lost their lives, and more, over similar misunderstandings. He gasped for air and desperately sought a dignified way out of his predicament.

Big Youth was at a loss as to what to do now, and seriously thinking of bolting.

Then Grandmother materialised in the yard, having walked all the way from her gate unnoticed, and they had never been so glad to see her.

"Who is this making so much noise here in my daughter's house?" she asked them. "What is this *thing* taking up the whole hearth?"

They turned and there she was, regarding Broker's car with total incomprehension. Broker quickly sheathed his sword and leaned his weight on the walking stick. Having satisfied herself that the huge black thing, with four shiny wheels, was indeed a car, Grandmother shuffled up to Broker and squinted up at him.

"What is this?" she asked of him.

"It's me, Grandmother," Broker said to her. "It's me your Broker."

His joy at seeing her was genuine and it earned him many points with Big Youth. Anyone who could genuinely like Grandmother could not be all bad.

"You are still alive?" Broker asked the old woman.

"Were you waiting for me to die?" she asked.

"Same old Grandmother," Broker laughed. "How old are you now, one hundred? One hundred and twenty?"

Grandmother turned to Janet and asked, "Who is this fool?"

"Ask him," Janet told her.

"I'm Broker," Broker said to the old woman.

Grandmother's eyes narrowed doubtfully. Was he playing a joke on her?

"You don't remember me?" Broker sounded disappointed. "You must remember me, Grandmother. I'm Broker. Bakari Ben Broker. Your son-in-law."

"Janet's husband?" she said uncertainly. "You are Janet's husband?"

"The very same?" he said to her.

"You are alive?" she asked, seriously.

"I think so," he laughed. "Yes, I'm very much alive."

"I thought you were dead," she told him.

"Dead?" he laughed till Big Youth had to join in. "No, Grandmother, I'm not dead yet."

"I remember that foolish laugh," Grandmother finally smiled. "Not a care in the world. So you finally remembered you had a wife and children?"

"I never forgot, Grandmother," he said, happily. "Not for a day did I forget about them."

"Then why didn't you come home sooner?" she asked him. "Where have you been all this time?"

"Working for them," he said to her. "I worked like a donkey, Grandmother. But now I'm back and everyone must be happy to see me."

"What have you brought them?" she asked him. "Is this your car? How did you get a car as big as a house?"

Broker, sensing an ally in her, laughed heartily and decided to keep her amused.

"I bought it," he said to her. "With my own money."

"You bought it?" Grandmother looked him in the eye and asked seriously, "You did not steal the money, did you?"

"No, Grandmother," he said. "I worked like a dog for it. I had to work day and night for it."

"Good," she said, nodding with satisfaction. "I told you stealing would get you nowhere."

"I remember, Grandmother," he said and nodded vigorously.

"Will you now stay?" she asked him.

"I will never leave again," he told her.

"Good," she smiled happily. "Your wife has been dying for the lack of a man. You see these two men here? They are always here. They have been hovering around her like hungry vultures. They think I don't know what they are after."

"Grandmother?" Janet warned.

"What?" Grandmother said to her. "You think I don't know what they are after? Especially this one?"

She swung her walking stick at Frank. He stepped back and smiled tolerantly. She turned to Broker and, lowering her voice, shared some secrets with him.

"Your wife has not been the same since you left her," she said. "She has been very lonely and always unhappy. I have been trying to find her another man, but now you are back. She can be happy you are back."

"Grandmother ..." Janet tried to stop her.

"What?" cried the old woman. "You don't want me to tell the truth? You don't want your husband to know how you cried for him till you fell sick? How I had to care for you and to feed you like a baby till you got your strength back?"

She turned to Broker and said, "She wanted to kill herself. She was so unhappy that she wanted to die. I had to lock her in the house and watch her day and night to stop her killing herself. But she is happy now that you are back."

"Leave me to speak for myself," Janet said to her.

Grandmother ignored her and said to Broker, "See how old she looks. Some people say that she has got the plague. But it's not true; it's just the worries that have eaten her up. From the day you left, till now, she has not stopped worrying."

"She can stop worrying now," Broker turned to Janet. "Your man is home again."

Janet was rooted to the spot, thinking of a bloodless way of getting rid of both of them.

"You heard your husband," Grandmother said to her. "You don't have to worry anymore. Your man is back to do all that for you."

"Enough," she cried, finally. "You go back to your house now!"

"I'm going, I'm going," Grandmother said, laughing happily. "You two must have a lot to talk about. Didn't I tell you I dreamt something good would happen today?"

"Stop dreaming for me," Janet said to her. "Leave me to speak for myself."

"I am happy for you," said Grandmother.

"Don't be," Janet ordered.

Grandmother grumbled about the ingratitude of children. Frank cleared his throat and Janet turned on him, irritated.

"I'm about to cook dinner!" she told him.

"But there is no need for you to stay," Grandmother added quickly. "Her man is back now. You may all go home now."

Frank picked up his jacket and made for the gate, feeling thoroughly misused and wishing he had left Crossroads the day before. Janet watched him go and wished there was a way to make him stay.

Grandmother sought Big Youth with her eyes and said to him, "You too, nosey boy. You may go home now!"

"I'm not a boy," Big Youth said to her. "I'm a man now."

But he picked up his things and his rolled-up posters and followed Frank out of the gate. Broker sighed with satisfaction and Janet died inside.

"This is a good day for me," Grandmother said to Broker.

She had finally managed to get rid of the begging pair, for the first time ever, and her son was home again.

"Do you still eat *matoke*?" she asked Broker.

He still loved it, he reported, especially the way Janet cooked it. He had eaten bananas in Pwani but he had not tasted anything as delicious as Janet's cooking.

"Come to my house," Grandmother ordered Janet. "I have bananas for you to cook for your husband. I was going to take them to the market but, now that my grandson-in-law is back, you must cook them for him. This is the greatest day of my life!"

"Mine too," Broker said, sitting down in the seat formerly occupied by Frank. He lit a pipe and watched the two women walk away, still arguing.

"What are you trying to do?" Janet was saying as she ushered Grandmother out of her compound. "Why are you behaving like a drunken old woman?"

"I'm drunk with joy," declared the old woman. "Are you not happy your husband is back?"

"After the way he treated me?" Janet asked her.

"Are you still bitter?" Grandmother was astounded.

"I'm still bitter," Janet told her. "I'm very bitter, now that I think about it. And so would you be, if your husband had done the same thing to you."

Grandmother's happy laughter rang through the place. It irritated Janet and made her angrier.

"Men," Grandmother told her. "You will never understand men."

Men were impossibility, a curse that women were born to. Men were never happy when their life was quiet and simple. Everything had to be hard and complicated for men to appreciate. So that they could beat on their chests and crow how strong they were or how good they were at solving problems. Men were like that.

"Why do you think they make wars?" she said to Janet. "So that they can afterwards make peace and get praises for that too. Your grandfather was a master of this confusion. He brooded when I nagged him and he raged when I did not."

145

"But he did not desert you for ten years," Janet pointed out.

"There are worse things than to be left by your husband for ten years," Grandmother said.

"Such as?" Janet asked her.

"Such as coming home drunk, every night, to bother you all night," Grandmother, said.

"Exactly what Broker did before he left," Janet told her.

"But he left you three fine children," Grandmother said as they arrived at her house. "Three wonderful children for which you must be grateful to him. And he has come back to you in a big car and full of remorse. What more do you want?"

"Much more than a big car and sweet words," Janet told her.

She wanted certainty, the assurance that this was not the beginning of another lifetime in hell. She wanted to see sorrow branded on his face with a flaming knife, to see him suffer and bleed tears of remorse for every single, miserable day she had endured on his account; to see his anguished repentance and true contrition, not the insincere and expansive show of remorse that she remembered only too well. She wanted to see Broker down on his knees before her, grovelling and begging for forgiveness.

Grandmother laughed and said, "The women of today will never understand men."

Then she showed Janet the big bunch of green bananas she had been saving for the market day and gave it to her to go cook some for her husband. When they had carried the bananas out of the house, she said to Janet, "Let me tell you a secret. Never try to humiliate a man. It makes them as stubborn as bulls and as hard as rocks and impossible to reason with. That is how many women end up all alone, without a man. If it is revenge that you want, smile."

"Smile?" Janet was baffled.

"As wide as you like," said the older woman. "Just smile and go about your business, as if nothing bad had ever happened between the two of you."

"Then?" Janet asked. "Then what?"

"Then he will go mad," said Grandmother. "He will go mad, but not in a bad way. He will go mad with guilt and shame. He will be mad from thinking why you are not angry with him. The madness will eat at his heart like an army of jiggers. And he will love you like he never loved anything in his life."

"And harass me as he did before," Janet said.

"He will never touch you again," Grandmother promised. "You see that old-dog look in his eyes? He is not the rampant bull he used to be. The fire is gone out of him and he is as gentle as an old goat now. He will be so grateful to you, for taking him back, that he will have you tell him what to do. He will never touch you again."

"I am sure he will never touch me again," Janet said, resolutely. "He is leaving right now."

"*Woi!*" Grandmother squawked. "Not like that."

That would be cruel and unacceptable. Even a complete stranger had a right to bend his knees and rest a while. Even the most unwanted visitor was entitled to a drink of water and some hospitality.

"You cannot deny him rest," she said to Janet.

"He has rested enough," Janet said.

"And food," said Grandmother. "Even an unknown beggar is entitled to some food."

Janet considered it. One part of her, the woman and mother part of her, the part that had kept her sane against all odds, said that this was the same man she would have given her very life for but a short ten years ago. Take him back, the inner voice said, accept him again, for all his manly faults, forgive him, give him another chance and see what happens. But the Janet part of her, the part that men found insurmountable and called shameless, told her to wake up and smell the dung heap; the leopard did not shed its spots, for all the deer in the forest, and a snake without fangs was still a snake; and Janet was not a naïve village girl with a sack full of innocence over her head. She was not so innocent as to believe that a man who carried a concealed weapon at all times could possess a gentle and harmless soul.

But she had accepted the bananas, on his behalf, and could not now deny him food.

"I'll cook him these," she said to Grandmother. "I will give him food."

"And a little talk," Grandmother encouraged. "He must have a great deal to say for himself after all those years. Listen to what he has to say and let us laugh about it tomorrow."

She stopped at the small gate and laughed merrily. She was convinced that she had won the battle for herself, if not for both of them.

147

Janet carried the bananas through to her compound. Before turning the corner to the front yard, she stopped to calm her heart and to silence the thumping in her head.

She had never missed Frank and Big Youth as she did now.

Chapter Seventeen

They talked little over dinner. Broker made several futile attempts at conversation and jollity, but he was quite alone in his effort. Janet remained painfully tense and the children had no idea how to relate to the stranger who claimed to be their father. They ate quietly and smiled politely and, when dinner was over, bid Broker goodnight and withdrew to their room; leaving their mother exposed and insecure and thinking of what to do if he attacked her.

"Nice children," he said.

Janet sat dead still, hardly breathing, as she fought to suppress the rage. He let her brew and was determined not to break the bubble himself. He was in no hurry. He was home again and he was not going anywhere again, ever. The silence was unnerving.

"You have brought them up well," he said.

She hardly heard him; so preoccupied was she with her fears. Broker's cane, with its concealed sword, was leaning on the wall to the left of the door. Her *panga*, the razor-sharp machete she kept by the door at night, was concealed behind the cupboard to the right of the door. She could reach it before he got to his sword, but this was not the way she wanted it to be.

"I'm proud of you," he told her.

Her nails dug into her fists and she repressed the rage until it was about to tear her bosom apart and break out in sobs.

"Speak to me," the silence was getting at him too.

She rose abruptly and started to clear the table, making such a terrible clatter, in her dark rage, that he was tempted to ask her to stop it. She carried the dishes to the kitchen and lingered there a full moment in the dark, and was on the verge of shedding some tears. Then she remembered him and rushed back to the living room, afraid to leave him alone too long, in case he started to relax and settle down. But once back in the living room, the silence was killing her again. She stood in the middle of the room, uncertain what to do next.

Broker smoked his pipe and watched her, an aura of infuriating calm surrounding him.

"Would you like some tea?" she asked him.

"How about some cocoa?" he asked her. "Like in the old days?"

She bit back the shrieks rising up inside her and asked again, very quietly and very carefully, "Would you like some tea?"

"Yes," he said nodding. "I would like some tea. I would like that very much."

She turned to go and he added, "Not too strong, mind you, and with lots and lots of milk and sugar. Just like in the old days."

She stopped in her tracks. The commander was back, as brazenly self-assured as ever. She put her throbbing head in her hands and groaned painfully. Her entire body was now on fire, every nerve aflame; an open wound into which poured hot oil, and she thought she was about to die.

"What's the matter?" Broker asked her.

"I can't go through with it," she said with a groan.

"Go through with what?"

She was silent for another exasperating moment. Her eyes were closed tight, her bosom heaving with sobs that tried to break free. When she looked up again, she had changed. In that agonized moment Janet had turned into a different person altogether.

"Do you have money?" she asked him.

"Sorry?" he was taken by surprise.

"Do you have money?" she repeated.

"Do I have money?" he puzzled.

"You heard me," her voice rising.

"No need to shout," he said calmly. "You will wake the children. Do I have money?"

He chortled, that carefree laugh that even Grandmother recognised for arrogance. They were getting somewhere now, he was thinking.

"Do I have money?" he repeated sucking on his pipe. "That's an interesting question."

"Then answer it!" she said harshly.

"I have money," he admitted. "1 have lots and lots and lots of money. More money than you can count. More money than most people ever see in their lives. More money than you ever dreamt of. Yes, I have money. How much of it do you want?"

"I don't want your money," she said ruthlessly.

"What do you want then?" he smiled benevolently. "Just name it."

"I don't want anything from you," she told him. "I want nothing at all from you; but 1 will make you a nice cup of tea."

"Just like the old days?" he asked hopefully.

"Just like the old days," she said. "Then you must leave."

"Leave?" the shock was very real.

"Leave," she was quite clear about that.

"Leave?" he could not believe his ears. "Leave to go where?"

"Back wherever you came from," she told him.

"I can't go back there," he protested.

"You will have to," she told him.

"At this time of night?" he asked plaintively.

"Now!" she said decisively.

She was dead serious too. Now that her mind was made up, her head was lighter and she could see clearly to forever.

Broker saw the change in her and was dismayed. He prided himself in being a master persuader and he had not met a woman yet who could resist his natural wiles. What was required now was a quick change in plans. If he could persuade her to let him stay the night, she would be laughing with him by the morning. He begged her to let him stay. It was late and he had nowhere to go.

"Have you forgotten Highlife Lodge?" she asked him.

"Highlife Lodge?" he was lost.

"Where you found your fat barmaid," she told him.

"My fat barmaid?" he groaned with deep-down pain. "Do you have to keep bringing that up?"

"Where did you leave her?" Janet asked him. "Did she send you ahead to find out if the foolish wife is still alive?"

"No," Broker said calmly. "Can't we discuss this in the morning?"

"You can't sleep here," she said firmly.

"But this is my house," he tried.

"Your house?" she choked on her fury.

She strode to the door, threw it open and pointed out into the night, at the crumbling ruin visible in the bushes; the dark brooding thing, the haunting thing in which dwelt the family curses and the demons that tormented her some nights. Many times she had thought of demolishing it, razing it to the ground and planting a thorn tree in the place. Now she was glad she had left it standing, all these years, just for this moment.

"That is your house," she said to Broker. "The cow-shed you built for your devoted village cow, while you spent your best years and money with your town women. You go share it with the rats and the snakes tonight. But tomorrow you must go away from here."

"Go away to where?" he asked dismally.

"Back to those with whom you squandered your life," she said,

"That is not possible," he said to her.

He was through with all of them. That was the reason he had come back to her.

"For you," he assured her. "For ever."

"Don't say that," she could not bear the thought. "I'm not here for you. Can't you understand that? Go back, wherever you have been, and forget you ever had a home here."

He feigned outrage. He raved and ranted for a bit and threatened to resort to extreme measures. Then, on realising that it was getting him nowhere, he said calmly, "My dear ..."

"Don't call me that," she warned.

"I'll sleep anywhere you say," he told her. "Even here on the floor. I really don't mind, I can sleep anywhere. Anywhere you say. But, please, don't make me sleep in the bush like a hyena."

"You can't sleep here," she said, firmly.

He was thoughtful for a moment. This was not the way it was supposed to be. Nothing was going as he had envisaged it. He had tried charming her and he had tried bluffing her. He had tried bribing her, all to no avail. Nothing was going according to plan and he could not understand why. What had he done wrong? Was he perhaps trying too hard or too fast or had she really changed that much?

He dragged on his pipe and weighed his options.

"All right," he said finally. "I'll sleep in your store."

"My store is full," she told him.

"Full of what?" he asked her. "Condoms? Does anyone here use condoms?

That did it.

"Out!" she bawled at him.

"What about the nice cup of tea?" he asked.

He had just talked himself out of it.

"Out!" she said.

Broker did not budge. He sucked on his pipe and reconsidered his options. At the moment, the options seemed very few, indeed, and diminishing by the second. He could wield his cane, like in the old days, and reclaim his throne by the sheer force of right. Or he could get down on his knees and beg for it. But neither of these options was in line with his envisioned, dignified return, or with any of his long-term plans. He would have to redraw his plans.

He heaved a sigh and struggled to his feet.

"I didn't mean to upset you," he said quietly. "But, since you feel so strongly about it, I shall now leave you and go find myself a bed for the night. I'll be back; you can be assured of that. The Highlife Lodge, you say?"

"Your wives may be there still," she said to him. "If they are still alive."

Then, as he looked about for his walking stick, she opened a carton, took a box of condoms and thrust it in his hands. He had no idea what he was receiving until he looked at the box. Then he looked at her, confounded.

"We don't want you spreading whatever you brought back with you," she told him.

She was gravely serious. He studied her solemn face, soft in a hard and mature way, and was amazed at how beautiful she had turned out to be. Astonishment turned to amusement and a sad smile broke out on his face.

"Now she gives me condoms," he said, with sad composure. "Now she gives me condoms."

His amusement annoyed her. She thrust another box in his startled hands.

"Here," she said. "Take this one too. Take another one. Take more. Take them all."

She was nearly hysterical as she piled the boxes in his hands until they spilt on the floor.

"Now get out of my life!" she screamed.

He was no longer smiling. His face had taken on a sickly ashen hue and his lips twitched uncontrollably. The boxes fell from his hands onto the floor. He made no attempt to pick them up. He picked up his walking stick instead and weighed it thoughtfully in his hands and was tempted to play his last card, He was looking at Janet, regarding her with a hard, cold look.

"When my name was Broker," he said waving his cane in her face. "You would not have dared treat me this way."

Then he turned and stepped out into the dark night.

Janet quickly shut and bolted the door behind him. She took her machete from behind the cupboard and leaned it in its reassuring place beside the door. Then she slumped into a chair, put her aching head in her hands and fought to control the shaking and the pain that tore at her heart. Broker heard the terrible sobs and went away convinced it would work out exactly as he had planned it.

It was pitch dark outside, he suddenly realised. His eyesight, like the rest of him, was not what it used to be, and he had some trouble finding his way to the car. He manoeuvred the huge car out of the yard and back onto the overgrown cattle trail that led to more overgrown cattle trails; one of which he knew would eventually take him back to the highway.

But the cattle trails, the old roads that had not been trodden by a car for decades, had been reclaimed by the vegetation in the time he had been at Janet's house. It was hard to tell in the dark where the trail ended and the pasture began. Somewhere between her house and the highway, he made a wrong turn and spent the next few hours trying to extricate himself from the untended fields and the cul-de-sac that led to abandoned homesteads and overflowing graveyards.

Around midnight, completely lost and unable to find his way back to Janet's house, he gave up altogether. He stopped the car and spent the rest of the night staring through the sunroof up at the heavens; counting the stars and marvelling at the comets and at the Milky Way and wondering how he had never seen these things before. And in between his marvels, he dozed intermittently and listened to the crickets and the hyenas and the thousands of night sounds that were made by creatures he had never ever seen.

He fell asleep before dawn, a deep, trouble-free sleep from which he did not stir until a worried herds boy woke him up at midday to ask him if he was alive or dead.

Chapter Eighteen

Only two souls were alive on the entire street.

The beggar sat by his phone booth watching Big Youth work his way up the street, sticking posters to walls and telephone poles as he came. When he was within earshot, the beggar hailed him with his usual greeting.

"You, *Bro,*" he called out. "Give me money."

Big Youth saw that he was the only person on the street, and laughed.

"I'm a beggar like you," he said. "I have no money."

He proceeded to stick a poster on the door of the old phone booth, stepped back to admire his work and said to the beggar, "What do you think?"

"What is it?" the beggar asked.

"It's a poster," Big Youth told him.

"A poster?" asked the beggar.

"I made it myself," Big Youth said with some pride.

"What is it for?" asked the beggar.

"It tells you to use a condom," said Big Youth.

"*Kodom?*"

"Condom," Big Youth corrected. "See, it says here, Man plus Woman minus Condom equals Babies plus Aids. But Man plus Woman plus Condom equals Life minus Aids. I call it the life and death equation. What do you think? Truly?"

The beggar nodded vaguely and said, "Truly, I have not eaten for many days."

"I'm a student," Big Youth told him. "Truly."

"But you have a job?" said the beggar.

"This is not a job," Big Youth told him. "It has no pay."

"No pay?" the man was horrified.

"None at all," Big Youth said.

"No money at all?" incredulously.

"Not a single cent," Big youth confirmed.

"You are a fool," the beggar concluded.

Big Youth laughed and said, "I don't think so."

Musa stepped out of the teahouse to stand looking forlornly up and down the street. He saw Big Youth talking to the beggar and called out to him.

"You!" he said to Big Youth. "What is that you have there?"

"It's a poster," said Big Youth.

"What is it for?" he asked.

"It tells you about Aids," said Big Youth.

He crossed the road to the teahouse and showed the posters to him. The posters had no pictures and, therefore, made no sense to Musa and he was not at all impressed.

"I want to put one up here on your wall," Big Youth told him.

"There is no Aids here," he said.

"Just one poster," Big Youth pleaded. "For the customers."

"Go away from here," he said, suddenly offended. "Go to Highlife Lodge."

"They won't let me in," Big Youth complained.

"Go hang them in your mother's house," Musa advised.

"I have no mother," Big Youth pleaded.

"Go find one," Musa said, impatiently.

Uncle Mark had followed Big Youth's progress up the street through the window and now came out to see what the angry altercation was all about.

"Tell him, Uncle," Big Youth said to him. "Tell him this is for the good of all."

Uncle Mark read the poster, laughed, and said, "That business again? Will the woman never give up?"

Then he took the can of glue from Big Youth and slapped some glue on the door. After that he took the poster from Big Youth and pasted it on the door of the teahouse.

"There, old bull," he said to Musa. "A communal problem demands for a communal spirit."

Musa was flabbergasted. He looked from the poster to Uncle Mark, roughed his hair and made some grumbling noises deep in his throat. He started to tear down the poster, saw the bemused smile on Uncle Mark's face and stopped. He huffed and puffed and was about to bash Big Youth's head in but Uncle Mark laughed and told him that Big Youth was a harmless big boy, just doing his job, a necessary job. No purpose would be served by beating his brains out; and Janet might just come around and hang her accursed posters herself. Musa lowered his fist and stormed back to the kitchen and the *mandazi* he had been making when solitude drove him out.

Uncle Mark winked at Big Youth, patted him on the back and asked, "Is it true that you don't get any money for this?"

"Janet has no money to pay," Big Youth reported.

He patted him some more and said, "I don't think you are a fool."

"No," agreed Big Youth. "I'm not a fool."

"Who wrote this?" he asked of the poster he had pasted on the door.

"I did," Big Youth said. "I call it the life and death equation."

"You are definitely not a fool," Uncle Mark told him. "On the contrary, you are a very smart boy."

"You think so?"

"Very smart."

"My teachers don't think so," Big Youth revealed. "They say I'll never make it."

"Never make what?" Uncle Mark asked.

"I don't know," Big Youth said seriously. "But I know I will."

Uncle Mark gave him some encouragement and sent him on his way. Then he returned to his window table, wondering how to get Musa to like life once again. He was afraid, one of these days, he would wake up to find Musa dangling from the end of a rope in the kitchen of the teahouse. It was a terrible thought to go to sleep on every night.

He sat still for a while, staring at the sun-drenched street and wondering what he would do without Musa. Where would he go? He sat for a long time thinking these terrible thoughts.

He looked up as a huge black car turned off the highway onto the main street. He sat up, intrigued, to watched it drive slowly down the street and stop in front of the post office. The driver stepped out and stood in the middle of the road, looking about in absolute wonder, at the derelict post office and the potholed street and the ruined buildings.

"You, Boss," the beggar called out to him. "Give me money."

"Why?" asked the stranger.

"I don't have any."

The stranger laughed and observed that was a good enough reason to beg. Uncle Mark saw him reach into his pocket and hand over some money.

"Thank you, Boss," the beggar shouted, so loud he was heard all over Crossroads.

The man reached into the car for a walking stick, then shut and locked the door.

"Watch the car," he said to the beggar as he started across the street.

"Musa," Uncle Mark called urgently to the kitchen. "You have a big, big one coming."

Musa grumbled, as he always did, and remained in the kitchen.

Heavy, dragging steps approached the entrance and stopped. Uncle Mark guessed that the stranger was reading Big Youth's poster, and a loud guffaw confirmed this. It was a good clean laugh, a good sign. Then the stranger entered the teahouse, leaning heavily on his stick and looked about.

"Greetings," he said loudly.

"Greetings," Uncle Mark said, astonished at how puny the stranger appeared from close up, away from his car.

"Musa," he called to the back.

"What does he want?" Musa called back.

"Breakfast," the stranger said to Uncle Mark. "Lots of breakfast."

Uncle Mark hesitated, before relaying the order to the kitchen. He noted that the stranger carried a sword concealed in his walking stick. Then he looked the stranger in the eye, smiled knowingly and conveyed the order to Musa in the kitchen, via a loud holler. There was a strange quiet from the kitchen, an ominous angry void full of torment.

"Tell him to order something sensible," Musa shouted back. "Or to go away and leave us in peace."

Uncle Mark laughed and said to the stranger, "He hates sophistication. Otherwise, feel free to order anything the heart desires, except pork. Whatever you do, don't order pork."

The stranger smiled, a thin, tolerant smile, and decided that, breakfast or no breakfast, he was going to like the man in the kitchen.

"Coffee?" he asked.

"This is a teahouse," Uncle Mark informed.

"Tea and toast then," he said.

Uncle Mark laughed and said, "I think you better ask him that yourself. He will be out in a moment. Sit down, make yourself comfortable. Do you play draughts?"

"For money?" the stranger asked.

"Money?" Uncle Mark smiled. "What in the world is that?"

"I never do anything without purpose," the stranger said.

"What a pity," Uncle Mark said very amused. "Money is such an alien concept here in Crossroads."

The stranger laughed and sat down opposite him.

"Is it always this quiet?" he asked.

"Always," Uncle Mark assured him.

Then Musa came out of the kitchen, arms grey with soot and charcoal dust, and looked about the place. And not finding the big one announced by Uncle Mark earlier, he walked to the window to look out and discovered the car. He gave it a long, thoughtful look before looking up and down the street for the owner. Not a soul in sight. He turned to the stranger and regarded him with great suspicion.

"What do you want?" he asked.

"He wants coffee," Uncle Mark told him.

"This is a teahouse," Musa informed him.

"I have told him," Uncle Mark said.

"Some tea then," said the stranger.

"Anything else?" Musa asked him.

"Breakfast?" the stranger said.

He saw the sudden change on Musa's face and added, "I'll settle for a poached egg."

Musa shook his head and said, "We don't have that kind of eggs here."

"Beef sausages?" the man asked hopefully.

Musa turned to stare out of the window at the car.

"I didn't say Musa has everything," Uncle Mark said quietly to the stranger. "He knows what those things are, that's all."

The stranger nodded agreeably, smiled, then turned to Musa and asked him, "What about bacon and sausage? Have you got pork sausages?"

Uncle Mark groaned loudly. Musa turned from the window and regarded this unlikely heap of refuse that would utter such a vile word in his place.

"This is a respectable house," he said severely. "We don't serve pigs here."

"House rules," said Uncle Mark to the stranger. "Every house must have rules, you understand."

The stranger nodded again, shrugged and said to Musa, "Give me whatever is allowed here."

Musa weighing him for a moment then nodded quietly and vanished back in the kitchen.

"Is he always this friendly?" the stranger asked.

"Always," Uncle Mark confirmed.

"He does not like customers?" the stranger wondered.

"He loves customers," Uncle Mark said. "He just does not get enough of them."

He rearranged the tops on the draughts board. The stranger took a deep breath, filling his lungs with the dust and the odours of the place, and seemed much better for it. He had driven through Crossroads on his way here, and witnessed the decay and the squalor that lay over it, and he was convinced this was the place to be. He picked up a piece and moved it one square forward.

"Where is everybody?" he asked.

"This is the funeral hour," Uncle Mark informed him.

"The funeral hour?" the man marvelled. "You have an hour just for funerals?"

"Otherwise we would be at it all day," said Uncle Mark. "Musa! Make that two teas."

Then he turned to the stranger and said, "The plague hit us like a mad bull from hell."

The stranger nodded and said, "I see."

He picked up another piece and moved it one square forward. He was surprised how easily it all came back. He relaxed and started to enjoy the game.

Musa came back with his huge black kettle and two glasses and poured the tea for them. He returned the kettle to the kitchen and brought them a plate of *mandazi*. Then he went back to the kitchen and brought the stranger the most confounding omelette he had ever seen. It was grey and yellow, and was speckled with red and green, and Musa insisted it was a Biri Biri omelette. It smelled of wood smoke, and was as chewy as wax, but the stranger ate it anyway, hoping it would improve relations between himself and the cook.

"You, Boss!"

They looked up to find the beggar, hungry beyond caution, standing by the doorway. Musa swung a hand at him and he jumped back startled.

"Leave the man alone," the stranger said to him. "I'll buy him some tea."

"You will?" asked the beggar incredulously.

"Take the table in the corner," the stranger directed. "And keep your mouth shut."

The beggar rushed to obey, tried to lift the table and take it away.

"Sit!" Musa ordered and reluctantly went to fetch him tea and *mandazi*.

After serving him, Musa went back to the window to keep one eye on the street as he watched the stranger tackle the omelette. Uncle Mark watched the man eat too; and wondered about that face. When he had eaten the whole thing, the stranger washed it down with a cup of tea and paused to listen to his stomach.

Musa eyed him inquiringly, waiting for the verdict. Finally, the stranger belched loudly and said, "Is there more?"

"You want more?" Musa was taken completely by surprise.

"Not right away," the stranger said quickly. "Give the rest to the Boss there."

He belched again, filled and lit his pipe, and appeared in no a hurry to leave. It intrigued Musa enough to ask, "Is that your car?"

"All of it," the stranger confirmed.

"It's not a small car," Musa observed in true Crossroads understatement.

In truth, it was just about the largest vehicle he had ever seen that was not a bus.

"You know what they say in Pwani?" the stranger said to him trying to be friendly. "If you must eat a pig, eat a fat one."

It was an old saying from the streets of Pwani, a cautionary tale, which even zealots took in good humour, and the stranger voiced it without malice. Musa, however, saw nothing humorous about eating pigs, thin or fat, and regarded the man with utter contempt.

"We don't eat pigs here," he informed.

"I noticed," said the stranger.

He had encountered several ferocious looking pigs in some of the abandoned homes he had strayed into the night before.

"Pigs eat filth," Musa said.

The stranger was in the process of filling his pipe and not paying much attention to the exchange. Now he stopped and looked up at Musa, then at Uncle Mark and back at Musa.

"Pigs are unclean," Musa added. "We don't eat filth."

"Oh," said the man. "I see."

Uncle Mark shrugged, at the stranger's questioning glance, and Musa asked, "Where are you going?"

"Going?" the stranger asked, confused.

"From here," Uncle Mark said. "No one comes here to stay. Even Musa has had enough of this Crossroads and wants to leave us."

"Why?"

"He thinks this is the worst place on earth."

"On earth?" The stranger laughed. "Obviously, he has not seen the world."

"I keep telling him so."

"Right now, I think this is the best place I have ever been to," the stranger said. "And I have been to places that you, my friend, would not believe."

"I bet you have," said Uncle Mark remarked, with a knowing edge in his voice.

"I want to live here," said the stranger. "Set up business here."

Uncle Mark and Musa exchanged puzzled glances.

"Business?" asked Musa.

"What sort of business?" Uncle Mark asked.

"Service business."

"What sort of service?" Musa asked, watching him with renewed suspicion.

"I see you have no service station here," the stranger said.

"Cars don't stop here," Musa informed him.

"That will change," the stranger told them. "Are there any good mechanics? What happened to Tae Lever?"

"They buried him last month," Musa informed.

"Life has not been kind to us," Uncle Mark confirmed. "But why would anyone in his right mind want to set up business here?"

"For money," the stranger told him.

"There is no money in Crossroads."

"Look at this place," said Musa. "No one comes in here anymore, not even for tea."

"All that will change," the stranger promised. "We'll change all that and more. As a matter of fact, we'll change everything in this old dump."

Musa peered out of the window at the car. The windows were too dark to see who else was in the car.

"How many are you?" he was obliged to ask the stranger.

"What is the business population of Crossroads?" the stranger asked him.

Musa scratched his head. The last census was before the plague and the new highway.

"Five," Uncle Mark helped out. "Six, if you count the beggar over there."

"Not very many," the stranger agreed. "But all that will change. Trade draws people like flies."

He sucked on his pipe, a faraway look on his face. Meanwhile, the old men watched him and waited for what would happen next. The beggar finished his tea and slunk out of the place without thanking his benefactor. Uncle Mark studied the stranger's bony face, the staring eyes and the wasted features, and wondered. Musa looked from the car to the man and missed the connection. He was increasingly convinced of his first hunch. This was the legendary *wa Guka,* the bank robber everyone talked about. He wondered if there was still a reward for his arrest.

"Where are you from?" he asked the stranger.

"From all over," said the stranger. "But I was originally from Crossroads.

"I don't remember you," Musa declared.

"Nor I you," said the stranger. "How long have you been running this dump?"

"Many years," Musa said.

"It was not always a teahouse," reminded Uncle Mark. "It was a butchery first, then a dairy, a barber's shop and, finally, a teahouse."

"I remember you now," the stranger said to Musa. "You cut my hair badly."

"I don't remember your head," Musa said thoughtfully.

"I had more hair then and not a single grey."

"I remember you," Uncle Mark told him.

"Who is he?" Musa asked.

"Bakari Ben Broker," Uncle Mark had only then remembered the man's name.

"Who?"

"Spanner," said Uncle Mark. "He worked at the service station."

Musa searched his memory. He was silent for a long time, staring at the car and searching for it in his head. It was only when he gave up looking for the car that he finally found Broker. But the Broker he hauled out of his memory looked nothing like the man sitting in the teahouse with a sick smile on his face.

"Spanner Boy?" he asked.

"You seem to remember," Broker laughed.

"Egg Seller?" Musa asked.

"He remembers," Broker laughed.

For the first time since the stranger's arrival, Musa appeared pleased to see him. He offered a handshake.

"Ten years," he said. "Ten years I have waited for you and I nearly didn't know you. Pay the money you owe me now!"

"What money?" Broker asked, surprised.

"For the haircut," Musa told him. "Before the fat woman came for you. You said you would come back, and then I heard you had left for Pwani with the woman. Don't tell me you don't remember!"

"Otherwise you'll fetch your *rungu*," Broker laughed. "Relax, old man. While it's true I don't remember owing you any money, I'll pay."

He tried to remember what Musa had looked like then, before the big belly and the soot on the face. The people he remembered in connection with teahouses, butcheries and lodgings had been robust characters with an eye for business.

"How much was the haircut?" he asked.

Musa had the exact figure. Perhaps, Broker conceded, the old man was not such a crook, after all. He took out his wallet, searched through a sheaf of notes and handed one to Musa.

Musa took the money and examined it carefully. It was all new, very smooth and very clean and it smelt of freshly sawed wood.

"What kind of money is this?" he asked doubtfully.

"Legal tender," Broker told him.

It was like no money Musa had ever seen.

"We don't use this kind of money here," he said, giving it back.

Uncle Mark took the money from him and scrutinised it expertly. He had seen enough counterfeit money in his time to consider himself an expert. Up in the north, where he had once been a goat trader, among many other things, Uncle Mark had encountered people who would try to pay him with everything including homemade currency. A nomad had tried to pay him with monopoly money he said got from a bank in Kakuma. Uncle Mark had, knowingly and otherwise, helped circulate a lot of creative currency during his life as a desert traveller.

Now he felt Broker's money with his fingers, held it to his ear and rubbed it between the fingers and listened to its rustle. He held it to his nose and smelt it. Then he held it up to the light and read its secret numbers and, finally, he declared it to be genuine paper money.

"It is real," he announced, giving it back to Musa.

"Have you seen how big it is?" Musa asked him. "I can't change this."

"Keep it," Broker told him.

"Keep it?" he was astonished.

"I have been informed that you have the best rooms in Crossroads," Broker said.

"Who told you that?" Musa was now, more than ever, convinced this was the famous bank robber everyone wanted to catch.

"Never mind who told me," Broker said to him. "I would like to rent one of the rooms."

"What for?" he asked suspiciously. "You have a house and a wife. Why don't you stay with her?"

"Because I want to stay here," Broker said firmly. "For the moment, anyway."

"You want to stay here?" Musa was confounded.

"Unless you are full," Broker said.

"No," Musa said. "We are not full, we are not full at all. In fact, we have never been full."

He examined the note again and, thoughtfully, put it in his pocket. He shook his head in wonder and said, "So you *were* Janet's husband! But you look so ..."

"Finished?" Broker laughed. "No, not yet finished; not by a long haul. What other kinds of businesses can one do here?"

Uncle Mark and Mzee Musa looked at each other doubtfully. Was the man serious? Or was he, perhaps, quite mad? They shook their heads simultaneously. Musa retreated to the window to stare out at the car. The last time he had seen a car nearly so huge it had been a hearse bringing home the mortal remains of Big

George Ganga. It depressed him to see it parked outside his teahouse.

Broker, watching him, wondered what was bothering him.

Uncle Mark, in turn, watched Broker and plain wondered.

"Have you been to see her?" he asked finally.

"To see who?" Broker asked. "My wife?"

"Janet," Uncle Mark said.

Broker's eyes twitched. Uncle Mark noted how his grip tightened on his walking stick, and wondered some more.

"I have seen her," Broker said relaxing his grip and smiling nervously.

He did not offer any more information and they left it at that. But Broker was unsettled, it was plain to see, and Uncle Mark wondered if he should worry about it at all.

Broker got down to business straight away. He had no time to waste, he told the old men. He had mountains to level and bridges to rebuild. He had impossible burdens to unburden and a terrible journey to retrace, through neglected and vastly altered landscape, and had no time to waste.

Mzee Musa had no idea what Broker was talking about, but Uncle Mark nodded and said it was never too late to right a blatant wrong and save one's soul. Which Musa understood even less.

When Broker was not at Janet's, trying to break her abhorrence of him and win back her affections, he was at Grandmother's, fanning her support for him. Or with the children, shamelessly worming his way into their hearts. Or with anyone he thought could help him warm his way back to Janet's heart. It was a long and frightful journey.

The rest of the time was spent surveying Crossroads, assessing old buildings and making plans for their restoration. He had enough plans for a whole lifetime of rebuilding.

And when he despaired of trying to move mountains, Broker played draughts with Uncle Mark for money. Always he lost. And the more he lost, the more he tried to win. It embarrassed Uncle Mark to take his money so easily, but Broker insisted on playing for money, in total defiance of another of Musa's house rules, and would not settle for less.

The day Broker learned that Frank had officially joined Janet's condom army, he tried to play Uncle Mark for five big notes, the ones that only he, and now Musa, possessed in the whole of

Crossroads. Uncle Mark declined, embarrassed beyond reason, and decided it was time to go comfort one of his widows, instead.

Broker brooded for weeks after that.

Chapter Nineteen

The condom campaign had been going strong for some time now, but the condom message itself made little headway. The condoms came in from Sokoni, arriving promptly at the end of each month, and filled her store to capacity, then overflowed into her living room and into her bedroom and finally into her children's bedroom.

Women, as always, were receptive and agreeable. They suffered the most under the burden of childbearing and rearing and had the most to lose and also the most to gain. But they were only collaborators in the population issues and few men indeed cared for Janet's lectures on the matter. Some men nervously accepted her offer of free condoms, but it was doubtful they ever used them. The youth, however, were the greatest consumers of condoms. They could not seem to get enough. And Janet began to worry.

It did not take Frank long to find out what was happening. Big Youth and his gang were selling the condoms to other youths, and to the few grown-up men who grasped the logic of using condoms but were too proud, or too shy, to accept them from a woman. More pertinently, some unknown people were buying the condoms from the youth and collecting all the free condoms they could lay their hands on and smuggling them over the hills and across the borders to faraway places, where they did not have free condoms, and selling them for a fortune.

Frank passed on the information to Janet. She had nothing to worry about, he told her. The Crossroads youth were not using the whole alarming lot of condoms themselves.

Janet was relieved. All they had to do now, Frank suggested, was to find out who was trafficking in Crossroads' condoms and stop him. Meanwhile, Frank had found a solution to the problem of the mountain of condoms that threatened to swamp her

"Sell them," he said to her. "Sell the condoms."

"Are you mad?" she was more than astonished. "The condoms are free. Free to us and free to them."

That was exactly the problem, he told her, the reason no one seemed to care about them. That was why the men laughed at

168

condoms and gave them to children to play with. A token price, Frank suggested, would make men value them. Something small, something that everyone could afford. The condoms were useless unless, and until, people used them.

Janet did not need to think long about it. The condoms were not for sale. Frank tried to convince her that she had a duty to use any method that would make Crossroads accept condoms. She was quite clear in her mind, and that was the end of that line of thought.

Meanwhile, Big Youth and the boys had fun with condoms. Condom exchange became a popular pastime in schoolyards and anywhere boys congregated. The condom came to be the currency of the Crossroads youth. Wagers were made, games were played with condoms and even debts were settled with condoms. The Japanese condoms were known as the yen, the German ones became marks and the American ones were dollars. But, for some reasons which had little to do with the real yen, the Japanese greens were the most sought after. Great myths were created around them, inspired by the strange inscriptions on the packaging, and there was no end to the feats they were said to be capable of. They were also rumoured to glow in the dark, and to perform many wonders besides. If one lost his condom in the dark, all he had to do was to whistle and the Japanese wonder came running.

The most common condom, however, was a no-name blue; a malformed blue balloon from some unidentified source. The boys said that the funny ones were made by *jua kali* in Pwani, at a sausage factory that had closed down. It was the lowest in value.

Uncle Mark and Frank were playing neither for condoms nor for money when Big Youth rushed to the teahouse to warn them that the Chief's henchmen were out to arrest Frank.

"What about?" wondered Uncle Mark.

"They didn't say," Big Youth told them.

Frank wondered if Big Youth had been hanging posters that he did not know about. Big Youth assured him he had not. Frank had nothing to fear and he played another game with the old man. He was setting up for a third game when they came for him.

"They want to see you," they said simply. "The big men want to see you."

"Which big men?" Frank asked them.

"All of them," they said.

As they led him across town to Chief Chupa's office, they kept shaking their heads and clucking their tongues in an ominous manner and hinting at how Frank was a finished man now. And, as befitted a wanted criminal, they took him the long way round, so that everyone in Crossroads could see that they were useful to the community and appreciate that they enforced the law without fear or favour.

People stopped to wonder and laughed at the henchmen, when they boasted what a dangerous man they had apprehended.

"What has he done?" people asked.

"Many things," the henchmen said.

What they would never admit was that they were menials, to whom no one ever explained their orders. So they acted important and bragged on and on until they came to the Chief's camp and handed Frank over to the lynch party.

It was the monthly *baraza*, the people's court convened to deal with legal wrangles that were too minor to take to Sokoni. It was presided over by the Chief, assisted by the elders and other relevant Government officials. Every one of them was there, and they were angry and clamouring for blood.

Janet had been rounded up too, along with dozens of others who had committed unforgivable crimes against the community; crimes that ranged from illegally cutting down their own trees to build their own houses, to illegally diverting public streams to irrigate their own land. Quite a few were there too for refusing to pay the Chief's own illegal development fund and the arbitrary seasonal goat tax.

Chief Chupa was flanked by the usual retinue of community leaders, church elders, Government officers and their followers and hangers-on.

The land cases, and the license and tax cases, were tackled first and quickly dispensed with. The bribes had been offered and accepted and the decisions made. The losers quickly lost and grumbled, while the winners praised the court for its wisdom and went home to celebrate their victories.

Then the case against Frank and Janet was called out. They were accused of corrupting the morals of the youth again. A simple case. It was, however, complicated by the self-interests of all concerned. Everyone, it seemed, was offended by Janet's condom campaign and had something to say against her. It was immoral and sinful, it was embarrassing to the community and it encouraged the youth to engage in indecent behaviour. And it had to be stopped.

The school heads had the biggest complaint of all. Their pupils, many of them hardly old enough to wipe their own noses, were suddenly so afraid of Aids they were threatening their teachers and demand to be told how to avoid the plague; asking that they be taught things the teachers themselves did not know. What were the decent, hard-working teachers supposed to do about that?

"Teach them," Frank suggested.

"Teach them?" cried the school heads. "Who'll teach them?"

"I'll do it," he offered. "I'll teach the class myself."

"How?" they cried. "You are not a teacher."

"But I can teach," he told them.

"How?" cried the Education Officer. "We cannot pay you."

"You don't need to pay me," he told them. "I'll do it for free."

Which confounded the assembly even more and stoked their suspicion of him. In their view, no sane person did anything without pay. Not in Crossroads.

Then the Education Officer spoke up, and announced to one and all that Frank had no teaching certificate and, therefore, he could not teach. The Health Inspector jumped in to inform the court that it was missing the pertinent point. His concern was for the health of the children who, he had it from reliable sources, were using the condoms as playthings.

"You can't blame us for that," Janet told him. "Blame the people who throw them away."

"Who are these people?" the Chief wanted to know. "They must be punished. Show us these people and we shall punish them at once. Where are these people?"

She turned to the assembled men. They avoided her eyes and looked elsewhere, while the henchmen eagerly awaited orders to pounce on someone and beat him into the ground.

The Health Inspector saw how the situation he had created was degenerating into dangerous witch-hunting and tried to defuse it.

"We don't need to beat up anyone today," he said to the henchmen. "What we need is more information."

"Why?" asked the Information Officer, afraid the suggestion meant more work for him.

"Because information is power," said the Education Officer.

"What?" cried Chief Chupa.

Power was the private domain of the big people; the leaders, the chiefs and the headmen. Power was his department. What did the children and these others have to do with power?

"Not that kind of power," the Education Officer explained. "I'm talking about the power of information, the power that is knowledge."

"Knowledge of what?" asked an old villager from the midst of the audience. "I know of the many corruptions that obstruct the process of justice in this hyenas' court, and yet I have no power to stop them."

The elders groaned and grumbled, and the henchmen offered to beat the insolent peasant into the ground. Other villagers protested; what the old man had said was indeed true, they said. Everyone knew of the corruptions of the *baraza*. The rich did not respect the courts anymore and the poor were tyrannised by the law. The elders howled their protest, the Chief fumed and the henchmen again offered to clobber someone and this time extended the offer to cover the whole impertinent mob.

The assembly was in danger of digressing into acrimonious absurdities when Janet brought it back to order.

"That is not what he means," she told them all. "What the man means is that we must educate the children. We must teach them to know what is right and what is wrong. Only then can they decide to do what is right."

A church leader quietly observed that it was a well-known fact that education led to arrogance and corruption. What would stop the children from experimenting with their newly acquired knowledge?

"You have little to fear from knowledge," Frank told them. "It is ignorance that you have to worry about. Because ignorance is irresponsible.

"And ignorance kills," Uncle Mark said, suddenly pushing his way through the crowd.

The big people had not seen him come, else someone would have moved to forestall his disruptive intrusion. Now all they could do was watch in silence as he pushed his way into the assembly, where he had no business at all, and turned to face the leaders.

"Ignorance is also bliss," he said to them. "We all know that. That is why Crossroads cherishes ignorance."

172

That was why Crossroads did not want to know anything at all; whether it was about the over-population, the starvation of the orphans or the many things that ailed the land, Crossroads just did not want to know. How many bicycle tyres had the brave Janet worn out carrying the burden of that knowledge from hill to hill? Yet the people of Crossroads remained happily as ignorant as ever.

"We all know about Aids," he told them. "The disease we like to believe kills only thieves and prostitutes and those that God does not love."

Crossroads buried them everyday. So what else could anyone tell Crossroads? About education? What had education done for the youth of Crossroads, except to confuse and to disenchant? About religion?

"Ask our very own Pastor Batoromeo," Uncle Mark told them. "A man on good terms with the Almighty. A man whose church is dying from the lack of worshippers while he battles the devil single-handed. And who can beat our Chief Chupa for dedication to duty? You tell me that. What else do we need?"

"Wisdom," said the old villager who knew of the corruptions in the court.

"We are all wise men here," Uncle Mark informed him.

"And women?" Janet asked.

"And women too," Uncle Mark agreed. "But what good is our wisdom, if it merely confirms what our mothers taught us at birth; that he who ignores wise counsel cannot ignore the consequences? Look among yourselves and tell me what you see. How many of you will be here tomorrow to bicker about whether or not to tell your children about the plague? How many children will be here to be told?"

The lynch party began to grasp the drift of Uncle Mark's words. The elders looked at one another and wondered whether they should be angry about it or not. They turned to their Chief for guidance. But Chief Chupa was himself staring down at his besieged Government boots in deep and unfathomable thought. The wise elders followed his example and adopted the same inscrutable pose.

Uncle Mark turned to Janet and Frank.

"If there is anything Crossroads hates," he informed them, "it is to be told anything it does not already know. So I suggest you take your newfangled ideas and your revolutionary family education projects and take them over the hills to the communities that have nothing better to do than to worry about the health and the education of their children."

At this point, Pastor Bat leaned over to Chief Chupa and whispered that the trial was taking too long and that he would have to leave soon. The rains were coming and the roof of his church was full of holes.

Chief Chupa nodded in agreement, glanced at his watch and turned to Uncle Mark.

"Conclude," he ordered.

"Crossroads is happy," Uncle Mark said in conclusion. "But Crossroads will perish from its bliss if Crossroads does not accept change."

The Chief nodded importantly and announced the meeting adjourned until after the rains. The lynch mob sighed with relief and everyone was suddenly eager to go home and forget the whole sordid business.

"What about the children?" Janet asked them.

"What about them?" demanded Uncle Mark.

"Do we leave them to go on blowing on condoms?" she asked him. "Or do we tell them what condoms are for?"

"That," said Uncle Mark, "is up to our wise, old leaders."

Janet turned to the leaders.

"Do we or do we not?" she asked them.

The leaders were suddenly in a hurry to leave. The mob too, rightly guessing that there would be no lynching today, had started to disperse.

"Wait," cried the Health Inspector. "The woman has a point. The children may be blowing on used condoms."

No one understood or cared. Janet stepped up to the fleeing leaders and demanded an answer.

"Tell us right here," she said to Pastor Bat's face. "Do we or do we not?"

"We not," said the Pastor exasperated.

"Not what?" she insisted.

Pastor Bat, thoroughly disconcerted, turned to Chief Chupa.

"Tell her," he said to the Chief.

"Tell her what?" the Chief was equally bewildered.

"You are their chief," Pastor Bat reminded him. "You are the one who is always telling them Government things. Tell her now."

"But I am a Government man," Chief Chupa pleaded. "I must do my job."

174

"Then do it fully," Janet told him. "Tell us."

"Tell you what?" said the Chief, trapped by his own fatuousness.

"Tell us what we want to hear," suggested Uncle Mark. "Tell us that our survival does not depend on you or on the Government or on those foreigners who send us condoms. Tell us that our health and that of our community depends on us, ourselves, and on our individual action. On all of us, united as one people. Tell us that."

"I can't do that," he said uneasily. "I'm not authorised to do that."

"So you tell us to go to hell," Uncle Mark said in despair.

Chief Chupa was not authorised to do that either. He looked about confounded. He was not used to being told what to do, least of all by unpalatable pariahs from the fringes of the community. That was not why the Government had appointed him chief. He turned to Pastor Bat for administrative solidarity.

"Do your job," Pastor Bat said encouragingly.

Then he turned and marched purposefully away. A large crowd of elders and leaders went with him, leaving the Chief and the Health Inspector to sweat it out alone.

"What shall we do now?" they asked each other.

"Stop fighting us," Janet suggested. "Let us forget the past, forget the reasons for which you were appointed chief, and let us work together for the good of our community. We are all on the same side; people with a common goal."

Both men hastily agreed. None of them, however, had the vaguest idea what that meant, how such a partnership might work.

The way it finally turned out was quite simple. They would, it was agreed, stop harassing and ridiculing Janet. On condition that Janet refrained from attacking their ineffective authority. On condition that they got all the credit for all the ideas that worked. On condition that Janet accepted blame for all the ideas that did not work. On condition ... there were so many conditions they finally lost meaning altogether.

But soon Janet was officially visiting the bars and the teahouses and the lodging houses and everywhere where men congregated for whatever purpose. Sometimes she was accompanied by the Health Inspector and sometimes she went with Frank. But most times she went alone, and the men were not amused. When she told them all about condoms, and about their proper use and disposal, they laughed at her and said they knew all about *kodoms*, for they were not born yesterday, but they did not need *kodoms*, for their ways were the old ways and they could not change. They were proud old bulls, they said, and old bulls did not take kindly to new yokes

Chapter Twenty

Uncle Mark had never had it so good. When Frank was away, doing whatever it was that he did with Janet, Musa played draughts with him. And when Musa was in another of his legendary sulks, Uncle Mark played Broker for money, always small sums of it. He won most of the time and would never understand why Broker insisted on playing for money.

Meanwhile Musa ran amok in the kitchen and terrorised the crockery, or stood morosely by the window counting the traffic on the highway and wondering if Crossroads would ever resurrect. Broker, from time to time, assured him that it would.

"You keep promising," Musa grumbled. "The service station is still closed and nothing has happened."

"Good things, like good wine, take time to mature," Broker said to him. "Great things, like great people, take a lot of time to be actualised."

"To be what?" Musa exclaimed.

"Never mind," Broker said irritably. "Just be patient."

He had had another cold morning at Janet's, trying to get her to notice him, and his confidence was at its lowest ebb. She used to be easy to talk to, to understand and to persuade. Now she was harder to convince than a bar room full of barmaids. He had come back with ringing ears, mostly from the echo of his own voice, and a heart that was full of self-doubt. He could not tell Musa this, but everything was now dependent on Janet.

He rearranged the board for another game, his movements hard and violent.

"Your move," he said to Uncle Mark.

A shadow fell on the table. They looked up simultaneously to find the beggar's scrawny face grinning down at them with hunger written all over it.

"Buy me tea, Boss," he said to Broker.

Broker shot an angry backhand at him and yelled, "Get away from here!"

The beggar leaped back, mortally astonished, and scrambled back to the middle of the road, where he stood for a long time undecided while the sun beat mercilessly down on his bare head.

Finally, having made up his mind that Broker was in no mood for friendship, he slunk back to his booth to await death by starvation.

Uncle Mark played his turn, uneasy about the angry air Broker had brought back with him and now beginning to worry about his winnings. It was plain robbery; theft from a blind man. Almost as though Broker was trying to lose everything he had. Sometimes Uncle Mark made deliberate mistakes, in the hope that Broker would take advantage of them and win, but Broker did not. He did not try to win at all.

Uncle Mark watched him anguish, and anguished about it himself, until he could not stand it any longer and his whole being cried: enough! He turned to Broker, intending to say what he had to say and be damned, but Musa beat him to it.

"Have you told her?' Musa asked Broker.

"Told who what?' Broker asked him.

"Janet," Musa said. "Have you told her?"

"Told her what?" Broker asked.

"The real reason for your returning," Uncle Mark said.

Broker paused. He looked from Musa to Uncle Mark and asked them, "Have you two been talking about me?"

Musa shrugged. Broker turned to look out of the window.

"You, Boss," he called out across the road at the beggar.

The beggar scrambled to cross the street, paused uncertainly by the doorway.

"Enter," Broker ordered.

The beggar looked warily from Broker to Musa, then took a step forward.

"Not too close," Broker said to him. "See the table in the far corner? That is your table from now on. You want to talk to me, you do it from there, you understand? Now go take it... I mean sit down at it, and order anything your heart desires."

The beggar did as directed and waited for Musa to take his order.

"Have you told her?" Musa asked again.

"Yes!" Broker said angrily. "Now give the man some service and leave us to our game before I lose my patience."

"Told her everything?" Musa asked him.

Broker looked up again, regarded Musa for a long, tense moment, his hands gripping tightly round the handle of his walking stick. "Is it any of your business?" he asked Musa.

"Yes," answered Uncle Mark.

Broker turned to the game, picked up a piece, paused before completing his move and again looked from one to the other of the old men. They were both watching him intensely, waiting for him to make his next move. "Have you?" Musa asked.

Broker was on the verge of unleashing a verbal onslaught, then thought otherwise and refrained from doing so. These were his friends, he tried to convince himself, the only friends he had in Crossroads and right now he needed all the friends he could gather around him. He turned to the game, completed his move and said, "She has not given me half a chance. The woman will not talk to me."

Musa nodded and went back to brooding out of the window. The two resumed their game. But the interruption had spoilt it for them. Broker got angry when he lost, rose abruptly and picked up his stick.

"My keys."

"What keys?" Musa asked, staring out of the window, his back as last week's *mandazi*.

"The keys to my room," Broker said offensively. "Remember me? I live here!"

"Not anymore, you don't," Musa said unperturbed.

Uncle Mark saw how hard Broker was fighting to control his anger and wondered how long it would take before the dam broke.

"I have paid six months in advance for a room here," Broker said to Musa. "So I do have a room here."

"You cannot stay here anymore," Musa told him. "It is not good for business."

"What business?" Broker bellowed. "Even fleas don't live here anymore."

The words hit Musa like a falling tree, crushing his ego and resounding painfully in his brain. His felt his head swell up and his chest contract. His arm muscles went into spasms and his nostrils flared dangerously.

"You have no right to say that," he said advancing from the window.

They faced each other, Musa with balled fists and Broker with his right hand over the ivory grip of his concealed sword. Bloodshed was imminent. But neither of them threw the first blow. They needed each other and they knew it. After a brief moment's standoff, Uncle Mark shook his head at them saying,, "This is no way for old men to behave."

"This is my place," Musa said. "He has no right to talk like that."

"And you have no right to deny him his right," said Uncle Mark. "Give the man his key."

"I have a right to do what I want here," Musa insisted.

"Give the man his key," Uncle Mark said wearily. "He is the second lodger you have had in years."

"I'm here to stay," Broker warned.

"Only for tonight," said Musa.

"We'll see about that," Broker said. "The keys?"

Musa paused, just long enough to recover his bruised dignity, then said to Broker, "Behind the kitchen door."

"I thank you kindly," Broker said and limped away to the kitchen.

When he was gone, Musa flexed his aching muscles and sat down opposite Uncle Mark.

"Who does he think he is?" he fumed.

"A customer," Uncle Mark replied. "But I never thought I would live to see you sink this low."

Musa shook his head as he rearranged the board.

"What about me?" the beggar asked from his table.

"You get out of here!" Musa barked.

The beggar scuttled from the table and ran out of the teahouse back to his phone booth.

"Who does he think he is?" Musa fumed. "Bringing beggars to my place. Who is he?"

Uncle Mark chortled quietly to himself and decided to keep his thoughts to himself.

Chapter Twenty-One

Big Youth was alone in Janet's house when Broker called to see her. The car stopped in its usual irritating place, right in the middle of the yard, as if staking a claim to the compound, and Broker hauled himself out. He had had a bad night. He drunk stale beer at Highlife Lodge, eaten bad food at the teahouse and slept badly on Musa's screeching, spring mattress. He was not feeling well and he was sweating profusely.

"Janet?" he called, limping into the living room.

Then he saw Big Youth, and the dozens of cartons of condoms he was sifting through, and hesitated significantly.

"Greetings," Big Youth said, cheerfully.

He was the only person in the whole of Crossroads who smiled unreservedly at Broker and, as a result, he had earned himself a special place in Broker's heart. But Broker's mind was in turmoil now and he had no time to be nice today.

"Where is my wife?" he asked.

"Janet?"

"Don't be clever today, I can't stand it."

"Janet's out," Big Youth told him.

"Out?" he wiped the sweat from his brow with a white handkerchief. "Out where? Who is with her? Frank?"

"Maybe."

"Why is she always with him?"

"They work together," said Big Youth.

"And you," Broker asked him. "What are you to her?"

"Nothing," answered Big Youth. "I'm just here."

"Are you her slave too?" Broker asked him.

"No," Big Youth said, unhappily. "I'm not her slave."

"Then why are you always here?" Broker asked him.

Big Youth, realising Broker was in a sour mood, decided to humour him.

"I like Janet," he said with forced cheerfulness. "So I help Janet; everyone must help Janet. A communal problem ..."

"Don't give me that nonsense," Broker warned. "When will she be back?"

"Whenever," said Big Youth.

Broker paced the room restlessly, wiping sweat off his face and neck, touching this and that and, finally, pausing before the old family photograph. He studied it for a long time. The photograph had been taken when Janet was young, full and rounded, and as fresh as a fragrant *dodo* mango. Her skin, he remembered, was smooth and silky and the colour of freshly roasted coffee. Her breath was as fresh and clean, and as warm and sweet as that of a newborn calf. She would have done anything for him in those old days, and the memory of it drove him mad with jealousy. Now she was older and hard-edged and maddeningly rustic and had the intoxicating odour of a lascivious lioness.

He stopped by the window to look towards the hills and the deserted mansion. For weeks now he had passed it on the way here and every time, he had been frightened and depressed by the state the place was in. The doors were vandalised and every windowpane was broken. Cars and farm machinery lay rusting away in the yard while in the well-planned and sprawling orchards, fruit ripened and fell down and rotted away on the ground. Broker had thought of the place often and wondered, but was afraid to ask, for fear of what he might find out. Now, hoping that Big Youth, of all people, would break it to him gently, he turned and asked him, "Who lives in the big house?"

"The one on the hill?" Big Youth asked without looking up.

"The one with the collapsed roof," Broker said.

"No one," said Big Youth. "No one at all lives there now. It belonged to George Ganga. He died."

Broker knew he should not have asked.

"Big George Ganga died?" he asked overwhelmed by the news.

"You knew George Ganga?" Big Youth was impressed.

Big George had been the richest man in Crossroads. Big and rich and a very feared man. No one had thought that he could die. Then he had died, and disappointed and despaired them all.

"What ate him?" Broker asked hopefully. "An accident?"

"Not an accident," Big Youth said. "Aids ate him up. His wife and children too. They all died."

The plague had eaten them all up. Only rats and vandals lived in the big house now. Big Youth had been to the big house once, to pick the fruit that now belonged to no one, and had seen the ghost of the big man watching from one of the broken upper windows.

"His face was all rotten and eaten up by Aids," he reported.

Other people must have seen the ghost too, he believed, for no one went to pick the fruit that lay rotting on the ground.

"Big George was a good man," Big Youth said. "But everyone feared Big George."

Broker had gone to school with George Ganga. They had nicknamed him the Man of the People. A very disciplined man with a big and courageous heart, a warm and benevolent heart, a heart with an overwhelming sense of justice. A good man. A man so good and honest and generous that they had bet he would die a poor man.

"You were all wrong there," laughed Big Youth. "He died richer than any of you."

"Don't be so sure," Broker said with incomprehensible irritation. "But if Big George is dead, then it's true this Aids will finish us all."

He paced the room some more, poked into the cartons and things with his cane, and brooded in a way Big Youth had never imagined him to be capable of. In Big Youth's eyes, Broker was a giant among giants, a rich and powerful man, and a man who could get anything on earth that he wanted. He had no reason to worry as he worried now.

"Why did you come back?" Big Youth asked him.

This was a place to go away from, to leave, to forget. To be thought of as in the past, not in the future. This was not a place to come back to.

Broker regarded the big youth, a faraway look in his sunken eyes, and was lost for meaning.

"People die like animals here," Big Youth told him.

"People die like animals wherever they die," he said.

"Not like here," Big Youth said. "No one dies like here."

He shrugged and said, "Here or there, death is the end. The end is the end everywhere."

He stopped to stare at one of the posters on the wall.

"Who did this?" he asked tapping at it with his cane.

If the school head had asked the same question, with the same air of awful authority, Big Youth would have lied about it without a second thought. Now he braced himself for the worst and said, "I did it."

"Very clever," Broker said.

"You think so?" Big Youth asked surprised.

"I know so," Broker nodded. "And very sensible too. You are not all stupid."

"I know," said Big Youth.

Broker went on nodding as he said, "I think you are quite a smart boy when you try."

"I think so too," agreed Big Youth. "But my teachers don't think so."

"What do teachers know?" Broker said.

"I don't know," said Big Youth. "They don't like me very much at school."

Teachers hated smart boys, Broker told him. His teachers never tired of telling him, even as they marvelled at his antics, that he would be a failure in life. A poor man, an ox happy to toil and die in other men's fields. A big and notorious nothing, they had said. The best he could hope for, they had told him, as they whipped his bottom raw, was to be a celebrated jailbird.

"Can you imagine that?" he asked Big Youth. "Telling something so base to a struggling, poor boy?"

Big Youth could not. He had been called all sorts of unfriendly things by his teachers, but never a jailbird or a big nothing.

"No wonder I ended up all inside out," Broker said. "That's teachers for you. They don't appreciate demonstration of any undue independence in a boy. I bet they are still wearing holed shoes and pushing old bicycles to school."

The thing to remember, he said to Big Youth, was to never let the teachers discourage him. The real purpose of life was not, as the teachers would have every schoolboy believe, solely to be able to read and write.

"But I like your poster," he said, resuming his pacing. "Did you write the one at the teahouse?"

"And all over Crossroads," Big Youth confirmed. "It was a lot of work."

"I can see that," he said. "How much did she pay you?"

"Nothing," Big Youth said.

"Nothing?" Broker stopped surprised. "You mean you did all that work for nothing?"

"She can't pay for anything," Big Youth said. "Janet has no money."

184

"Maybe she has no money," Broker said to him. "But don't go working for other people for nothing. You will die a poor man."

Big Youth nodded, thoughtfully, and said he would keep that in mind.

Broker finally sat down on a chair, a little exhausted from all the pacing and the restlessness, and watched Big Youth work, adding up long columns of numbers. They were silent for a while, each lost in his own thoughts. Broker tapped his thoughts out on the floor with his cane as he thought them and Big Youth found that very profound indeed. Then they heard the sound of a bicycle bell and Broker rose to peer out of the window.

"It's not her," he said watching Head Faru ride into the compound, looking hot and dusty and thoroughly demoralised.

The Headmaster dismounted by Broker's car and paused for a moment to wonder what the thing was doing there. Muttering to himself, as old teachers did, he approached Janet's house. He leaned the bicycle on the wall and entered without knocking.

"Greetings," he said loudly as to a whole classroom.

"Greetings," they said.

His eyes searched the room for Janet, missed Broker, but found Big Youth.

"Where is Janet?" he asked him.

"She went to teach," Big Youth said.

"To teach whose school?" he asked. "Today is not a school day."

"That is what she told me," Big Youth informed. "I don't know where they are."

The Headmaster was at a loss. He continued disregarding Broker as he thought out his next move. Should he brave the midday sun again and go back home to mend the broken fences, or should he rest here awhile and wait for her? It was a big decision to make.

Broker watched him think and waited to be noticed. When it was clear the man would not acknowledge him, he cleared his throat and said, "Greetings, teacher."

"Greetings," said Head Faru.

"Do you remember me?" Broker asked him.

The Headmaster finally looked Broker in the face. He saw a strange, hard-boned face, heavily lined with pain and suffering, and eyes that seemed to peer out from a dark, deep cave. He shook his

185

head and walked to the door to look out at the car. Like many people in Crossroads, the sight of the car aroused in him the urge to leave Crossroads.

"Is it yours?" he asked Broker.

"It is," Broker replied.

"I thought it belonged to a big man," he said.

Broker laughed, thoroughly amused, and Big Youth grinned behind Faru's back.

"When are you leaving?" the Headmaster asked.

"Leaving?"

"Crossroads," he said. "Going away."

"Never," Broker said. "I'm not leaving at all. I'm here to stay."

"Stay?" he sounded dismayed. "Stay here? Doing what here?"

"Business," Broker told him.

"Business?" he suddenly looked suspicious. "What business?"

"I don't know for certain yet," Broker said. "Any business that makes money. I have many things in mind and I might re-open the petrol station."

"What for?" asked the Headmaster. "There are no cars in Crossroads."

"Correction," Broker now laughed the full laugh Big Youth liked, and tried to imitate. "There is one car in Crossroads. More cars will come when I get down to business."

"Cars will not stop here," the Headmaster was convinced of it. "They are afraid to catch the plague and die."

"We'll take care of that," he assured. "We'll show them one cannot catch Aids by stopping for a refill and a cup of tea. The rest will follow naturally."

The Headmaster shook his head doubtfully. He was not used to such foolish optimism. Such thinking could only come from a stranger, someone who did not know Crossroads at all.

"I am looking for a good mechanic," Broker told him.

"There are no mechanics here," he said, adamantly.

There were no artisans or craftsmen of any sort left in Crossroads. The Polytechnic taught all sorts of skills, but the students left almost immediately to escape from the plague and to seek their fortunes elsewhere.

186

But why would anyone, in his right mind, want to set up business in Crossroads? he wondered. Broker confessed to having been asked that question countless times since his return.

"I can assure you I'm quite sane," he said to the Headmaster. "I never venture into anything without a purpose."

"There is no money in Crossroads," the Headmaster said.

"I have been told that too," Broker admitted. "But we'll change all that."

"We?" the Headmaster marvelled. "How many are you?"

"For now, just one," Broker told him. "I hope to interest the business community in my new ventures. What is the population of Crossroads?"

The Headmaster had no idea. But he knew it was not the same as it was yesterday.

"This is a dying place," he said. "Where are you from?"

"Me?" Broker laughed. "From here."

"How come I don't know you?" he said.

"I have been away a long time," Broker told him. "The name is Broker. Bakari Ben Broker. You tried to teach me arithmetic."

"I remember all my students," the Headmaster said. "Which year were you in my school? What was your name?"

"Everyone called me Ben Broker," Broker said.

"Ben Broker?" Head Faru thought.

Broker waited. Big Youth tried to be insignificant, as he went on counting condoms behind the Headmaster's back.

"There was a noisy boy at the back of the class," the Headmaster said, doubtfully. "But he got nought and was not good at anything. What did they call him?"

"Spanner Boy?" Broker laughed.

"You knew him?" the Headmaster asked.

Then he saw the amusement on Broker's face and asked, "Were you that boy? The boy who thought everything was funny?"

"I was," Broker admitted.

"You were that boy?" the Headmaster marvelled. "The boy who could not get anything right? Are you Broker, the Spanner Boy?"

"The very same," laughed Broker.

"When did you come back?"

"Some time ago, now."

"But I haven't seen you about," said the Headmaster.

"You have seen my car," Broker said.

The Headmaster nodded. It was the biggest thing in Crossroads, he observed.

"Do you live here now?" he asked.

"Not at the moment," Broker told him. "Janet and I have decided to live apart, for the moment."

"Has she divorced you then?" the Headmaster asked.

"Where do you people get the idea that she will ever divorce me?" Broker sounded irritated. "I'm here to stay."

"I see," he nodded thoughtfully. "I am very happy to see you back."

"You must be the only one," Broker said laughing.

"Now you can pay me for the eggs you took from my farm," said the Headmaster.

"What eggs?" Broker asked and laughed.

He had paid so many forgotten debts since he had been back, that he was now not surprised at all when complete strangers demanded payment from him.

"Didn't you use to sell eggs?" the Headmaster asked him.

"I did," he admitted.

Then Head Faru reminded him of a long forgotten debt of eggs that Janet had refused to pay for because they were not consumed at her house. She did not know it, but the eggs had gone to Jemina's place where, it seemed, they had had even less to eat.

"You remember too well," Broker said, taking out his wallet. "How come only the people I owe are happy to see me?"

The Headmaster had no idea.

"One box of eggs, you say?" Broker asked him. "How much was it?"

"One hundred and twenty," said Head Faru.

He accepted the proffered money and studied it for a moment, exactly as everyone else had done the first time they had encountered the money he had brought back. Finally he was forced to ask, "What is this?"

"Money," Broker said, amused.

The Headmaster marvelled. It was new paper money, in new and big denomination notes, and it was clean and crisp and smelt like a new book. But Crossroads had not seen any new money in years and did not know what to do with it.

"We don't use this kind of money here," he said.

"It is perfectly legal tender," Broker told him.

"I can't change this," he tried to give it back.

"You keep the change," Broker said to him.

"Keep the change?" Faru was appalled. "We don't do such things here."

"Then consider it interest," Broker told him. "For the years I have owed it to you."

"Interest?" he nodded agreeably. "I understand interest."

Why hadn't he thought of it himself? He examined the money again, carefully.

Broker had heard, from the old men at the teahouse, that his money was causing a serious disruption to commerce in Crossroads. Market women had now to travel all the way to Sokoni to change it to smaller and more comprehensible denominations.

Head Faru finally put the money in his pocket. Then he looked at Broker and shook his head in awe.

"So you are Broker, the Spanner Boy," he marvelled. "The boy we said would come to nothing. So you did make something of yourself, after all?"

"In a manner of speaking," said Broker laughing a little.

"We teachers are always happy when a student of ours proves us wrong," said Head Faru. "But what happened to you? You were so big and strong even my teachers were afraid of you. How come you are now so ...?"

"Finished?" Broker laughed heartily. "Life has not been too kind to me either. But I'm not complaining."

He had given as good as he had received. No, not quite true. He had received a whole lot more than he had bargained for. But that was all in the past now. He was a new man now. A man with new dreams, new hopes, new aspirations and a whole new destiny.

"What business can one do here?" he asked his old teacher.

"Grave digging," said Big Youth quite unasked.

"Grave diggers do well here," agreed the Headmaster. "They are making a killing right now."

"Anything else?" Broker asked him. "Something less morbid? Something in the line of buying and selling."

"Coffins," said Big Youth, again unasked.

Broker swung his cane at him. Big Youth dodged and ran out of the house.

"The boy is right," the Headmaster confirmed. "Coffin makers do well too. The waiting list for coffins is as long as your arm. This is a town of death."

"You begin to convince me," Broker nodded slowly.

"You are not serious about staying, are you?" the Headmaster asked.

"Dead serious," he said.

"But why?" asked Faru. "Why have you come back? Why do you want to live here? No one does that."

"I was born here," Broker reminded.

The Headmaster scoffed at that.

"Many people were born here in Crossroads too," he said forcefully. "But they have all left, never to come back. No one comes back to Crossroads except to die."

"I have been told that too," Broker said.

Big Youth came back to look for something less tedious to do. The Headmaster hesitated on seeing him enter, then decided to speak his mind, all the same.

"She got used to living without you," he said.

"Are you talking about my wife?" Broker asked him.

"Janet," he said. "I'm talking about Janet. I know it is not my business."

"You are right," Broker said turning suddenly hostile. "It is not your business."

The Headmaster, not used to such talking-back from his pupils, hesitated. He cleared his throat and said, "I'm your old teacher and I must tell you the truth."

"I'm not a boy anymore," Broker said. "I know a few truths now and some of them are personal and very important to me."

"You are not going to make her life impossible again, are you?" the Headmaster asked. "Because, if you are, you will have a lot of people to answer to."

"Such as?" Broker asked him.

"The son of Mateo," he said. "Frank is devoted to her. He will not let you hurt her again and he will do anything to stop you."

"Him and who else?" asked Broker.

"Everyone in Crossroads," he said. "People who watched Janet grow up and saw what you did to her."

"I married her," Broker said. "She is my wife."

"Was," said Big Youth.

190

"You keep quiet!" Broker barked at him. "You were not yet born."

"I was in class two," said Big Youth.

"Then keep out of this," Broker ordered.

He turned to the Headmaster and stated again that he had not divorced Janet.

"You deserted her for over ten years," Faru said.

"How come everyone knows how long I have been away?" Broker said, exasperated. "Just that and nothing else. How come no one remembers any of the good things I did for Janet?"

"What things?" asked Big Youth.

"I gave her a home," Broker told him. "And three children."

He turned to the Headmaster and added, "I may have wronged her too, but I'm ready to make amends. All I want is a little understanding from all of you."

"Understanding?" the Headmaster was outraged. "After what you did to her? You want understanding from us? We who watched her suffer and watched her recover and saw her grow to be a strong and respectable woman?"

He turned to Big Youth and said incredulously, "He wants understanding."

Big Youth shrugged, for he liked Broker a great deal, and stayed out of it.

"She is still my wife," Broker said evenly. "And I love her."

"Everyone loves Janet," the Headmaster informed. "That is why we do not want to see her hurt by you again."

"I have no intention of hurting Janet," Broker said exasperated. "I want to make it up to her."

"How?" asked Big Youth.

"You keep quiet," Broker ordered.

"I know your type," the Headmaster said finally. "You think you can silence anyone, that you can buy anyone to keep quiet while you do them wrong. Have you any idea how many rich men have tried to buy Janet?"

"How many?" Broker asked.

"All of them," he said.

"I'm her husband," said Broker.

The Headmaster left him, took his bicycle and pushed it to the gate. Before mounting his bicycle, he stopped and took out the money Broker had given him. He held it up to the sun and examined it carefully.

"It's real money!" Broker bellowed out of the open window.

The Headmaster glanced back, startled. Then he pocketed the money and rode away.

"Is he always like that?" Broker wondered.

"Always," Big Youth confirmed.

Head Faru owned a grocery in Crossroads, he revealed. When the boys were not driving him insane in school, the customers were doing so with their incessant pleas for credit.

"What does he sell?" Broker asked.

"Farm produce," said Big Youth. "From his own farm."

Broker nodded, thoughtfully. He started pacing the room again, stopping now and then to glare in the direction of the gate and wonder what was keeping Janet.

"Are they always gone this long?" he asked.

"Always," Big Youth said.

"Just the two of them?"

"Just the two of them."

Big Youth was enjoying Broker's discomfiture and added, with certain mischief, "Sometimes they don't get back until after dark."

Broker digested this information.

"Where do they go?" he asked.

"I don't know," said Big Youth.

Broker resumed his pacing, walking slowly from the window to the door and back. He paused by the cartons of condoms and glared at them thoughtfully. Finally, he turned to Big Youth and asked him, "Would you like to work for me?"

"I'm still in school," Big Youth said.

"After school," he said. "You could earn yourself some money."

"Doing what?" Big Youth asked.

"Selling."

"Selling what?"

"Whatever I tell you to sell," Broker said impatiently. "And stop asking foolish questions. Do you want to make money or not?"

"How much?" Big Youth asked.

"More than she pays you," Broker told him.

"Janet does not pay me," Big Youth said.

"I know," said Broker.

Big Youth considered. He could buy himself some books. And a new dress for his grandmother. He could do lots of things with money. He could even buy himself a radio, and a ticket out of Crossroads.

"What do I have to do?" he asked finally.

"Start calling me Boss," Broker told him. "And tell Janet I must see her."

Then he picked up his cane and limped out of the room. Big Youth watched out of the window, intrigued, as Broker rushed to his car and drove urgently away.

Chapter Twenty-Two

When Broker had left, Big Youth carried the cartons back to the store. He took out some more to work on.

Janet and Frank arrived a while later, both exhausted and in need of peace and rest.

"Your husband was here," Big Youth said to her. "He says he must talk to you."

"What does he want now?" she wondered.

"He offered me a job," said Big Youth.

She scoffed at the thought.

"Remember what I told you," she said to him.

"To forget everything he says," said Big Youth. "But Broker says so many things it is impossible to forget them all."

"You must try," she told him.

Frank stood in the midst of the cartons and things looking confused.

"Sit down," she said to him. "I'll warm up some food."

She gave him a stool by the doorway, took the rolled up posters and teaching aids from him and carried them into the house. While she was in the house, Grandmother came through the small gate, leaning heavily on her stick, and holding the hand of Jeremiah. She was dressed in a colourful, new dress Broker had bought for her and wore it with great pride.

She paused on seeing them and asked with great concern, "Don't you two have anywhere else to go?"

"Nowhere," Big Youth said cheerfully. "Greetings, Grandmother, you are looking beautiful today."

She regarded him with her usual disdain of him and mumbled unhappily.

"We like Janet," Big Youth answered.

"Find another woman to like," she said to him. "Janet has a husband now. You don't have to watch her all day."

"Why are these two always here?" she asked Janet, when she appeared.

Janet ignored the question and enquired after the children. Grandmother had sent them to visit their aunt and maybe get something to eat there. She had had nothing to give them, she complained.

"They have been crying all day like motherless children," she said.

Janet glanced at Big Youth. He shook his head at her. He had been at her house most of the day and, though he had not seen them, he had not heard the children cry from hunger. On the contrary, he had heard them laugh as they pestered Grandmother for bananas.

"We were delayed at the school," Janet said to her.

"Are you now teachers?" she asked.

"No," Frank said. "But we teach."

She was not interested in his opinion and repeated the question to Janet.

"We are now teachers," Janet admitted. "We talk, we make noise and we teach. We do everything. Nobody wants to do anything for anyone, not even to tell the children what they want to know. If I was a man ..."

"Manhood doesn't make man," Grandmother said, glaring at Frank.

Frank smiled tolerantly and Big Youth laughed out loud.

"Manhood may not make a man," Janet said to her grandmother. "But they listen no matter what manner of man speaks out. When a woman speaks out, they laugh in her face and call her *malaya*, a shameless prostitute."

She sighed wearily and said to Grandmother, "I'm about to heat up some food for lunch. Have you eaten?"

Grandmother ignored her and went on glaring at Frank. She weighed and re-weighed him and came to the same conclusion as always. He was worth exactly nothing.

"Why do you spend all your time with another man's wife?" she asked him. "Have you nothing better to do?"

"I help her out," he informed her.

"But she is another man's wife," she said morosely. "Why don't you go help someone else?"

He would, he assured her, as soon as he reopen his clinic and made enough money.

Grandmother was not at all pacified. She grumbled about the moral outrage of it; a man must not spend so much time with another man's wife, no matter what.

"Grandmother," Janet said patiently. "We are tired from arguing with difficult people. Sit down and eat something with us or go back to your house."

"I'm going," she said. "You don't have to chase me out like a dog."

But she made no move to leave.

Big Youth finished what he was doing and, declining to join them for lunch, left to go do his homework. Janet went to fetch the food and Grandmother resumed her interrogation of Frank.

"Is it true you have the plague?" she asked him.

"It is true," he answered.

"You don't look sick to me," she said. "Not like the people I have seen with the plague."

"I'm not sick," he told her. "But I have in me the virus that causes Aids."

"So you will also get sick and die?" she asked.

Frank, detecting the hopeful tone in her voice, smiled patiently and assured her it was still a probability. But it could take a long time, he told her.

"Then why don't you get a wife of your own?" she asked him. "Have your own children before you die from the plague?"

"And leave them orphans when I die?" he asked her. "Like Jeremiah? Like all the others? Grandmother, I don't think that it is such a good idea."

She looked for a way round his reasoning. Finding none, she grumbled, "But this is another man's house. Another man's wife."

He laughed and assured her there was nothing but respect and honour and good intentions between him and Janet. She was not convinced.

"Come, Jeremiah," she said to the boy who was almost an extension of her arm. "Come take my hand for we are not wanted here."

The boy took her hand and they went back across the yard and through the small gate as they had come.

Janet came out with a tray of food and was surprised to find them gone. She had served something for Jeremiah too and she took it back into the house.

"She tries my patience like no one else," she said as they sat down to eat. "But I think we did well today. Let us hope they will soon open more doors to us."

Frank agreed with her, but wondered how they would cope with it all. There were so many schools, so many youths. Would they ever reach them all?

"We must avoid despair," she told him. "I wouldn't be sane today if I spent every night awake, worrying about rejection and counting the condoms that I did not give out. We must live in hope and take it one day at a time. Tomorrow we'll do better."

She was an amazing woman.

"Tomorrow we shall do better," Frank said.

"After lunch, I will make you a nice cup of cocoa," she promised him.

It was something to look forward to. This, however, was not to be.

They were not quite finished with their lunch when Broker returned. They watched silently as the huge car pulled up by the grain store and Broker hauled himself out of the driver's seat, full of energy and bursting with enthusiasm.

"Where have you two been?" he asked them. "I have looked for you all over the place."

"We have been working," Frank said with a good feeling born of a job well done and a good meal. "We gave a talk at the Polytechnic today."

"Don't you people get tired of talking?" he asked them. "What do you talk about?"

Janet's tolerant smile immediately vanished. Broker was sniffing the air and eyeing Frank's food and did not notice.

"Banana mash," he said, enthusiastically. "It's my favourite dish."

Janet ignored the hint and asked him, "Why were you looking for me?".

"I'm very hungry," he said. "May I have some too?"

"Was there no food where you have been?" she asked him.

"I wasn't anywhere," he said. "I have been driving around looking for you."

"Why are you looking for me?" she asked him.

"I have discovered a way to make Crossroads men wear condoms," Broker told her. "But I am very hungry. May I have a little food? I don't need much, two mouthfuls will do."

Janet considered. He would have to sit down to eat the food and she would have to sit and listen to his endless lies and to empty promises and to his pathetic pleas for forgiveness. She was not strong enough for that today.

Before leaving Pwani to return to Crossroads, he had known for certain that it would not be easy to regain everyone's love and acceptance. But he had promised himself to outwait them all. He would bombard them with his presence, smother them with his patience. He would suffocate them with his shadow, crowd them till they forgot he had ever been away. He would wear Janet out with his endurance, the same way he had worn out countless other women before and after her.

Now he stood before her, like a patient, old vulture in his baggy black suit, and waited. He had come home prepared to wait.

Janet realised he would stand there forever, unless she gave him something to eat, and rose to fetch him some food.

Broker immediately took her stool and asked Frank where they had really gone.

"Everywhere," Frank told him.

"So?" his tone suddenly changed. "You think you are a smart operator, don't you?"

Frank had no idea what he was talking about.

"Hanging around my wife like that," he said. "Making yourself available?"

"Available for what?" Frank asked him.

"Making her need you?" he said.

"Need me how?" Frank asked a little fed up. "What are you talking about, Broker?"

"About need," Broker told him. "About ... you know very well what the devil I'm talking about."

"Janet doesn't need any one of us," Frank said shaking his head. "Janet does not need anyone, at all. Thanks to you, she is cured of men."

"Don't change the subject," Broker said severely.

He was about to respond in a similarly unfriendly manner, when Janet returned. She paused significantly, noting the tension in the air and the way they avoided her eyes, before giving the plate of food to Broker. He dug into it hungrily, like the famished man he was. After one mouthful he spat it all out and tried to give back the rest of the food.

"*Pili-pili*," he cried. "Too hot."

"But you love chilli," Janet told him. "You always loved it hot."

"Not anymore," he said, belching painfully. "It would kill me now."

Spicy food turned his insides on fire, he said. The pain was incredible. But he was really, really hungry. Could he have something less spicy?

Janet regarded him for a full moment, convinced this was another one of his manoeuvres, and considered ejecting him forthwith. Frank read her thoughts and shook his head at her. She took the plate from Broker and stormed into the house.

"I have got craters in here full of fire-spitting dragons," Broker said to Frank.

And that was just one of the many complications, he added. He could tell Frank tales, about living with the disease, that would curl his imagination.

Frank nodded and tried to concentrate on his food.

"Some people have to suffer the full range of problems," Broker went on. "Aids is a terrible, terrible disease. You don't know how lucky you are to be free of infection. Believe me, dying is the easiest part."

Frank nodded again.

Janet returned with the food she had served for Jeremiah, before Grandmother had hustled him away, and gave it to Broker. He sniffed at it, tasted it guardedly.

"I haven't had a decent meal in days," he said eating voraciously.

Janet stood over him, with a mixture of pity and loathing on her face, and watched him eat.

"I wish someone would teach Musa how to cook for people," he said to Frank. "Have you had his *exodus special?*"

Frank had to smile. Everyone who stayed at the teahouse had to try Musa's *exodus special;* Musa made sure they did. As far as Frank could tell, the dish was made out of offal, or hoofs or whatever meat was going cheap at the slaughterhouse that day, and vegetables and anything that Musa could fit in the same pot. Musa claimed that the *special* contained manna, collected that very morning from the slaughterhouse, but Frank suspected the ingredient was, in fact, the sheep's brain that Musa got as discount from the butchers.

"About the condoms," Janet said to Broker.

"Condoms?" he seemed momentarily lost.

"You said you had a bright idea about condoms," she reminded. "Or was it just another scheme to get yourself a free meal?"

"I really do have an idea," he said. "Many ideas, in fact."

He turned to Frank and said, "Now I know why you never eat at the teahouse. This stuff is the real thing."

"The condoms?" Janet pressed.

"I have been thinking," he said.

He had been doing a whole lot of thinking lately. What else was there to do at night at the teahouse? He had thought himself into migraines sometimes; thinking about his past and his future and about Janet, and how he could help her with her work. He had considered giving her money, but then it would not do to bribe men to use condoms. That would never work. He had experienced bribery at its most blatant phase, in the harbour at Pwani and he knew it to be very short sighted incentive.

"You know, you have a tough job here," he told her. "It is not easy to convince men that a condom does not affect their proud virility; especially such pig-headed total men as you have here. I should know, I was one of them."

He took another spoonful of food. He was in no hurry, and it drove her mad with impatience. She watched him chew, slowly and thoroughly, and she wrung her hands impatiently.

"Well?" she prompted, when she could stand it no longer.

He had thought a great deal, he emphasized. He had thought back to something Big Youth had told him. A communal problem called for a communal solution, the boy had said.

"He is not completely foolish, that boy."

He took another mouthful, exactly calculated to drive Janet insane with apprehension, and it did.

"Get to the point!" she yelled.

He finally did; in his own devious and unhurried way.

He was not used to doing things for communities or for anyone, other than himself, he revealed. Wherever he had lived, in the cities and in the towns, and in such like places, people thought, and were indeed encouraged to think, only of themselves. Selfishness was the key to success, they learned. They were encouraged to be individualists, to lie, to cheat, to rob and to plunder their own people in order to satisfy their insatiable hungers. They were taught that their avarice, their megalomania and their raging carnal and spiritual hungers could only be slaked

200

by the sacrifice of fellow humans; by the rape, torture and murder of their own kind.

Broker had witnessed it all as he had hobnobbed with the real scum of the earth - the traders who imported condemned grain from Europe to sell to their poor people, their own kith and kin, knowing very well that it would eventually kill them. He had wined and dined with apparently sane and educated men who had prospered by selling radiation-contaminated powdered milk to poor mothers to feed their starving children on. Still Broker had done business with others who stole public lands, toilets and bridges, in broad daylight and, without any scruples whatsoever, removed man-hole covers from the pavement, leaving gaping holes in which their brothers occasionally broke a leg or two. And all these things had been done overtly, blatantly and without fear, shame or remorse, by husbands, fathers and brothers; all of them men who claimed to be lovers of children and fearers of God.

"I tell you, it's a dog eat dog world out there," he said, as he continued to avoid Janet's eyes.

"About the condoms," she reminded.

"Sell them," he said.

"Sell whom?" she asked, momentarily lost.

"The condoms," he said. "Just sell the condoms, it is that simple. Stop giving them out free and sell them. Just sell the condoms."

He turned to Frank, expecting some sort of male solidarity and found none. Frank was staring at Janet and worrying about the extreme expression on her face. Broker turned to find her regarding him with a contempt that went far beyond hatred.

"Is this the bright idea that is supposed to make my work easier?" she asked him, calmly, fighting the urge to lift him up bodily and throw him into the latrine.

He nodded and said smugly, "In a nutshell, yes."

"You are sicker than I thought," she said quietly, grappling with the screams of fury boiling up inside her. "You are sicker than a dead dog."

"And dead serious too," he said, giving her his empty plate. "Is there more food?"

"No!" she screamed.

She snatched the plate and was about to take it into the house, thoroughly outmanoeuvred, when a sudden thought stopped her. She stopped and looked back at Broker, and there was pain in her voice, as she asked him, "Is this the big job you offered Big Youth?"

He nodded.

"Selling condoms?" she asked him.

"Yes," he said.

"Selling Government condoms?" she could not understand this kind of greed.

Broker nodded again and she was at a loss for what to do with him. He turned to Frank, a smug expression on his face.

"The boy talks too much," he said. "But he is a clever and hard-working boy, full of promise. We must not let him go to waste."

"So you are now going to teach him to be like you?" Janet was scandalised. "A dealer in other people's property?"

"I'm only trying to help," he said.

"Trying to help whom?" she asked. "Haven't you learned anything from your life of debauchery? Hasn't your condition taught you any amount of humility?"

"Why else would I be here?" he asked trying to sound reasonable. "Why else would I return to Crossroads?"

"You tell me," she said, putting the plates down on a stool and crossing her arms to listen.

Broker was trapped. He looked from her to Frank and found neither support nor escape from that quarter.

"I came back to be with the people I love," he said, with strained sincerity. "To give back some of the things that I took with me from Crossroads."

The love, the friendship, the energy that had kept him going when he thought the world would fall down on him.

"And to help my people," he said.

"By selling them what belongs to them?" Janet asked him.

"In any way I can help," he said. "I know for certain that no one will buy condoms to throw away. So I'm certain that they will use them."

"Do you, seriously, believe people will buy something that they don't want for free?" she asked him.

"Why not?" he said. "People do the stupidest things. I have dealt with people before and, believe me, I know people."

"You don't know people," she said severely. "You have never known people. Those were not people you dealt with out there, wherever you were."

"People are people," he told her.

"Real people do not think like you," she told him.

Real people did not look for the slightest excuse to exploit their brothers' ignorance and to make money out of them. Real people did not seek to make profit out of the free Government condoms. The very idea was immoral, disgusting and contrary to the terms of her employment.

"And it might work," he told her.

"You are mad," she finally concluded.

"But gifted," he said, smiling disarmingly.

He used to beat her to submission in this manner. With persistence, tenacity and a diabolically convoluted logic she could not withstand. He would keep at it till she was too tired to resist him, till she realised she would have to give something for him to let go.

"Remember when we sold eggs for a living?" he said, laughing.

"You sold eggs," she corrected. "I did not."

He reminded her of how he had sold eggs he did not have and made money by getting the sellers and the buyers together. She had not complained then. It had given them a start in life. This new venture was another such break. Only this time the gain would not be in money but in recognition and in influence and acclaim.

"You will be famous," he told her.

"Famous for what?" she asked.

"For doing your job," he said. "Just trust me."

"Trust you?" the words stuck in her throat. "How can I ever trust you again?"

"You have nothing to lose," he told her. "The condoms are free."

"Have you any idea what would happen if they found me selling their condoms?" she asked.

"It makes more sense than throwing them into your latrine," he said to her.

"Who told you about that?" she asked.

"This is Crossroads," he told her.

Everyone knew everything in Crossroads.

"And what do you suggest I do with the money?" she asked him. "Give it to you to buy another car?"

"I don't need another car," he said to her. "I have enough money to buy several cars, in fact. But there are lots of widows and orphans in Crossroads who could do with some money."

"Why don't you give them your own money?" she asked. "If you are so concerned about their welfare."

He could not do that, he told her. His money was for his wife and children. But money was not the issue here. The issue was how to make Crossroads appreciate the prevailing epidemic conditions and accept the condom. That was the goal. How they got there was immaterial.

"Don't worry about the selling," he told her. "I have sold everything from red mercury to goats' powder."

"Goats' powder?" Frank had never heard of it.

"Ground goat's ... you know, *things*," Broker said. "I must have saved some few rhinos too, I think. So you see, I'm not completely selfish."

"Does it work?" Frank asked, intrigued.

"Does rhino horn?" Broker laughed, suddenly his old self again. "I'm a broker, not a scientist."

Janet was following their little exchange with incredulous amazement, and disgust.

"Give me one carton of condoms," he said to her. "If it's not sold out by this time tomorrow, my name is not Broker."

He said it with such sincerity, and earnest intention, that it sickened him. And, seeing him so true and ingenuous, Janet wavered. She still did not trust him, but he was right in one thing. Anything that made Crossroads condom-friendly was worth a try. She turned to Frank.

Frank was busy, being studiously uninvolved, but the expression on his face was enough. He did not have to say "*I told you so*".

"Frank?" she asked him.

He shrugged.

She turned back to Broker, her mind made up.

"Just one carton," she said to him.

"You will never regret it," he assured her.

"But let me warn you," she said, her voice hard and businesslike. "If this is another of your schemes to lose me my job ..."

"I don't work like that anymore," he said to her. "You will see."

She hesitated for a moment before picking out a carton of condoms for him.

"Take that one," she said, pointing to a half empty one.

Broker pounced on it, like a life raft. He tried to lift it and found it too heavy. Frank rose to help him carry it to the car.

"Are you going to town?" he asked, as they loaded it in the boot.

"Directly," Broker said, once again bursting with excitement. "I'll deliver you right to your door."

"I'll be back as soon as this one is sold," he said to Janet. "I promise you, you will never regret this."

She knew, deep down in her heart where love and hate, despair and hope resided, down there where reason held no sway, that she would regret it for the rest of her life.

"And don't worry," he said before driving off at high speed.

But she did worry

Chapter Twenty-Three

She sat down, now all alone in her large compound, and worried about Broker. She worried until she worried she might go after him and take back the condoms she had given him.

"Greetings," hailed Teacher Paulo.

He was leaning on his bicycle in the yard, right in front of her eyes, and Janet had not seen or heard him come. So great were her worries.

"Greetings," she said, a little startled.

Teacher Paulo was the Headmaster at Crossroads only surviving village Polytechnic. Like all suffering school heads, he was a simple and humble man.

"You are all alone?" he observed.

"Frank has just left," she told him. "Broker too was here."

"I did not know Broker was back," he said.

"You must be the only one that did not know it," Janet told him. "He has been going round Crossroads telling everyone that I'm his wife."

The Headmaster was silent, thoughtful. He had been a Headmaster for a long time. A good and honest man, as all of Crossroads would testify. He sometimes stopped by to wish her well or to call his greetings over the hedge as he rode his bicycle to and from school, but he had never thought of Janet as someone to be seduced and corrupted. He was not immune to her magnetism, no man could be, but, like Head Faru, he had never come to bother Janet with vulgar propositions. Like everyone in Crossroads, he knew of the hardships she had endured under Broker and he sympathised with her.

"You will not let him abuse you again," he said firmly.

"He cannot abuse me again," she said, convinced of it. "It will never happen again. But I thank you for your concern. What brings you here today?"

The question caught him off guard. He had been so disturbed by the news of Broker's return that he had forgotten the purpose of his visit.

"I had a word with the School Board," he told her.

He paused uncertainly. He was a meticulous man, economical and careful with words. Words, he often said to his students, were more than mere articulated animal sounds. Words, he told them every day, were mightier than machetes. Words could heal, but words could also kill.

"I passed on your request," he said to her.

"And they turned it down," Janet concluded from his hesitation.

The Headmaster nodded. She had not expected much, she told him. Not from a School Board made up of illiterate, power-hungry hyenas.

The Headmaster winced at her choice of words and said to her, "They said that sex education is not education at all. They cannot allow you to teach it in my school."

"Great sadness," she said. "But I thank you for trying."

Again he was silent, choosing his words with care. He was not against Janet or her work. He understood everything she was trying to do for Crossroads. But he was a school head and he had to do as the Board and the Government said. He had just come to tell her that, he said.

"I understand," she said to him. "Sit down and have some tea."

"I can't stay long," he told her.

His late brother's wife was to be buried that day. And two of their children were so sick only God knew how long they would live. It was a shame and a great sadness.

There was not a single child in his school who had not lost a family member to the plague. It made him sad to see how they grieved. And no one, except Janet, seemed to care about stopping the plague.

"The plague has brought us all great sadness," she said to him.

"You do a good and important job," he told her. "But I'm not allowed to say that."

"I understand," she told him.

He was quiet for a moment, thinking what to say next.

"I hear they let you teach at the other school," he said.

"Too little, too late," she told him. "They have lost half the girls to pregnancy already."

"My school is all boys," he told her. "Girls do not like to learn carpentry."

He said it with the heavy resignation of a long suffering parent and teacher. Like Janet, the grief he carried was not all his own.

"Come in and have some tea," she said to him.

She coaxed him into the living room and made him sit down. He rose as soon as she left to go to the kitchen to make the tea, and paced the room restlessly. When she came back with the tea, she found him admiring Big Youth's *Life and Death Equation*. She didn't think much of the poster, which she found simple and almost silly, but then that was Big Youth - endearingly simple.

"Did Big Youth do this?" he asked her.

"And more," she told him.

"All by himself?" he marvelled.

"All by himself," she confirmed.

"He is not entirely foolish, I see."

On the contrary, Janet found Big Youth both intelligent and gifted. He was also very quick and eager to help.

"I'm happy you find some use for him," he said to her. "He is quite useless in school."

He had taught Big Youth for several years and, like everyone else who had ever taught Big Youth, despaired of him.

Janet laughed and told him they did not know Big Youth. Then she poured the tea in two large enamel mugs and they sat down to it.

"You have nice children," he said, admiring the old family photograph.

"They are much bigger now," she told him. "They go to the old mission school."

Where she had gone to school. Where Broker and Frank had gone to school. And where Teacher Paulo had taught for many years, before moving over to the Polytechnic; when it was sick and dying from the theft of funds, corruption and mismanagement, and it appeared that no one could save it. It was where everybody went to school before the proliferation of the self-help schools that were now closing down for lack of pupils.

"How many children do you have?" she asked him.

"Children?" he looked up startled. "Very many."

He had several boys and two girls. But, if he could start all over again, he would have fewer children. Of that he was certain.

"They all say that," Janet observed.

But he was sincere. Sad and sincere. A teacher's salary was no longer enough for his large family, and for his numerous relatives with their numerous children, all of whom claimed a right to it by virtue of blood relationship. If they had all had fewer children, life might have been easier for Teacher Paulo.

By the time he had finished his third cup of tea he had managed to reveal to her what he had really come to tell her; that she was free to come and talk to his students as well, as long as she did it discreetly and with a minimum of fuss. And having at last said it, he rose to leave.

"I'll be glad to talk to your students," Janet told him.

"I hope we can do it quietly," he said to her. "I would hate to lose my job over a foolish misunderstanding."

"You will not lose your job," she assured him. "Go well."

"Stay well," he said, looking a little lighter.

Then he rode away on his rickety, old bicycle.

Janet watched him go and was pained to realise, once again, that people who worked the hardest in their lives also lived the saddest of lives.

Chapter Twenty-Four

Everyone in Crossroads knew that condoms were free. They could not comprehend it, therefore, when Broker turned up among them, all excited and offering them the very same condoms for money. They had to scrutinise him, long and hard, before agreeing that he appeared quite sane. Some could not help but wonder what kind of fool he had turned out to be.

"Don't you know it, man?" they said to him. "*Kodoms* are free."

"Correction," he told them. "Condoms *were* free. Condoms *are not* free anymore. Condoms *will not* be free again and condoms *will never* be free again, understand? Not ever again! Do you understand?"

They could not understand. Just yesterday, Janet was there, down on her knees, begging them to take the condoms away from her, to do with them whatever they wanted to do with them. How come now they could not have condoms but for money? They laughed in his face and told Broker to go try his tricks somewhere else.

"Tricks?" he laughed at them too. "You just don't get it, do you? There's nothing for free anymore; this is the new world order."

They did not believe him. No matter how hard he told them, he could not convince anyone he was serious, that they had used their last free condom, ever, and they would not be getting another free condom for as long as they lived.

"Never again," he said harshly. "From now on, you will have to pay up, and pay up well, if you want to go on using condoms."

"We don't use *kodoms*, man," they said to him. "We are total men. That's why Janet gives them to us for free."

He had news for them, he told them patiently. He would turn off their supply of free condoms for ever.

"*Si* you turn it off," they said defiantly. "*Kwani* what are you waiting for?"

"Turn it off?" Broker laughed. "I just did; turned it off and threw away the key."

"But you can't do that," they reasoned. "Only Janet can do that. You are not Janet."

"That's right," he told them angrily. "And you have no idea who I am."

Most of them were toddlers when he was the Spanner Boy. They had not experienced Broker in those old days; when women would count their daughters and men their goats after Broker had been to visit. But he had no intention of wasting a whole day arguing with young fools and went in search of real men; men who, like himself, understood well the uncompromising principles of supply and demand.

The men heard him out, mostly out of politeness, but could not understand a word he said. He gave them all the deal of their lives, an offer he said would never be repeated. But they, too, refused it all the same. Like everyone else in Crossroads, they knew that *kodoms* were free. They dared him to turn off their supply.

Broker was defeated, but not discouraged. He called them unflattering names, told them they were as foolish as their drooling sons, and went in search of total men; the entrepreneurs who had kept Crossroads ticking over all these years, against insurmountable odds. But they too knew condoms to be free and were certain they could never sell any.

Broker was sweating heavily, and going mad with frustration, when he finally called on the proprietor of Crossroads General Store, the oldest retail business in town. The man was away in Sokoni for supplies and the wife, who ran the shop most days, said she knew nothing about condoms and that Broker would have to wait for her husband.

To pass the time, Broker called on the girls at Highlife Lodge. They were all new faces, most of them barely past their teens. They had enough education to understand half the instructions on the condom wrappers and asked him to tell them what the rest meant.

What happened to a condom when it expired? they asked him. Did it go stale, like old *mandazi* or did it disintegrate and fall apart like an old wig?

Broker answered their questions the best he could. He told them everything he knew about condoms and what he did not know he made up on the spot, determined to satisfy their hunger for knowledge. But the girls were only half listening. Alice, a

211

rustic beauty with dark eyes, was looking at the huge car outside and then at the famished man with his carton of condoms under his arms and trying to put the two together.

"Is that your car?" she asked him.

He assured her that it was, all of it.

"Then why are you selling condoms?" she asked him.

"I believe in condoms," he told her.

She had never met a man who believed in condoms before; none of them had and they were all very amused.

"You may laugh all you like," he said to them. "But I'll break the neck of the first cow to call me the condom man, you hear?"

They heard him and laughed even louder and decided to like him. He had to be a rich and important man, they said to themselves. How much money did he have, they asked him. He had not come to buy, he told them, impatiently.

"Will you stop asking foolish questions and listen to me?" He said harshly.

He flattered them, told them how important they were, how they were the vital vanguard in Crossroads' war against the plague. Only they could stop Aids dead in its tracks and save themselves and the community from certain death. They had the power to do it, and he had the equipment to do it with. What they had to do was to insist that their clients use a condom.

"Men don't want condoms," Alice told him. "They pay us not to use condoms."

"You must insist that they use condoms," he said to her. "Think of yourselves first; do you want to die painfully like a dog just because men don't like to use condoms? You have to protect yourselves, you understand? Otherwise you and your ignorant men will soon be as dead as donkeys."

"You don't know men," they said, laughing at him.

"I'm a man," he reminded.

"Would you wear a condom?" Alice asked him.

"Would I be selling condoms otherwise?" he said to them. "Believe me, I have my best interests at heart too."

But, more importantly, he had the girls' welfare in mind too. They could make lots of money from the deal he was offering them, if they bought the condoms from him and sold them to their clients for a profit.

The girls were better read than he had thought and could read well between the lines. They let him talk himself hoarse, then laughed in his face again and wondered where he had come from.

"Real men don't wear condoms," Alice informed him. "Even Janet knows that."

And that was that.

"You foolish cows!" he suddenly went wild, on realising he had wasted his precious time and flattery on a herd of village sows. "Don't ever say you were never told. Don't ever say I did not warn you, when they pack up your wasted carcase in a matchbox and stick it down a rat hole."

The girls were stunned at his sudden change of humour. They could not understand his anger at all and fled from him in fear of their lives. He picked up his carton of condoms and stormed back to the general store, in a dark and seething rage. The man was not back yet, and the woman still knew nothing about condoms. Broker moved on, called at other lodging houses and tried to persuade the proprietors to include condoms in their room charges and insist on their guests using them.

"We can't do that," they said, drowning in embarrassment. "We have nothing to do with that business. You must talk to the girls."

"What?" cried the girls. "We can't do that, we'd lose our customers and our jobs. Do you want us to lose our jobs?"

At this point, Broker seriously considered dumping his carton of condoms in the nearest dustbin, then jumping in his car and driving till he fell off the edge of the earth. He could see no light at the end of the dark anymore, no way at all to penetrate the swamp of ignorance and apathy around him. Then he remembered why he was doing it and soldiered on.

He found the proprietor of the general store on the third try and offered him the deal of the year. The man promptly refused it. He knew, like all the others did, that *kodoms* were free.

"Not anymore," Broker said, as he had said to all the others. "There will be no more free rides here."

The man was not interested in rides, free or otherwise.

"I'll give you a special price," Broker offered, in desperation.

"What for?" he asked.

For the best condom he had never used, Broker told him. Not the standard Government issue but the real thing. Gold-wrapped and all. Guaranteed to stay fresh forever. It was made from very special rubber, a latex-rich medicinal rubber from a genus of rubber trees that grew in only one place on earth.

"Have you heard of Kasai?"

"Kasai who?" the trader asked.

"Kasai is a place," Broker said, wearily wiping heavy sweat off his face and neck. "It's a place deep in the Congo. You have heard of the Congo. You have not? It's the largest equatorial forest in Africa; so vast its inhabitants have never seen its outside, and believe they are the only people on earth. Well, Kasai is right in there, at the heart of this mighty jungle, and that is where the best rubber comes from."

"So?" said the man, a little intrigued. "It is still only a *kodom*."

"Only a *kodom*?" Broker acted scandalised. "This is the best condom in the world. Here, take a good look at it."

The trader took the condom and examined it curiously. Like many people in Crossroads, he had never before seen a condom at such close quarters, and was now surprised to see how simple and ordinary it looked.

"But do not underrate this little bit of latex," Broker warned him. "The only thing it will not do is sing to you."

The man was examining the condom with undivided concentration and wondering how such an innocuous bit of equatorial jungle could create so much *maneno*, so much hullabaloo, all over Crossroads. Was it possible, he wondered, that it really did contain medicine that revived the flagging libido of old men, as he had heard it mentioned once in passing? He was loath to ask.

"I will give you a really special discount," Broker was telling him.

"Discount?" the man glanced over his shoulder.

His wife was at the back of the shop, cooking his supper. There was no one else in the shop, except himself, Broker and the cat sleeping on a sack of flour in the corner. But he lowered his voice all the same, as he asked, "How special?"

"Very special," said Broker. "Something like ... thirty percent?"

"Only thirty percent?" the man asked.

He knew a thing or two about discount.

"This is a very special condom," Broker said to him.

The trader scrutinized the condom, glanced again over his shoulder and finally asked, "How does it work?"

"How does what work?" Broker asked him.

"*Kodom*," said the man.

"How does a condom work?" Broker asked, confused. "What do you mean how does a condom work?"

"Does it have batteries?" asked the man.

"What for does it need batteries?" Broker asked.

"You say this *thing* can sing," said the man.

"Did I say that?" Broker was devastated. "No, I did not say that."

He fought to keep his collapsing face straight, and his raging temper under a tight leash.

"I did not say the condom could sing," he said, calmly. "I said ... I said ... Listen, condoms can't sing or dance. Condoms don't perform, not by themselves, anyway. What am I saying? Listen, it doesn't require any batteries at all, OK? Condoms don't use any batteries. Are you listening? You wear them over your ... *you know*. To stop your wife having a baby. And to protect yourself."

"Protect myself?" the man wondered. "To protect myself from what?"

"From disease," Broker was on the verge of despair.

This cannot be, he was thinking to himself, this is not possible. He had heard of famine in the midst of plenty, but this went beyond mere dearth of information.

"From disease?" the man was studying the condom in his hands, and not quite listening to Broker.

"Have you ever heard of STDs?" Broker asked him. "Diseases such as Aids?"

The man suddenly looked up, "Aids?"

"Please, don't ask me what that is?" Broker pleaded.

"I know Aids," the man smiled. "Aids is the disease of men who *manga-manga*."

Broker nodded vaguely, not wanting to be embroidered in any more of the man's ignorance, and pointed at the condom.

"What do you say?" he asked.

The man glanced over his shoulder.

"I will take two," he announced.

"Good man," Broker clapped him on the shoulder. "I like doing business with smart, decisive men."

The man was flattered.

"I'll have your two cartons delivered within the hour," Broker promised.

"Cartons?" asked the man, confused. "What cartons?"

"With the condoms," Broker said. "Your two cartons of condoms."

"Two cartons of *kodoms*?" the shopkeeper was now bewildered. "Two cartons of *kodoms*? What shall I do with two cartons of *kodoms*? I want two *kodoms* ... two *kodoms* like this one."

"Two condoms?" now it was Broker's turn to be confounded.

"Two like these," said the man.

"Two pieces?" Broker finally despaired. "You want two condoms? Two pieces of condoms? What on earth do you want to do with two condoms?"

"I'm an old man," said the trader reasonably.

"I can see that," Broker said. "The condoms are not all for you."

"My wife is old too," said the trader.

"I understand that too," Broker told him. "I don't want you to use all the condoms by yourself. I mean, I want you to stock them for sale. For your customers."

"My customers?" the man said scandalised. "My customers do not buy *kodoms*. *Si* they can get free *kodoms* from Janet."

"Not anymore," Broker struggled to remain calm and composed. "I thought I told you that already. I thought I made that quite clear. Can't you understand anything, man? There will be no more free condoms from now on. Never again. Can you understand that?"

"No one uses *kodoms*," said the trader, reasonably. "I told you my wife is too old to have children and I don't *manga-manga*."

He was ordering the two condoms so as not to waste Broker's time. He could see that Broker was an honest and hard-working man and, therefore, wanted to help him out.

"I thank you very much," Broker said, his voice strained. "That is very considerate of you. But what I'm telling you is this, from today on, anyone who wants a condom will have to go to a shop. If I give you a monopoly now, in a few weeks' time, men will be lining up to buy condoms from you. Think about it. All of Crossroads will have to come to you for their condoms. That is how fortunes are made, my man. And I'll do even better. I will give you sixty percent discount. Imagine that; a whole sixty percent."

"Sixty percent of what?" said the man rationally. "The silly things are already free."

216

"Not anymore," Broker tried to suppress the outrage rising in his voice. "Don't you understand anything, man?"

"I understand everything," the trader said, suddenly offended. "You want to make money out of me, that is all you want to do. I don't like that and I don't need your ... *things*. I have no use for them. Take them back."

"Wait!" Broker ordered. "Listen to me. We can make a deal."

"What sort of deal?" the man asked.

"Something beneficial to both of us," Broker told him.

Broker wanted to make money, yes, but he also wanted the trader to make money too. He wanted to be friends with him and to help him. There was a whole lot of business ahead, for the both of them. He would get the trader something to revive his virility too. That was how much he wanted to be friends with him.

"You can't get rhino horn anymore," the trader informed.

"Rhino horn?" Broker laughed contemptuously. "That is all old hat now, haven't you heard that? No one uses rhino horn anymore. I'll get you something very special, very powerful. Have you ever heard of Super GTP?"

The old man had never heard of it.

"That is because it's very new," Broker told him. "I invented it myself."

He had also conjured up the lofty sounding name himself, after the patent office rejected the original name.

"It's a secret recipe," he said to the trader. "Here are your two condoms. I really wish you would consider stocking condoms for your customers. You will never regret it, I assure you. I know money is not your problem, but who ever said no to more money. Look at me, look at my car. Wouldn't you like to drive a car just like mine? How do you think I got such a car? Not by saying *no* to good business opportunities, I assure you of that. You too can have a car like mine, anyone can. The secret is in selling. Selling anything and everything. You have talent, I can see that in you. You can sell anything you want to, I can see it in your eyes. And I'll give you a really super deal on the Super GTP too. You must stock it also. The two go together, like tea and *mandazi*. You will be a famous man, not to mention very rich. You do want to be rich, don't you?"

The man considered. He had been working at getting rich the whole of his life. The half-empty general store was the closest he had come to realising his dream. He had a grandson who would soon be on his way to University and he would need all the money he could get. He did not have to think too hard about it; he wanted money, lots and lots of it. He nodded.

Broker talked on, not giving him time to think or ask any more questions. By the time he had finished, the trader was nodding vigorously at his every word and soon they were talking orders. Cartons full of orders and advance payments and all. Then, as the man was about to hand over the down payment for his first ever stock of condoms and GTP, his teenage grandson arrived home from school and broke the spell. The trader swept the two free condoms deftly off the counter into his pockets.

"Sorry," he said, suddenly remembering he was old enough to be Broker's father. "I can't help you. I only stock things I can sell."

It took Broker a full moment to realise he was serious. Then, waving his sword-stick menacingly at him, he swore at the trader in the foulest language ever head in Crossroads; the shockingly dreadful language Malindi fishermen used to such devastating effect it was known to have shamed attacking sharks into fleeing. It brought the alarmed wife out of the back room of the shop to stand with her son by her husband's side and wonder what on earth had transpired.

"What is the matter?" the boy asked, confounded.

"Nothing," said the father, trying to remain calm. "You go to the back, Anderea. You too, Grandmother, this has nothing to do with you."

"Wait," Broker said to the boy. "You might need some too."

"Some what?" asked the boy.

"Nothing," answered his grandfather. "Go, Anderea."

Then he turned to Broker and pleaded, "The boy is only fifteen, for heaven's sake!"

"In that case," Broker said, full of malice. "He will need twice as many as the father."

"Twice as many what?" asked the boy.

"Nothing!" said his grandfather. "Get out of my shop!"

He picked the carton of condoms off the counter and hurled it into the street. Then he took the two condoms from his pocket and threw them after the carton. One of them bounced off Broker and landed at the boy's feet. The boy picked it up and handed it to Broker.

"Keep it, son," Broker said to him. "It's on the house."

"Thank you," said the boy, pocketing the condom.

"Anderea!" his grandfather barked. "Give it back, at once."

The boy threw the condom at Broker. He caught it deftly and put it in his pocket. Then he winked at the boy and went out onto the hot street to collect his condoms, where they were scattered all over the dust.

"What was that about?" asked the trader's wife, confused.

"Nothing!" he said. "Go back to the back."

She led her grandson to the back of the shop, leaving him to sort out his thoughts.

Broker returned to the teahouse at sunset, in a tired and depressed mood. He found the old men sitting out on the veranda, reading the latest batch of old newspapers to arrive on the *Far Traveller*, and enjoying the last warmth of the dying sun. Uncle Mark stopped him to ask if he knew *wa Guka*.

"No," he said, brusquely.

"You don't know the most celebrated bank robber in the world?" Musa asked, incredulously.

"No," he said.

"Really?"

"Should I?"

Musa shrugged and let it go.

"We just thought you might know him," Uncle Mark said, lamely.

"I don't," Broker said, with a little too much anger.

He declined Uncle Mark's offer of a game and rejected Musa's offer of a free meal, which he knew he would pay for anyway, and left them. He retired early to his simple lodging room to lie awake the whole night, staring at the sooty roof and trying to convince himself that he was still Broker Ben Broker, the monarch of Pwani brokers.

Chapter Twenty-Five

Grandmother was surprised to find Janet all alone. She was certain she had heard voices over the fence that morning, one of them clearly a man's voice.

"An old friend was here," Janet told her. "He has left."

It had been quite a while since Grandmother had heard the voices. She had hoped it was Broker, talking and laughing with Janet, and was unhappy to learn that the man had just left.

"Why do men come to see you?" she asked Janet. "What do you give them so that they cannot stay away from you?"

"Talk," Janet said to her. "Good words are sometimes tastier than good food."

She scoffed at that.

"Women come to see me too," Janet reminded her. "They too just want to hear good words."

"Can't they see that your husband is back?" Grandmother asked her.

She laughed, tiredly, and said, "Has Broker been to bribe you again?"

"He is my son-in-law," Grandmother said. "He can visit me whenever he likes. He is still your husband."

"I'm not still his wife," Janet said to her. "I have told you so already. Was it not you who taught me never to let a man break my heart again?"

"I had to do it," Grandmother acknowledged. "I had to make you strong."

But, now that Janet had grown so strong that no man could move her, she had to be generous to men. Especially to her husband who had come crawling back to her like a beaten dog.

Janet shook her head and said, "We have had this conversation before, haven't we?"

And they would have it again and again, Grandmother confirmed. They would keep having it until Janet came to her senses.

"You must talk to him," she urged. "Talk to your man."

"I talk to him all the time," Janet said.

"Not the way you talk to those other men," Grandmother told her. "Talk to him like a wife. With love and respect."

That was impossible for Janet to do, to have any more love or respect for Broker. Her love he had betrayed and her respect he was yet to earn.

But how could she not respect him, Grandmother asked. Was he not a man, like the rest? Was he not the best dressed man in Crossroads, the most admirable? Was Broker not the most generous man Crossroads had ever seen? And had he not left Crossroads on a donkey and returned in a big car, his own car? How could she not respect such a man?

They were so engrossed in this argument that they did not hear Broker's car until it pulled up in the yard.

"Be kind to him," Grandmother hissed. "Be kind now, you hear?"

"Greetings, Grandmother," Broker called cheerfully, limping across the yard to where they stood.

"Greetings, my son," Grandmother was delighted to see him.

"Greetings, my dear," he said to Janet.

She choked on the reply. He had been gone for over a week and she had started to hope he had gone back to wherever he had come from. The pain in her head, the headache that had started the day he arrived back from Pwani, and which had started to wane, now returned with a vengeance. She clenched her fists and tried to will it away as she listened to his lies.

"It took a little longer than I thought," he was saying gleefully. "But I sold the whole consignment, as agreed. Not a single condom left."

The time factor not withstanding, Janet was amazed.

"Every single one of them, as agreed," he affirmed.

He did not bother her with it, but he had also been down with fever, and battling with the fear of death and with the demons of uncertainty and failure. And, in his delirium, he had determined never to give Janet up again, ever.

He handed her the money he had obtained from the sale, as proof of his diligence and of his honesty. She took the money, counted it once, twice and wondered. It was all in small denomination and was old and tattered and extremely filthy; the kind of money one obtained from a chicken sale in Crossroads market. Broker was already famous for his endless supply of large, new notes; so much so that the new money was nicknamed *broker*.

Anything that cost a whole *broker* was considered quite special indeed. Rumours were rife that Broker was the notorious bank robber, *wa Guka*, himself. Janet too was beginning to wonder.

He noticed the kettle and cups on the stool by the door and asked if he could have some tea. She replied there was no tea left. Could she make him some? He asked.

She did not reply. She was looking at the disgustingly smelly money in her hands and, again, wondering what to make of it. She had not said *no* to the question of a cup of tea, Grandmother noted and smiled her crafty old smile. Then she left them to work it out by themselves and walked away to her gate, quietly praying that Janet would wake up from her foolish arrogance, before her husband gave up trying to be good to her.

Janet counted the money once again and, once again, wondered what to do with him. Finally, she invited Broker into her house and made him some tea.

While he took the tea, she turned things over in her mind and wondered some more. Was it possible that he had really changed? Did she dare trust him again? She longed so to believe that he was a new man, someone she could trust with her dreams, her feelings and her innermost fears. But did a leopard ever change its spots?

"I can't believe you sold condoms," she confessed.

He laughed loudly, nervously.

"Who bought them?" she asked him.

"Everyone," he said.

At first they had pretended they had no idea what condoms were or what they were supposed to do with them. Broker had told them everything, with a lot of imaginative embellishment. Then they had started talking. Finally, they had admitted knowing what *kodoms* were but never having tried them. From there, it was downhill, all the way.

"I have a list of orders this long," he told her.

She nodded thoughtfully and wondered again whether she could ever believe in him again. She longed so to be able to believe him. To believe that he had actually changed, and was now an honest and caring person, capable of understanding her. His absence in the past one week had stirred up some unreasonable compassion in her being. But she could not admit to this, not even to herself. Finally, she gave him back the money.

"You keep it," she said. "Keep it till we know what to do with it."

His heart rejoiced at her choice of words. He would get her back yet, he thought as he put the money back in his pocket. Then he noticed the pile of books the Headmaster had forgotten on the table.

"He was here again?" he asked unhappily. "Is he also after you?"

"He likes to talk," Janet told him. "I like to talk to thinking people too."

She saw the look of disappointment on his face.

"This is my house," she said. "Everyone has a right to visit me here."

"Everyone except me?" he complained. "The one person in the world who loves you? Didn't you ever miss me in all the time I was away?"

"All day, everyday," she told him. "For about a week."

She had watched the gateway and prayed; prayed that he would reappear, as suddenly as he had disappeared, and lie to her that he had lost his way home, as he had often done. She had dreamt of his return in milliards of different visions. In her dreams, he had returned home on foot, on a bicycle, on horseback and, once, in a coffin. But she had never, ever imagined it the way it had finally happened.

"All I ask is forgiveness," he said to her.

She had forgiven him the day she stopped crying over him, she told him.

"And tolerance?" he asked her.

If by tolerance he meant her watching helplessly, while he wasted away in disease and died, the answer to that too was no.

Broker was overwhelmed. Not that he had expected his illness to remain a secret forever. He had only hoped, really hoped, that he would be able to reveal it to her himself, to break the news to her as gently as possible, when they were friends again. Now he remembered Uncle Mark remarking that no one returned to Crossroads, except to die, and wondered how many more knew the real reason for his returning.

"I'll take care of myself," he said to Janet, and meant it.

"But for how much longer?" she asked him.

"For as long as it takes," he told her. "All I need is patience. I don't ask more than friendship."

Friendship hurt too, she told him. All her adult life she had been a woman alone, with children and responsibilities. She did not need any more responsibilities now.

"Why don't you just go away?" she was close to tears.

"I can't," he said firmly.

"For my sake?" she said. "For the sake of the children?"

He shook his head adamantly.

"Then stay away from here," she begged.

"I can't do that either," he told her. "You know I can't."

She was on the point of breaking down. She fought back the tears, just as she had fought them back when women had scorned her after her husband had run away with a prostitute. She swallowed back all the hurt and the sadness, for she knew, from experience, that the pain would not kill her.

"How did you sell the condoms?" she asked him. "Who bought them?"

"You don't want to know," he told her.

"What did you tell them?" she asked.

"You don't want to know that either," he told her.

But she did want to know. She wanted to know everything that he did in her name, without exception. So Broker told her the other version of the story. The decent version where there was no mention of the pain and the anguish of the past one week, the desperation when he realised that he had lost his bet with her and was about to lose any chance he had of getting her back. He was glad she had not mentioned the time factor; and he did not tell her about the raging profanity, and the grave threats he had issued to persuade Crossroads to buy condoms. He did not tell her of the lies either, the false promises he had made to nearly half of the population in Crossroads. He told her a whole bunch of colourful lies, instead. She did not believe any of it, anyway, so lying to her was easy.

Afterwards she gave him another cup of tea.

"You don't have to lie to me," she said to him, as she poured the tea. "I don't believe you sold condoms to Crossroads men."

"I have the money to prove it," he said, giving it back to her.

She counted it again, slowly and carefully. It looked, felt and smelt Crossroads. A smell like that of a rotting corpse.

"Still I do not believe it," she said, giving it back.

He put it back in his pocket.

"It will go directly to the orphans," he promised her.

224

But could she be certain of it, though? Could this not be just another ploy to win her back?

"I don't work like that anymore," the very thought offended him. "How many times do I have to tell you that?"

She thought some more and wondered if it was really possible that nothing was impossible. A camel, as Pastor Bat warned Crossroads, would pass through the eye of a needle before the rich man. As of Crossroads men using condoms …

"You can be certain of that," he assured her. "No one buys to throw away."

He was having a bit of a problem with the shopkeepers, though, he said to extend the friendly conversation. The shopkeepers would not accept that there were no free condoms anymore. Some of them were buying, and reselling the free condoms Janet gave out and were unhappy with the new arrangement. They vowed to resist it with all their might.

"We may have to open our own shop," Broker said to Janet.

"A Condom Shop?" she asked, suddenly dismayed.

"With condoms from all over the world," he told her.

In Pwani, he said, they had shops that specialised in everything from buttons to beans.

"We'll do condoms," he said to her.

Now she was more than dismayed. She was shattered. The leopard did not change its spots, she was sad to realise. It only said that it had.

"You are mad," was all she could think of him.

"We'll be famous," he told her.

"You'll be in prison," she promised him. "You can't set up business selling stolen condoms."

"Donated," he corrected. "Donated, not stolen. And, as we too shall donate the money to orphanages and homes, everything is respectable."

This was one of the many great ideas he had pondered during his one week in limbo. He was not quite certain himself just how sincere he was in this, but the more he talked about it, the more he liked the idea.

"That's right," he enthused. "We shall donate it all to orphanages."

Janet informed him that there were no such places in Crossroads.

225

"We shall build them," he declared, his head spinning from the loftiness of it. "I shall name them after you. Imagine that! Janet Broker Home for Orphans and Old Folks. Your name will live forever! Imagine that!"

Janet tried imagining it. But, no matter how hard she tried, she could not focus on such fantastic madness. All she could see were her name and her career destroyed beyond retrieval, her reputation dying in a swamp of infamy and her life forever trapped in the web of greed and deception spun by this incurably sick man who was once her adored husband. She listened, with mounting alarm, as he ranted on and on about the fantastic new journey they were about to embark on together.

When he finally paused for breath, she asked, full of concern, "Are you feeling all right?"

He laughed till he nearly collapsed from laughter.

"I've never felt better in my life," he said.

If anyone had intimated that he would go from selling goats' *things* to flogging multicoloured condoms, he would have said they were raving mad. But now ... no one would ever say he, Bakari Ben Broker, had not lived. And if he could do it all over again, he would do it the same way.

"But this time," he said affectionately, "I would take you and the children along."

That did make her smile a little. The curtain of madness had briefly parted and, through the haze and the smoke, she had a glimpse of the dark interior, the place where the horned beguiler dwelt and where he was now busy pounding on goats' things and plotting more unscrupulous assault on friend and foe alike. That was him in there, the old Broker, the devil she knew, thinking only of himself and promising things he could never deliver.

"You are not serious about the Condom Shop?" she asked, hopefully.

"I'm dead serious," he said to her.

She worried like she had never worried before in her entire life.

Chapter Twenty-Six

There was no stopping Broker now.

With no delay, and little hullabaloo, the Condom Shop was built. When it was done, it was nowhere near as splendid nor as grand as he had painted it with his words, but it was solid and had as much promise as any of the other sheds in the midst of the ruins.

Frank and Big Youth did most of the building, with old materials and only the bare minimum of tools. They knocked the old animal clinic back into shape, with old timber and tin drums and iron sheets, and anything they could lay their hands on. When it was done, Janet and Broker helped give it the finishing touches, and a new coat of whitewash.

"What shall we call it?" Big Youth asked them.

He was up on a ladder by the entrance where, having erased the original name, he had decided to give their new creation a proper identity. He had got as far as *THE* when creativity, once again, eluded him.

"Boss," he called out to Broker. "What shall we call it?"

Frank and Broker were fixing the door back onto its rusty, old hinges and Janet was giving the side walls a final coat of whitewash.

"Call what?" Broker asked him.

"The shop," he said. "What shall we name it?"

"This is not a shop," Janet told him. "It is a centre."

"Centre?" Big Youth was lost. "Centre of what?"

"Centre for family life education," she told them.

"But it's only a kiosk," said Big Youth. "It's not even a shop."

"It's not a kiosk," she told him. "Not anymore."

Big Youth turned to Broker for confirmation.

"Boss?" he asked.

"Do as she says," Broker said, to avoid conflict.

There had already been one precarious moment, when they had failed to agree on whether the door should open inwards or outwards and had argued forever about it. Janet had prevailed in the end, but the matter had left everyone sour and tense.

Big Youth did not like the name suggested by Janet, and was glad when he counted up all the letters in the name and found them too many to fit on the name board.

"Too long," he announced triumphantly. "Boss?"

They all turned to Janet.

"Must we name it anything?" she asked them.

"Yes," the men said in unison.

"All right then," she said, to placate them. "You name it."

Big Youth at once suggested they name it the *Aids Awareness and Birth Control Centre*. Again too long for the board.

"What about *The Condom Centre*?" Broker suggested wearily.

"No," Janet said, straight away.

"*The Condom Shop*?" Big Youth asked hopefully.

"Brilliant," said Broker, eager to be rid of that problem. "It's simple and to the point. Perfect. Write it."

Big Youth had already embarked on the task, without waiting for further approval. Frank and Janet appeared stunned.

"We can change it later," Broker told them. "Right now we have more important issues at hand; so let's forget about naming anything and get back to work."

Thus *Frank's Animal Clinic* became *The Condom Shop*. They watched anxiously as Big Youth painted the new name over the doorway, giving the job his entire attention, as he did with any job he found to his liking. A month before the construction started, Broker had promised him he would be the first general manager of the new venture. Big Youth had not stopped smiling since.

"Which reminds me," Janet now said. "How are we paying him?"

"Are we paying him?" Frank was puzzled.

"Are we not?" she asked.

They turned to Broker. Broker tried to ignore the question, shrugged and said, "That's my department, so don't worry about it now."

But they worried.

"We can't afford salaries," Janet said.

"I know," he said. "I'm not paying him any money. Big Youth wants to be a salesman."

"Selling what?" Janet was suddenly alert. "You are not going to teach him to sell goats' ... *things*, are you?"

"I said not to worry about it now," Broker said, a little touchy.

"I want to know now," she insisted.

228

Broker turned to Big Youth and said seriously, "Lesson number two: never, ever, go into business with a woman."

Then he turned to the fuming Janet to attempt an explanation.

"The boy is wasted in school, anyway," he said to her. "We can all see that."

Janet could not see it. He turned to Frank, but Frank merely shrugged.

"It's not our duty to decide how or when Big Youth will drop out of school," Janet said firmly. "Our responsibility is to encourage him to stay on in school, for as long as possible, and hope that he comes out of it with something that is good for himself."

Broker nodded vigorously, not even trying to absorb any of it, and was glad when the next distraction came along.

Pastor Bat was walking down the road, a briefcase in one hand while his other hand held up a black umbrella to ward off the afternoon sun.

"What is he doing here?" Janet wondered.

The Pastor hardly ever came to town at all, except to attend the monthly lynch party, the *baraza*. There was none scheduled for the day and, with the rapacious Crossroads wind blowing dust in his eyes, and trying to deprive him of both his umbrella and his cassock, the old Pastor was a sad sight to behold; forlorn and lost and in dire need of a friend.

"I'll go talk to him," Broker said, wiping his hands on his trousers.

"What about?" Janet asked him.

This was not the time to try to explain to anyone what it was that they were building.

"Don't worry," he told her. "I'll not bring him here."

He crossed the street to intercept the preacher outside the teahouse. The beggar was crying out for money, from inside the phone booth where he had somehow locked himself in and from where he had been trying to extricate himself for the past several hours. Musa and Uncle Mark, playing draughts by the window, were well aware of the beggar's predicament, but had offered no assistance, as none had been requested yet.

"Greetings, Pastor," Broker said, cheerfully to the old man.

Pastor Bat had not seen Broker approaching. He stopped abruptly and looked about. He seemed startled to hear such a powerful voice from such a gaunt character as stood before him.

"I was about to come to see you at your church" Broker said to him.

The Pastor studied Broker, read him like a book, from left to right and from head to toe and back, and decided he had never seen him before.

"I'm Broker," Broker said to him. "You baptized me in your church."

Pastor Bat had baptized most of the people in Crossroads, and he prided himself on knowing most of them by name and family, but he could not place the man with sunken eyes who now stood before him.

"Bakari Ben Broker," Broker tried. "You insisted on calling me Nebuchadnezzar."

"Nebuchadnezzar?" that rang a bell.

It was Pastor Bat's favourite christening name for troublesome young men; there was no better way to anchor them down than with a good and solid biblical name. But, as far as the Pastor could remember, there were not many Nebuchadnezzars left in Crossroads today. Broker himself had stopped using the name as soon as he could pronounce it. Pastor Bat could think of only one living Nebuchadnezzar and that one was ninety-three years old.

"I married the daughter of Maalim," Broker tried again. "I'm Janet's husband."

"Janet?" that name he remembered. "I know Janet."

"She's my wife," Broker told him. "You married us, remember?"

Again, Pastor Bat had married everyone in Crossroads.

"You must remember us," Broker insisted. "Her father called the police on you."

Pastor Bat smiled faintly at the memory. Janet was the only Muslim in Crossroads ever to convert to Christianity, and that was only because Janet's parents had rejected Broker. Pastor Bat, however, had accepted the couple with open arms and pronounced them man and wife, even as policemen waited outside to arrest him for defying a court order banning their union.

"I haven't been to your church since that day," Broker confessed.

Most of the people Pastor Bat married never returned to his church, he observed. Only a handful of them returned in coffins, leaving it to their confounded relatives to account for their long absence from the church in a bid to convince Pastor Bat to bury them.

"I haven't been to any church at all since," Broker now confessed. "Except for a wedding or two and funerals. To tell you the truth, Pastor, I haven't been a very good man."

Pastor Bat nodded and observed that confession was the first step towards salvation.

"I pray that you will one day see the light and be saved," he said.

"The light?" Broker laughed amused. "I have seen the light and what a light! As for salvation, I don't know if anything can save me now. But thanks for your prayers, all the same."

"Prayers are free," the Pastor told him. "But the sins must be paid for and only you can atone for your sins."

All Broker had to do to pay for his sins was to get down on his knees and pray. Pray with all his heart and with all his mind and, in sincere remorse, ask God for forgiveness. Only then could he hope for salvation.

"But I think that is not the reason you have stopped me on this hot road today," he said.

"No at all," Broker admitted. "It's about the orphans."

"Orphans?" Pastor Bat was momentarily lost.

"The orphans," Broker said. "The children without parents."

They were all over Crossroads, like the rats and the bedbugs, and every home had more than its share.

"Death, widows and orphans are three things you cannot escape from in Crossroads," the Pastor conceded. "And their numbers grow faster than the weeds in April."

He had a recurring vision, he revealed. In the vision, he saw the entire land unruly with weed; weed that ran riot and with great abandon, where millet once ruled the fields. It did not need a prophet to tell him what the dream meant. The world would soon be as riotous with poverty, as the land of his vision, when all the able-bodied men and women were dead from the plague.

"Who will tend to the fields then?" he asked Broker. "Who will look after the young and the old then? Who will protect our homesteads? These are the questions that keep me awake at night. But I'm sure that is not the reason you have stopped me on this hot road today."

"About the orphans," Broker told him. "We must build a home for them."

"Have they no homes?" the old Pastor sounded surprised.

"They do," Broker agreed. "But most of them are overgrown and abandoned ruins, dead homesteads surrounded by endless graveyards. Homes so poor that the orphans would be turned out by their occupants but for the fear of the God."

"The fear of God is a great incentive," said the preacher.

"We need a centre for them," Broker told him. "A place where the orphans can be fed and taken care of. People in other places have such houses where they take care of their orphans and their old. It is a shame we have no such houses here. We must have them."

"We?" Pastor Bat looked about for the rest of them.

"The people of Crossroads," Broker said.

The Pastor looked about again and asked, "Which people do you speak of, young man?"

"Us, all of us."

"Where do you come from?"

"From here," Broker said. "You baptised me."

"And you have not noticed how there are no people left in Crossroads?" the Pastor asked him.

"There are enough of us left to make a difference," Broker said. "We must believe that."

Pastor Bat smiled sadly and asked, "Have you seen my church recently?"

"I drove by there the other day," he said.

"Did it look to you like the church of a people who can build anything?" he was almost angry about it. "Look at me. Do I look to you like the Pastor of a people who can believe in anything?"

Under different circumstances, Broker might have agreed with him. The Pastor was a scrawny old thing, a relic of the times. The only thing that distinguished him from the old beggar struggling to free himself from the dead phone booth was the dusty cassock that he wore.

"I have raised some money," Broker revealed. "But I need a plot of land to build on, a communal place, where good people can bring their goodwill and their assistance. Somewhere close to the people's hearts, somewhere like a churchyard."

Pastor Bat suddenly looked up. He scrutinised Broker again and read him for a longer moment this time.

"Have we had this conversation before, young man?" he asked.

"Not with me," Broker said.

The Pastor wagged his head. He had never, knowingly, allowed unrepentant sinners into his church and he was not about to start doing so now. He would never allow the fruit of sin to flourish in his backyard.

"You are quite right, Pastor," Broker said, working hard to remember the rest of the stuff he had had to learn for his marriage. Righteous people do not turn their church into a market place, a stamping ground for sin. Good people do not allow their only church to fall into such a sorry state. It breaks my heart to see it."

The church roof was caved in and the walls were full of cracks. The windows and the doors had long been vandalised, stolen by people who did not respect or fear God anymore. It was hardly fit to be called a House of God.

"It's enough to shame any God-fearing man," Broker said. "And yet we must hate sin and not the sinner. Isn't that what you taught me, Pastor? That is why I have decided to use my own money to help out the community, pious and sinners alike. I would like to start with your old church, by donating new windows and doors, doors that can be locked at night to keep out thieves, vandals and impenitent sinners. The roof of the church will be repaired too at some expense."

The Pastor listened with greater concentration now, as Broker outlined to him how he intended to spend his own money for the good of the community. By a blessed coincidence, the Pastor was on his way to an emergency Committee meeting to discuss the budget estimates for the repair of the church roof, which was leaking right above the altar. Broker wasted no time in taking control of the situation.

"I know a man in Makutano who makes good tiles," he let be known.

He had noticed also that the Pastor's house was in no better shape than his church. He would see to its repair too, along with anything else that the Pastor wanted seen to.

They talked for nearly half an hour, standing in the hot, dusty street surrounded by its many ruins and decrepit buildings. The Pastor finally sighed and asked, "How much land would you need for this ... orphanage?"

"Not much," Broker assured.

When they parted, moments before the beggar extricated himself from the phone booth and came charging out to ask for

233

money, Pastor Bat was more than ever amazed at the might of his God. The Lord did, indeed, work in mysterious ways.

Chapter Twenty-Seven

Crossroads carried on doing what Crossroads did best it continued to die quietly and without fuss, to sink in its dark pit with only the barest of a sigh as of a weary soul abandoning a vexatious body.

But, since the return of Broker, the old town had slowed down in her gradual slide into the crypt. With the opening of the Condom Shop, Crossroads paused to take note, and waited to see what would happen next.

What happened next was simply that Mzee Musa gave the old teahouse its first coat of whitewash in over ten years. The job was accomplished through the courtesy of Broker's crafty bargaining and the gallons of whitewash left over from the Condom Shop. When it was done, the teahouse looked almost alive.

Impressed by the results, and in anticipation of the new business boom that Broker promised everyone would soon descend on Crossroads, other traders were thinking of doing the same sort of renovations to their own decrepit premises.

Meanwhile, Mzee Musa embarked on the arduous task improving the menu. He doubled the amount of milk and sugar in his tea, tripled the number of eggs in his *mandazi* and whipped the dough thrice as hard. He increased the number of potatoes if his stews, introduced onions and tomatoes in his recipes and cooked everything twice as long. At Broker's instigation, he did away with goats' offal and started experimenting with real meat, cutting it so small it disappeared in the stew altogether. Then he discovered Ethiopian *pili-pili* and went mad with it.

But all that, Broker told him, was hardly good enough for a future boomtown. He would have to try a lot harder. He would have to redesign the entire menu.

"Take the tea, for example," Broker said to him. "It's not sufficient to throw water, milk, tea leaves and sugar together and boil them till they cry enough"

Everything, the boiling included, had to be done in proportion.

"Take your *mandazi*, for another example," Broker went on. "They are too fat, too ugly and only half cooked. That is why no one ever asks for more, and no amount of sugar or eggs will improve that. Then there is your *sambusa* ... what can I say? Not even a starving dog will eat *sambusa* stuffed with sheep's brain, no matter how cheap it is."

Musa sighed and said, "Meat, as you know, is expensive."

"Have you ever considered using vegetable instead of offal?" Broker asked him.

"Cabbage *sambusa*?" Musa asked doubtfully. "In this dry season?"

"Just one idea," Broker said. "The possibilities are limitless."

Musa listened with mounting bewilderment as Broker told him of every little thing that ailed his business. Everything, it seemed, had serious flaws. The food was unpredictable and the service grudgingly given. And then there were the flies and the ants, not to mention the overfed roaches and the rats strutting around the place like senior partners. Broker did not mince his words. He enumerated all the multitude of things that needed improving and laid them bare on the table between them. Musa was flabbergasted, and about to concede defeat and forever remain the same, but Broker urged him not to despair. All he required was a totally fresh approach.

"You have to cook to a recipe," Broker told him.

"Recipe?" Musa finally despaired.

"A plan," Broker said to him. "So much of this, and so much of that. If you stick to the same proportions, the food will taste the same, whatever sort of a mad day you are having."

Musa considered the suggestions. They were too many, too complex and, as far as he was concerned, too unnecessary a clutter in his simple and uncomplicated life. He turned to Uncle Mark. Was it true, that his cooking was so bad it cried for a new cook?

Uncle Mark nodded diplomatically and answered that, at the least, his cooking called for a new approach.

"Don't get me wrong, old bull," he said, careful not to hurt his friend's feelings. "But a woman might breathe new life into that old kitchen of yours."

Musa regarded him for a full moment before asking, "How come you never told me before, old bull?"

"I wanted to be your friend," Uncle Mark said to him.

"So do I," Broker said quickly. "But I also want you to do well too and to make a lot of money."

Musa considered. They were his only company and they had nowhere else to go eat. If they really did not like his food, there had to be something not quite right with it. But if they thought that he would hire a woman to cook for them, they had another thing coming. Finally, after some serious thought, he nodded agreeably and declared he was up to the challenge. If they wanted good food, he would cook them good food. He would cook them the best good food they had ever eaten.

Then he stormed off to the kitchen, seething with suppressed rage, to dream up the most incredibly atrocious recipes ever seen in Crossroads. And Crossroads took note.

"Why are you doing it?" Uncle Mark puzzled.

"Doing what?" Broker asked him.

"Whatever it is that you are doing to Crossroads? You know we'll never thank you or love you for it."

Broker laughed suddenly and vigorously.

"Who said I was doing it for Crossroads?"

"You expect to make money from giving it away?" Uncle Mark was flabbergasted.

"I'm not giving it away," he said. "I'm not giving anything away."

Now it was Uncle Mark's turn to laugh, that old laugh of his, the all-knowing chortle that infuriated Broker so.

"You can laugh at me, old man," Broker said irritated. "But I'm not as foolish as you think. You will see."

And, to encourage greater optimism, he bought the old petrol station from Janet, for a scandalous sum of money, and hired youths to clear the debris and the rubbish from it. He was convinced that it was the key to Crossroads revival. Next, he brought oil executives from the refinery in Mombasa to look at the location with a view to contracting him as their official representative in the Crossroads region.

The executives patiently accompanied him on an inspection tour of the place and he showed them everything; showed them what had happened to the old place, since the station had closed down. They discussed it among themselves for a long time.

"Why don't you build it in Makutano?" they asked him.

"I want to revive Crossroads," he told them. "Not to kill her again."

"You'd make more money there, on the new highway," they pointed out.

"I know that," he said to them. "I know all that, but would you wish a fate such as this to befall your own home town?"

"Certainly not," they said.

But they would not build a bank on a graveyard to make peace with their ancestral spirits either, they told him. They recommend he relocate his dream to Makutano, where there was more traffic, otherwise he would lose every single cent he sank into Crossroads.

"It's my money, damn it," he said impatiently. "I'll revive this place, whether you like it or not. All I'm asking from you is recognition and the endorsement of the filling station."

They were walking among the old ruins as they discussed his project. Finally, when they were so sick of looking at ruins, and avoiding funeral processions, that they were numb with shock, he took the oil executives to the teahouse and introduced them to Musa. Over a lunch of Biri Biri omelette and something else that Musa insisted was vegetarian, they talked some more.

"You have seen our farmlands," Broker told the executives. "A land drowning in fertility, a land throbbing with natural resources and a dynamic people ready to die for it."

They had not seen any of those things, but they nodded politely and ate their lunch.

"What they need now is a new impetus," Broker told them. "A new purpose and direction. And we, gentlemen, can provide that."

The executives listened and dug into Musa's confounding Biri Biri omelette, so loaded with Ethiopian *pili-pili* it melted the plastic plates it was served in. When they had eaten their fill, Broker asked them what they thought of Crossroads.

"It's dead," they said.

"I know that," he told them. "What else?"

"Very dead," they said.

"What about potential?" he asked them. "Have we got any potential?

"The potential you have," they agreed. "The potential is there."

"That's all I needed to hear from you," he told them.

They finished their lunch and he escorted them to their car.

"We'll discuss your project," they promised him. "Then we'll let you know our decision."

"You do that," he told them. "But be quick about it, I haven't got a lifetime."

The speed with which they boarded their executive vehicle told him they would not be hurrying back. He watched them drive away, then walked slowly back to the teahouse.

"How did it go?" Uncle Mark asked him.

"Quite well, considering."

"Considering what?"

"Considering no one gives a damn about an inconsequential community dying a hopeless death in the heart of nowhere."

There was anger brewing deep down inside him and Uncle Mark decided to leave him alone to work it out by himself.

"Did they like the food?" Musa wanted to know.

"The food was the only thing they liked about Crossroads," Broker told him. "They said they have never eaten anything quite like it."

Then he saw the beggar, lying down on the dust by his phone booth like a dead thing, and called out to him.

"Hey, Boss!"

"Boss?" the beggar suddenly sat up.

"Come over here," Broker called.

The beggar scrambled to cross the road, followed by a horde of flies and the pungent smell of years of neglect.

"When was the last time you had a wash?" Broker asked him.

"Wash?" asked the beggar.

"Bathe," Broker told him. "When was the last time you had a bath?"

"Bath?" asked the beggar.

Uncle Mark laughed and said, "Where would he get water to bathe himself?"

"What's your real name?" Broker asked the beggar.

"Name?"

"You do have a name, don't you?"

"Me?"

Uncle Mark chortled quietly and said, "What does he need a name for? No one ever calls him but you."

"Is that so?" Broker said to the beggar. "From now on you are the Mayor, you hear? You can call me Mayor too. You and I are the only people in the world who care a damn about this old place. Now go to your table and order whatever your heart desires."

The beggar rushed to his table to await Musa's pleasure. The old men looked at each other and did not know what to make of it. Broker left them to their doubts and returned to the Condom

Shop to ponder his next move, battling the doubts, and the screams of failure resounding in his brain, by reminding himself, again and again, that he had left Crossroads with no luggage, no money or return fare and returned in the biggest car Crossroads had ever seen. He was very far from beaten.

The water-seller came by a little later, pulling on a cart that was loaded with water containers, and asked Broker if he wanted to quench his thirst. The water seller was a new phenomenon in town, an optimistic, free spirit lured back from the tomb of despair and oblivion by the promise of a new beginning. Since the opening the Condom Shop, he would come by several times a day offering fresh spring water; which everyone knew came not from any spring but from a stale, old well on the other side of town, which had been dormant and forgotten for years. But he was a fresh light in town, a sign of the dawn, and everyone loved him and forgave him for it.

Broker assured the water-seller that did not want to quench his thirst now. In fact, he said, would never want to quench any of his thirsts again, ever. The man went away, pulling on his cart with three uneven wheels and singing happily for all to hear.

"*Maji safi! Maji safi!*"

Broker sat on a stool by the entrance and dozed off.

"Meya."

He opened his eyes to find the beggar hovering over him.

"What?"

"I have eaten," said the beggar.

"Good," Broker closed his eyes again.

"Meya!

"What now?"

"I have had some tea too," said the beggar.

"Then get out of my sight," Broker said impatiently. "And don't ever disturb me again when I'm thinking."

The beggar scuttled away and Broker closed his eyes. He was about to doze off again when he heard the old men approaching. They walked fast and purposefully, like men with a long way to go and an important mission to accomplish. He opened one eye, saw the way they hurried across the street and closed it again, feigning sleep.

It was a rare thing, indeed, for the two of them to call on Broker at the Condom Shop. Musa did not believe in condoms. Musa did not believe in anything, other than in Allah and in Death, both of whom were never far from his mind, and it bothered him that anyone seeing him at the Condom Shop might conclude that he was there to purchase condoms. He had gone as far as suggesting that they move the abomination farther down the street, and remove the shame from his face. Janet had laughed him into silence and the suggestion was ignored. Now he contented himself with keeping as faraway from the despicable place as he possibly could and it intrigued Broker, therefore, to hear him now approach the shop with such single-minded purpose.

"Broker?" Uncle Mark said, without wasting time with niceties. "We want to talk to you."

Broker opened his eyes, yawned and stretched, and waited for them to state their business.

They stood there before him, looking extremely embarrassed and ready to apologise for the intrusion, and they appeared to have suddenly forgotten whatever business had brought them there.

"What can I do for you, old bulls?" he asked them.

"You tell him," Musa said to Uncle Mark.

He was highly agitated and on the verge of being unreasonable. When Musa was unreasonable, words fled from him in terror and he fetched his machete and let it do the talking instead.

Uncle Mark cleared his throat, but he too could not find the words.

"Tell me what?" Broker asked him.

"Tell him," Musa said again to Uncle Mark. Uncle Mark cleared his throat again, feeling like a fool, and Broker had never seen him so unhappy.

"Well?" Broker prompted. "Do you know *wa Guka?*" he asked.

"You have asked me that question before," Broker reminded.

"I know," he said. "But Musa here wants to know. He wants you to assure him that you are not *wa Guka*. So tell him. Tell him you are not, and we can all go back to our businesses and have our peace of mind."

Broker studied the old men for a long moment. He saw the sad concern on their dusty faces, and the grim determination that was almost comical, and burst out laughing. He laughed till his stomach ached. Then he coughed till his chest was about to rupture.

The old men watched him, baffled; watched him laugh himself into a delirious bundle of mirth, then watched him cough nearly to death, and felt very foolish indeed. When he was done coughing and laughing at their absurdity, Broker had no breath left in him to say a thing more.

"See that now?" Uncle Mark turned to Mzee Musa. "See that, old bull?"

Then he turned and walked back to the teahouse, thoroughly disgusted with himself, and Musa followed him, very perplexed indeed. Watching them walk away thus, defeated by their own curiosity, Broker burst out in fresh gales of laughter.

Back in the teahouse, Uncle Mark returned angrily to the draughts table, and the bundle of old newspapers that had inspired the ill-advised expedition. Musa sat down opposite him and continued to brood.

"He lies," he said, after a moment's consideration. "You know he lies."

"Of course, he lies," Uncle Mark was angry for exposing himself to such ridicule. "But that is no proof he is who you think he is."

"He does not fool me," Musa said to himself. "He does not fool me at all."

The latest bundle of old newspapers lay scattered on the table between them. According to the papers, top police agents had left Makutano for Sokoni and Crossroads to track down the elusive bank robber. The report was patchy and worrying. Though the police had an old photograph of the fugitive, they admitted having never set eyes upon him. They had confiscated his picture from a jilted lover, of whom he had multitudes.

He had last been sighted in Biri Biri, where he had robbed the local bank, the local post office and the local farmers' cooperative society, all in one busy morning, before heading in the direction of Crossroads.

The report perplexed all of thinking Crossroads. The whole world knew Crossroads was a dead and dying place. It had no banks to rob, no post offices, no farmers' cooperatives or anything that could attract the attention of a bank robber of *wa Guka*'s class. Even businesses left their doors open at night in Crossroads.

"Why Crossroads?" Musa puzzled.

"Will you forget the man?" Uncle Mark said exasperated.

Musa could not. He was afraid he was about to discover that he had entrusted his dreams, his entire future, to a man who was about to meet with a particularly violent end. It made him so angry he rose abruptly and wandered off to his kitchen; the only place in the whole world that made any sort of sense to him.

Broker was starting to doze off again when Big Youth rushed up all excited.

"Boss?" he called loudly.

"What?" Broker said, his eyes closed.

"I have to talk to you," said Big Youth.

The day was turning out to be an especially vexing one, indeed. Big Youth never sought to officially talk to him. He usually came out and said whatever it was he had to say and left it to be understood in whichever way anyone chose to understand it. Now he appeared anxious to be understood, and this bothered Broker.

"Make it quick," he said brusquely.

"It's serious, Boss," Big Youth said.

"So is my time."

Big Youth hesitated significantly. Broker heaved a sigh, opened his eyes and sat up. Big Youth was covered in sweat. He had run all the way here, he reported. He was nervous and agitated, and Broker had never seen him so upset.

"What's up, big boy?" he asked him.

"Terrible trouble, Boss," said Big Youth. "Very bad trouble."

"Spill it out," Broker ordered.

Big Youth did. There were strange people, in strange big cars, driving all over the farmlands in Crossroads asking all sorts of worrying questions. Rumour had it that they were policemen looking for the fugitive *wa Guka*.

"Here?" Broker wondered.

"Here," said Big Youth.

Rumour also had it that *wa Guka* had a wife and children in Crossroads and was hiding out among his family and friends.

"In Crossroads?" Broker mused.

He rarely read anything, except bank notes, and was, in that respect, more ignorant than old Musa when it came to current affairs.

"They say they will shoot him dead, Boss," Big Youth was very worried. "They say they will kill him, the same way they have killed all the others. They say they will shoot dead whoever is hiding him too."

Broker reflected some more.

"Is that all?" he asked.

"Yes, Boss," said Big Youth.

Broker sighed and said "He who lives by the sword ..."

"Boss?" Big Youth was lost.

Broker laughed and said he wished *wa Guka* well, whoever he was, wherever he was. Then he settled back in his stool and Big Youth could not understand it at all.

Like everyone else in Crossroads, he wanted so to believe that Broker was the famous *wa Guka*. He could not now understand why Broker refused the honour due to him as the most famous person ever to come out of Crossroads. Now he was about to die in a hail of bullets, still refusing to acknowledge and accept he was who he was.

Broker watched Big Youth anguish, smiled comfortingly and asked, "Is there more?"

"No, Boss," Big Youth said.

But there was more, Broker could see that. Big Youth feared. Big Youth feared that his dream was about to implode; and Broker would die before he had taught him everything. Before he had taught him how to be rich, world-wise and free. Big Youth did not know how to articulate this anxiety, so he leaned on the shop wall, crossed his arms and brooded.

Broker closed his eyes and thought. They stayed like that for a long time. When Broker opened his eyes, he rose abruptly, startling Big Youth to attention, and announced he was leaving for Makutano.

"What for?" Big Youth was horrified.

"Business," he said.

He would be gone for several days.

"Several days?" Big Youth was in a panic. "Why so long?"

He had many things to do, he said.

"You take care of business here until I return," he said to Big Youth.

"But I have to go to school," Big Youth protested. "I must go to school."

"You'll manage," Broker told him. "Is there anything you would like from Makutano?"

Big Youth shook his head, thoughtlessly, and lived to regret it. The offer was never to be repeated, and he would forever dream about the radio he should have asked for.

But the most significant thing about the whole episode, at least to Big Youth, was that the strange cars disappeared from Crossroads after Broker left for Makutano.

He was gone for nearly two weeks, two intolerably long weeks, during which Crossroads seemed to have come to a standstill. Big Youth started to dread, and Janet to hope, that Broker had left for good, that he would never come back again. Then he returned, loaded with gifts and things, for anyone who had cared to ask, and more. He brought back toys and clothes for his children, a colourful dress for Grandmother and a Parker pen Big Youth did not need.

"Keep it," Broker told him. "It may come in handy one day."

Uncle Mark had not asked for anything either, but he got a proper draughts board and men. Musa too had not asked for anything, but he got colour magazines with enough *impossible* pictures to keep him amazed for a long, long time.

For himself, Broker brought back a trunk load of maps and plans and architectural designs of incomprehensible proportions. He had plans and drawings for everything, from the petrol station to the proposed orphanage. He also brought back two mysterious items for himself. One of them was a small charcoal brazier, whose use he refused to discuss with the old men at the teahouse. The other one was a heavy item, wrapped up in thick jute bags, which he had Big Youth swear never to open and not to disclose its presence to anyone until after Broker's death. He also brought back a rocking chair, which he installed outside the Condom Shop, and ordered Big Youth never to sit on it.

He was as excited as a small boy, when he showed the plans to Janet.

"You are serious," she was shocked.

"Dead serious," he guaranteed her, as he gave her the presents he had brought back for her. "These are for you."

She tried to refuse them. He insisted, promised they had no strings attached to them, and assured her he would not leave unless she accepted them. She opened the bottle of perfume first, sniffed at it and seemed satisfied with it.

"And what is this?" she asked, of the other package.

"A book," he told her.

"A book?" she puzzled. "What sort of a book?"

"Open it," he said.

245

She opened the package, with a lot of apprehension. Broker watched her keenly as she discovered the book. It was a huge, hardcover volume and she regarded it with some trepidation as she examined the cover. She read the title, quietly to herself, then looked up and asked, "Where did you get such a book?"

"I knew you would love it," he said excited. "Open it, look inside."

Janet opened the book and Broker watched her peruse it. He had perused it himself at the bookshop in Makutano and had thought about it for a long time before purchasing it for her.

He watched her turn the pages, one after the other, one after the other, and waited for her to retch, slam it shut and return it to him. The first time he had seen the photographs he had quickly looked away. Janet did no such thing. She calmly turned the pages, one after the other, and went on turning them and studying page after page of bleeding lesions and open sores. When she got to the last page, she shut the book, looked Broker in the eye and said, "Thank you."

And seemed to mean it.

"Show them that," he said pleased. "Show them that and, I promise you, they will never laugh at your job again."

Janet nodded again and said, "Thank you."

Then she invited him to a cup of cocoa.

While he had his cup of cocoa, she picked up the book and turned it in her hands and thought about it and nearly despaired. Until now she had thought that she had seen everything that she knew everything there was to know about the plague. Until now she had thought that nothing could frighten her.

Broker, watching her suffer, read her thoughts and said, "Yes, my dear, it really is that bad, and worse. But the worst of it is that we haven't heard the last word."

She closed the book and wondered what to do with it.

Chapter Twenty-Eight

The children had left for school. The homestead was still, and the silence was driving Janet insane. She worried about the book.

She had showed the book to a few people in Crossroads. The women had cried out in horror and staggered away in shock. The men had braved the sight for a moment, then they too had turned away shocked and accused her of showing them shameful pictures. Now she did not know what to do with the book. It worked, she knew it did, just as Broker had said it would, but she had no idea to what ends it worked and how to make it work to the desired ends.

She did not have to go out to work yet and she decided to do something hard to keep her mind from her worries.

She was weeding her vegetable garden when the letter came. It was delivered by one of the Chief's henchmen, a man she knew to be an immoral and unscrupulous ox.

"Where is it from?" she asked him.

"From Sokoni," he told her.

Sokoni was the nearest post office, miles away on the old highway. All letters to Crossroads came via Sokoni, so the ox was not telling her very much.

Janet examined the envelope. Apart from the fact that it had been steamed open, courtesy of the post office mail thieves and Chief Chupa's inept spy system, the envelope also told her nothing. The postmark was a black smudge and the envelope bore no sender's name or address. She wondered if the letter had anything to do with the book.

She opened the letter and read it with some anxiety.

"What does it say?" asked the ox.

"Nothing to you," she said to him. "You may go now."

He left, reluctantly, and she watched him ride away on his rickety old bicycle that had uneven wheels and rocked and wobbled like an aged, mechanical hyena.

Janet was thoughtful for a long while after the ox had left. She considered the letter and all its chilling implications, and tried to make sense of what it said.

Finally, she took out her bicycle and rode to Crossroads.

At the Condom Shop, Big Youth had taken over from Broker and was busy doing what he did best - organising the merchandise and pointlessly stock-taking; doing his calculations on a large piece of paper torn from one of the cartons that the condoms had come in. There was not much to calculate. In six months they had sold a hundred and twenty condoms, all of them at discount to Alice of Highlife Lodge.

Broker was dozing in his rocking chair by the entrance, a position that was increasingly beginning to feel like the throne of the Mayor of Crossroads. People who had any business with him sought him there; people who thought he had money to give away, or that he knew someone in Pwani who might find their only son a job at the harbour; and people who merely needed his reassurance that there was no need to kill themselves now, that Crossroads was about to resurrect and to be again a jolly and glorious place to live in. Broker heard them all out, rocking in his chair, eyes closed, and nodding every now and then, to show them that he was awake. And when they had talked themselves out, he sorted out their problems, as fast and as expediently as possible, and they went away and left him to his dozing and to his apprehension over his own predicament, which no one could help him solve.

He was confident there was no danger in leaving Big Youth to run the shop unsupervised. There was no money to steal and, anyway, the big boy had a bias towards honesty that was even more disquieting.

Halfway through the afternoon, an old woman came by and discovered the shop for the first time. She had not been in town for months and wondered what it was.

"A Condom Shop," Big Youth told her.

She was happy it was so close to the road and asked to buy a pound of sugar. Broker heard her and decided to stay put, eyes closed, and let Big Youth deal with it.

Big Youth did not disappoint him. Rising to the occasion, and in his characteristic candour, he explained to the old woman that he could not sell her any sugar as he only sold condoms. She asked what that was, and he told her it was a *thing* younger people needed. To forestall further inquiries, he pointed her down the road to where she would find plenty of sugar.

She was wondering why Big Youth did not sell sugar, in such a colourful shop, when Alice from Highlife Lodge rushed up with an emergency order. Of all Crossroads, Alice seemed to be the only one determined to survive.

"*Biggi*," she said to Big Youth. "Give me one box of co ..."

Then she saw the curious grandmother standing by her side and said, "*co ... bbage.*"

"*Cobbage?*" Big Youth asked her.

She indicated with a gesture what she wanted. Big Youth laughed and said, "Oh, that *cobbage.*"

"Greetings, Grandmother," said Alice.

"Greetings, my child," said her grandmother. "You come all this way to buy cabbage? But the market is only ..."

"They don't have any down there," Alice said.

"And they don't have sugar up here," said the grandmother. "What has this town come to?"

"There is sugar down there," Alice informed her, accepting the box of condoms from Big Youth and stuffing it in her bag. She received the change and counted it carefully, while her grandmother watched and marvelled at the cabbage she had bought.

"Show grandmother where to buy sugar," Big Youth said to her.

As the two left the place, Hanna Habari came by on her way to the market and was surprised to find Big Youth behind the counter of the Condom Shop.

"Where is Janet?" she demanded.

"Janet does not run the shop," Big Youth informed her.

"Don't you go to school anymore?" she asked him.

"I do," he told her. "What can I do for you?"

"Nothing," she said, disdainfully.

She wanted pills, but she could not bring herself to ask for them from a boy. Broker was dozing in his chair nearby, but like most people, she did not talk to him unless she had to. He was a cold and arrogant man; a distant and hard-hearted man, and perhaps even dangerous. Everyone agreed Broker should be left quite alone. She was about to walk away disappointed when Janet arrived, riding up in a turbulence of fresh perfume and hot dust. She hopped off her bicycle before it had stopped and leaned it on the wall.

Broker sat up, expecting trouble. Janet never came to the Condom Shop, except to complain and to berate. He had not done anything she might consider unethical in recent months, but he braced himself for a hard confrontation all the same, as she strode up to him and slapped an envelope into his hand.

"Read it," she ordered.

The letter was from the Ministry of Health and it was addressed to the Family Life Education Officer. Broker's relief was overwhelming.

"It's addressed to you," he said, trying to give the letter back to Janet.

"Read it," she ordered.

"Is it good news?" asked Hanna.

"Or is it bad news?" asked Big Youth.

"What does it say?" demanded Hanna.

"Tell us what it says," said Big Youth. "What is the matter? Is it that bad?"

Janet took the letter from Broker and gave it to him to read for himself. Broker took the letter back from Big Youth, unfolded it and read it out loud.

"*Dear Janet*," he started.

He turned to her and said, "They know your name at the headquarters."

"I work for them," she said impatiently. "Read it."

Broker read it.

A team of officials from the North-South Commission would be visiting the country shortly to inspect and assess their ongoing projects, with a view to determining which ones should be upgraded and which ones should be discontinued.

"Louder," said Hanna. "We all want to hear."

"Janet?" Broker asked.

"Read it aloud," she told him.

Broker obliged.

Among the projects to be reviewed by the funding organisation was the Crossroads project. They had heard good things about Janet's work with her community and they considered her success a prime example of a functional bilateral *bla-bla-bla* ...

"In short," Broker said, slightly out of breath, "they are happy with your work."

"But who are they?" she asked him.

"The North-South something-something?" he said. "I've never heard of them before!"

Janet worried.

"But, since the letter came via the Ministry of Health," he said, to ease her anxiety, "it is safe to assume that they are the people who pay for the condoms."

Janet worried even more.

"What's the matter?" he asked her. "They are happy with your work. They even call it a prime example of ... whatever."

"They have never been to Crossroads," Janet said. "They don't know how impossible the people are."

"That is not your fault," he said to her. "You have done your job. You have told them all about condoms."

"But when these people get here and see for themselves?" she was beside herself with worry. "How little has been achieved?"

"They already love you at the headquarters," Broker told her. "Why can't you be happy and love yourself too?"

There was the shop, she reminded him. The shop was at the core of her distress.

"The shop?" Hanna asked, puzzled.

"The shop?" Broker laughed, really amused. "They will love this shop."

"It is a pretty shop," Hanna affirmed.

"We sell their condoms, for heaven's sake," Janet informed her. "They won't like that."

"They won't know that," Broker said.

"How can they fail to find out?" she cried in dismay. "Just look at it."

They looked and were pleasantly surprised to find that she was quite right. The Condom Shop stood out like a jewel in a refuse dump. It was the brightest thing in Crossroads. A bright light in the midst of rot and destruction. It was indeed the prettiest thing in Crossroads, Hanna attested.

Big Youth cleared his throat.

"Boss?" he said.

"Quiet!" Broker ordered.

"May I speak?" Big Youth asked.

"Silence!" Broker ordered.

Big Youth had new orders from Broker never to speak unless permitted to do so. No one permitted him now, but he judged the situation serious enough to warrant a breach of regulations.

"We can hide it," he said to them all.

"Hide a shop?" Janet was, for once, thoroughly disgusted with him too.

"Just the name," said Big Youth. "We can call it the cabbage shop and sell cabbage and sugar instead."

She was appalled. She regarded him as she would have done a strange creature that crawled out of a dark and smelly latrine. Big Youth shuffled his feet uncomfortably and turned to Broker.

"What do you think, boss?" he asked. "Just for a few days?"

It was not the most obtuse idea Big Youth had expressed that day, Broker observed patiently, but it was too simple. An idea for first class morons and early quitters. For cowards eager to disengage and disperse before the commencement of battle. Broker had no time for such mundane ideas. He had not made it to where he was by taking the easiest, or the safest, first option.

"Any more ideas?" he asked all around him.

Janet had exhausted hers on the way to Crossroads and Hanna had no idea why such an appealing little shop should cause so much bother to anyone. But Big Youth had some ideas. They ranged from demolishing the shop and rebuilding it after the inspection tour, to lifting it off its foundations and hiding it behind the post office. He was bubbling with ideas, but not one of them was bold enough or combatant enough for Broker, and he suggested that the boy take the rest of the day off from thinking.

"Let's not think like morons," he said to them. "We must think straight. Where is Frank?"

Straight thinking was Frank's forte. But Frank was out treating cattle, no one knew exactly where, and they did not know when he would return.

"We better wait for Frank," Broker said. "We may be missing an opportunity here. Let us wait for *Daktari*."

He sat back down, slightly out of breath, and watched Janet fret. This was it, she moaned. This was the end of her career, the end of everything she held dear. Why did she ever let herself be dragged into this mess?

"Dragged you?" Broker sat up. "Mess? What on earth are you talking about, woman?"

"I had no idea the trouble you were sucking me into," she said to him.

"Sucking you?" he was dismayed. "Where do you learn such mean language from? I'm telling you, there's no reason to despair. Stop moaning like an old woman and think straight. The situation may be drastic, but it's not impossible. Just don't panic and stop worrying about the shop. I will take care of everything."

"I could lose my job."

"Not over this," he told her. "Leave the shop to me. You go worry about the condoms at home."

He glanced at the letter again.

"Wait a minute," he said, studying the envelope. "This letter is over three months old. Where has it been all this time?"

"It came through the Chief's office," Janet told him.

So they had to assume that it had been steamed open, deciphered for the Chief's consumption and digested before being passed on to her.

"But that can't take three months?" Broker puzzled.

"Everyone must have read it," she observed.

Sometimes, letters addressed to activists were copied and sent to the various officials so that they may know what they were dealing with and exact the appropriate penalty when processing application forms for trade and liquor licences, or for any of the numerous official permits required to live or die in Crossroads - birth certificates, circumcision licences, death certificates and funeral licences.

"The North-South people must have changed their minds," Broker announced.

Janet wished she could believe that. Too many unexpected things had happened to her in the recent past for her to expect any good news.

"Cheer up," he told her. "If they come, they will find me. I'm not simple, you know."

She smiled reluctantly, for she understood that more than anyone else around.

"And don't undervalue yourself," he told her. "You have done a commendable job. The letter clearly says so here. Look, it says here, you can have anything you need to make your work easier."

"Anything?" Hanna marvelled.

"Does it really say that?" Big Youth asked.

Broker gave him the letter.

Big Youth read the paragraph that promised Janet anything she needed. All she had to do was ask. He read it twice, once for himself and again for Hanna, who was looking over his shoulder.

Janet wondered out loud if this was the good thing Grandmother had dreamt for her the previous night. Hanna laughed her shrill laugh and said it was a good thing, whoever had dreamt it up. Janet had laboured in vain for too long, she said. It was time she got something out of her labour.

"Ask for a video machine," Big Youth advised.

"Are you mad?" Janet was aghast.

Crossroads' electricity supply had gone the way of the highway; along with the post office and the filling station; the telephone and everything else that had made sense. But that was not the point.

"I don't need a video," she told him.

"Not for you," he said to her. "For me."

"They did not ask you," Hanna reminded him, before turning Janet to say to her. "Janet, listen to me. I'm a woman and I know what it means to have nothing, nothing at all, that you can call your own. Don't waste your choice on foolish wishes. Ask for something big."

"Like a video," said Big Youth. "We could have shows at the shop. We'll get many customers that way."

Not a wholly stupid idea, Broker observed, but again it was too simple. Janet shook her head too and admitted it was impossible to think of any one thing that would solve all her problems. She needed so many things she could not begin to count them.

"Ask for a farm," Hanna suggested. "A big farm with a big house and a big tank for water. This is your only chance to have these things."

"But what has a farm got to do with my work?" Janet asked her.

"Your work?" she laughed her shrill laugh again. "Do you want to do this work all your life? Don't be foolish, woman, get something for yourself."

"Ask for money," suggested Big Youth. "Lots of money."

"Can she do that?" he asked Broker.

With money she could buy whatever she really needed. With money, many things were possible.

"Can she ask for money?" Hanna wanted to know.

"I don't know," he said, smiling sadly, for his mind was on loftier ideals. "The letter does not say anything about money. Would it be dishonest?"

He shrugged and gestured vaguely. It happened all the time, he told her. The big men in charge of the Government coffers did it all the time themselves. And those in charge of the donor funds often found better use for the funds than that for which they were originally intended. Some diverted the funds, under dubious circumstances, to satisfy personal needs and those of their friends and close relatives. Big cars were bought and expensive mansions acquired. Huge consignments of drugs, worth millions of money, were sometimes ordered, paid for and delivered to nonexistent hospitals while remote health centres died for lack of drugs. Broker did not know, he admitted, but the whole business of Government, it appeared, was to enrich the governors and to impoverish the governed.

"There," he laughed without any cheer at all. "I told you it was a madhouse. There are probably millions of condoms you have never received, which have, nevertheless, already been paid for and, at least on paper, been delivered to you."

Janet was horrified.

"Such things happen all the time," he assured her. "Sometimes funds are stolen outright, and the donors know about it. Most times they look the other way."

"Why?" she asked.

"Why?" he seemed surprised by the question. "That is a question you don't hear asked often enough. Many have lost their jobs or gone to prison for asking why; sometimes it is safer not to know why."

"How?" she asked, awed.

"Don't ask me," he said, suddenly exasperated. "I have done it myself."

"But that is stealing," she was dismayed.

"It is," he agreed.

"I would never do such a thing," she said, more to herself than to him.

"No, not you," Broker's head was beginning to throb. "But the are many of us who would never forgo the opportunity."

Janet was regarding him with that special look she reserved for things that crawled out of dirty latrines. Her loathing for despicable things and people was famous. She was about to vomit.

"Don't look at me like that," he said to her. "Some people think it's foolish to be honest among thieves and cheats. Some people believe that we must embrace every single opportunity to advance ourselves and to improve our personal finances. I don't necessarily agree with all of them, but that is up to each of us to decide for ourselves."

Janet thought deep and hard. They waited for her to make her mind and decide for herself. The water-seller came by, pulling on his strange contraption, and asked them if they needed a drink of water to quench their thirst. They did not want to quench their thirst and he went away, ringing his bell and yelling that he had sparkling spring water to sell.

Hanna shook her head sadly and remarked that she walked such a long distance to the river to fetch her domestic water, that a water tank would save her life.

"I would ask for a water tank," she announced.

A water tank would ease Janet's burdens too, it was true, but only as far as water was concerned. What about the other things? What about her work?

"You could ask for a clinic," Broker proposed. "A real clinic with doctors and nurses and dressers. The whole works. They would build it right here in Crossroads. Then you would not have to fill your house with condoms."

An attractive proposition, Janet considered, but a little too fantastic to imagine coming true.

"Let us be realistic," she told them.

"Ask for money," said Big Youth.

"A big house," suggested Hanna.

"Lots of money," insisted Big Youth.

"A water tank," said Hanna.

The two went through the whole list of things they thought Janet really needed. There were so many of them that Janet thought they would never stop.

"Stop it!" she screamed at them. "Stop this madness at once. I must think for myself."

"What about a car?" asked Big Youth.

"A car?" Hanna exclaimed. "Have you gone mad?"

"A small car," he said.

"A small car?" Janet asked him. "How small is a small car?"

"Like the one the DFO uses," he told them. "Chief Chupa had one too which … "

"Rots in his goat-yard for lack of service," Janet reminded him.

"Yours will not die," he promised. "The boss will reopen the garage. Ask him."

She turned to Broker astonished. He shrugged and frowned at Big Youth, warning him to keep his big mouth shut. But there was no danger of Janet being impressed by Big Youth's revelation, for Hanna suddenly reminded them that the Chief would never allow a Janet to drive a car in Crossroads.

"Why not?" demanded Big Youth.

"She is a woman," she stated.

"Big George's wife had a car," said Big Youth.

"Bought for her by her husband," Hanna glanced significantly at Broker. "Her husband was a big Government man. But what do you need a car for, Janet, when you don't even have a farm?"

"Have you seen the way she has to travel to do her job?" Big Youth asked her.

"She can't even drive," said Hanna.

"I will teach her," he offered.

"You?" she laughed, the full force laugh Crossroads women used to reduce men to boys - the equivalent of a kick to the crotch. Women had refined to an art, and little girls could deliver it to great effect without any idea what they were doing.

A twitch appeared on Big Youth's left cheek.

"Broker will teach me to drive his car," he said.

"He will?" Janet asked, surprised.

"So that I can drive to Makutano to buy him things."

"In his car?" She turned to Broker, utterly amazed.

Broker shrugged again and wished the boy would shut up. He was not feeling too well, his headache seemed to be galloping out of control and all this marvellous talk of free cars and things was wearing him out.

"Only rich people have cars," Hanna reminded. "Janet is not a rich woman."

"The Government people are rich," Big Youth assured her. "They can give her anything she wants to do her work. Isn't that so, Boss?"

"What have televisions and farms and sewing machines and God-knows-what got to do with her work?" Broker said tiredly.

"She must also get something for herself," Hanna said. "She hasn't got anything for herself."

"That is not the purpose of the letter," Broker tried. Then, suddenly realising that he would have to kick the two dreamers out of the decision-making process in order to advance the plot, he said harshly, "Why don't you two just shut up and let Janet make her own decision? Better still, why don't you go home and leave us to make up her mind?"

"Go home?" Big Youth asked incredulous.

"Hey, Janet is my friend," said Hanna. "I can't leave her to make such an important decision alone."

They had known Janet all their lives, they said. She was one of them, their own kind, and they wanted to see her succeed for once.

"This is your only chance," Hanna said to her forcefully. "Don't waste it. Think and think hard or you will always be poor like us. Think."

Janet thought. She had never had this much choice before. Although deep down in her heart she believed it to be an exercise in futility, she thought about it. She thought of the many things she had never had and always longed for. A stone house with a large kitchen, a borehole so that she would not have to trek two kilometres to the river and back, and a water tank, so she could capture rain water for herself and her grandmother. She needed a radio, so she could keep in touch with the world outside of Crossroads, and a bicycle with a better carrier - so she could carry her cartons of condoms more convincingly when she went out to give them out. And money. Not mountains of money as Big Youth wished for her, but enough money for her and her children, and for her Grandmother and for her friends and for anyone who needed it. Especially for the poor souls who called her selfish for not sharing the bags of money they imagined that she earned working for the Government.

Then Big Youth rudely and violently interrupted her thoughts, exclaiming, "Look!"

A white car had suddenly entered Crossroads and was approaching down the main street.

"Oh, my God," cried Janet. "They are here."

"Don't panic," Broker told her. "Just relax and let me handle it."

Her heart was thumping away and she was choking with dread as they watched the car approach. It came slowly on, the occupants looking out of the windows as though looking for a particular address among the broken and twisted ruins. When it finally drew level with the Condom Shop, the car stopped and the occupants regarded the group gathered outside the shop.

There were four men in the car. Four dark hulks with stern faces and red eyes that could see through walls. For a brief, uncomfortable moment, the two groups stared at each other. And, in that brief moment, Broker recognised the men for what they were.

"This is not the North-South gang," he said to Janet.

"Who are they?"

"A different gang altogether," he told her.

"What do they want?" Hanna asked.

"I don't know," he said. "I'll ask them."

He rose tiredly and limped to the vehicle.

"Good afternoon, gentlemen," he said loudly. "You seem to have lost your way. Can I be of any assistance to you?"

"Maybe you can," one of them said.

The rest of the brief exchange was held with Broker leaning over the window of the car, obscuring their voices. Then he stepped back, apologised for not being of any help and the car drove faster than it had arrived. Broker limped back to the shop.

"What did they want?" Big Youth was more concerned than the others.

"Directions," he told them. "Would you believe they had never heard of Crossroads until today."

" Where are they from?" Janet asked him.

"Makutano," he told her.

"They are policemen, are they not?" she observed quietly.

"They didn't tell me," he said to her.

She had known him far too long to be fooled with half answers. He read her mind and said, "Don't worry. Everything will be all right, you will see."

"Have you decided?" Hanna asked her, suddenly getting back to important matters. "We must know what you have decided before I leave."

She vowed she would not leave before Janet had made up her mind. So Janet thought and they waited. She thought and thought.

They waited.

When she finally decided, and told them of her decision, they groaned in unison and wondered if she too had gone completely mad

"What I would really like," she told them, "More than a car, more than a big house, more than TVs and water tanks and money, is to know how many people in Crossroads are free from Aids."

"What has that got to do with this letter?" Broker was unable to contain his anger and disappointment.

"Everything," she said.

"Why?" Hanna was equally dismayed. "What do you want to know such a thing for?"

"I'll tell you," she told them.

It would do more than make her work lighter. It would give it direction and purpose - give it a new lease of life. Despair and ignorance were the biggest enemies in her war against the plague. The numerous people who, because they mistakenly believed that they were already infected with Aids, did not care for their lives or make any effort to protect themselves. If she could establish how many of them were infected, then she might know what to aim for in her campaign against Aids.

They did not understand her at all. None of them did; not Broker, not Big Youth and certainly not Hanna, who observed sorrowfully that she had let condoms get into her head. There could be no other explanation for such irrational thinking.

"What you mean is test everyone," Broker commented quietly. "That is impossible, you know."

"Why impossible?" Janet asked him.

"The will never agree," he told her.

"We'll only test those who agree," she said.

"Have you any idea how much it would cost?" he asked her.

"No," she admitted, her earlier optimism beginning to fade.

"The earth," he told her fervently, his head pounding in earnest. "A fortune of the kind no one will waste on such an inconsequential place as this one. It would cost the earth."

"And save lives," she told him. "And make my work easier. Isn't that the whole point in all of this?"

"Would they pay that much?" Big Youth asked.

"I don't know!" Broker said, harshly. "What is the population in Crossroads?"

"What does it matter?" Janet asked them. "We have to start somewhere. We'll never know anything until a proper survey is done. We can start with the youth. We can test them first."

"Does it hurt?" Big Youth asked her.

"No," Broker said to him. "They take a little blood sample, is all there is to it."

"I heard that a woman fainted after giving blood," Hanna revealed.

"They don't take that much," Broker assured her.

"Is it safe?" Big Youth asked next. "Do they use a big needle?"

"You will not feel a thing."

"But all this is idle talk," Janet stirred herself awake. "Nothing at all will come of it. We all know that."

"But there is no harm in asking," Hanna told her. "You never get what you don't ask for."

Janet nodded and said she would certainly ask, as soon as she could think of something sensible and realistic to ask for. She had been promised the moon too many times before, she told them.

Broker looked down at his shoes, feeling thoroughly rotten, and swore to himself that she would get her wish out of the letter, however absurd that wish turned out to be.

"The fate of Crossroads is up to the people of Crossroads themselves," she said, steeling herself and changing into her invincible demeanour. "That is you and me."

"And Frank and the Boss?" added Big Youth.

Everyone was welcome to contribute, even people with uncertain names and motives who promised not just the moon but the stars as well.

Hanna laughed and said, "Janet, listen to me. I'm a woman like you and I know the suffering you must endure to get anything of your own. Don't let these men mislead you. Ask for something you need, not what they tell you. Ask for yourself and yourself alone. Do you hear me? Ask for something to make you happy. I must go now. Stay well."

They were quiet for a long while after she had left.

Chapter Twenty-Nine

The homestead comprised of five mud and thatch huts, overgrown with weeds and in various stages of despair. Two of the huts were completely dilapidated, overwhelmed and boarded up. Behind them stood a half completed stone house - dead and grey and glaring down at them, like an old family curse. The tile roof was only half done; but it was rotten and collapsing into the sad interior. It was a huge and ambitious structure, with many rooms and large windows into which nature now poured with orgiastic abandon.

A hungry dog rose from the shade, gave a half-hearted bark and lay down again when Broker's car pulled up in the middle of the well-trodden yard.

Broker alighted and stood for a moment, looking round the deserted compound. All the doors were closed and padlocked. Smoke rose from one of the huts. He could have sworn that he had seen movement as he turned in at the gate. But, apart from the dog, frail and starving and now watching him without interest, there was not a living soul in the compound.

He walked about the yard, tapping at things with his walking stick, and discovered a world of used-up dreams; a broken chair here, a rusty pot there, an old shoe, a battered toy no one used any more and ragged clothes and blankets and things that had been spread out on the grass to sun. Memories, and ghosts of memories, leaped at him from every place and every object that his eyes landed on.

He remembered sneaking here late at night with Jemina. He remembered the torrid nights in one of the now derelict huts and he remembered creeping home to his unsuspecting Janet before it got too light. He remembered Jemina's parents, simple country folk with as numerous problems as they had children. He remembered their quiet acceptance of their daughters' occupation; that the girls had to work at the lodging houses to bring home the money, without which their fatherless children, most of them conceived in the process of earning their siblings a livelihood, would have been much worse off. Jemina had never told him whether her family knew exactly what she did at the lodging house, or if they knew that she was running away with him to seek her fortunes in Mombasa.

She had just asked him, "When are you leaving?"

And he had told her, "Tomorrow."

"And when are you coming back?" she had then asked.

"When I'm rich and famous," he had said, only half in jest.

Jemina had nodded and said, intractably, "I'm coming with you."

And there was no way of dissuading her. The following morning they had left on the *Far Traveller* to Makutano, and from there they had boarded an overnight *Coast Express* to Mombasa.

Jemina had lived with him for three years. Then she had found her German and married him and gone off with him to God knew where. And he had not seen her again. But before she left to pursue her fate, she and Broker had had their last supper together; and talked a lot and wept some, as they reminisced on their long and hopeful journey from Crossroads. Then they had promised never to forget each other and to seek each other out when they were rich and famous; when they had made it and had something to share. Then they had gone their separate ways.

For Broker, a man, with nothing to sell but his tongue, it had been a long and hazardous journey from poverty. But he had made it at last, as promised to himself. And he was now rich and, in his own way, famous. And he was back home where he had started. He could now begin to earn the true renown he had promised Jemina and himself; by being first famous to his own people.

But why was he here, at this dead homestead, at this time of day? What did he expect to find here? The respect she, and others like her, had lost in him? Or the triumphant homecoming that Crossroads had denied him by dying on him?

As he approached the house, whose interior he knew too well, the armed gang emerged from hiding and descended on him. There were about twenty of them, all rugged and dusty; emaciated creatures with hungry and hostile eyes. They came at him, with hoes and machetes and other farm implements.

"Greetings," he called out, fearfully.

The sound of his voice checked their advance. They had not expected such a big voice from such a puny person and they were uncertain what to do next. Broker too had no idea what to do now.

"Is there no grown-up here?" he asked them.

They quietly surrounded him, brandishing their crude weapons and seeming ready to do him serious harm. They examined him from head to toe; studied him from every angle. And none of them was a day over thirteen. When he turned and walked slowly back to the car, they followed him and proceeded to give the car the same thorough scrutiny they had given him. But they made no attempt to stop him opening the door of the car and preparing to retreat into the safety of its interior. Then he paused and asked them, "Is there no one here with you?"

They made no reply.

"Who is your leader?" he asked them.

A hard-boned girl, of indeterminate age, stepped forward. She was about four feet tall, stunted and dried out and prematurely aged. Only her hair and her bosom confirmed that she was a girl.

"Who are you?" she asked him.

"Broker," he told her. "I'm Broker. Jemina's friend. You know Jemina, don't you?"

"Aunt Jemina," said a boy.

The girl kicked him into silence.

"Do you mind if I look around?" he asked her.

She did not reply. He shut the door of the car and walked round to the back of the huts and the incomplete house in the overgrown fields.

There was a burial plot, next to the grey stone house; with about a dozen graves, half of them recent. There were no markers on any of the mounds and the graves lay untended, mysterious and unsettling in their anonymity. Broker paused by the most recent of the mounds of earth, higher than the rest and just beginning to be reclaimed by the weeds and the grass, and wondered if it was a grave of anyone he remembered. The boy who knew Jemina came to stand next to him.

"Aunt Jemina," he said unasked. "She died."

Feeling suddenly faint and breathless, Broker leaned on his cane to steady himself. He closed his eyes and blanked out his mind and concentrated on staying on his feet. When the pain had passed, and he could think again, he thought of their last days together, and of Jemina's resolution not to return to Crossroads until she had fully realised her goals.

When and how had Jemina returned home? Had she come back, as she had left, in a bus? Or had she returned in a hearse?

264

Had she returned in a big, expensive car like his, or in a simple wooden coffin? The burning question was - had she found the fame and the fortune she had strived for, or had she come back as insignificant and as futile as she had left? Had she finally made it? The half-finished stone house seemed to suggest that she had not returned as she had left.

He did not know how to grieve for her. He was not surprised she had come home. He had known it from the beginning; as indeed they had all known all along, that it was just a matter of time before life caught up with them. He had come hoping that it was not so.

One day, in Mombasa, when they were still good friends and struggling together to make it, they had sat in the tourist bar where Jemina plied her trade and talked about many things. They had also talked about the plague; how unfair it was, how malicious it was to have singled out the most vital of all human activity as a way of transmission. How could anyone hope to survive it? How were men and women expected to live without each other? How were they supposed to find husbands and wives, with death poking at them from every nook and cranny?

Jemina's closest friend, had died a most horrible death at the local hospital and Jemina was inconsolable. Only a few months before Farida's death, they had talked about their dreams. Broker had overheard them from the next table, where he sat with a Russian sailor to whom he was selling a two-kilogram bottle of old nails and red paint, disguised as red mercury.

The sailor, who spoke no English at all, and even less Swahili, had only half his mind on the deal in progress. His imagination had been seized and was held captive by Farida's beauty. Twice she had turned down his offer of a night to remember, by explaining to him patiently, in impeccable Swahili, that she had had enough of one-night encounters, with hard-up sailors, and she was on the lookout for true romance - a wealthy tourist and a lasting relationship.

Two battleships, with six thousand American sailors on board, were due to dock later that day and the whole city was ecstatic.

"If one of them offered you a lot of money," Farida had asked Jemina, while waiting for the sailors to disembark, "Would you do it without protection?"

"No," Jemina had needed no thinking about it.

"What about a thousand?" Farida had asked. "Would you do it for a thousand?"

"No," she had said without any hesitation.

"For ten thousand?" Farida had asked.

"No," Jemina had said.

"What about one million?" Farida had finally asked. "Would you do it without a condom, for one million?"

Jemina had hesitated.

Farida had laughed and said, "Me, I would."

She came from a poor family to whom money was everything. With money, she could rush home and build a large, stone house for her mother. She could buy clothes for her children, and for the children of her brothers and sisters, and send them all to school. She could make her parents happy, and make her relatives proud of her, for once. She could eat good food and have some nice clothes and good things, for once. A girl could do a lot of things, for once, with that kind of money.

Jemina too may have made her relatives proud of her, for once. But there was no big stone house for her mother here. Just an orphaned, half-finished structure, all rough and mouldy, as depressing as sin and as unsightly as a miscarried foetus. The children, including those of her brothers and sisters, were all half-naked and out of school. No one, it seemed, had benefited from whatever irresistible offer she had accepted in exchange for the remainder of her life. Aids had got to her first.

Broker left Jemina's grave a thoroughly troubled man. The boy took his hand as they walked back to the huts and the other children. Two of the huts were now open. Broker pushed a door to look into a dark and dank room, smelling of urine and poverty. Rats scrambled from the floor and ran up the walls to their nests in the thatching. There was not a stick of furniture in the room. The entire floor was covered with sacks and sleeping mats. The second house was in the same dismal condition; one vast sleeping place where rats ruled most of the day. A scrawny milk goat, with twisted horns, leaped out of the house, startling Broker half to death, and bolted.

"Who lives here?" Broker asked, of the padlocked huts.

"Grandmother lives here," said the boy.

She had gone to the church to look for food, the boy said.

So this was what it all added up to, Broker thought. One poor grandmother and dozens of mouths to feed. What had happened to Jemina's brothers and sisters, the men and women who had so diligently produced all those children? Were they dead too? Or had they simply fled from the despair?

Broker opened the boot of his car and off-loaded the shopping he had brought with him. He gave it to the girl, who bore a striking resemblance to Jemina.

"We thought you were a thief," she said to him.

That was the reason she had locked up the old milk goat in the house when she saw his car. Broker laughed and said, "No, I'm not a goat thief."

He had been many things in his life, he assured her, but he had never been a goat thief.

Chapter Thirty

Uncle Mark and Frank were having a quiet game of draughts when Broker arrived back in Crossroads. They watched out of the window as he parked his car by the post office and saw the angry manner in which he shut the door. They heard his rude answer to the beggar's greeting and knew then that all was not well.

He limped into the teahouse and, without a word to anyone, went through the kitchen to his room at the back.

They exchanged worried glances and resumed their game. A moment later, there was the smell of burned hair in the air and sudden heavy pounding coming from Broker's room. They abandoned their game and rushed to ask what in the world was going on.

"Go away," Broker thundered from inside the locked room. "It's not your business."

They went back to their game. They were about to embark on a new game, when the henchmen came for Frank.

"They want to talk to you," they said, rudely.

"Who wants to talk to me?" he asked them.

"All of them," they said.

Frank had made his peace with Kata, by agreeing to treat Kata's cows without payment for the rest of his life, and he could now think of no other enemies to look out for.

"Go tell them I'm busy," He said confidently.

"You better come with us," the henchmen insisted. "They are very angry."

"Angry?" Frank was suddenly uneasy. "But I have done nothing today."

He had not left the teahouse at all that day.

"You come, anyway," they urged. "They have sent for your friend as well. They have sent for the *kodom* woman."

Frank turned to Uncle Mark for counsel. Uncle Mark shrugged and played his turn. They wound up the game and Frank left with the henchmen. They had gone some way down the road before he realised that they were leading him away from the Chief's office.

"Where are you taking me to?" he asked them.

"You will see," they said, ominously.

They walked across an open field, jumped several fences and crossed numerous abandoned fields to the old mission school. Frank began to relax. So far he had had very little to do with Head Faru's school. But as they jumped over the last fence, he began to wonder at the rumbling sound coming from the school building.

"You will see," the henchmen promised.

Doubts whirled in his mind.

Halfway to the school buildings, his mind was equally divided between fleeing and facing it like a man. Then they turned a corner to the front of the school and came face to face with the source of the noise.

Everyone was there. The Headmaster, Frederick Faustian Faru, the teachers and the School Committee were all there. The pupils were drawn up in ranks in front of the school office, the youngest in front and the oldest at the back. Also present were Chief Chupa and his sycophants, the church elders and their hangers-on and the school's Board of Directors. They stood in one discontented line in front of the Headmaster's office, a bunch of impatient and restless elders.

In front of the angry teachers and elders were three terrified boys with their hands behind their backs and their eyes cast down on their bare feet. Next to them stood Janet, her feet and hands black with the mud from her garden, and for once, she looked old and harassed.

The noise died down when Frank showed up. The henchmen shoved him next to Janet and left him there.

"What happened here?" he asked her.

She smiled feebly and shook her head. Frank turned to the Chief, who then turned to the Headmaster.

"Do you know these boys?" Head Faru asked Frank.

Frank did not.

The Headmaster turned to a junior teacher and said, "Bring them out."

The teacher ducked into the Headmaster's office. The assembly waited expectantly. When the teacher came out again, he had three well inflated, coloured condoms floating on strings.

"Quiet!" the Headmaster barked.

No one had spoken. He turned to glare at Frank and Janet, while the teacher with the condoms sweat with embarrassment and awaited further instructions. When none were forthcoming, he looked for the fastest way to get rid of the condoms. He settled for handing them out to the guilty boys. The boys refused to take them and the Headmaster barked, "Take!"

They took. They knew which one belonged to whom and swapped them immediately.

"Explain," the Headmaster said, turning to Frank. "How did these boys get these ... *things*?"

"No idea," Frank admitted.

"No idea?" the Headmaster roared. "No idea? What do you mean no idea?"

"I don't know," he said.

"You don't know," Faru was apoplectic with fury.

"Why don't you ask the boys?" Janet suggested.

He was in no mood to accept suggestions from anyone. She turned to the boys and posed the question to them. They looked at one another, wondering if they should trust her and tell her.

"Answer!" Head Faru ordered them.

"We found them," they said.

"Where?" he barked.

The boys were terrified.

"Where did you find them?" Janet asked them.

They had found the condoms on the road, they said. The condoms had fallen from a lorry. The Headmaster chuckled dryly and said, with great foreboding, "Try another one."

Even Janet had to admit the strain on the imagination; seeing three condoms falling from the back of a moving lorry. But this was school and, no doubt, the Headmaster had heard it all before. In the old days, when the highway had passed through Crossroads, all manner of impossible things had appeared in the community and were said to have fallen off passing vehicles; including once a white child who was, inexplicably, unharmed and who confirmed that he had indeed fallen out of the rear window of his parent's station wagon. But this was a different matter altogether, and Janet asked why it had been deemed necessary to drag her here to ask the boys such a simple question.

"Is that all?" she asked the Headmaster. "Can we go now?"

"Not yet," he said harshly. "We are not through with you two. We know that you have been teaching children to..."

He stumbled on the words.

"To what?" she asked him.

"Sex education," he said.

270

Janet shook her head sadly. Whenever anyone had a problem with discipline or control, in Crossroads, they found an easy escape in blaming it all on society. Failing to find a convincing scapegoat, they turned on her campaign. She could not deny she was responsible for the proliferation of contraceptives and condoms in Crossroads.

"We don't teach what you think," she now said to her accusers. "We teach how not to end up pregnant and out of school, or dead."

Pastor Bat squawked in disgust. In less tolerant societies, he disclosed, people like her and Frank would be stoned to death.

And who would be casting the first stone, Janet wondered. Who, among the elders, did not have children? Who among them had not made babies?

The Committee looked down in embarrassment. That was not the issue here, the Headmaster pointed out. The children were too young to know of such things.

"Too young?" Janet turned to the pupils on parade. "Is there anyone here who does not know where babies come from?"

There was general discomfort all round. A small boy, with an intelligent forehead and large, sincere eyes raised his hand. Everyone quickly ignored him.

Chief Chupa cleared his throat and said sombrely, "That is not what we came here for. We came about those ... *things*."

"The condoms?" Janet asked him.

The Headmaster caught his breath painfully; *did she have to insist on using that name?* and the Chief nodded calmly and said, "Yes, the *kodoms*."

"What about them?" she asked him. "We have established that they fell from a lorry. Are you afraid the boys will find out what they are really for?"

"No," he said, ill at ease. "But they must not blow them up like that."

"Certainly not," Janet agreed with him.

But it was merely a matter of information and education.

"Your department," she said to the junior teacher who had fetched the balloons.

"My department?" cried the teacher. "I'm a history teacher. I'm not a..."

The words would not leave his mouth. He turned to point an accusing finger at the Headmaster and said, "He is the teacher of biology."

The elders grumbled, wondered what this had to do with learning, and started to question the wisdom of summoning Janet to the disciplinary assembly.

"Quiet!" the Headmaster barked at them all.

The noises stopped at once.

"That," he pointed at the balloons with his cane, "that is not biology! Those *things* are not in our curriculum and we can't teach such things here. We are responsible educators here. We teach important things, useful things, things that will benefit the pupils in the future. We have to prepare them for the future."

"What future?" Janet asked him.

What future could there be without living? she asked them. She, at least, taught respect for life and living. Without her teaching, the future the teachers claimed they prepared the pupils for would never be realised. That was why it was necessary that the school committees allow her to teach family life education in their schools.

"You need not fear these," she said taking one of the inflated condoms and bursting it in her hands. "The children know what these things are."

She turned to the assembled pupils and, raising the other balloons over her head, asked them, "Who knows what these are?"

Only an imbecile would claim that knowledge in front of the Headmaster and the School Board. The small boy raised his hand and said, "Balloons."

"Anyone else?" Janet asked. "The big boys at the back?"

No one dared know. They mumbled among themselves and groaned and tried not to be noticed. The Headmaster, the teachers and the committee started to relax. They had been right after all; the children's minds were virgin lands, rich and fertile and full of promise. They had to be tended with care and planted with the best and the most useful of seeds; not to be sown with useless information and rebellious and disgraceful ideas.

Frank leaned over to Janet and pointed out her error.

"Wait," she said to the pupils. "I will rephrase that question. Who does not know what these are? Raise your hands."

Not a single hand went up.

"See," she said to the School Committee. "They know what these *things* are. Now all you have to do is teach them their use and purpose."

"Us?" cried Chief Chupa.

"How?" demanded an elder.

"I'll show you," she told him.

She gave the condoms back to the boys, turned to the history teacher and asked him to fetch her a board and chalk.

"Draw me a man and a woman," she said.

"What?" the teacher cried in dismay.

"Don't tell me you didn't learn that much biology," she said to him.

"But why me?" he wailed.

"You are the teacher," she told him.

"But I'm not the only teacher here," he complained to the Headmaster. "Why does she pick on me?"

The Headmaster was at that very moment realising what a serious mistake he had made by sending for Janet, and he was busy thinking of a way to put an end to the whole affair.

The Chief watched Janet thoroughly and sincerely humiliate such learned men, and fell madly for her again.

"But, but ..." he stuttered, "I can't draw."

Janet threw her arms up in despair and the odour of perspiration and perfume hit the Chief and he thought he would faint from the rush of blood to his head.

"Who can draw?" she asked them. "Anyone?"

The small boy raised his hand.

"Anyone else?" she asked.

The Headmaster cleared his throat; her excited odour was getting to him too.

"We haven't got time for this sort of nonsense," he said.

Frank, who up till now, had watched and waited impatiently for Janet to be done with humiliating everyone so they could all leave and forget the whole matter, cleared his throat, and said, "I will draw. Bring me a board and chalk."

The history teacher was eager to oblige him. Frank took the balloons from the boys and handed them to another teacher. The mortified teacher let go of the strings and the condoms floated over the heads of the School Committee. They ducked their heads and the wind blew the condoms out to the playing field.

"Bring some chairs for your elders," Frank said to the boys.

273

The boys rushed to obey and everyone realised they were in for a long day at school. They mumbled and grumbled, but only the chairman had the audacity to moan out loudly that he had important matters to attend to.

"More important than the education of these children?" Janet asked him.

He made fatuous noises but sat down when a chair was offered.

Pastor Bat suggested they punish the boys, as had been originally intended, and be done with the whole business. Chief Chupa suddenly remembered he had a funeral to attend.

Janet ignored the excuses and herded the Committee into their chairs, while Frank finished his drawings. They were good drawings of female and male figures, simple but complete and clear in every detail.

She took the Headmaster's stick from him, leaving him feeling naked and powerless, and used it to point at the large board.

"Now, boys and girls," she said to the rapt students, "We are going to learn how babies are made."

The Headmaster put his head in his hands and groaned loudly.

"And how this knowledge may save your life," Janet added.

The Committee groaned in unison, and squirmed in their seats and stared into space, and wished they had sent their apologies as usual.

As Janet launched into her practised lecture on reproduction, Pastor Bat rose abruptly, announced that he had better things to do with his time and stormed away. Chief Chupa, whose idea to humiliate Janet had so miserably backfired, rose and followed the Pastor.

The rest of them sat it out, too embarrassed to stay but too cowardly to leave, and had their first ever public lecture on human reproduction.

At the end of the lecture, they were all very surprised that they had survived. And, though none of them would ever admit it in public, most of them were glad they had stayed.

Chapter Thirty-One

Frank had left to go back to Crossroads, and Janet was busy at her weekly washing when Head Bakora rode up on his old bicycle, a little sweaty and out of breath.

"Greetings," he hailed.

"Greetings," she said, a little startled.

The Headmaster dismounted and stood leaning on his bicycle, uncertain how to proceed. Like most men in Crossroads, he stood in awe of Janet for her defiance of all social norms and traditions, and for her reputation of not only arguing with men but also insisting on winning the arguments. Had she been an old and ugly woman, her behaviour might have been more easily understandable. Had she been a barren old widow, or deformed in some manner, that too might have been mitigation enough. But Janet was young, healthy and attractive and, at her age, was expected to be fragile and subservient; like a woman, like a daughter, a younger sister or a third wife. And Janet refused to be any of these things.

She continued her washing, trying hard to ignore the thumping inside her head. She had swallowed four aspirins that morning and still the pain persisted; it appeared that she would have to live with this pain for the rest of her life.

He stood and watched her work, bent over the basin full of soapsuds, her movements firm and decisive. Her shawl was tied tightly round her waist to stop the wind lifting her skirts, but it was not doing a good job of it.

Embarrassed as much by the straying shawl as by her silence, he cleared his throat loudly and said, "I have come about ..."

He searched for the words. Janet looked up but went on washing, rubbing the clothes firmly and busily. When their eyes met, the visitor cleared his throat again and said, "I'm not unhappy about you; about what you did to my school."

What she had done was to display posters on his school's notice board without his authority, and without a written permit from the Government.

"My teachers are still angry about it," said Head Bakora said to her. "I have come to tell you that."

"I had to do it," she said.

He had no say in the matter, he informed her. He had to answer to the School Board and to the PTA.

"Between the Board and the Government," he added, "they decide what will be taught in my school."

"But you know better what should be taught in your school," she said to him. "You should have a say in these matters."

"Alas, it is not so," he shook his head sadly. "I'm employed by them. I must do as they say."

She straightened up and shook the suds from her hands and arms, sending them flying in all directions.

"What about the children?" she asked him. "Doesn't anyone care what happens to the children?"

"I have been a teacher for forty-five years," he said sincerely. "I would not still be a teacher if I did not care about children."

He stood in the middle of the yard, leaning on his bicycle, looking sad and tired. A hard-working man after a hard day's work. Janet could not help but think what a simple and gentle man he was. A caring husband, no doubt, and a good father. She wondered why Grandmother had never proposed him as a potential husband. She had recommended most men in Crossroads, after all.

"Sit down," she said, wiping her hands on a corner of her shawl. "I will make you a cup of tea."

He declined. He was in a hurry, he said. He had stopped by just to tell her that he was not against her or her work.

"It was very kind of you to come," she told him.

Still he lingered. He had more to say, it seemed, but he did not know how to say it. He cleared his throat several times. Finally, in too many words, he let her know that he was not like other members of the School Board. He was an educated man and a civilised man. He understood a whole lot more than he was allowed to. He also let her know that he liked her. He liked her, in spite of all that was said about her. It would be all right for her to come again to his school and teach about those *things*.

"About condoms?" she asked, to be certain they were talking of the same *things*.

He cleared his throat, nodded and added, "And the other *things*."

It was the kindest thing anyone had said to her that day.

"Unofficially, of course," he added.

"You must sit down now," she insisted. "I will now make you a nice cup of cocoa."

Before he could plead his business further, she was off in the house fixing him a cup of cocoa. Reluctantly, he leaned his bicycle on the wall of the grain store and sat down. He sat uncomfortably for a moment, then rose and moved the stool away from the direct view of the gate.

Janet brought out the teakettle that was rarely empty or completely cold, and two large enamel mugs. She smiled knowingly on observing that her visitor had moved the stool away from the direct view of the road, and poured the cocoa.

"How many children do you have?" she asked him.

He had seven girls and five boys. Four of the girls were married, three of them to men of dubious existence, the fourth to a high-school teacher, a good, honest and hard-working man. One of his boys was a Government man, the other a student of medicine. The old teacher had not much to regret in his children. But, if he could start over again, he would have fewer children.

"That's what you all say," Janet commented.

"I have never said it to anyone before," he said uncomfortably. "No one would understand."

"Your wife?" Janet asked.

"I don't think she would either."

Following on this line of thought, they talked about family planning; how alien and suspiciously diabolical the idea seemed when a man was young and virile and invincible, and ready to populate the entire earth, and how sensible it appeared to be later on in life, when one was older and balder and drowning in a molasses of hardships, and just about to be vanquished by family life itself.

"That is how experience teaches us," Janet told him. "Always too late."

He laughed and said that he liked her cocoa. She poured him another cup. Then they talked about her job. He thought it was a good idea to teach the youth about sexuality, about pregnancies and venereal diseases. But he thought that chastity was the answer, chastity, not the condom or the pill.

"That is what children were taught in the old days," he said, sadly. "That and discipline and self control. Harlots and wayward men got their just rewards and sinners would burn in the fierce fires of hell. We cared about such things then. The whole society understood abstinence."

Janet observed that that may have been true before the plague, when youth could stray a little without having to pay so dearly with their lives. Now the whole society had to rethink its approach to these old problems. The new plague did not know old from young, good from bad or priest from prostitute.

"How many wives do you have?" she asked him.

"One, of course."

"How many girlfriends?"

"Girlfriends?" he smiled sadly. "How come you ask so many questions?"

"Does it embarrass you?"

He laughed nervously, shook his head and said to her, "It is true what they say about you; you are completely without shame."

"Shame?" she too laughed with true mirth. "Do you want to know what I think shameful? Do you want to know what is really shameful?"

He was not certain he wanted to hear it, but she told him anyway.

"Crossroads is shameful," she told him.

Crossroads' greatest shame was to let embarrassment stand in the way of truth and reality; to allow so many of its people to die so needlessly. That was the worst shame of all. And it was that shame that had decided Janet to set her own shame aside, and to utter the unutterable and to mention the unmentionable and to teach the un-teachable.

"Because of my shame at what we have become," she told him. "So who are you to tell me I have no shame?"

"It is what they say," he said apologetically.

"Where is the shame in fighting for life?" she asked him.

"There is none," he agreed. "But in the old days ..."

"Forget the old ways," she told him.

Taboos had to be eliminated, to make way for meaningful progress. Old beliefs and assumptions were the biggest handicaps in the battle against Aids. People who still believed that they were safe from Aids, because they had many wives, and so-called *safe* partners, and did not *manga-manga,* or consort with prostitutes. But their *safe* partners too had their own *safe* partners, who also had *safe* partners; in a endlessly long chain of *safe* partners that was a recipe for a terrible catastrophe.

278

"I have only one wife," he assured her.

He had no girlfriends and no *safe* partners either, and he was certain his wife was an honest and faithful woman.

"Then you have little to fear," Janet said to cheer him up again. "But you do understand the gravity of my work?"

"I do understand now," he rose.

"Am I still welcome to talk to your students?" she asked.

"I hope we can arrange an appropriate time," he said, picking up his bicycle. "I thank you for the tea."

"Cocoa," she corrected.

"Cocoa," he said. "Thank you for the cocoa."

"And I thank you for coming," she said.

He rode away thoughtfully. She watched him go and felt a sudden surge of affinity for the quiet man with so many problems. Like herself, he was a victim of his conscience, a thought wandering in the Crossroads wilderness.

She resumed her washing.

Grandmother hobbled through the small gate, her eyes roving here and there looking for something to criticise. Janet watched her come, noted how unhappy she looked, and braced herself for the onslaught.

Having found nothing real to complain about, Grandmother sighed wearily and asked to know who she had been talking to.

"To Head Bakora," she told her.

The old woman mumbled something about Janet finding time for everyone but her own husband.

"Has Broker been to bribe you again?" Janet wondered.

"Why do you hate him?" she asked her.

Janet did not hate Broker. True, there was a time she had hated him with all her being, detested him with the kind of passion reserved for one's mortal enemies. Now she had nothing but pity for the creature who once was her feared and revered man.

"He needs you now," Grandmother said firmly. "He needs you, like you once needed him."

"I don't need him now," she said.

How could she not need him? Grandmother wanted to know. Was she not a woman, like other women?

"Manhood doesn't make man," Janet reminded her. "You taught me so yourself."

"What was true yesterday is not important today," Grandmother said, wishing she had never uttered those words.

"Your husband is a total man. A man of vision and ability, a man strong enough to look after his own. Did he not catch you and tame you, when you were a young and wild thing, and make you into a woman? Did he not give you three good children and build you a nice house?"

"A nice house?" Janet gestured towards the old ruin, sending soapsuds flying onto Grandmother's face. "That house over there or another one?"

He could build her a better one now, Grandmother pointed out. But Janet did not want a better house from Broker. The one she had was sufficient for her and her children.

"You taught me never to depend on a man again," she said, resuming her work. "You taught me very well."

Grandmother smiled, a rare, pleased smile, and said she was happy Janet had learned the lesson well. Maybe she had learned it a little too well. She had grown strong and wise and formidable to men. She was no longer an innocent who had to be protected from the wolves in men's clothing. No man could cheat her, misuse her or abuse her again. Now she could afford to be generous, even to men. Especially to the man who had made her what she was.

"Made me what?" Janet wanted to know.

"A woman?" Grandmother said. "That is what you are, and don't you ever forget it."

Janet laughed, a bitter and dry laugh devoid of mirth.

Grandmother finally sat down, to demonstrate her good will, and continued her tirade. Janet had made her point, she said. Janet had proved that a woman could be just as bull-headed and as stubborn as a man. But it was imperative now, especially now that her man was back in the saddle, that she return to her natural role of wife and mother.

Janet laughed again, the same weary laugh that frustrated even Grandmother. Grandmother laughed too and was determined not to be put off. They argued for a while, a semi-friendly, verbal match at which they were both adept players. They talked till Janet had washed, rinsed and hung the clothes out to dry.

Then they heard Broker's car coming, from way down the old cattle trail that was now well trodden and marked with his tyre tracks. Grandmother listened expectantly as the sound grew louder and louder, and watched Janet fret and wait apprehensively for the car to appear. It was the biggest car Crossroads had ever seen. It gave her a thrill; a strange, forgotten sensation, whenever that impossibly huge car penetrated her granddaughter's gateway and parked in the middle of the yard. It fulfilled her enormously to know that it was all owned by her grandson-in-law, the man they had all said would come to nothing.

"Be kind," Grandmother said, watching Broker haul himself out of the driver's seat. "He is your husband."

"Greetings, Grandmother," Broker said, limping across the yard to them. "Jeremiah must be giving you something very good, for you get younger every day."

Grandmother laughed and said, "You don't have to flatter me, my son. You will always be my favourite man."

"I have some things for you in the car," he told her.

Then he noticed the kettle and the cups and asked if there was any tea left.

"No," Janet said, immediately.

"May I have a cup?" he asked her.

"No," she said again.

He laughed and said not to worry. Grandmother would make him some tea, he was certain. Janet said it was all right with her, whatever Grandmother did for him. She wanted nothing to do with him, and the sooner he understood that the better.

"You know I'm a total man," Broker said laughing. "I don't give up easily. Ask Grandmother here."

Grandmother smiled, that crafty old smile, and limped away to her compound.

"You must stop bribing her," Janet said firmly.

"Me?" he feigned innocence. "Bribe Grandmother?"

"All those things you bring her," Janet told him. "She tells me everything, you know."

It was not like that at all, Broker said. Grandmother and he went way back. She was the very first person to accept him in the Maalim Juma home; arguing, as always that manhood did not make a man. He had never got around to asking her whether it was meant as an insult or as a compliment. But it had served its purpose well.

"I like to give her things," he said to Janet. "To help her and Jeremiah. After all, who have they got to look after them?"

"How do you think they survived before you came back?" Janet asked aggravated. "Me, they have always had me."

He apologised and tried to make light of the matter. He had not come to make trouble. He had come to make peace. He agreed with her, and suggested that he too might have fared better, if he had let her take care of him. See what the others had done to him!

It made Janet angrier, remembering the time she had wasted watching the gateway, yearning for his return, longing for his carefree presence, and praying that he would return. It hurt her that her prayer had been answered ten years too late. Now she prayed he would disappear again, just as suddenly as he had reappeared, and never come back again. But she knew there was no hope of her prayer being answered a second time. He was here to stay, to haunt her and to pester her for the rest of her life.

"I don't ask more than kindness," he said, reasonably. "Is that too much to ask?"

It was.

"Even a dog deserves some kindness," he pleaded.

If kindness meant giving of herself and her life, to be shredded and wasted again, that was too much to ask.

Broker thought of things to say, to ease the tension, but nothing he tried today seemed to work. He rose and announced that he would go talk to the old woman for a while, come back when Janet was in a better mood.

"Don't hurry back," she told him. "And bribing Grandmother will get you nowhere."

"We'll see," he said and laughed wearily.

He limped back to his car and drove away, defeated. Watching the car turn out of the gate, Janet was, for the first time since his return, torn between pity and loathing. She put her head in her hands and pressed hard to suppress the pain.

Chapter Thirty-Two

Broker sat outside the Condom Shop and watched the traffic rush by on the highway. It was not much traffic, but it was enough to make him want to get into his car and drive to the end of the earth; an urge that had been with him for as long as he could remember. It was pent up rage, the potential to explode into unbridled fury to purge himself of the demons of his flawed past; the dark terrors and the nameless creatures and things that dwelt deep down in his tortured soul. He knew of only one way to confront these anxieties - by hurling himself onto the jagged edges of perpetual darkness itself, by jumping into his car and driving himself to the very mouth of death itself. But his car was parked in the yard behind Musa's teahouse and he did not have the energy to walk there.

His body was on fire, his feet and hands were cold and tingling and his vision was blurred and the pain in his chest was unbearable. He had been this ill only once before, at the beginning of the ailment that was now part of his life. Doctors had prescribed for him all manner of medicine and recommended rest. The medicine, which he had carried with him ever since, was in his suitcase in his room at the teahouse and he had no energy to go for it either.

He saw Big Youth come swimming in the mirage towards him and surmised, by the way the boy moved, that some evil was afoot, and braced himself for the worst.

"Greetings, Boss," Big Youth said cheerfully.

"Greetings," he responded.

Big Youth dashed into the shop without another word to him. His unease grew when he heard a carton rip open and Big Youth rummage urgently inside it.

Musa emerged from the teahouse and the beggar hailed him as usual, saying, "You, old man! Give me money."

Musa waved him away and glanced up and down the street. There were no customers in sight, not a sign of the hoards Broker had promised. Broker waved at him. Musa ignored him too and continued to regard the empty street with anger. He had given up trying to make Broker declare his true identity, or leave Crossroads forever, and he shook his head and went back into the teahouse.

Broker watched Musa waddle back to the teahouse and wondered. He turned back in time to catch Big Youth slip a box of condoms inside his shirt.

"What are you up to, big boy?" he asked quietly.

"Being smart," Big Youth said just as calmly.

"It is called stealing," Broker said. "Put them back."

"Janet lets me," Big Youth said to him.

"Lets you do what?" he growled. "Put them back or pay for them. There will be no more rackets here, as long as I'm boss."

Big Youth sulked. It was a sight to behold. He was not used to sulking and it made Broker laugh to see how hard he tried to appear unhappy.

"Put them back," he ordered.

"But, Boss," Big Youth said reasonably. "I have not received my salary."

"What salary?" Broker asked. "No one gets paid a salary, you idiot. We are all volunteers."

"But, Boss," Big Youth tried protesting. "You said I would die poor if I worked for nothing."

"Put the condoms back," Broker told him. "And don't think that I don't know you have been selling them behind Janet's back."

"Janet doesn't mind," said Big Youth. "The condoms are free."

"Not here," Broker said. "You know that."

"But I don't want to die from Aids," Big Youth pleaded.

"Then wait until you get married," Broker advised. "You should not be indulging in sexual activities at your age."

"How will I ever get a wife?" Big Youth asked seriously.

"Don't worry about that now," Broker said irritably. "There is a wife and a husband for everyone out there, including the ugly and the stupid. Finish with your education first. Read, learn and educate yourself, then ... here, give me those."

Big Youth looked balefully up and down the street and handed the condoms to Broker.

"You are too young to be thinking about a wife," Broker said to him. "There are enough young people here wearing out their lives with wives and children and things they could do without. I'd hate to see you grow up to be just another dead-end village scoundrel like them. A nobody."

"I'll not be a nobody," Big Youth said and meant it.

"I certainly hope not," Broker said. "A man must strive to rise above his birth and circumstances; grow to be somebody."

"Somebody like you?" Big Youth asked him hopefully.

"No, don't be like me," he said quickly. "Be like ..."

"Like Frank?" asked Big Youth.

"Like Frank," he said uncomfortably. "Someone like Frank."

Frank was the perfect role model. He was clean, smart, educated, and disturbingly honest. He also had dreams, most of them antiquated and mundane, but no man was ever complete without a few wild ideas to keep him going.

"Yes," Broker said convinced. "Be like Frank."

"How come he got Aids?" Big Youth asked him.

Broker was suddenly sick to his stomach. Cold nausea rose from his liver and spread to his stomach.

"You didn't know Frank had Aids?" Big Youth asked, worried.

Broker's hands trembled as he took the box of condoms and handed it back.

"Here," his voice quaked when he spoke. "Take your stupid condoms and go away. Go away, get away from here!"

Big Youth took back the box and regarded it dejectedly. He had never before seen the crushed look that was now on Broker's face, the despair and the utter despondency that were now suddenly branded on his face.

"You really didn't know," he said to himself.

"Go away," Broker yelled at him.

He was perspiring heavily from the heat and the fever. Then came the stomach cramps and the excruciating pain.

"I'm sorry,' said Big Youth.

"Just go away," Broker hissed. "And don't ever come back here."

The urge to jump in his car and drive over the edge of the earth was overwhelming. Rivers of sweat ran down his face and his body shook feverishly. It enraged him to see himself so utterly helpless and out of control; exhibiting such moronic weakness.

"Get out of here!" he barked, so loud he was heard inside the teahouse.

Big Youth left him alone and walked slowly away, weighed down by guilt and by the dismal despair his revelation had caused Broker.

Broker watched him go, shuffling his feet in the dust; and, for the first time ever, ignoring the beggar's pleas for alms.

When he got to the end of the street, Big Youth glanced back ad the hulking figure seated in front of the Condom Shop, paused briefly, waved and then crossed the old *Hell Run*, without looking out for traffic, and he did not see the grey Government car, approaching fast from the direction of Biri Biri.

Broker leaped to his feet and let out a strangled cry that was heard all over Crossroads. But Big Youth did not hear the warning cry, so deep had he descended into his private hell, and he stepped right out into the path of certain death. Brakes screeched and dust flew, obscuring the crossing. When the dust cleared, the car stood inches from the indifferent youth, having missed killing him by a hair's breadth. The driver, gone mad, was cursing loudly, so loudly that Broker, the beggar and the old men looking out of the window of the teahouse, heard every nasty word and every shameful name he called the reckless boy. It incensed them all, but the curses did not reach Big Youth, any more than the beggar's pleas had, and he went slouching on his way.

Broker sat down again. He was shaking violently, his throat was lacerated from the jagged howl it had emitted and his chest was on fire. His head ached like it had never ached before and his heart was thumping at a frightening rate. Sweat poured down his face and back and his hands shook when he lit his pipe. He smoked and rocked in his chair and wished he could fall asleep or, better still, die right away, to escape the agony.

Uncle Mark, who had watched the encounter with Big Youth through the window of the teahouse without comprehending it, came across the road to find out what had transpired.

"Nothing," Broker told him.

"Fancy a game?" he asked.

"Just leave me alone," Broker said to him.

Uncle Mark nodded and went silently back to his draughts table.

A funeral party came down the old road, the entire cortege comprising of two old pallbearers, a woman and seven children.

Broker watched it go by, too weary to rise, and Musa stepped out of the teahouse to ask who was in the box. It was Sabuni, the dhobi, they told him, the last practitioner of the old craft of the hand-washing clothes. The teahouse and all the lodging houses in Crossroads depended on him and now he was dead.

"Great sadness," Musa said.

"Great sadness," said the woman.

There was nothing more to be said.

The funeral marched on and Musa was left standing alone in the middle of the dusty street, a thoroughly distressed man. Of all the nasty things that could happen to a man, of all the multitude of causes that Crossroads died from, the washer-man had to go and die of malaria. It was almost as though Sabuni had died of a phantom accident. It was no way for a respectable, hard working and God-fearing, family man to go.

The sadness and the anger swelled up inside him. They whirled and swirled and crashed like thunder inside his stomach. They ate out his insides and chewed on his vital force, leaving him hollow and light-headed and cold. They sucked on his very soul and, like a hot and hungry devil wind, eddied and rose up in his chest and swelled out till his lungs and his heart were on the point of bursting. Then the fury erupted in his throat, in a tortured, nerve-jarring, guttural cry.

"*Hauuuu!*" he bellowed, like a mortally wounded bull. "*Hauuuu!*"

His howl was as loud as it was terrible and it crashed in the air and reverberated over the old ruins, and Crossroads heard it and trembled with dread.

"It's not fair!" he roared. "It's not fair, at all!"

The beggar ran into his booth to hide and Musa stormed back to his teahouse to beat up the crockery.

And Broker brooded in earnest.

Janet found him near total defeat, slumped in a pitiable bundle in his chair outside the Condom Shop, and wondered what was the matter. He answered her that it was nothing, and not to worry about it.

"Is Frank back yet?" she asked him.

"I haven't seen him."

She leaned on her bicycle, studying the haggard, dusty figure in front of her and trying to suppress the upsurge of helpless pity. She had not seen him for some time and had started to miss his pestering presence and now she was shocked by the extent of his decline.

"How is business?" she asked him.

He shook his head wearily. If he sold condoms to Crossroads for a living he would starve to death, he informed her.

"I'm cooking bananas for dinner," she told him. "Would you like to come over? About seven?"

"I'm not hungry," he said.

She lingered, fighting off the cold guilt which rose up in her heart, and which she knew to be unjustified. She steeled herself and told him she had to do some shopping. Then she rode away and Broker brooded in earnest.

Half an hour later, she passed by on her way home.

"If you should see Frank ..." she said to Broker.

"I'll tell him seven," Broker said, sucking on his pipe.

She watched him and worried. All her children sucked their thumbs when they were worried.

"Are you all right?" she asked, with some concern.

"I'm fine," he told her. "I'm just fine. Don't worry about me."

But she worried.

"I'm going home to do some washing," she told him. "Have you got anything I can wash for you?"

He hesitated. All his suits were dry-cleaned in Sokoni, twenty-five kilometres down the old highway, and his shorts and shirts were washed by Sabuni, the dhobi whose funeral procession had just passed by. The clothes he wore now were dusty and filthy, even by Crossroads standards.

"In my room," he said picking up his cane.

He struggled to his feet and led the way to the teahouse. Janet pushed her bicycle after him, noting how heavily he leaned on his cane, and worrying about it. She left her bicycle on the wall next to the notice that forbade it, and followed him into the teahouse.

As they crossed the tearoom to the lodgings at the back, Broker asked Uncle Mark to watch that the beggar did not steal anything from the Condom Shop. Uncle Mark laughed and commented that he did not believe the old beggar would steal anything he could not eat right away. But he would watch the shop, all the same.

Mzee Musa was on a mat in the middle of the room, prostrating himself exactly as Maalim Juma had done at this time of day in his office at the petrol station. They avoided him and walked through the cluttered kitchen to the back of the teahouse.

Broker's car was parked in the middle of the yard, dark and solemn like a waiting hearse. Big Youth washed and polished it every morning, on his way to school, but it was always covered with a fine layer of grey Crossroads dust by evening.

"Wait here," Broker said at the door to his room.

She obeyed, and he entered the room alone.

The yard was overgrown with weeds and grass, across which a thin footpath snaked from the kitchen to the latrine in the corner of the yard, and two lines of tyre marks led from the back gate to Broker's car. The bathroom at the far end of the yard had a gunnysack for a curtain and the smell of mould and decrepitude was pervasive. Everything was black, rotting or dead. The grass and weeds were unnaturally grey as though someone sprayed something evil over them. There was no sign of joy.

Janet had never been to the back of the teahouse before and was shocked at the filth. So this was how men lived without women, she thought. It depressed her.

A gasp from Broker's room brought her sharply back to the present.

"Ben," she called out.

There was no reply.

"Broker," she called.

She heard a strangled gasp from inside the room and shoved the door open. Broker was slumped in the only chair in the room, jaws clenched and hands pressed to his chest.

"Broker?" she was terrified.

"I'm fine," he said. "I'm just fine."

He gave her a faint smile to reassure her.

"Absolutely fine," he said. "It's nothing new. It comes and goes. I have holes inside here full of broken and dying things."

"What things?" she asked.

"You don't want to know," he said coughing painfully. "If only they would die less dramatically."

His attempt to laugh it off provoked a fresh outburst of coughing, his wasted body bouncing up and down on the seat, and it was painful to watch. The thumping in Janet's head, the pain which had started the day Broker returned and would not go away, now started again.

It was a small, bare room, devoid of furniture. There was a mattress in a corner of the room, the bedding on it in a messy pile. There were unwashed clothes everywhere, and on a string across the room and on nails on the walls. A suitcase lay open on the floor and was piled high with clothes. There were also several cartons of condoms, stacked up against the wall, and numerous empty beer bottles by the makeshift bed. Gambling was not the only house rule Broker disregarded.

The smells of pipe tobacco, sickness and death were palpable. But there was also another disturbing smell — a strange, acrid odour that emanated from a small soot-blacked brazier in the corner and reminded Janet of the Hindu crematorium at Makutano.

"What's that smell?" she asked.

"What smell?"

"That," she said, finally recognising it for what it was, the odour of singed hair.

"Oh that?" he laughed. "You don't want to know about that."

"Why not?" she asked.

"This is my office, as well as my private residence," he told her. "That's why I said to wait outside."

The room was stuffy and inhospitable. She opened the window and said, "You should not smoke in your condition."

"Nor drink nor stress myself," he said impatiently. "What else, *Daktari?*"

"You must eat a healthy diet," she told him.

"In this place?" he laughed at her.

"I'm serious," she told him.

"So am I," he laughed feebly. "Say, who is the expert here?"

"Just telling you," she said.

"Telling me what?" he asked. "You stick to pushing condoms. Better still, stick to pushing pills and leave the condoms to me and your boyfriend."

"Frank is not my boyfriend," she said, hurt.

"Why is he always with you?" Broker asked her. "Why does he live here?

"He does not," she told him. "And that would be no reason to detest him. I can't believe you hate Frank that much."

"What do you expect?" he said to her. "He spends all his time with my wife, while I spend nights with the rats."

"You left," she told him.

"And came back," he said.

"Too late," she told him. "Years too late."

"But I came back," he said. "Came back to you."

"No, not to me," she said, firmly. "To yourself. You came back to yourself."

He had come back to his own conscience, to settle scores with his own demons. Janet and Frank had nothing to do with that. They were good friends who worked together and enjoyed each other's company.

"That's all."

Broker snatched up his laundry bag, angry at himself for being so transparent. Losing control frightened him more than death.

Janet watched him sort out the dirty laundry and stuff it in the laundry bag. It was getting harder for him to hide the fact that he was a very sick man. But he was admirably brave about it, and it more than upset her to realise there was little she could do to help. He had all the money he needed to buy medicine and nursing care and all sorts of solace for himself. But he had chosen to live in this squalor and to make everyone feel bad and hate her for it.

"Did you ever rob a bank?" she asked him.

He looked up, startled. Janet stood by the window, regarding him with great concern. He smiled bravely, but a shadow crossed his eyes, something dark and chilling and so flitting it was gone before she could see it for what it was.

"What makes you ask me such a question?" He looked puzzled.

"Did you ever?"

"Rob a bank?" He laughed uncomfortably. "You mean with a gun and a *panga* ? Like *wa Guka?*"

"Did you ever?" she asked, impatiently.

His laughter had no body to it.

"Did you shoot people?"

"Why do you ask?"

"What happened to your leg?"

"Mob justice," he said, then, seeing the horrified look on her face, he said quickly, "No, no, I'm just joking, that was an accident, jus an accident. I used to live recklessly, like a madman too. But I was young and thought that I would never die."

He resumed stuffing clothes in the laundry bag in a sombre and angry mood. She watched him for a while, before finally asking him, "Would you like to come back home? With me and the children?"

She had no idea what made her ask him that. It was not just pity but something bigger and deeper; the primordial goad that drove poor people to take in injured animals and stray dogs they could ill afford.

"I get it now," he said laughing with relief. "You draw the line at thieves and murderers."

Janet smiled and added, "And Godless heathens and child molesters.

He assured her he had never been any of those things. He was amazed and pleased about her too, he said. He had never known her this way at all; he had never known her to make him laugh so, when he wanted so to cry. It made him angry to realise how little he had known her.

"I thought there was no room at your house," he said to her.

It pleased her to hear him say those words.

"There is room in my house now," she said to him. "The condoms are in the shop now."

Broker considered. She waited. Since discovering the nature and the severity of his illness, he had resolved he would never be an object of pity for anyone. Now he heaved a heavy sigh and said, "It is amazing how things grow on you."

Then he lifted the laundry bag to his shoulder and carried it out of the room saying, "Shut the window."

Janet shut the window and the door and followed him to the front of the teahouse, where she had left her bicycle. It was still the only bicycle in Crossroads that could be left leaning on the wall of the teahouse without Musa tossing it out into the middle of the street.

As they tied the laundry bag on the carrier, Musa came out to watch and to grumble how she set a bad example riding a bicycle. She ignored him completely.

"Your laundry will be ready in a day or two," she said to Broker.

"Thanks," he said.

Janet finished tying the bag to the seat and mounted the bicycle.

"No hard feelings?" she asked.

"No hard feelings," he said, and meant it.

"And no more snide remarks about Frank?" she asked.

"No funny remarks," he confirmed.

She noticed Musa eyeing her lewdly and pulled her skirts over her knee.

"I'll bring the laundry back when it's ready," she said to Broker.

Then she rode away, leaving Musa breathless with excitement and Broker smiling sadly at him.

"Is she now back with you?" he asked.

"You better believe it," Broker told him.

"Women," Musa said despairing. "I will never understand women."

Broker patted him on the shoulder and said to him seriously, and amicably, "Frankly, old friend, neither will I."

Now that they were such good friends again, Musa felt compelled to reveal that he did not think it was such a good thing for Broker to keep them awake all night, every night, with his roasting and pounding.

"All right," Broker patted him on the shoulder some more. "If that's the way you feel about it ..."

"You'll stop?" Musa asked, taken by surprise.

"As soon as I have perfected my new formula," Broker said.

"How long will that take?"

"Scientific research is a tricky thing," Broker said. "You never know when to expect any results."

Musa, correctly, understood that to mean he would have to lie awake at night with the smell of singed goats' hair in his nostrils listening to the dismal pounding. They turned and entered the teahouse together.

"You know what?" Broker said cheerfully. "I'm suddenly very hungry. What have you got?"

"Nothing," Musa told him.

"Why don't you go whip up a good old Biri Biri omelette for me?" he was feeling quite reckless.

"No eggs," Musa informed.

"Do they matter?" Uncle Mark wondered.

Musa glanced sharply at him, sighed and said to Broker, "I can make you exodus special."

Broker groaned, "I thought we did away with all that nonsense."

"It's quick," Musa pointed out.

"Forget it," he turned to Uncle Mark. "A game?"

"Why not?" said Uncle Mark setting up the draughts table.

Musa watched them set up the game and wondered what to do next.

"Give us some tea, old bull," Uncle Mark suggested.

Musa did not budge.

"Why do you do it?" Uncle Mark asked, when the game was well under way. "It's not like you need the money?"

"I do it for science," Broker said.

"For science," Uncle Mark laughed his wise old laugh. "You really believe the stuff with the goats' things really works?"

Broker laughed with him and remarked that that was what he was trying to establish.

"The whole purpose of research is to find out things," he said. "To discover if and how they work."

He had received encouraging reports from his retailers too; but he wanted to be certain himself. Now he was approaching the critical stage and he would soon need volunteers on whom to test his new invention; some reliable old bulls with nothing to lose; and he was confident that his dear old friends would oblige him.

Musa's mouth fell agape.

"Meaning us?" Uncle Mark asked astonished.

"I have no other friends here," Broker said to him.

The conversation died a sudden death. The old men looked at each other, quite lost for words. Then Musa sighed, deep and sad. Finally convinced that Broker was beyond all redemption, He went to cook real poison for him. Uncle Mark, in his turn, decided the time had come to thrash the little creep to death; to pulverise him and win from him every single big one he had left.

"Now I have heard it all," he said to himself. "Now I have finally heard it all."

"Your move, then," Broker said, pleased with himself.

From where he sat, he could see all the way down the street and keep a lookout for customers at the Condom Shop.

"Tell you what, old bull," he said rubbing his hands together happily. "How would you like to win five big ones today?"

Uncle Mark regarded him quizzically for a moment, then burst out laughing.

"I thought you'd never ask," he said.

"I must warn you, it won't be that simple," Broker told him.

"We'll see about that," Uncle Mark chortled as he reset the table.

As the new game commenced, the beggar emerged from his booth, scratched his backside and, raising one leg, freed a resounding fart.

"You, Mayor," Broker called out to him. "What's up?"

The beggar waved and went back into his phone booth to sleep.

"He used to be a decent hard-working beggar," Uncle Mark observed with some disapproval. "You have turned him into a corpulent sloth like the rest of us."

Broker laughed, "Don't worry, you'll all survive."

"Shall we now?" Uncle Mark wondered.

"I guarantee it," he said seriously. "Your move."

Chapter Thirty-Three

Janet was alone when Hanna called to see her.

"Thank God you are alone," she said on realising that neither Frank nor Big Youth was about. "I must talk to you."

She had come to return the book, she said. But she also wanted *those things*.

"Pills?" Janet asked her.

"Not those," Hanna said. "The others."

"Condoms?" Janet asked doubtfully.

Hanna nodded and burst into nervous laughter.

"Condoms?" Janet was incredulous. "But your man hates condoms. Hanna, my dear friend, what have you been up to?"

"Nothing," Hanna laughed uncomfortably. "I have read your book. I have read it, from the first page to the last page, and it frightens me. I don't want to die like that."

She had shown it to her husband too.

"What did he say?" Janet wanted to know.

"Nothing," she laughed again nervously. "He was shaken to his root."

She had had a long talk with him after that. They had talked and talked and, finally, she had realised his problem.

"He is afraid," she said to Janet. "He is afraid that men will know about it and consider him a coward. So I must not tell anyone, not even my best friend, about it."

"Grandmother did tell me something good would happen today," Janet said, suddenly brightening up.

She had not imagined it would be this good. She took a carton and started to open it, but she was too excited to do it.

"Let me help you," Hanna offered.

Together they opened the carton and inspected the contents.

"I can't believe what I'm hearing," Janet said to Hanna. "Tell me again. How did you make him agree to use condoms?"

It had not been that hard, Hanna said, beginning to relax. Her husband had a younger wife.

"She is mad after men. He will get the plague from her and die."

"Did you tell him that?"

"It made him so angry he got up and left."

But, before leaving, he had promised to come back and beat her senseless. She had never seen him so angry. She was packing to go back to her mother's house, when he returned, a little drunk, and informed her he had been to the funeral of his closest and dearest friend, a man who did not deserve to die so young. Then he had talked death, how it was not fair anymore, how good people died while bad people lived to old age. How the peacemakers died while tyrants lived forever. How infants died from hunger while cannibals thrived. She had never heard him talk so crazy and had never, in all of their life together, thought him capable of such heavy thoughts.

"He was so angry he wanted to kill somebody," she said to Janet. "I was shaking like a coward, waiting for him to take his stick and beat me senseless. But he did not do it. Instead, he told me not to leave him, that he loved me, and that he had thought over what I had told him, about his younger wife, and he had decided to take action."

"I think he is a wise man," Janet said.

"A wise man?" Hanna laughed. "I don't think so. He is afraid to die."

"Like all of us," Janet told her. "But you were very brave to tell him off like that."

"I was dying from fear," she said. "Waiting for him to beat my little brains out, as he had promised."

"But you had the courage," Janet said.

"I don't think so," she said uneasily. "I fear it may be too late."

"Then go for a test," Janet suggested. "It will give you peace of mind."

"I'm not so courageous," she conceded.

"At least you will know," Janet told her. "You will not worry about nothing."

"I could not live with such knowledge," she said convinced.

"A lot of people do," Janet told her. "People just like you and I."

"No, not people like me," Hanna laughed. "It would kill me. I am a screaming coward."

"You are not," Janet said to her. "You have just proved it. You have faced up to your greatest fear and made him see reason."

"That is different from knowing you are going to die," she said.

"We shall all die," Janet said to her. "We all know that, yet the knowledge does not kill us."

"But we do not know when or how we shall die," she argued. "I don't want to know that."

"We can never know that for certain," Janet assured her. "Not even when we know for certain that it will happen."

Hanna knew for certain that she did not want to know anything about her death. It would take the spice out of her life. She could never laugh again, and that would kill her.

"Have you been tested?" she asked Janet.

Janet had not.

"So you don't know either?" she asked.

"No," Janet said.

She did not know for certain either. She had not done any of the things that caused one to get Aids.

"Is it really true," Hanna asked her seriously, "Really, really true you have not had a man since Broker left? I'm your best friend and I'll not tell anyone."

It was Janet's turn to have a really, really good laugh.

"It's really, really true," she said laughing. "I have forgotten about it, I think."

"You are a very strange woman," Hanna said with some awe.

"That is what they tell me," Janet laughed with her.

"You know, I'm a bit like you," Hanna confided. "I can't stand the thought of another man touching me. I'm not one of those women who say there is spice in variety. Like that woman of Lewi? The young one he brought from Nairutia? I heard that she told Kongo's wife that her sister told her that another woman had told her that ...

When Hanna left, an hour later, after a refreshing session of hot, Crossroads gossip and explosive laugher, Janet had enough reason to smile. Now she knew for certain that it was possible to make Crossroads use condoms.

Chapter Thirty-Four

Years of living by herself had taught Janet self-sufficiency. Her vegetable garden was never without ready vegetables or seedlings, and her chicken house was never without chicks. She was the first out with the seeds, when the first rain of the season fell, and she was always busy planting, weeding or harvesting. Most times she did it alone, but sometimes Big Youth helped her. Sometimes Frank helped her too, when he despaired of trekking over Crossroads treating animals whose owners could not pay him.

They were in the vegetable patch behind the house, planting for the short rains, when she finally asked him, "Do you have a bed?"

They were elbow deep in soft, black earth, surrounded by seedbeds, and Frank had no idea what bed she meant.

"To sleep on," she said.

Of course, he had a bed, he told her. The teahouse was not as primitive as it appeared from the highway.

"Broker sleeps on the floor," she informed him.

"Broker wants to sleep on the floor," he said to her. "It's his own choice."

Broker had paid Musa to take the bed out of his room and to provide a second mattress. Broker paid Musa extra rent every week because his idiosyncrasy made his room that much harder to clean.

"Why does he want to sleep on the floor?" she asked perplexed.

"He's doing penance," Frank revealed.

Janet had never heard of such absurdity.

"But you have heard of Christians tearing off their rich clothes and wearing sackcloth to atone for their past sins and excesses," Frank said to her.

That she had.

And as for past sins and excesses, Broker probably had more than his share. Frank had heard him brag to the old men how he had slept in every hotel and boarding house and in every kind of bed ever invented by man; from bunk beds in roadside motels to waterbeds and featherbeds in luxurious five-star hotels. He had had more than his share of beds.

"And not cold ones at all, if you know what I mean," he had told them.

But, in order to find himself, he had had to return to his roots; right down on the ground where he was conceived, where he was born and where he would most likely die.

They were about to embark on a serious unravelling of the statement, when the ox rode up on his mechanical hyena and ordered them to the Chief's office.

"What has happened now?" Janet asked him.

"Nothing," he said.

"Then why are you here?" she asked him.

The Chief wanted to see her, he said. The Chief and the PC and the DC and the DO and the DHO and the DIO and the whole lot of them.

"The white men also," he added.

"White men?" she was suddenly alert.

"Which white men?" asked Frank.

"From the world," said the henchman. "The world ... something or something."

"Your visitors," Frank said to Janet.

"The North-South people?" Janet was astounded.

She had started to believe the whole thing a hoax, a bad joke played on her by some heartless bullock back at the Health Ministry's headquarters.

"What shall we do now?" she wondered out loud.

"Clean up and change," he said to her. "Then we'll go and meet them."

There was nothing else to do now but face them and find out what they wanted from her.

"I should have known," she said, gravely, as they walked back to the house.

For a moment there she had been too carefree, too happy for it to last. Now she was back in the real world, the world of worries. She put her hands to her temples and pressed hard. The migraine that had started with the return of Broker, and which she had thought she had overcome, was back. Her head throbbed.

"Go tell them we are on our way," Frank said to the henchman.

The henchman rode away and they set about tidying themselves up for the encounter with the outside world.

"Don't worry," Frank said to her. "Take them to one of your group meetings. Or take them to a school. They are here to see things, not to hear words. Show them the posters, they'll be impressed by the posters."

While she washed and changed, Frank racked his brain for what to do next.

On the way to the Chief's office, they stopped by the Condom Shop to warn Broker. He was already aware, having been alerted by the noisy arrival of a convoy of vehicles the like of which had not been seen in Crossroads since the death of the old highway.

"Don't worry," he said to Janet. "Go meet your important guests."

"And then?" she asked.

"Show them the sights," he said. "Then bring them round."

"Bring them here?" she cried.

"In a couple of hours," he said.

"Here?" she could not believe her ears. "To the shop?"

"To the shop," he said.

There was nothing to fear. Everything would be just fine.

"Trust me," he said.

She loathed the very words. She clenched her jaws, planted her feet firmly on the ground and put on a determined air. Broker smiled as he watched the fury build up in her and seethe and bubble and swell, until she transformed into the indomitable warrior that Crossroads knew her for and she was ready to take on the world.

"Go get them," Broker said to her. "Frank, you stay here! Can you drive?"

"No," Frank confessed.

"Never mind," Broker told him. "Get the old men from the teahouse. Get everyone you can. We shall need the beggar too. Where is Big Youth?"

Frank had no idea.

"Never here when you need him," Broker said with some annoyance. "Not to worry, we'll show them yet. Now here is what we must do."

The Chief's office was packed with people. Many of them were strangers but Janet recognised a few; the administration, the

301

community leaders and the regular lynch mob from the weekly Village Council.

Chief Chupa was there too, at the centre of a great confusion, and way out of his depth, trying to communicate with the visitors through the ox. There were seven white people, six men and a woman, all covered with the dust of their long journey from Pwani to Crossroads and unable to get a glass of water from the henchman who claimed to understand their language.

Chief Chupa had never been so happy to see Janet.

"*Hiyo*," he said to the visitors in a language they did not understand. "There she is. Ask her yourselves."

The visitors turned to Janet. One of them introduced himself as Don Donovan.

"We are looking for Janet Juma," he said to her.

She was Janet Juma, she told him.

"Then you know who we are," he said, with great relief.

She had received a letter, she said to him.

He shook her hand and introduced the team. Janet forgot their names almost instantly. She was so worried about what to tell him that she could hardly think.

"As we explained in the letter," the man was saying to her. "We are not here to inspect but to appreciate. Not to criticise but to compliment. We have heard very encouraging things about your work."

They had come to see for themselves what she had achieved and to assist her, in whichever way they could, to achieve greater success.

Janet smiled bravely and managed to welcome them to Crossroads, on behalf of herself and on behalf of the Chief and of all the assembled community leaders and of the people of Crossroads, a few of whom were assembling in the background waiting for the visitors to start handing out gifts. All of Crossroads had heard about Janet's letter, through the Chief's letter-steaming henchmen, and were certain that such generous visitors would not come and go and leave them empty-handed.

"Unfortunately, we haven't got much time," Don Donovan was saying to Janet.

They had lost precious time finding their way out of unmarked back roads and cattle trails, and still had several places to go after Crossroads. Now they were placing themselves in her capable hands and looking forward to an exceptionally successful tour.

"Show us everything," he said.

"Everything?" she was still in shock.

"Everything you can show us in the next three hours," he told her.

They started with the schools.

She decided to show them the schools she visited, especially those that were faraway and over the hills, in the hope that when they returned to Crossroads it would be too dark for them to see the Condom Shop.

When the convoy of rugged vehicles suddenly pulled up at Head Faru's school, it took everyone by surprise; it startled the teachers, and amazed the pupils, and disrupted lessons so thoroughly the Headmaster was alienated instantly.

"What do you want here?" he demanded of Janet, speaking in Crossroadian. "Why have you come here?"

"We are here to show the world the good work you are doing here," she said to him.

"What good work?" he asked confused.

"Educating the youth about Aids," she told him.

He was about to protest he did not teach such things, then saw all those people, most of them strangers, and some of them even white, and all of them listening. He took Janet aside and asked her what, in the name of the Almighty, she was trying to do to him.

"I thought I told you I don't want to lose my job," he said to her. "Who are all these people?"

"Friends," she told him.

"Whose friends?" he asked her.

"You will not lose your job," Janet assured. "We'll be gone in a moment."

"Have you cleared it with the Ministry?" he asked her.

While she thought of an appropriate reply to that one, the last vehicle in the convoy brought Chief Chupa and Inspector Iddi. Faru saw them arrive and, at once, knew that everything was in order. Inspector Iddi was the head of the DSS, a nebulous gang of law enforcers whose job was to silence dissenters and to shadow any foreigners that the Chief thought might disrupt the peace and stability prevailing in Crossroads. Faru welcomed the visitors, profusely urging them to feel at home in his school.

He conducted them from class to class where, in truth, they taught everything except condoms, and along the verandas, where that very week the Headmaster had, for the first time, allowed Janet to hang three of Big Youth's largest posters. The visitors saw the posters and were very impressed. The journalists took pictures of everything and the television crew filmed every step of the tour.

One journalist remarked that he had not, during their travel through Crossroads, seen any signs of organised garbage disposal. Indeed, he was disturbed by the amount of environmental pollution he had witnessed; the numerous plastic and paper bags blowing in the wind and hanging on fences and on trees all over the place.

"What do you do with your used condoms?" he wondered out loud.

The question was not addressed to anyone in particular. It was one of those anonymous missiles that journalists love to fire at smug authority, a terror cannon not aimed at any particular coordinates, and for a moment, no one dared touch it. But this was Head Faru's school and, like a natural host, he accepted the question.

"Used condoms?" he asked, even before the words had sunk in his brain. "Why do you ask me?"

"Into the latrine," Janet said quickly. "Not out in the compost with the household waste."

"Very good," Don Donovan sounded pleased.

He commended Faru for running such a well organised school and Faru was pleased too. Then the journalist wanted to interview some students.

"What for?" Faru asked bewildered. "They are only children. They don't know many things. Why must you talk to them?"

"To see what they know about the campaign," Janet said to him.

"What campaign?" he asked.

"The family life education campaign," she told him. "This is official."

Which Faru could tell, by the number of confounded Government officers who had come along for the show. His eyes met those of Chief Chupa, who was at that very minute wishing he had missed this thoroughly tedious expedition, and the Chief smiled reassuringly. There was nothing either of them could do now, for Janet had completely taken over leadership.

She led them to the senior class, where she was allowed to lecture to the seniors once a week; out in the field, away from the teachers and the younger pupils. The pupils were eager to be on television and some of the boys, it turned out, knew a whole lot more about condoms than Janet had taught them. The girls, on the other hand, knew just enough to pass their examinations, or so they let on. It was a free and lively discussion and everyone had fun. Everyone, except Head Faru, who was sweating his career away, and the teachers who had no idea what to do with the credit they got for teaching sex education.

Chief Chupa, and most of his entourage, had no idea what was said, and, wisely, kept out of range of the cameras. But Inspector Iddi, who was keenly listening to every word, understood a great deal. He would come back later with his DSS gang, and the Provincial Security Team, to grill Head Faru and his staff and find out if they really taught sex education

The visitors left the school impressed.

Their next stop was at Pastor Bat's church. The repairs had been completed and the foundation for the orphanage had been dug. About fifty children were playing in the field behind the church, while waiting for their meal, which was prepared in a makeshift kitchen under a tree.

"We are here to show the world what you have done for the orphans," Janet informed the Pastor.

"What have I done for the orphans?" he asked.

"You have given them a place to come to," Janet told him.

It pleased him to be thought good and generous, and he welcomed the visitors with open arms. He took them around his humble church and showed them everything there was to see. Such important people had never visited his church before and he agreed to be interviewed by them. Not even Janet understood a word he said.

Afterwards, she showed the visitors the true extent of the devastation that Aids had wreaked on Crossroads, the places where it had harvested every man, woman and child and left the homesteads empty and deserted. She took them to homesteads that were occupied only by very old people and to others where very young children had long learned to live by themselves.

Finally, thoroughly depressed by what they had seen, the delegation asked to see Janet's office. The request caught her completely off guard.

"My office?"

She had worried about everything except this. Why should they now wish to see her office? Their allotted time was long over and they should have been jumping into their big cars and going away.

"We would like to see how you work," Don Donovan told her. "How this great work is coordinated."

She had no idea what he meant by coordinated. What coordination was there to do? She did the work she had to do, any which way she could. Offices and coordinations were tools she did not possess. But he was a friendly man, and his big-toothed smile inspired trust, and she felt called upon to tell him the truth.

"I have no office," she confessed. "I work from my house."

"Very well then," he said. "Take us to your work place."

Before she could think of an excuse, he had hopped into his vehicle and the others followed his example. Janet got in beside him and the magnificent convoy rocked its way to her house.

Broker lay half asleep on a sack by the grain store while Frank sat on a stool by the door of Janet's house. They were both equally exhausted, having walked and worked like they had never done before in their lives.

Janet had expected them to be in Crossroads, winding up business and demolishing the Condom Shop and she was puzzled to find them at her house.

The yard was impossibly clean and there was not a single old stool, wastepaper or any sort of rubbish littering the place. It appeared like someone had swept the compound clean and disposed of the chicken droppings as well.

"This is not my place," she thought as she looked around.

She did not ask Frank and Broker what they were doing there and they did not offer any explanation. They just watched quietly from the background, as she took her visitors on a tour of the place.

Then she opened the grain store, throwing the door wide open for Don Donovan to behold the tons of condoms she had not been able to give out.

Don Donovan peered in the store, made some satisfied noises and informed her she was out of stock. Janet looked in the store and was amazed and astonished to find only one carton of condoms in an otherwise spotlessly clean store.

She turned to Frank and Broker and found them excessively busy avoiding her eyes.

"Do you have a clinic," Don Donovan asked her.

"Not here," Broker said stepping forward. "The clinic is in Crossroads."

Janet grabbed at the doorframe and held on to it to stop herself falling to the ground from shock.

"I'm Bakari Ben Broker," Broker said to Don Donovan. "Janet's assistant."

Janet's vision suddenly blurred. The earth spun in her eyes and she leaned on the grain store, faint from shock. She watched in horror as Broker grabbed the visitor's hand, and pumped it vigorously, and spewed a stream of words that were completely meaningless to Janet. Her head was about to explode from the hammering within and her ears were on fire. Why did she ever trust this man? Why? Why? Why?

"This place is too small for a clinic," Broker was saying to Don Donovan. "So Janet thought it wiser to locate the clinic closer to the people. I'll take you there, if you like."

"We'd like," Don Donovan said happily.

Janet gasped and, mistaking her reaction for modesty, he smiled and said to her, "We'd like to see your humble clinic, if you don't mind."

Everyone piled back into the vehicles. Janet, almost dead from despair and migraine, got in next to Don Donovan. Broker and Frank rode in the back, squeezed in among the camping gear and the luggage. As the vehicles rocked along the cattle trails, she turned to Broker and, speaking in Crossroadian, asked him what in the name of sanity he thought he was doing to her.

"Helping," he told her.

"How?" she had hardly the strength to ask.

"You will see," he said and smiled. "You will see."

She turned to Frank, her last hope for some truth and sanity, and asked him where all the condoms had gone to.

"Don't worry," he told her.

But she worried. To put her mind at ease, he informed her that he had shifted the boxes of condoms to Grandmother's place. Broker had taken the rest of the condoms to the Condom Shop, where the convoy was now headed.

"Don't worry," he said again. "Everything is safe."

"And the shop?" she turned to Broker. "Did you have to bring that up?"

"They'll love the shop," Broker assured her. "You will see."

They travelled the rest of the way in tense silence.

Chapter Thirty-Five

Janet was beside herself with worry, as the convoy of vehicles drove down the potholed street past the teahouse to the Condom Shop. The shop was still standing, for the whole world to see.

Her worry turned to horror when she saw the line of boys waiting in front of the Condom Shop. And that was not all. The word *Shop* was gone from the board above the door and in its place was a hastily scrawled *Clinic*. The paint was still wet and glistening, and in places beginning to drip, but it hardly mattered now. Janet's career was over, her job gone to hell, and there was nothing to do now but go home and wait for her letter of dismissal.

Big Youth sat behind the counter with his arms folded in the manner of a serious shopkeeper and waited for the order to start dishing out condoms. The visitors alighted and Broker gave the pre-arranged signal. The boys surged forward and Big Youth started handing out condoms, keeping the tally on an exercise book by his elbow.

"Condom Clinic?" Don Donovan enthused. "Marvellous! How does it work?"

"Very simple," Broker said, effectively taking over from the exhausted Janet. "Just as you see, the customers ... the clients queue up here to receive their requirements of free condoms."

"Free?" Janet was truly puzzled.

"Of course," Broker told her.

"Free," Frank confirmed.

Janet's relief was overwhelming.

"Can I film this?" the cameraman asked her.

"Be my guests," Broker said to him.

The crew got busy with their equipment.

Uncle Mark and Mzee Musa ventured out of the teahouse to join the growing number of curious onlookers and to wonder what in the world was going on.

Janet had only the vaguest idea and Frank and Broker were too busy to answer questions. Broker noted, with some satisfaction, that Big Youth was using the Parker pen he had brought him from Makutano to scribble figures in the exercise book.

One of the journalists was concerned about the ages of the clients and wondered how many condoms they received.

"Six," blurted Big Youth.

"Six?" Broker exclaimed.

"They are young, boss," Big Youth said grinning happily.

Broker summoned him aside and demanded to know if he had gone completely mad.

"No, boss," Big Youth answered.

"Then why are you giving so many condoms to these boys?" Broker asked him.

"I asked them how many condoms they wanted," Big Youth explained.

"But six condoms?" Broker was about to explode. "Have you told them they must return them at once?"

"At once, boss?" Big Youth asked uncertainly.

"As soon as the visitors have left?" Broker said to him.

"I forgot to, boss," he said fearfully. "But I'll tell them now."

"Not now, you idiot," Broker told him harshly. "I'll kill you for this, I promise you. Wait until the visitors have left."

Don Donovan was, in the meantime, engrossed in discussion with Janet. Broker joined them to ask her, in Crossroadian, if she had told the white man her wishes yet. She replied that he had not asked and she had not had the chance and, besides, she did not think it was such a good idea to ask for anything at all.

The cameraman interrupted to ask Broker if he would kindly organise the queue for visual variety.

"A few mature faces will do," the man said. "A face such as his and his and his."

He was pointing at Chief Chupa and his henchmen.

They stared back at him, dumbstruck, then cried in unison when Broker translated the request.

"Who, me?" Chief Chupa cried, dying from embarrassment. "I can't do that. I am their Chief here; tell the white man that I can't use *kodoms*."

"What about you?" Broker turned to the DO

"Who, me?" said the DO "I am a Government man too. We are all Government men here. We must not be photographed using *kodoms*."

The others with him agreed vehemently and Broker was at a loss. He turned to the cameraman and said, loudly, "They are all camera-shy. I'll have to do it myself."

He stepped forward, hoping to encourage others to do likewise, but no one joined him in the line.

"Musa?" he called out. "Come here, old bull."

"Will they pay me?" Musa asked him.

"Don't be foolish," Broker told him. "Join the line!"

Musa stayed put. The beggar jumped in the line, unasked, and they let him stay. Uncle Mark, after a moment of serious doubts and self-searching, joined them too and dragged Musa into the line. Musa grumbled, but stayed in the line.

"This is for Janet," he said to Broker.

"I know," Broker said.

The line inched forward. The camera zoomed in on Broker.

"I'm HIV positive," Broker said to the camera. "I'm a total man, but I'm careful. I know that I can live an active life in spite of having Aids."

Broker said many more things besides; answering questions that the journalist thought about but did not believe anyone in the ramshackle town could understand. He told the journalist of the poverty of the people, the conditions that rendered the community incapable of affording the most basic hygiene and medicine, let alone latex condoms.

He talked of the ignorance that shackled the people to the earth like beasts of burden and the illiteracy that made it impossible for the community to understand Aids, and its potential for annihilation. And, of course, there were not just the economic and the literacy factors to consider. There were also the cultural and the social dimensions as well. For Janet, a woman in a land of men who prided themselves on being the most virile and the most total men in the world, to stand up to them and tell them they were wrong took a lot more than dedication to duty.

Broker talked at length about Janet, what a good and honest person she was and what a tough battle she had to put up, against insurmountable odds, in her determination to educate Crossroads on the monster that was about to devour them all. He talked about his own, not too meagre role in the campaign to save Crossroads from Aids. He said so many things about himself that the camera ran out of tape.

The assistant changed tapes and the cameraman moved on. He sought another old face in the line and found that of old Musa, wrinkled like old leather, streaked with soot and ashes and as angry as a rhino with a poacher's arrow up his rectum.

"What do you have to say, old timer?" the journalist asked him.

Musa had no idea what they wanted him to say. He turned to Uncle Mark for interpretation. Uncle Mark was himself staring at Broker with utter consternation and marvelling at the man's incorrigibility. He had never, in all his travels near and far, been much of a talker, and he was astounded at how easily Broker span yarns and how convinced he seemed of the things he said. So what was Musa supposed to do now? Speak the mundane truth? Admit he had no idea what the fuss was all about or tell lies?

He turned to Uncle Mark and asked what the *mzungu* wanted from him. Uncle Mark translated the white man's question.

"Me?" Musa asked in Crossroadian. "You know I don't do that business, Old Bull."

"If you did," Uncle Mark said to him, "Would you?"

"Me?"

"You," Uncle Mark said. "That is what the *mzungu* wants to know."

When he had woken up that morning, no one had told Musa that by the time the day ended, he would have been questioned about *kodoms* by strange white faces with recording machines. He, in any case, had not seen one until recently, had never used a *kodom* and his opinion of *kodoms* was unspeakable. So what was he supposed to say?

"Something wise," said Uncle Mark. "Something to help these young bulls who must face life as it comes."

He was about to turn about and go back to his teahouse, when Broker stepped in smoothly and saved the day.

"Tells us," Broker urged. "A world-wise man like you, surely uses a condom."

"I do?" Musa was now scandalised.

"Why?" Uncle Mark nudged him again.

"Why what?" he asked, confounded.

"Come on, old bull," Uncle Mark leaned over and spoke to him in a language only old bulls understood. "You don't have to know anything at all; say whatever you know and make the white face smile and all of us happy."

Musa did not want to say anything for anybody. He wanted to be out of there, with his reputation intact, and back to where he had control. But he and Uncle Mark went way back and, as far as Janet was concerned, he had never dreamt he would live to see the day she would need him this much.

"Why do I need *kodoms*?" he asked himself, turning to face the camera.

Then, remembering the number of times he had teased Janet with the same question, he smiled and tried to remember all the things he had heard about condoms since the Condom Shop opened.

"Why do I need *kodoms*?" he repeated to himself. "Because *kodoms* are good. Yes, *kodoms* are good. *Kodoms* are good because ... because they stop women being pregnant."

And that was just about it. That was all he could think of to say about condoms. Everything else he had heard about condoms was just too preposterous for a respectable old man to repeat in public. He looked around, feeling very foolish and inadequate indeed, and was encouraged to see them all nodding wisely and agreeing with whatever it was that he had said.

Broker made the translation. His translation was even less adequate, judging by the pained expression on the white journalist's face.

"*Kodoms* also prevent plague," Uncle Mark added, to help his friend out.

"If everyone used *kodoms*," Musa went on, encouraged. "There would not be so much dying as there is now. So I think that *kodoms* are good. They are also very cheap."

"Free," Broker informed.

"Free?" Musa was genuinely astonished.

"Absolutely free," Broker confirmed.

"But just this morning ..."

"Free," Broker said tersely. "OK?"

"OK," Musa said. "They are free, absolutely."

Then, having said so much regarding something that he knew absolutely nothing about, he turned and marched angrily back to his teahouse.

The camera moved on, to everyone's relief, and sought out another interesting face in the queue. It found that of the old beggar, grinning from ear to ear and happy to be a part of *whatever-*

on-earth-was-going-on. Certain that now his turn had come, he stuck his hand out at the camera and said promptly, "Give me money."

Where upon Broker grabbed him roughly and shoved him out of the line.

"Forget this madman," he said to the journalist. "Talk to this other old man here. Uncle Mark is the wisest man in Crossroads. Ask him, he knows everything."

The journalist turned to Uncle Mark while Broker took the beggar aside and gave him money and ordered him to take the rest of the day off. The beggar went happily back to his telephone booth and Broker went to see how Janet was getting on.

She was deep in discussion with Don Donovan. The visitors were more than happy with her work.

"Are you married?" he was asking her.

She hesitated to answer and Broker interrupted to ask what the visitors thought of her clinic.

"Brilliant idea," said Don Donovan.

He was more than impressed by what he had seen in Crossroads. He expressed his gratitude to Chief Chupa and to Janet for running such an effective campaign. Chupa was ecstatic, pumping the visitor's hand repeatedly.

"Before we leave," Don Donovan finally asked Janet. "Is there anything you would like us to do for you?"

Janet was overwhelmed.

"Anything that would enhance your work?" he asked her.

She had dreaded this moment since the visitors' arrival. There was no doubt in her mind, and she knew exactly what she wanted, but it seemed all so absurd now that she could not get it out of her mouth.

"Transport," Broker said to Don Donovan.

"Transport?" Don Donovan asked puzzled.

"A vehicle," he said. "A car, to be exact."

"A car?" Chief Chupa understood that much, and he was not at all amused.

"A small one," Broker said, still addressing Don Donovan. "Like one of those Japanese wonders that go everywhere."

He was pointing at one of them in the convoy that had brought the visitors from Pwani.

"A Jeep?" the Chief was apoplectic. "What on earth for? What do you need a car for?"

"For her work," Broker was still talking to Don Donovan, and trying to control his rage. "You have seen the distances she has to cover to make house calls. She carries her wares on her head, inside those giant cartons you saw at her house."

"On her head?" exclaimed the Chief's henchman. "But she has a bicycle?"

No one heard him.

"The cartons disintegrate when it rains," Broker was saying to Don Donovan. "They cannot withstand wetness. They just fall apart when wet."

And the contents spilt out and floated away in the gutters and the ditches, from where they were swept into the waterways to pollute the streams and the dams and the rivers.

"It's not a healthy sight, I can assure you," Broker concluded.

Don Donovan nodded in agreement and thought that it was not an unreasonable request.

"*Lakini* she can't drive," the Chief told him in Crossroadian.

"She will learn," Broker assured the Chief.

"*Lakini* she is a woman," the Chief said ardently. "She is only a woman."

Broker smiled nicely at him, as to a well-meaning but very misguided imbecile, and asked him to pick up his fat behind and get lost, as this discussion had nothing at all to do with him.

The Chief grumbled and promised to have Broker arrested for disrespecting him. He was the Chief, the Government man, and he had to know everything that went on in Crossroads.

Don Donovan had no inkling what the fat, old fool was grumbling about and turned to Janet, who stood with a transfixed stare on her face, smiling as if the whole exchange had nothing to do with her.

"I like your assistant," he said to her. "He's a very astute man."

This inspired Broker to ask, "Well, what about it?"

"Cars don't come cheap," Don Donovan said.

"I know that," he said. "I have one of my own."

"A Jeep?" Don Donovan asked.

"A *BMW*," he said.

"My last car was a *BMW*," Don Donovan told him.

"Mine was a *Volvo*," Broker said.

"A *Volvo*?" Don Donovan was impressed. "I own a *Volvo* myself. What model was yours?"

Janet watched helplessly, and quite disgustedly, as Broker hijacked her guest and led him on a wild chase into unfathomable, egoistic labyrinths, where truth had no meaning whatsoever and only cars mattered, and they forgot about Crossroads. They discussed cars for a long time, while Janet fretted and Chief Chupa seriously worried that Broker might survive to usurp his throne.

"We'll look into the budget," Don Donovan promised Broker. "We should be able to afford a Jeep for her."

Then Janet opened her mouth and reversed every gain that Broker had made in the last half hour. What she really wanted, she said it loudly so as not to be misunderstood, what she really wanted, more than a car and more than anything else, was to have a free medical test for Crossroads.

They were startled into silence. Sensing something vital was at stake here, Chief Chupa turned to his henchman and asked what she had said. The ox had no idea, but Broker overheard them, and he was incensed enough with Janet to tell them exactly what she had asked for.

"*Haui!*" cried the Chief horrified. "You mean to test everyone?"

"Everyone who consents to it," she told him.

"Do you know what it would cost?" he asked her.

Broker patted him gently on the shoulder and assured him that it would cost the earth, but asked him not to lose any sleep over it, for it was not his money and he had exactly zero to do with it.

"Can anyone pay?" Don Donovan asked.

"No," Janet told him.

"What is the population of this place?" he asked them next.

No one had any idea.

"The last meaningful census was thirty years ago," Janet told him.

Before Aids made its first appearance. Since then, people had died like flies and everyone had lost count.

"Many people are ill, anyway" Broker said. "We are talking very small numbers, indeed."

"So you think it's a good idea too?" Don Donovan asked him.

Broker saw the anguish on Janet's face, but this was a once-in-a-life-time and he decided to speak his mind and be damned for all time.

"No," he said, speaking the absolute truth for the first time that day. "I don't think it's such a good idea at all."

The money could be better off used in providing medical support for those who were sick and protection for those who were not. That was his honest opinion.

Janet was so disgusted she was about to spit in his face.

"But it's all up to Janet," he added. "She knows best the problems of Crossroads."

Don Donovan nodded thoughtfully and said, "We'll look into the budget."

Then he thanked them all for a very enlightening tour and promised to get in touch in due course. The delegation piled into their new vehicles and left Crossroads, in the same rush they had arrived in.

The last vehicle had not completely left Crossroads before Broker called back the boys and ordered them to surrender all the condoms they had received from Big Youth. The crowd dispersed, and were no better off, or worse off, than when they had arrived; except for the few youths who had had the foresight to disappear before Broker demanded the condoms back.

A few old-timers lingered, and were heard to complain that they had not come all this way and waited all this long in the sun for nothing; and they now wanted the presents that the visitors had brought for them. What had happened to the money that the visitors had brought? they asked. Why was it not being dished out? They wanted answers to these questions, and they wanted them now, and they refused to go home empty-handed.

They confronted Chief Chupa and demanded the money that his henchmen had promised would be distributed by the visitors with the many cars.

Chief Chupa, totally confounded by the news himself, turned to Janet for help, and Janet obliged him, as only Janet could.

Giving vent to the anger and the fury she had endured since Broker told Don Donovan about the clinic, she responded by giving the old men a tongue-lashing the like of which they had never had before. What was the matter with Crossroads' men? she asked them. Did they grow up and turn to animals or were they hyenas from birth? Did they think with their heads, with their stomachs or with their tails? When would they mature, start behaving like men? When would they realise that they were husbands and fathers, and not scavengers?

She insulted them for a full ten minutes, and no one dared answer back, but, when she was done, they grumbled some more and swore not to leave before the money and the presents had been distributed. They were not fools, they said, they were total men and they had not come all the way out here to be insulted by a woman, not even one who shaved every morning. They insisted that their Chief discipline the insolent woman and force her to hand out the money they knew she had been paid. But Chief Chupa had received the visitors himself, and had been with Janet all day, and he knew of no such money or presents, and he suspected that there wasn't any, and he too was helpless against this tempestuous woman.

It was going to sunset before most of them understood, and believed, that there would be no communal eating happening that day, and dispersed. They went away disgruntled, and lamenting it, all the way to their homes to vent their anger on their own hapless women.

Thus ended another great day in Crossroads, arguably the greatest day since Mobil brought out the giant cranes and tractors to exhume and carry away the corpses of the old fuel tanks from the impotent belly of Juma's service station; the underground fuel reservoirs that they had thought the town would never again need.

And Uncle Mark and Mzee Musa retreated to the teahouse veranda, from where they watched the cynics depart, reluctantly, to return to their accustomed oblivion.

Mzee Musa marvelled -, without real surprise - that, with such a gathering camped nearly for the whole day at his doorstep, he had not sold a single cup of tea. What was wrong with people?

Uncle Mark nodded wisely and tried to shrug the rising melancholia from his weary shoulders. With the parting of the crowd, something moved, something dark and sinister like the ghost of a looming disaster. Something cold and encircling like the belly of a swamp toad. Something apocalyptic, like the first labour pangs of a death too long in the womb.

Crossroads had silently, and without a struggle, sunk another foot in its yawning grave.

"Will anything come out of this?" Janet wondered to herself.

"Just might," Frank said encouragingly.

"But don't bet on it," Broker told them all.

He had witnessed many such a grand circus before. Tomorrow the show would be somewhere else, doing something else equally vital to the people it concerned. And also living and making a living for the wives and the children and the *Volvo* back home. As for Crossroads ...

"You said it yourself," he said to Janet. "It's up to Crossroads itself."

Sadness and gloom covered them with grief.

"But we gave it a fair shot, didn't we?" Broker added, laughing sadly. "No one will ever say we did not try."

"Did you get the car?" Big Youth asked Janet.

"No," Janet told him.

"What did you get?" he asked.

"I don't know," she said.

"You got nothing," Broker informed her, with a touch of bitter resentment.

"Nothing?" Big Youth was appalled.

"Zero," Broker told him. "That is what she got."

"You mean we did all that work for nothing?" Big Youth was devastated.

"No," Janet said. "I don't think so."

"Yes!" Broker said harshly. "You did all that work for nothing."

She did not argue with him. She was about to die from disappointment herself and Frank did not know what to do about any of it.

Then Big Youth remembered he had his bookwork to do and they released him. Janet had to go home to cook for her children, and to think things over, and they released her too. Broker offered to drive her home, but she wanted to walk, alone, and to do her thinking on the way. She asked them to come around for dinner later on in the evening. Broker declined. He too had thoughts to think and things to do and he had to remain open a little longer and see what happened. Besides, Highlife Alice had not come for her daily supply of condoms.

Then he looked up and saw again the false sign hanging over the door of the shop and remembered.

"Hey you!" he called after Big Youth. "This is a Condom Shop!"

Big Youth looked back confounded and spread his arms to ask, "So?"

"Get rid of this *clinic* nonsense!" Broker commanded him.

"Tomorrow," he promised.

"And get back the free condoms you gave to your friends," Broker shouted after him.

Big Youth laughed and went on his way.

When they were all gone, Broker sat down to think the day over and to wait for the one sure customer in the whole of Crossroads. He could not help but feel that, all in all, the day had gone much better than anyone could have hoped.

Chapter Thirty-Six

They were waiting for dinner, when Julia called, all excited and wanting to talk to Janet, alone.

Frank withdrew to the kitchen, ostensibly to see how the food was cooking, and left them to it. When he was safely out of the way, Julia reached under her shawl and handed Janet back the book she had borrowed.

"Did you show him," Janet asked her.

"He was horrified," she said.

Kata had been so shocked by the pictures in the book he had finally talked about those *things*.

"Condoms?" Janet asked her.

"Not so loud," she said.

"You talked to Kata about condoms?" Janet lowered her voice with difficulty.

"I did," Julia was ecstatic.

"You talked to Kata about condoms?" Janet said flabbergasted. "Did you hear that, Frank?"

"Will you now tell the whole world?" she said uneasily. "That is why I can't tell you everything. Kata will kill me when he finds out I told you."

"But this is good news," Janet said to her. "How did you do it? How did you make Kata talk about condoms?"

Julia had started by reminding Kata of her own fears over his inheriting his brother's wife. At first, he had raved and ranted and refused to talk about it. He was a man, he said, and he could do exactly as he wanted. He did not have to discuss his personal things with his women. Then Julia had threatened to leave him, unless he sat down and discussed their future together. Kata had raved and ranted some more, but he had finally sat down, after making certain that there was no one about to witness the scandalous event. Then she had brought out the book and shown it to him.

"Where did you get this?" he had asked after turning a few pages.

"I told him you gave it to me," Julia said to Janet. "To show him what would happen to him if he did not change his ways."

"Will that sister of yours never cease to annoy me?" Kata had asked, shaking his head in despair.

Then he had turned a few more pages, and a few more, until he came to the very end of the book. When he finally closed it, his face was the colour of a dead lizard. His stomach had quaked and grumbled loudly, and his heart had heaved to the roof of his mouth. He had swallowed it back and, clenching his jaws like a man, had forced it back way down in his body and sat on it. He had sat very still for a long moment. Julia had left him to fight it out with himself, like a man, and he had fought it out till he had finally triumphed and life had returned to his face. Then she had asked him what he intended to do about it all.

"We talked about everything," Julia said to Janet. "He said he must inherit his brother's wife, that is the tradition. His clan expects it and the clan must have its way."

"But he must not share her bed," Janet warned.

"He doesn't want to," she said. "She will live in her own house and he will visit her from time to time, to see that she is all right and to give her help. He said he would never sleep at her house."

"And you believed him?" Janet was incredulous.

"I'm not stupid," Julia told her. "I know how mad men are. From now on, no taking chances."

"And what did he say?" Janet asked.

"I am your man," Kata had said with fire in his mouth. "I will protect you!"

"Just like a man," Janet observed.

"Just like a man," Julia agreed. "But I told him that was not enough. I must also protect myself. He was not very happy about that."

Then they had talked and talked, for nearly the whole night.

"If I ever catch you with another man," he had finally said to her. "I will kill you. Do you hear me? I will kill you!"

"Just like a man," Janet observed.

"Just like a man," Julia agreed.

"But I'm so happy for you," Janet told her. "You have won a great victory today."

"But are those things safe?" she asked apprehensive.

"Much safer than not," Janet told her.

"You mean they are not completely safe?" she sounded disappointed.

"Nothing is completely safe," Janet told her. "Only total abstinence is absolutely safe."

Julia wagged her head, uncertainly. She was a hot-blooded woman and not much given to self-denial. She had been that way ever since discovering men at the tender age of sixteen, when men were really mad after her. Then she had met Kata. Men were still mad after her now, but Kata's reputation with his circumcision knife was enough deterrence to keep them away from her.

"I will not lie to you," she now said to Janet. "I can't live without Kata. And I don't even know what those *things* look like."

Janet promptly opened a box and showed her a condom. She unwrapped it and let Julia look at it.

"I'm sure your husband knows what to do with it," Janet said to her. "It's really quite simple; but, if he doesn't know, bring him for a quick lesson!"

"I can't tell him I told you," Julia said.

"Where will you say you got the condoms?" Janet asked her. "He knows about the book, and he knows we talk about it."

Julia had no choice. Could she have one of those *things*?

"Just one?" Janet laughed merrily. "You have so many things to learn, my sister. But you have made me very proud of you today."

She gave her a whole box of condoms.

"We must not give Kata any excuse to go back to his old ways," she said. "The instructions are on the boxes."

"You won't tell Grandmother, will you?" Julia asked worried.

"So she can tell the world?" Janet laughed. "No, I won't tell Grandmother."

Julia wrapped the box in her shawl and left in a hurry.

"Frank," Janet could hardly contain the excitement. "Did you hear that, Frank?"

He had.

"She is a new woman now," Janet told him. "She has solved the Kata problem by herself."

"Not completely," Frank said, returning from the kitchen. "There is still Kata. Can she persuade him not to cut everyone with the same knife? And to disinfect his knives between jobs?"

"One hurdle at a time." Janet said. "One at a time."

"Shall we ever get there?" Frank wondered.

"The important thing is ..." Janet started.

"Never to despair," he said and shook his head in admiration.

He had just earned himself more than a nice, hot cup of cocoa, she told him. But he would have to wait until after dinner for it.

Chapter Thirty-Seven

Don Donovan and his team never came back to Crossroads, just as Broker had suspected, but the rains did come and those who had had the strength to till their land, planted. Some of them would live to see their crops thrive, mature and ripen, but most of them would be walking corpses by then, physically ravaged by Aids, sucked empty of all the vitality of life and too weak to harvest.

Then, one harvest day, a much smaller convoy came to Crossroads. They had been sent by the Ministry, they said, to carry out a survey. To find out how many people in Crossroads were infected with the virus.

Janet could hardly contain herself. No letter had preceded the visit and she was as surprised as the rest of the population about it. A makeshift consultation room was hastily cleared inside the derelict post office and word was sent out to summon the community. By mid-afternoon, a good crowd had abandoned their crops in the fields and gathered outside the post office. The Chief came with his gang of crowd busters, to find out what was happening, and to arrest anyone found making political speeches. They hastened away again when they heard it had all to do with Janet and her plague.

The hardest part, however, was getting the people of Crossroads to volunteer their blood for testing.

"Does it hurt?" they asked.

"Not at all," Frank assured them.

"Is it safe?" they asked.

"Absolutely," Broker confirmed.

"There is nothing to fear," Janet guaranteed them all.

"Then you go first," Big Youth said. "*Daktari*, you too go first."

Frank rolled up his sleeve and led the way inside the post office. Big Youth followed and some youths gathered enough courage to venture forth. A line formed. Soon a sizeable crowd was waiting in line to give their blood samples.

The beggar took the opportunity to go down the line asking for money from the steady stream of people entering the post office. Someone, probably Big Youth or one of his friends, had spread the rumour that there would be payment for the blood samples. However, the greatest crowd watched from across the street, vowing to never submit to any form of testing, paid or otherwise, for they were people, they said, not animals to be tested and examined and subjected to strange experiments.

"Why do they stand so faraway?" asked the European nurse who had come with the team.

"They are afraid to know the truth," Janet told her.

"In Europe too," she said to Janet, "there are people who would rather die than know the truth."

Her name was Janice, she had told Janet during their lengthy conversation while they waited for the community to assemble. She was from Ireland and was a volunteer with a European aid agency involved in the provision of primary health care to poor rural communities around the world. She had been all over, seen everything and nothing could shock her.

"You think your men folk are stubborn?" she said. "You should try talking to ours."

Which was enlightening, but not in any way comforting.

More and more people came, until Crossroads looked like a market day of old; people crowding the verandas of the post office, and of the teahouse, and sitting on the banks of the road while others climbed on trees to see better what was going on; which was nothing really, for all the action was inside the post office, where the medical team had a devil of a time convincing the volunteers that they would not die from giving a few drops of blood for testing.

By the end of the day, only a fraction of the population had given their samples. But they were adequate for the purpose of statistics, Janice assured Janet. They had samples from a whole cross-section of the community, old and young, male and female, literate and illiterate, rich and poor, and that was all they needed. The results would give Janet more information than she needed to plan her campaign. The results though would take a while to process.

The team went away, promising to return when the results were ready, and the crowd dispersed, grumbling about having wasted their whole harvest day for nothing.

Crossroads sighed back into its accustomed languor and resumed its normal state - that of continuous dying. Everything returned to normal; life stirred and went on as usual or, as was mostly the case, ceased to go on as usual. And Janet stepped up her campaign, certain now that change would come, that change was imminent, for the threshold had been breached, and there was no way to go now but forward.

Broker concentrated on his new passion, building. He spent long hours with all manner of builders and engineers. He brought out a Chinese constructor from Pwani to commence work on the service station and insisted that the constructor live at the teahouse. This endeared Broker to Musa a great deal. But, after only a few days of Musa's cooking, his Chinese contractor fled Crossroads, with Broker's money in his pocket, and Broker had to hire an Indian mason from Sokoni, who brought his own lunchbox to work, would not touch Crossroads water, and insisted on going back to Sokoni every evening after work.

Broker personally supervised the digging of the foundation for the orphanage. Everything was done with pick and shovel by a gang of labourers from Sokoni, for there were no labourers in Crossroads strong enough to wield these tools, and it took a long time. And when the projects were progressing to his satisfaction, he took time off to mind the Condom Shop, to work on his new formula *Goats' Powder* and to play a game of draughts with the old men.

Days came and went.

There were repeated reports of strangers in big cars roaming the countryside again and hopelessly losing themselves in the devastated landscape. Some reports said the men were prospectors from Johannesburg looking for gold. Other reports said that the strangers were Janet's cohorts, looking for those who had refused to donate their blood and they were going to take it from them by force this time. Still other rumours, no less fantastic, said the men were Government agents hunting for the legendary *wa Guka*. Whichever version one chose to believe, the rumours were terribly unsettling, for Crossroads was too weak to resist an invasion, even a friendly one.

The rumours were cause for lengthy, and often acrimonious, exchanges at the draught table, where Broker and Uncle Mark passed away the long evening hours before retiring to their lonely beds. There was no gold in Crossroads, Uncle Mark assured everyone. He had scoured those hills himself, in search of everything, from herbal roots to leopard skins. Had there been gold in under Crossroads, he would have found it long ago.

"Wouldn't it be just hysterical, though," he said one evening. "If God were to give us massive finds of gold moments before wiping us out with His plague?"

"It wouldn't surprise me at all," Broker grumbled. "Him and that old preacher must know something we don't."

He was hurting terribly, as he did most nights after dark, and was not in a good mood. In fact, he was outraged by the injustice of it all; the pain in his body was more than a man should have to bear.

"If the idea is to polish us all off," he said indignantly. "To nullify, to cancel out His greatest creation - why not send down the fire and brimstone the preachers rave about?"

"Plagues were promised too," Uncle Mark observed moving his turn.

"But not this plague!" Broker cried in anger. "We cannot survive Aids; man must have children. The human race must thrive, procreate."

"But do so sensibly," Uncle Mark said.

This plague was unfair, Broker grumbled, groaning with deep-down despair, and scratching an itch in his side that would not go away.

"He hit us too hard," he complained. "With one blow, He got everyone - father, mother and the children too."

"The sons shall pay inherit the sins of their fathers," Uncle Mark said with his irritating amusement. "That too is written down somewhere, I believe."

"But it hurts too much," Broker said through clenched teeth. "It hurts too much."

"It's meant to hurt," Uncle Mark told him. "Lest we forget who is mightier."

Broker slammed his piece on the table and swore in a most unfriendly language. What kind of crap talk was this? Who did Uncle Mark think he was, the prophet of doom? If Broker had wanted a sermon, he would have gone to Pastor Bat.

"What is the matter with you today?" he raged at the old man. "Can't you agree with me even a little?"

"I didn't know you wanted me to agree with you," Uncle Mark regretted.

"Now you know," Broker said. "Play on."

They played on, in tense silence. The smoky hurricane lamp hissed on over their heads and cast a pale light on the board between them.

Meanwhile in the hot and dark kitchen, Mzee Musa continued his search for new tastes with which to tantalise them. He had already, thanks to his willing guinea pigs, invented a new *mandazi* out of sweet potato.

A few days later, mayhem came to Crossroads.

It arrived suddenly and in a flurry of unmitigated violence. Someone, Broker never found out who, had directed the strangers in the big cars to the Condom Shop, with the assurance that, there they would find whatever it was that they were looking for. Dozens of large cars converged on Crossroads and descended on the Condom Shop, to disgorge a savage army of big, men.

They found Broker dozing in his chair, warding off the flies, and the pain, by dreaming up new projects for Crossroads, surrounded him and ordered him to lie down and identify himself or be shot to death.

Broker did not budge from his seat; he had long passed the stage where the threat of death could make him do anything. He watched them rave and rant, and behave exactly like a bunch of police savages he had once witnessed shoot a drunken man to death, for threatening them with a walking stick. He had dealt with the type before, and he knew where they were coming from; knew of their hungers, their fears and their insecurities that turned them into beasts. And, because he did not care whether they shot him dead on or not, Broker found them comical in extreme.

When he was through laughing at them, he invited them all to the teahouse and introduced them to Mzee Musa and his sweet potato *mandazi*.

They ate hungrily.

Crossroads, they revealed, was just about the hungriest place they had ever looked for a fugitive. They ate up all of Musa's *mahamri masala*, pumpkin *sambusas* and even *exodus special*. When no one dropped dead from it all, Broker gave Musa a discreet thumbs-up and signalled him to bring out the full works, the whole range of experimental delicacies, new inventions that had been lying under the kitchen table for weeks for lack of willing guinea pigs.

The strangers stayed with Broker for more than an hour, eating and talking like old friends. Then they had to go continue their manhunt and they promised Musa they would drop in on him from time to time, to see how he was doing and to partake of his delicious cooking. Musa thanked them all for their generous patronage and invited them to come back as many times as they liked. He would always be there to receive them and to serve them to the best of his ability.

Amused by the false civility, and the blatant insincerity, Broker smiled wearily and led the man hunters back to the Condom Shop. There he thanked them for coming, and wished them well in their hunt and, assuring them that Crossroads was more dangerous than even they imagined, sent them away armed with free condoms.

Chapter Thirty-Eight

Broker was alone at the teahouse when Janet called to see him. She had not seen him for a while and wondered how he was.

"Very well," he said to her.

He was in top form, all things considered.

"And you?" he asked her. "How are you?"

"I have no headache today," she informed him.

"Headache?" he laughed weakly. "How I wish I only had a headache."

His body was such a huge ache that a mere headache would have been an entertaining diversion.

"I've come to buy you tea," she informed him.

She looked around puzzled. Where were the idle old men? she asked him.

Uncle Mark had gone away on one of his mysterious visits. He had widows who needed solace, and spinsters who needed comfort and advice, and would be gone till dark. Then he would return extremely exhausted, having graciously partaken of their hospitality and eaten several dinners and drunk numerous cups of tea.

"Musa?" Janet asked.

Musa was in the kitchen dreaming up new recipes to poison his customers with.

"Musa?" she called to the kitchen. "Give us some tea!"

Broker regarded her with wonder. When he first met her, Janet was Jamila, a shy girl who would not look him in the eye, and was chaperoned everywhere she went. Now she talked loudly and clearly and men listened when she talked.

Musa brought them tea and *mandazi* and reported that he was about to embark on a new venture – kale-filled *sambusas*. Janet wished him well, but she decided to stay with his plain old *mandazi* that she knew. There were only a limited number of ways that *mandazi* could go wrong. As for kale *sambusas* - the very idea had flaws she did not have time to go into.

Musa went morosely back to the kitchen to invent some more. He paused at the door to ask Janet whether he should add carrots or *dhania* and onions to the kale *sambusas*. She informed him that his *sambusas* could not get any worse than they already were and suggested he add anything and everything he could think of and see what happened. He grunted and left them to their tea.

They talked about this and talked about that and nothing in particular.

Out of the window they could see the Condom Shop, where Big Youth lounged in Broker's favourite chair, waiting for customers who rarely came. It was a futile and tedious job. According to very suspect statistics, assembled by Big Youth during his long idle hours at the shop, the average Crossroadian used one and a half condoms a month. This was discouraging news for Janet. At that rate, the current stock of condoms at the shop would be moth-bitten and mouldy before they were all sold out. Big Youth's suggestion that they sell the condoms by the kilo had received a resounding and unanimous thumbs-down. Good intentioned, but extremely daft, Broker had warned, and ordered him to stop thinking like that, like a moron, and to refrain from compiling bogus statistics of any kind for a while.

Was it possible, Broker now wondered, that someone somewhere was under-cutting them; deliberately depriving them of their business?

Janet did not think so; after all, the condoms were going just as fast as they had when they were free; which was some kind of success.

Was it possible, she wondered, that Big Youth had a racket of his own of which they knew nothing about?

Broker did not think so. He had sealed all the possible loopholes and Frank kept a tight control on the inventory.

"You, *Meya*," the beggar materialised at their table.

"Not now, Mayor," Broker told him. "I'm talking to my wife."

"Is Auntie your wife now?" asked the beggar.

"You better believe it," Broker answered.

The beggar hesitated, then quietly withdrew.

"How come you didn't tell me that Frank had Aids?" Broker asked Janet.

"Would it have made any difference?"

"I would have known," he said.

"As you can see, he is not ill," she told him.

"He didn't tell me," Broker complained. "Not even after I told him so much about me. And how come he was accepted in the house when I was not?"

"That had nothing to do with it," she told him. "But you don't want us to go into that again."

"No, not again," he laughed nervously. "Not today."

So they talked about the other things; the orphanage and the children's home. The Indian constructor had abandoned the project and fled, distressed by the casket parade at the church gates during the funeral hour. Broker had sent to Makutano for another builder and the work was set to resume shortly. Plans for the reconstruction of the petrol station were at an advanced stage too. A new contractor would soon arrive from Pwani and serious construction could start soon. Janet did not know what to make of it all. She had seen what had been done so far, and it seemed almost real, but she dared not believe any of it would be completed.

She smiled sadly and said, "You know, you make it sound all so real."

"Big Ben never started anything he didn't finish," he said to her.

To get away from this fantasy, she changed the subject and they talked about the children instead.

"Do they know?" Broker wondered.

"I had to tell them," she said.

"How did they take it?" he asked.

"Like Crossroads' children," she said.

Death was a constant companion in Crossroads and children were acquainted with its every facet at an early age. They were not afraid of death anymore. Only sad and confused.

"They don't like me," he said.

"They don't know you," she told him.

He had picked them up from school on several occasions, driven them home and tried to bond with them. But the children had remained polite and distant.

"They have been too long without their father," Janet told him.

He had never been good with children, she reminded him. In the old days he would bribe them to stop wailing. When that failed, he would storm out of the house and go to town, returning late at night when all was quiet again. But, maybe if he could spend time with them alone, he might teach them to like him.

"I would like to take them to Soi," he said.

"To the hills?" Janet was startled. "What on earth for?"

"For a visit," he told her. "You may come along too, if you wish."

"No," she said at once. "I can't go back there."

She had been to Soi before, long ago when she had reason to go there. They had visited the mountain villages, so high up there was hardly any air, and drunk goat's milk and eaten goat's heads and stayed in lodging houses so derelict the guests slept on wooden platforms. And she had enjoyed it all so immensely. But that was in the old days, when she was in love and would go anywhere he went and do anything he wished. Now she had no wish at all to revisit old ghosts.

"Have they ever been up there?" Broker asked her.

"What for?" she asked.

"They would love the waterfalls," he said.

She thought to object. She thought about it for a long time.

"The waterfalls were beautiful," she conceded.

And he was their father, for good or worse, and, whether she wished to share certain memories with him or not, there was no good reason to deny the children a chance to experience their father.

They had their tea and *mandazi* and when they were done, she rose to go.

"Musa!" she called out to the kitchen.

"Permit me to pay for this," Broker offered.

"Didn't I tell you my headache was gone?" she said to him. "It started the day you came back. Musa!"

Musa came in, his face and hands white with flour.

"How are your kale *sambusas*?" she asked him.

"*Bado,*" he said indifferently. "They are not ready."

"Neither were your *mandazi*, if it's any consolation," she said to him. "The tea was terrible too and ... when will you learn to cook for people?"

Musa regarded her with impervious resignation.

"So you won't pay," he said to her. "OK then, don't pay."

"I didn't say that I would not pay," Janet said to him. "Today I will pay."

Musa, visibly surprised, received the money from her and counted it twice before dumping it in the till.

"Go *polepole* on the kale *sambusa*," she advised him. "Thoroughly cook the kale before you try whatever it is that you want to try."

Musa nodded agreeably, taking her all so seriously that Broker could not help laughing aloud and asking, "Are you sure you are up to it, old bull?"

"Of course he is," said Janet. "He has never had a woman to do anything for him. Stay well, you two."

"Go well," they said.

Then she left them, Broker to brood alone by the window and Musa to return to his innovations.

Out of the window, Broker thought he saw Big Youth pass a box of condoms to Highlife Alice without receiving money in exchange. But he was too tired to go raise hell about it.

Chapter Thirty-Nine

The old Soi, like the Crossroads people, was weary of its life of deprivation and misery; and a death too long in passing. But, unlike the people, the Soi could not run away from its fate, terrible as it was. The old river could not just pack up its belongings, its rocks and its fish and its crocodiles, hippos and river snakes and leave Crossroads for good.

Deforestation and illegal diversions had turned the once mighty river into a sickly, slimy stream choked with weeds and human waste. The water no longer ran but trickled, and the cataracts no longer roared but fizzled. The old lakes and dams were no more. They had long ago turned to marshy pools and mud-holes in which only herons, storks and water snakes thrived.

To enjoy anything close to Soi's original splendour, one had to drive for miles along long-disappeared roads and up the naked, rocky hills to the source of the river. There, among the rocks and the bushes, the river was white and alive and the children could dip their feet into its many pools without their toes rotting away and falling off. And in the cool shade of the last mahogany tree in the bleak land, one could unpack a picnic and momentarily forget the burdens of Crossroads.

They had stopped at Maili Nane, an old and despairing shopping centre, tottering on the brink of death on the side of the mountain, and bought food and drinks for the picnic. And, in the euphoria of the outing, they had bought enough food to feed a village.

As the children frolicked in the stream and fed the leftovers to the trout and the tadpoles, Broker informed Frank that this was the very spot he had brought Janet when he first courted her. How they had walked half a day to get there and had forgotten to bring any food along. But he had caught a fish and grilled it and Janet had refused to eat any of it.

"And that stump over there," Broker told him. "That was once a mighty ebony tree, hundreds of years old."

The largest tree in all the land; old and solid and meaningful, and no one had thought that it could so easily be destroyed. In its cool shade the eldest of Janet's boys had been conceived. And over there.

Frank was only half listening. Janet had asked him to go along with Broker and the children to keep an eye on things. What things? She did not know. Did she expect Broker in his condition to run off with the children?

"Just go along with him," she had insisted. "For my sake."

Now watching Broker watch the children, and speak so fondly of their mother, he realised he need not have come along. Broker cared for his children and adored them, in his own remote and selfish way.

"Do you have children?" he asked suddenly.

"No," Frank answered.

"Not even one?"

"I was never married," Frank informed.

Broker laughed and asked, "What did you do with your life?"

"School, mostly," he said, almost regretfully. "Then it was too late. You do know I'm HIV positive, don't you?"

"I know," Broker said. "I know."

There followed a strange silence, a silent moment when none of them knew what to say to the other.

"How did you find out?" Broker asked.

Frank told him about the routine check-up that had cost him his scholarship.

"I was unwell when I tested positive," Broker revealed. "I was ready for anything, when I took the test. But not for this."

"All I could think of was suicide," Frank said.

"I couldn't think at all," Broker confessed.

His brain had seized up. For days he had walked about in a daze. Then, when he had finally started to think again, all he could think of was that he was a walking dead man. But, even then, suicide was the farthest thing from his mind.

"It seemed to me then, as now, rather futile to kill oneself when you are about to die, anyway," he said to Frank.

So he had decided to live. He had said to himself, "Broker, the time for nonsense is over. Seize the day."

"Such wisdom comes too late," Frank observed.

"Don't I know it?" Broker laughed.

He had finally joined a support group in Pwani, a group of people like him, whose social status, expectations and outlook on life had been changed forever by HIV. With them, he had found the peace he needed in which to pull himself together. With them, he had found that he could talk, laugh and even cry without fear or embarrassment.

"That was eight years ago," he said.

Eight long years. Some of them had been great, others not so great, but he was still here.

They were quiet for a while.

"I was too cowardly to kill myself," Frank admitted.

He could not think of a way that was not messy or painful.

"And I was afraid of hell," he added.

So he had returned to Crossroads. He had come back determined to hide the truth and his fear of pain and of death. But everyone had soon found out, sooner than he could have told them, had he had the courage to. Some still held it against him, but it did not bother him anymore.

"My associates were not what you would call model citizens," Broker revealed. "But even they disappeared very quickly when word got out. After that, my wives and lovers vanished too. Not even they would give me the time of day."

"But for Janet, I would not be here today," Frank confessed.

It was Janet who had held his hand, looked him in the eye and told him it was all right to fear pain and death; and to even cry when that fear was too much to bear.

"Why me?" he had sobbed.

"Why anybody?" she had asked. "Disease doesn't know priest from prostitute."

She it was who had coaxed, nudged and bullied him back to a positive perspective.

"Why is it that women are so weak, when their men are with them, and so strong, when they have no one to lean on?"

"Don't ask me," Broker said to him. "I never went to University."

They were silent for a long moment, each locked up in his own private hell.

Frank remembered how Janet had taken him into her life and led him back to church. No one had believed him there either, but most had accepted him, as they did repentant sinners, and supported him, albeit at arm's length, and left him to get on with the rest of his life. None of them had cared to know the truth. Pastor Bat had pronounced, in his lofty way, that truth was a matter between man and God and left it at that.

"So now I knew something new," Frank laughed a little. "Now I could die in peace."

"Live in hope," Broker told him, exactly as Janet had done. "Finish the work we have started."

Broker had not been to church much himself but he understood well Pastor Bat's words. In his case, though, his conscience was a legion of demons. His Gods, until recently, had been money and sexual gratification. The truth, as he had told the Pastor, was that he had never been a good man. His fate had been sealed from birth; he had known it, from the day he was old enough to know anything, known that he was destined for a short, turbulent and extraordinary life. He had known this long before embarking on his Pwani adventure. But he had not worried about it then. He had not worried about anything until now.

Now he worried too much, he confessed, worried about things that had never bothered him before. Things such as pollution and global warming. And about people and about justice, and about people. About people who were too poor, too hungry and died too young. About the day of Judgement and about heaven and hell. Things such as had never bothered him before.

"That was how I realised that we had to build something while we still can," he said to Frank. "Something that will live on after we are gone. We must reclaim Crossroads back from the dead."

"We?" asked Frank.

"Isn't life a communal problem?" Broker said. "Crossroads must be brought back to life."

"Crossroads has no money," Frank reminded him.

Which Broker knew only too well. Crossroads had everything except money. And Broker had everything except time. What he needed was someone he could entrust with the several projects he had initiated. An honest man. A man like Frank.

"I know nothing about building," Frank confessed.

"Neither do I," Broker said. "But we must not let that discourage us; we shall hire qualified contractors to do the work. Mobil will oversee the reconstruction of the petrol station and the Church Committee will see to the orphanage. You and Janet will keep an eye on the budgets and things."

He had it all worked out, it emerged.

"But we have a job," Frank protested.

"It is all part of the same solution," Broker told him. "An hour here, an hour there and it's done. You will find the time."

Frank thought. There was not much to think.

"Have you asked Janet?"

"I'd like you to do that for me," Broker said. "Janet doesn't believe anything I tell her. So it is up to you."

Frank was certain she would not approve.

"I know," Broker nodded. "She is my wife."

"Was," Frank corrected.

"She still is," Broker said irritably. "Are you in love with her too? No, don't answer that. Just a thought going astray."

Strangely, he could not remember loving Janet. Desiring her, wanting her, possessing her, yes, but loving her, not really. Not until now.

"She doesn't love me," he admitted finally. "Not anymore. But she does not mention divorce."

"Would you grant it?" Frank asked him.

"No."

"But she doesn't love you."

"I just said that," Broker was beginning to hurt inside. "Not that it matters, anymore, not anymore. I want her to be happy, to have good things and to live a good life; to live to have a good memory of me. I don't want her to have to fight for my corpse, and my estate, like so many women have to do nowadays."

"Janet would never do that," Frank assured.

"Exactly," he said. "And yet she must. I would hate to think that all my sweat and labour will end up in the hands of the numerous vultures poised to claim it."

"Why not write a will?" Frank wondered.

"Write a will?" Broker laughed. "You are quite a simple man, for all your great education. How many corpses of prominent men are rotting away in mortuaries all over the land, while learned lawyers argue about the validity of their last wills and testaments? What is a man's last wish worth against the wills, the testaments and the greed of his wives, his clan and his tribe? I'd hate to suffer this form of posthumous debasement. That's why I pray for a swift death and a swift burial. And everything that I have goes to my wife and to my children. That's it."

He had tried telling Janet about the will, the bank accounts, of which he had several, and the deeds to properties she did not know he had. But Janet would not listen. She did not listen to him anymore. Not on any subject that demanded faith and trust.

"I will leave the documents with you," he said to Frank. "You must give them to her, make her believe and take an interest in these things. She must accept them, for her own sake, for my children's sake."

"I'll try," Frank said thoughtfully.

He could only try.

Then the children interrupted them wanting to climb the rocks up to the source of the waters but were afraid to go alone.

Frank rose to go with them.

"I'll just sit here and think things over," Broker said to them. "Suddenly I don't feel too well."

Frank left him to rest and led the children on the steep and dangerous climb to the place where the water trickled out of the rock face in tiny crystal clear drops - and the youngest observed that the mountain was so sad, it wept for her father who was going to die.

Chapter Forty

The giant crane groaned and grunted, and spewed clouds of diesel smoke, as it crawled to the next pit and lowered the giant tank in place. The first tank was already in its place and the army of labourers was filling in the soil.

The crowd of onlookers, of non-believers turned believers, braved the heat of the day and the dust to witness the greatest miracle of their life, the resurrection of an entire community.

Up till now, no one, least of all the old men at the teahouse, had believed the service station could be revived. Now the whole town watched in awe as the puny figure in a dusty, grey suit supervised the first stage of that miracle. One day they would be able to tell their grandchildren they were there the day Crossroads was raised from the dead.

Bakari Ben Broker, the saviour of Crossroads, was leaning a little too heavily on his ebony cane as he supervised the installation of the petrol pumps. The station building, a clean, red and blue structure, stood at the heart of Crossroads, a transplanted organ ready to start pumping life back into the corpse. But there was work yet to be done. The power generator was yet to be delivered and the air compressors and service machinery that Mobil had sent from Pwani were stranded in the vast savannah somewhere between Nipe and Nikupe. But, all in all, the project was progressing well and Broker was busy.

As the labourers buried the second fuel reservoir in its new womb, Broker limped back to his car and drove slowly away, wishing he could stop the reckless rush of time so he might catch up.

He was getting out of the car at the Condom Shop when the convoy arrived. It was composed of half a dozen Government vehicles and was led by the dusty jeep that, Broker recognized, belonged to the District Health Officer. The vehicles stopped at the post office and Broker at once knew who the visitors were.

The team was led by the same friendly Irish volunteer nurse who had led them when they had taken blood from the community. She too recognised Broker and introduced him to her team.

Broker sent Big Youth to fetch Janet and, while they waited for her, he invited the team to a cup of tea at Musa's. It was the largest single group Musa had ever served. Not only did he immediately ran out of tea glasses, he also run out of ideas on what to do with so many customers.

Broker took over, telling him what to do and giving orders, as if he owned the place, and Musa gladly obeyed and did exactly as he was told, and said he would be forever grateful to Broker for it. Broker suggested a fifty per cent reduction in his rent and Musa laughed happily and said Broker would have to work in the kitchen for a year to expect that kind of gratitude. When the visitors were contentedly gorging themselves on Musa's *mandazi*, he suggested serving his improved kale *sambusa*. Broker opposed the idea at once. These were big-time doctors who knew all about research, and experiments gone haywire, and especially about salmonella. They were, therefore, the wrong type of guinea pigs.

But, drunk on his success so far, Musa insisted they try his new recipe. He had added *terere*, he said, and *pili-pili hoho* and several indigenous herbs and some traditional ingredients that were known to kill stomach worms and to re-ignite old men's fires, and to cure all sorts of ailments besides. They just had to try them.

Broker was adamant. There would be no experimental food served to his guests today. But this was Musa's Teahouse and he could do as he pleased.

"Not today," Broker informed him.

Today he would do exactly as Broker told him and like it. The argument was about to degenerate into a fistfight, their newly found alliance disintegrating before it was fully cemented.

"Gentlemen, gentlemen," Uncle Mark intervened. "Why don't you ask your esteemed guests whether they want to try something out of this world."

"Have you any idea what he wants to serve them?" Broker was scandalised.

"The choice is theirs," said Uncle Mark. "Let him ask."

Musa asked and, to his delight, the visitors did want to try something new. Broker tried to discourage them, but it was all in vain. They were true scientists, and hungry to boot, and they insisted on trying. While they waited for Janet and the *sambusas* they talked about this and that. Broker learned, for the first time, that it was not a surprise visit at all. The nurse had written to Janet weeks before to arrange a date.

Janet arrived at about the same time as the kale *sambusas*. She had been on her way to Crossroads when Big Youth met her and she was excited that the reports were out. She was also apprehensive as to what the reports portended.

"Don't worry," the nurse said to her. "They are not as bad as we expected. We shall need several rooms for the counsellors and two rooms for the doctors."

There were lots of rooms in the post office, Janet assured them. She sent Big Youth off to prepare the rooms.

"Here is how we do it," the nurse told her. "The people will go through to the counsellors first. The counsellors will talk to them, ease their fears and prepare them for whatever reports they may get. The reports are confidential and the counsellors have no access to them. To get their reports, they will go to someone, who is trained to deal with such delicate matters. The whole exercise is handled with extreme sensitivity and in the strictest confidence. No one but the doctor in charge sees the reports. It's that simple. However, how the recipients react to the reports depends on their own psychological wellbeing."

Janet was to find out the significance of this statement at very short order indeed.

Presently, Big Youth came to report that the rooms were ready and they rose to leave. How did they find the *sambusas*? Musa was dying to know. Prudently, most of the visitors said they had no comment, while one doctor said he would wait to hear from his stomach and Janice, in her forthright and professional manner, informed Musa that his kale *sambusas* tasted like fresh cow pats. Musa was so impressed by her candour that he was not at all discouraged. He thanked her for her opinion and assured her he would add lots and lots of *pili-pili* especially for her next time she came to Crossroads.

Then Janet led the team across the road to the post office, leaving Broker to disentangle the hopelessly entangled bill. When he had done that to Musa's satisfaction and paid the bill, Broker sauntered onto the veranda to join Uncle Mark in watching the people gather.

Two long lines snaked their way out of the post office and halfway to the Condom Shop. And still more and more people were arriving.

"This should be something," Uncle Mark observed, in his perennially amused way. "This will be interesting."

A gross understatement, as it soon turned out. The lines grew and grew, and Broker nodded tiredly and sank into a chair, looking older than ever, and concentrated on ignoring the pain that tore his insides with fire. The lines grew so long they baffled even Janet. Why were there more people in line than had been tested? Had Crossroads finally woken from its slumber?

She did not know it then, but Crossroads' rumour mill had been at it again, firing up old dreams and creating scenarios that stirred the dullest of Crossroads' souls. The facts of the health team's last two visits not withstanding, many of those present had come seriously believing there would be money, or some sort of reward, handed out at the end of the exercise. But quite a few of the spectators, among them the old beggar, had no idea what the queues were for but joined them anyway.

The old men watched from the teahouse and wondered.

Then, just as they began to think that, maybe they were wrong, that everything would turn out all right, a man shot out of the post office, wailing and screaming like the devil himself was after him, and bolted to the highway. A few people ran after him, and with him, never to return for their reports.

"What's the matter with him?" Musa asked alarmed.

"He knows," Uncle Mark said to him.

"Knows what?" Musa asked.

"What the matter is with him," Uncle Mark said, chortling quietly to himself.

Musa regarded him, long and hard, and tried to understand what he had said. Unable to make head or tail of it all, he withdrew to his kitchen to embark on a hot, new venture, the first ripe banana *sambusas* ever invented.

Janet emerged from the post office, now unbearably hot and stuffy from the people and the sadness crammed in there, and joined Broker and Uncle Mark on the veranda of the teahouse. She was ominously quiet and was chewing on her nails, something they had never seen her do. As they watched, another man emerged from the post office, calmly put his medical report in his pocket and quietly sauntered away.

"Have you got Aids?" Big Youth called out to him.

"No," he said.

"Then why are you not happy?" Big Youth asked him.

"What is there to be happy about?" he asked calmly walking away.

345

Musa wandered back onto the veranda to wonder where on earth all those people lived, since he hardly saw them, except when there was some strange madness happening in town.

After the man came a girl from Highlife Lodge, looking confused and clutching her test report to her bosom like a precious deed. She was thoroughly bewildered, as if she had walked through the door and found herself in a strange new world. She stood there for a brief moment, looking about in confusion, then sank to the ground, unconscious.

The men watched confounded her colleagues from the lodging house went to her aid and carried her into the shade where they tried to revive her with the crowd milling about them and asking them what had happened to her.

The old men looked at one another. They did not know what to make of it.

"There must be another way of doing this," Janet said to herself.

"You heard the nurse," Broker said to her. "Some laugh, some wail. Others ... well, there's no telling what the others will do."

Frank joined them then, having just arrived back from Sokoni where he had gone to treat Inspector Iddi's cow. The inspector had given him lunch, thanked him profusely and dispatched him to other clients who had also tried to pay him with lunch and with their gratitude. All in all, he had earned three lunches, numerous handshakes and countless promises to be paid for his labours when money became available. He slumped into a chair and the old men briefed him on what had happened so far. Then he joined them in watching whatever-it-was unfold.

The people were coming out in droves now, and their reactions were turning stranger, more bewildering and even violent. The crowd, fearful of an outbreak of something dangerous and catching, started to disperse, slipping away as surreptitiously as was possible in broad daylight; pretending they had just been passing by or had come to escort a friend and had nothing at all to do with the lunacy brewing up around them.

Then Sikarame, the robust young man well known for his rakish behaviour, burst out of the post office, laughing and yelling with joy, and changed the tide.

"I'm well," he announced going mad with relief. "I'm well, thank God, I'm well."

The crowd stopped and looked back. Then they gaped and were dumbfounded.

If anyone deserved to drink the brimming bowl of God's wrath, and to suffer the whole measure of divine retribution, no one deserved it more than Sikarame. And if any person at all deserved to perish from the plague, and do so in a slow and singularly excruciating way, that person was the young man now celebrating his wellbeing.

How now, they wondered, was it possible that the one being everyone wanted to see drop dead from the curses he received daily from indignant mothers had been spared the rigours of the dreadful plague? How was that possible?

The crowd paused to consider. If Sikarame was indeed well, then wasn't there a similar chance that they too were well, that there was hope for all of them, after all? They started drifting back in line, determined to be brave about it all.

Janet was speechless. Was is possible? Was it really possible? She hurried back to the post office as Big Youth emerged from there, calmly controlled, hands in his pockets, and slouched across the road to stand next to Frank.

"*Daktari*," he asked in a low voice. "The man tried to tell me but, tell me again, what does it mean HIV minus?"

"It means HIV negative," Frank replied.

"Is it good news or bad news?" he asked.

"The best news you ever prayed for," Broker told him.

"Does it mean I don't have Aids?" his voice rose a notch.

"That's right," Frank told him. "You don't have Aids."

"You mean I don't have the plague?" Big Youth asked louder.

"That is what it means," Frank told him.

Only then did Big Youth have the courage to show him his report.

"I'm happy for you, Big Youth," Broker said to him. "You really are not a foolish boy."

"What does yours say?" Big Youth asked Frank.

"I haven't got mine yet," Frank said.

"Will you show me yours?" he asked.

"It's confidential," Frank told him.

"But I showed you mine," he said.

"You didn't have to," Frank told him. "Didn't they tell you anything in there? Anyway, you know my condition already."

Then Janet hurried back across the street and Big Youth pounced on her.

"Mine is minus," he told her excitedly. "What is yours?"

"I can't tell you," she told him.

"You must tell me," he insisted. "I told you mine."

She dismissed him with a wave of her hand, and turned to the solemn old men.

"It's very sad in there," she told them.

People were going mad in all sorts of ways, she reported. Some were broken by the reports, while others were reborn by them. Some were laughing, while others were sad and disconnected, in spite of the good counselling they were receiving in there.

"I have never seen such strange behaviour," she said, sadly.

"That's people for you," Uncle Mark observed. "That's people for you."

Before the day was over, he observed, some fool would have tried to take his own life or done something stupid like that. A sudden gloom descended on them as they watched Crossroads go quietly mad in its own way.

"This," Broker said to himself, "is not fun at all."

"But it's more interesting than watching Crossroads die," Uncle Mark thought to himself.

Julia Kata emerged from the post office and they all looked up expectantly. She stopped by the entrance for a moment, to reacclimatise herself to the searing white light, the crowd and the dust, then walked slowly across the street to Janet.

"I must talk to you," she said quietly. "Alone."

She was tired and scared, and quite distraught.

Frank decided to go for his report and leave them to their privacy. But Broker was tired, and Uncle Mark belonged there too, and they decided they were not going anywhere and stayed put. So Julia took her sister aside to talk to her there.

"I know you can't lie to me," she said handing her the report. "Tell me the whole truth. Tell me what it says."

Janet unfolded the report, with worse apprehension than she had opened her own. Suddenly, she took Julia in an embrace and pressed her to her bosom. She held her there for a long quiet moment, overflowing with joy, and expressing her love for her with hugs and kisses.

"I dared not believe those men," Julia said, when Janet finally let her breathe again.

The old men watched indifferently as they embraced again and celebrated their good fortune.

"Well," Uncle Mark observed quietly. "There is one we do not have to weep for."

Musa nodded thoughtfully and Broker grunted. His mind was fuzzy and everything, it seemed, was slipping way. A ruthless old devil was busy excavating his nervous system, with a rusty, old bulldozer, and he wished the pain would ease so he could doze a little.

"What about Kata?" Janet was asking her sister. "What about your husband?"

"Would he come?" Julia said.

"Then it is not going to be easy," she told her.

That was up to Kata himself, Julia was decided. He had had more than ten years of her life, and she had given him more than enough children. Now that she had her life back, she would do everything to keep it. Everything, including leaving him.

Janet walked her as far as the highway, expressing her love for her and her joy at the report.

"As of today," Julia swore to her. "I'm cured of men."

Then she went home and Janet returned to the teahouse to wait for the exercise to end. She arrived as Frank was emerging from the post office, report in hand and looking very puzzled. Big Youth pounced on the report and ran with it to the teahouse.

"Minus?" he exclaimed, when he stopped to read the report. "HIV minus? But this one is just like mine!"

Janet snatched the report from him. She glanced at it, looked up thoughtfully, and waited for an explanation.

"There must be a mistake," Frank told them all.

"Did you tell them?" she asked him.

"They said it was not likely that they had made a mistake," he told her. "They were extremely thorough with the tests."

"That is what they told me," Janet said.

But she had to be certain. She rounded up the nurse and demanded an explanation.

"Quite simple," the nurse told her. "The earlier reagents, that's the chemicals used to perform the tests, were not as efficient as the ones we have used here. With this new test, the margin for error is so small it's negligible. But we can repeat the test for you, if you wish."

Frank was totally confounded.

"Just to be certain?" Janet said to him.

"You'll have to give us another blood sample," the nurse said.

"But everyone knows that *Daktari* has Aids," Big Youth told them all.

"Go away," Janet ordered him. "Go to your friends and stay with them."

Big Youth left to tell his friends of the new development. Frank was in shock and the old men did not know whether to be happy for him.

"Cheer up," the nurse said to him. "Sometimes we have to believe in a miracle."

Most of the youth tested had been found to be free from infection, she had said to Janet, and that Janet knew to be a miracle in itself. Her prayers had been answered in more ways than she had ever hoped for.

The nurse went back to wind up the exercise and Janet hugged Frank. She clutched him to her bosom and held him there and embraced him with her whole being and felt him, and felt him feel her, and cared little what anyone thought of it.

Broker watched them quietly, a sad smile on his tortured, old face; and Uncle Mark decided it was not his business, and Musa went mad with jealousy.

Over Frank's shoulder, Janet saw Hanna emerge from the post office, dazed and confused and uncertain which way to go, Hanna paused by the exit, looking this way and that, and tried to compose herself. Janet's joy suddenly died. She quickly released Frank and rushed across the street to meet her.

"Have you got your report?" she asked her.

Hanna gave her the report to read for herself. Janet glanced at it and a sudden chill gripped her heart. Her mind was suddenly numb and her mouth dry and she knew not what to say.

Janet made to embrace her. Hanna stepped back and held out her arms to ward her off.

"Don't touch me," she said, through clenched teeth. "I'm all right. I'll be all right. I'm all right."

She was all dry and flaky inside; all light and airy and empty and dead and, if anyone touched her now, anyone at all, she would crumble to nothing and fall to the ground; explode like a puff mushroom and turn to smoke and dry powder, and blow away, and no one would be able to help her after that.

She walked slowly away from that awful place, slowly but determined and hardening inside. Janet walked with her, in a strained and gloomy silence, wracking her heart and mind for divine revelation, for something to say or do, one single word that could express the pain and the anguish that she felt for her friend.

They walked some distance in this sad silence.

Then Hanna began to talk, in a fast and bitter torrent that seemed to spew from her very soul. She would shed no tears, she said, for this was way beyond any tears.

"No, I will not cry," she said.

"No, do not cry," Janet told her.

"And I will not kill myself," she decided.

"No, do not kill yourself," Janet told her.

"I will kill the dog instead," she said.

"No, don't kill your husband," Janet told her.

They walked slowly on, Janet explaining how there was nothing to be gained from killing her husband; nothing but loss and more loss.

"Think of the children," she said.

"That is exactly why I must kill him," Hanna said resolutely.

Then she let out a tortured cry and ran for the highway.

"Stop!" Janet yelled after her. "Stop her, someone stop that woman!"

People turned and saw a woman rush hysterically down the road towards them. They stepped out of her way and she ran past them, so fast they hardly saw the tears raining down from her eyes.

Janet turned and ran back for her bicycle.

"Help me!" she pleaded to the old men.

No one moved. She mounted her bicycle and pedalled frantically after Hanna. Big Youth saw what had happened and ran after her. That was all the help Janet got from Crossroads that day.

The old men exchanged indifferent glances, shrugged, and went on doing what they were best at - nothing. The wheel that Janet had set in motion, with her grand ideas about change and about community service, was running full steam ahead. There was nothing they could do about it now, not even if they had the will or the energy.

They watched her pedal madly across the highway and disappear in the old cattle trails, after the wildly screaming woman, and knew that she would never catch up with her, never undo the harm she had done.

Musa watched another crowd disperse without spending a bean at his place, and was more than dismayed. He walked over to Broker to moan about it, and to wonder if it had anything at all to do with Armageddon and the prophecy that he and Uncle Mark talked endlessly about. Broker was tired and in pain and in no mood for conversation; but he assured Musa that religion had absolutely nothing at all to do with the events of the day.

"Then why are you building the churches?" Musa asked.

"I'm not building the churches," Broker informed him. "I'm just helping an old man with his roof."

"But you are repairing his church too," Musa accused.

Broker grunted and wished Musa would stop bothering him so that he could sleep a little. He wished he could sleep for a hundred years. He had enough exhaustion for a century's rest, but first he had to build the filling station.

"Will you repair the Mosque as well?" Musa demanded.

"What for?" he asked.

"So that we too can have a place to pray," Musa said.

"We?" Broker smiled thinly. "I know of only one practising Muslim in Crossroads."

"You used to be one of us," Musa reminded.

"I used to be all things," Broker said quietly. "I was Muslim when I courted, Christian when I married but now … That was a long time ago, a long, long time ago."

"You don't pray anymore?" Musa asked horrified.

"Oh, I do," Broker assured him. "I pray all the time."

Especially when the nights were so dark he could not see any hope at all. He prayed then, prayed, like everyone else, and prayed and prayed; prayed for God to reveal Himself and His purpose, and for the daylight to come and lift the veil of anxiety.

"But I don't face any particular direction, or assume any special position when I pray."

Musa regarded him with total incomprehension. For a seriously sick man not to pray for healing, it was all beyond his understanding.

"Didn't they tell you there is no cure for this plague?" Broker asked him. "This Aids thing has no cure, neither here nor in heaven."

To pray for a cure was like to seek for a resurrection.

"Frankly," Broker said to him. "It's a total waste of time."

He was cold, in spite of the feverish heat that brought out sweat beads on his nose, and he was so weak that talking exhausted him.

"To tell you the truth, old bull," he said to Musa. "I could do with a cup of tea right now."

Musa did not budge.

"May I have a cup of tea?" he asked firmly. "With lots of sugar, please?"

Musa was so thoroughly disgusted, to discover he had been living with an impenitent *kafiri* all along, that he did not acknowledge the order. Pigs and heathens were things he could not reconcile with.

Uncle Mark saw the approaching standoff and resolved to keep out of it.

Frank too discerned that Broker was unwell, and that Musa was offended by his presence, but he was too weary to help any of them. He had walked over numerous hills and valleys that day to treat livestock whose owners would never pay him, and he was not in a charitable frame of mind at all. Then the report springing such a surprise on him had left him fully drained.

After a long, disturbing moment, during which he wondered yet again whether life was really worth living, he rose quietly and, without a word to the old men, started out after Janet.

Uncle Mark, who saw everything, heard everything and normally understood it all, nodded quietly and admitted to himself this was all beyond him. In one short day, one girl had fainted, one man had gone mad and a woman had gone to murder her husband. And hundreds of other people had gone quietly home to do whatever it was that quiet people did when they knew for certain that their world was about to come crushing down on them.

This, thought Uncle Mark, would go down as the most calamitous day in the history of Crossroads. But perhaps even this was better than watching Crossroads die.

Chapter Forty-One

The children had left to school, and Janet was doing the things that mothers must do before they have to do everything else, when Big Youth rushed in to inform her that her husband was dying.

"Again?" she asked him.

She had had several such scares in the last few months and was used to them now. Broker's condition was bad and definitely getting worse, but Broker was in no hurry to die.

"I'll come as soon as I can," she said and continued doing her work.

There was no danger of Broker dying before she got to him. Broker would not die before he had turned her into a nervous wreck and driven her into the ground with worry.

"He is very ill," Big Youth said, in a panic. "He is going to die."

"He is not," she told him.

Broker would not die before his work was done. He had told her as much himself. He would not die before the seeds he had planted had started to flower; not before he had done all the things that he had come back to do. Not before then.

"You run back and tell him to hold everything until I get there," she ordered Big Youth.

Big Youth ran back, as urgently as he had come, and Janet resumed her work. She finished doing what she had to do and was taking out her bicycle to ride down to Crossroads, when Broker drove up. Big Youth was with him in the car, grinning from ear to ear and being happy with himself. Broker was nowhere near death and, in fact, appeared just as unhealthy as Janet had last seen him. His walk, she noted, was more unsteady than usual, and he was sweating heavily, partly because he wore a black suit on the hottest day of the year.

"Is this the man who is dying?" she asked Big Youth.

"That was Musa's idea," Broker confessed, grinning as mischievously as Big Youth.

Musa was determined that Broker should not die in his room at night and was keeping a strict watch on Broker's health. The slightest change had him sending for Janet, and on the carpet praying for Broker's recovery. He was also secretly rehearsing the Muslim prayers for the dead.

Janet helped Broker into the house, helped him take off his jacket and sat him in a chair. She gave him a glass of water to drink and offered to make some tea.

"Don't bother," he told her bursting into fits of coughing.

She looked on helplessly as his whole body erupted inside and shook and quivered in a cough that would neither come out nor stay inside of him.

"Are you all right?" she asked, when he had calmed down.

"This will pass," he said. "Then I'll be as good as new."

Big Youth was watching from the doorway, a worried frown on his face.

"Stop gawking and go wash the car," Broker told him. "No fingerprints on the mirrors, you hear? And stay out of the boot."

The last order was repeated every time Big Youth had to wash the car, though it was totally unnecessary now. Unable to resist the temptation, Big Youth had already looked in the boot of the car and seen what it was that he was not supposed to see; and it worried him.

Now he laughed and went off to do as ordered. He loved cleaning Broker's car and turned the radio on so loud that Janet had to go out and order him to turn it down.

"Would you like something to eat?" she asked Broker.

"I'm not hungry," he said.

But he looked frail and grey, and it worried her.

"I'll be all right," he told her. "I felt a little funny, that's all. It's nothing new. I'll be all right as soon as I have rested."

So she let him rest and looked for something to do while figuring out what to do with him. Meanwhile, Big Youth washed the car and played with the radio. He could not decide between the stations and switched from one to the other in a way that irritated Janet so much that she had to go out again to ask him to turn it off.

When she returned, Broker was half asleep, slumped in his seat and snoring lightly. The sweating was gone but his breathing was hard and irregular.

"Broker?"

He started awake and looked about in panic. Then he recognised Janet and relaxed.

"I'm all right," he said.

"No, you are not," she told him. "Get up."

"What for?" he asked.

"I'm taking you to hospital," she said firmly. "Get in the car."

"I can't drive," he told her. "Not in this condition."

"Where are your car keys?" she asked him.

She looked out of the door and called out to Big Youth.

"Help him to the car," she said. "Get Broker in the car. I'm driving him to hospital."

"But you can't drive," Big Youth said.

"Who told you that?" she asked him.

"You can drive?" Big Youth was astonished. "But you never told me you could drive."

"There are many things I never told you, Big Youth," Janet said to him. "Where are the car keys?"

"In the car," he said amazed. "I'll get them."

Broker laughed suddenly, hard and loud, startling Janet.

"Woman," he said, with much admiration. "You are so full of surprises."

He had forgotten that her father, Maalim Juma Maalim, had owned half of Crossroads and the only garage for miles around.

"But seriously," he said to her, "I can't go to a hospital; I have been in too many hospitals already."

"I must take you to a doctor," she insisted.

"What doctor?" he asked her. "I have seen them all."

From medical professors to witchdoctors and from herbalists to faith healers. In abject panic, he had turned to anyone who claimed to have a cure, and squandered a fortune on quacks of every type and derivation, and he had no wish to see any of them now.

"Don't waste your time," he said to her. "I can confirm to you, with absolute authority, that this thing is incurable."

Janet anguished. She could not just stand there and watch him suffer and do nothing about it. She had to do something or go screaming insane.

"You have no choice," he said smugly.

Pain and suffering were part and parcel of the thing. And physical pain of this nature could not be shared, not with the best love in the world. Therefore, there was nothing that she or anyone else could do for him, except, perhaps, to allow him to die with some dignity.

Big Youth came back with the car keys and Broker ordered him to go back and finish washing the car. They were not going to hospital or anywhere else soon.

Janet was thoroughly distressed. She looked about the room and wondered what to do, now that her day had been so frustratingly disrupted.

"I'll make some tea," she announced.

"Do that," Broker said, though he was not in any mood for anything but rest.

While she was gone, Frank arrived to find him slumped in the chair looking more dead than alive. He woke up immediately on Frank's arrival and asked what was new.

One old farmer had paid Frank promptly, and with money, for treating his old cow, and that was new. New and incredible. Frank had passed by the churchyard too, where the new orphanage was coming up, and the contractor appeared to be still on site, and his workers lying about in the shade, and so, maybe something new was happening there too. Otherwise, Crossroads was still her dying old self and there was nothing to report. Broker seemed content with the report.

"Is there anything I can do for you?" Frank asked him.

"Help me up," Broker said.

Big Youth gave a hand and they supported Broker out of the house to the latrine round the back. While they were thus engaged, Grandmother arrived in a rush, without her stick and without her Jeremiah and in great agitation, and called Janet out of the kitchen.

"Where is he?" she asked. "Where is my grandson-in-law?"

Janet looked outside and saw that the car was still there.

"He was here a moment ago," she said. "I heard him talking to Frank just now. They must be outside somewhere."

Grandmother had not seen anyone outside. She could not have seen anyone. She had dropped everything, and come just as fast as she could, when she heard the bad news about Janet's husband.

"How cruel can life be?" she moaned. "Just when I thought that now there was someone to look after you. Just when I thought that now I could die in peace!"

"Stop it," Janet said harshly. "You are upsetting me."

"You are not upset already?" cried the old woman. "Your husband is dead and you are not upset?"

"What husband?" Janet was now upset. "Who told you my ... Broker was dead?"

"Everybody knows your Broker is dead," said Grandmother. "They told me he died, they said that he dropped down dead like a donkey, right in the middle of the day."

"Broker is not dead," Janet told her. "Broker is here."

"Where is he?" she asked. "Where is my son, I want to see my boy."

"Sit down," Janet ordered. "He will be here very shortly."

She sat down, reluctantly, and Janet went to fetch her something to calm her down. She was pouring her a cup of tea when the men returned. Broker was a little breathless from the effort but he was looking much better and walking without support.

"Greetings, Grandmother," he said cheerfully.

"You are not dead?" she asked him. "I was told that you were dead."

"Who told you that?" he asked her much amused. "Who said that I was dead?"

"The whole town says that you are dead," she said to him.

"Not yet, as you can see," he said laughing.

But, though he laughed, there was pain in his eyes, and deep-down concern, as he asked to know who had said he was dead and how they had said it. Had they said it with gleeful smiles or with sad frowns? Had they announced it in anxious whispers or with loud rejoicing? How had Crossroads broadcast the false news of his untimely death?

"Tell me, Grandmother." She had never seen him so earnest. "Did anyone grieve as they told these lies?"

"No." She was never one to tell a lie. "But I would have shed enough tears for all of them myself, had I not shed them all grieving for your sad wife when you abandoned her. I believe they all think that you are really dead, the way they say it."

Broker laughed heartily, though in great pain, and said to her, "You know that I can't die without telling you."

"Stop it now" she said harshly. "No more foolish talk of dying; you are not dying before me, you hear? I'll not allow it. Sit down and rest yourself."

Broker sat back in his chair and Frank sat opposite him. Big Youth went back to the car to play with the radio.

"Give your husband some tea," Grandmother ordered.

"I'm making him some cocoa," Janet told her.

"Cocoa?" Grandmother exclaimed. "You didn't give me cocoa."

"I gave you what was ready," Janet said.

"Make him something to eat," Grandmother ordered.

"He is not hungry," Janet said.

"Not hungry?" She was quite excited now. "Who says he is not hungry? Men are always hungry."

Broker assured her he was not hungry. She would not hear of it. He had to eat something. Something nice and hot. His favourite food. She had a nice bunch of bananas at her house. She would go and get it right away.

"I don't want food," Broker pleaded. "Not right now."

"What do you want then?" she demanded. "Would you like sour porridge?"

"No, thank you," he told her. "All I want is some peace and quiet. And a little rest."

"And good food," she insisted. "Don't tell me you don't want food. I raised four boys and a husband and they were always hungry. I will go for the bananas."

She rose to leave. No more room for argument.

"You must not upset him now, you hear?" she said to Janet. "Give him anything he wants."

When the old lady had left, Janet poured some tea for the men. Then she sat wringing her hands and looking for something to do. Cooking the bananas might be the distraction she so desperately needed. Talking about a death, which they all knew was not only inevitable but imminent as well, had sapped her creative energies.

Broker watched her suffer and tried to think what was going on in her head. In his own head was a raging storm, churning his brains and sucking out his life, and the effort needed to think was too much to muster.

"What are you thinking?" he asked her.

"Nothing," she told him.

"What nothing?"

There was a time she thought he could read her mind. But that was way back when she was young, desperately in love, and as predictable as a teenage bride could be. Later, she had realised he had not read her mind at all but had deliberately, and manipulatively, planted the ideas in her mind in the first place.

Now she revelled in the secret knowledge that she could predict his every word and his every move in a way that he would never ever guess at. He had not changed at all in all the time he had been away. Despite his recent interest in the community, he was still the same Broker and would always be himself.

"Janet," he said, trying to lighten her mood, "Remember how we used to walk to Soi to watch the sun set?"

She did. They would sit for hours and talk about the things they would do when they were rich. They would talk with optimism and enthusiasm about their future. And they would make wishes. "You wanted to be a nurse," Broker remembered. "And you wanted to be rich," she reminded him. That amused him so much he laughed till he coughed. Those had been the best days of his life. Alone in the hills with his woman. He had never been so happy since.

"Your wish came true at least," she said to him

"So can yours," he said to her. "The hills are still there."

"I'm too old to make wishes now," she said sadly.

Besides, she did not think he was in any condition to climb any more hills.

"I would not have to," he said.

His car made the journey with little difficulty. He had driven up there several times and the tracks were no worse than the one from her house to Crossroads. The loggers who had turned the entire land into a treeless wasteland had also left their mark on the once impenetrable hills. Everywhere their bulldozers had been, there were great tracks and trails wide enough to drive a bus through.

"You are in no condition to drive," she reminded.

"I wouldn't have to," he said again.

She shook her head firmly. She had not been back up there since her eldest son was born. Besides, she still harboured fond memories of the place and did not want to spoil it now by going back there and discovering that her memory was flawed. "I will never ask again," he promised.

She thought and thought. It took her a long time to decide.

While she readied herself, Frank left to go down to Crossroads to reopen the Condom Shop. Big Youth came to report the car was clean and ready for inspection and Broker rose. He felt much stronger now and he grew more optimistic as he followed Big Youth outside. The car was, indeed, spotlessly clean.

Broker commended Big Youth for it and assured him of a great future at the new petrol station once it was opened.

"Washing cars?" Big Youth was dismayed.

"No, of course not," Broker told him. "But an assistant manager must know what every workman does at the station. That is what I was taught by a very wise, old man."

Big Youth was elated. Then he remembered and the grin slipped off his face.

"Boss," he said. "You are not dying right away, are you? You have too many things to teach me."

"You heard Grandmother," Broker laughed. "I'm not allowed to die before her."

"Good," said Big Youth. "Grandmother will never die."

Broker took him by the shoulder and gave him the most affectionate smile Big Youth had ever seen. Of all the people in Crossroads, Big Youth had grown to be Broker's closest companion, the younger brother he wished he had. Now he walked him to the grain store door and the fading poster of the life and death equation.

"Did you truly write that?" he asked.

"Yes, boss," Big Youth said with great pride.

"Then there is very little left for you to learn from me," he told him.

Big Youth agonized. He had determined not to grow up to be an ox, and Broker was his only chance. There was something that had bothered him for long now and he decided to get it off his chest.

"Boss," he said. "What is the purpose of life?"

"The purpose of life?" Broker was taken by surprise. "Many people will tell you different things. But it seems to me that to live honestly and decently, and live well, is a good enough purpose."

Big Youth beamed happily as they walked back to the car to await Janet.

"I don't want to be an ox," he said determined.

"I'm sure you'll not," Broker assured patting him on the back. "I want you to do me a favour, Big Boy."

"Anything, Boss," Big Youth said.

"I want you to take care of my children," Broker said. "Look after them like your own brothers."

"I'm always here, Boss," Big Youth said.

"I know," Broker patted him on the shoulder. "But I want you to teach them to be smart like you. To fear death and to take precautions."

"But, Boss," Big Youth said reasonably. "They are only children."

"I know that," Broker patted him some more. "They are my children and I want them to grow up to be smart, big youths like you."

"All right, Boss," Big Youth said. "But you'll let me know before you go?"

Broker laughed till he coughed. Grandmother returned with a bunch of green bananas, as he was coughing sickeningly and choking, and ordered him not to go anywhere before he had eaten.

Chapter Forty-Two

The *Far Traveller* was running late. It worried Uncle Mark, for he could not remember the bus ever being this late. He worried it might have had an accident or been taken out of service. It was so old and decrepit it should not have been on the road in the first place. He wondered what he would do if the *Far Traveller* stopped running. He would probably suffocate from the staleness of Crossroads news. He would have to finally pack up and leave Crossroads.

He was about to give up waiting and go back to the teahouse, to contemplate his departure, when he saw a cloud of dust approaching from the west. The *Far Traveller* was still on the road. It arrived a record forty-five minutes late.

The reason for this uncharacteristic late arrival became obvious the moment the bus pulled up. Behind the wheel was a ruffian face that chewed *miraa,* the intoxicating herb which experienced desert travellers ate in order to stay awake all night to fight off marauding hyenas. From the look on his face, the young scoundrel had also smoked things that sensible long-distance drivers did not smoke.

"Greetings," he said cheerfully to Uncle Mark. "Are you the one who reads old newspapers?"

"I am," Uncle Mark said, smiling evenly.

"I have something for you," he said and dropped the bundle of newspapers out of the window.

Uncle Mark, refusing to be offended, continued to smile evenly as he picked up his papers.

"The money," said the young man stretching out his hand. "And make it quick, old man, we have many miles to travel today."

Uncle Mark took the money from his pocket, the proceeds of his scandalous winnings at the draughts table, and counted it carefully before handing it over to the insolent young man.

"Where is Captain Speed?" he asked giving the money.

"Do you want to talk to him?" He turned and called to the back of the bus, "You, Captain!"

"What?" asked the gruff voice of the Captain.

"The old geezer is here," he said. "Will you talk to him?"

Captain Speed came up from the back, his driver's cap at a rakish angle, his shirttail out of trousers, and looking like he had spent the night in a bad place.

"Greetings, old man," he said to Uncle Mark. "Have you received your papers?"

"I have," Uncle Mark said.

"Good," said Captain Speed. "That lot's on me. You haven't paid the young rogue, have you?"

Uncle Mark smiled at the young driver. The driver shrugged, reached into his pocket and sheepishly handed back the money.

"Bad start, my boy." The Captain wagged a finger at him. "Bad start."

He reeked of something ripe and fermented, like sorghum wine. But it could have been anything, since the bus travelled through so many wine-drinking regions, cultures and peoples that it was a minor miracle it ever reached its destination. But the Captain never drove drunk and Uncle Mark could vouch for that.

"This is your new captain," Captain Speed said introducing the young driver. "I'm taking him up to Kakuma to show him the ropes. Then I'm going to hand over this old monster to him and settle down."

"Retire?" Uncle Mark was a little bewildered. "But you are still a sprightly young soul and full of life!"

The Captain laughed.

"The soul may be young," he said happily. "But it resides in a very old cage now."

He had done enough driving in his time, he said. Now he wanted to leave it to a younger man and sit down to read old newspapers like Uncle Mark did.

"You will never see me this way again," the Captain assured.

"In that case," Uncle Mark said sadly, "Would you accept a cup of tea, from a fellow old bird, as a sign of respect and of my gratitude to you?"

"You don't owe me a thing, old man," the Captain said.

"Except my undying friendship," Uncle Mark told him. "God knows, this place would have been impossible without you and your packages."

"If you put it that way," the Captain said. "Is there perhaps a glass of wine anywhere in this dead place?"

"Regretfully, there's no wine in this dead place," Uncle Mark assured him. "Not where I live, anyway. But there is a lot of tea and things to eat."

The Captain thought some more. The passengers raised their voices and grumbled that they were getting hungry.

"What do you say, Babu?" the Captain asked the young driver.

"No," the young ruffian answered. "We are running late already."

"Not us, you fool," Captain Speed said to him. "You are the one who is already late. I have driven this bus for fifty years and not been late once. I have repaired punctures and changed tyres more times than you have had a bath and not once did I run as late as you are running now."

To Uncle Mark, he said, "I accept your offer of undying friendship."

"Undying friendship?" the young man exclaimed. "You old bats will never see each other again."

"Is that so?" said the Captain.

And, with that, he hopped down and accompanied Uncle Mark across the highway and down the road to the teahouse. The young driver jumped out of the bus and followed them, pleading with the Captain to come back to the bus so they could recover the lost time. They ignored him and walked on to the teahouse, talking about the old days and the many journeys they had made together.

Uncle Mark introduced Captain Speed to Mzee Musa as the old man who brought them all those interesting old newspapers.

"Give him everything," he said to Musa. "Everything except your *ugali* cake. Give that to the troublesome young man following us."

Then he led the Captain to the draughts table and sat him down.

"This is how I live my old age," he said laughing.

Captain Speed was delighted. Draughts was his passion too. When he was not negotiating the monstrous bus through a God-forsaken landscape, draughts was his choice of relaxation.

"Care for a game?" Uncle Mark asked.

"No," the young driver said joining them. "We have miles to go."

"Why not?" said Captain Speed. "No one can fire me now."

Uncle Mark set the table, with a great display of ceremony, and said, "Your move."

Captain Speed was a good player. Talking and playing and asking questions about Crossroads as they played, he won two quick games in a row. Uncle Mark complimented him for this and wished he had such a playing partner. The Captain laughed and remarked that, had he known retirement was such good fun, he would have retired many years ago.

One by one, the passengers followed them to the teahouse.

"Give me money," the beggar called out to them as they passed.

Some gave him money and some passed without noticing him. Then they joined the drivers at the teahouse and ordered tea and food. Musa was soon so busy he could hardly cope, and was heard to wish Broker was there to tell him what to do.

"Is this place new?" they asked him.

"No," he told them happily. "The teahouse is as old as Crossroads."

"How old is Crossroads?" they asked.

"Very, very old."

"How come we never stop here?" they asked him.

It was a much better place than the old Bush Town, where they usually stopped for refreshments. An old *Far Traveller* confronted Captain Speed with the question.

"Don't ask me," Captain Speed said to him. "You ask that young rogue there. He is your captain from now on."

The young driver considered the request.

"Besides your lousy *mandazi*," he said to Musa. "What else have you got here?"

"A petrol station," Musa told him proudly.

"A petrol station?" the young driver was impressed.

"It will be opened very soon," Musa said. "And many more things."

"I'll think about it," said the new driver.

"You do that," said the old Captain. "You are the boss now."

"Not until I deliver you back to civilization," said the young man. "Then I'll see what I can do about it."

Musa was beside himself with excitement. His banana *sambusas* went big with the travellers. His kale *sambusas* were a major hit too, as was his *ugali* cake, which he slipped to the passengers without Uncle Mark knowing about it. He was so happy he hugged and kissed the teapot and promised to give it a thorough scouring, and gave Captain Speed an extra cup of tea on the house.

"On the house, you hear?" he announced for all to hear.

"Thank you," said Captain Speed. "I like you, and I like this old man too, and I like this whole place. Are all the people here as good as you two are?"

"All of them," Musa assured.

"I'll buy land here," he said. "I like this Crossroads place. I'll get myself a wife and settle down here."

There were plenty of wives in Crossroads, Musa assured him. Old and young and every shade of woman; what with all the men suddenly departing and leaving their women behind.

"Ask this old bull here," he said, indicating Uncle Mark.

Uncle Mark laughed his knowing, old laugh and said, "It's not such a bad place this Crossroads."

"It's the best place on earth," Musa confirmed.

Captain Speed laughed merrily and said all places were the best place on earth for those who had to live and die in them. But he was a free spirit, like Uncle Mark, and he had never found a place he would wish to die in.

"Did you ever make it to Djibouti?" he asked Uncle Mark.

"No," Uncle Mark answered.

"What about Cape Town?" he asked. "The place you wanted so much to go to."

"No," Uncle Mark said.

"Not even to Alexandria?" he asked next.

"I never made it to Earth's End either, if you must know," Uncle Mark said to him. "Nor to Tierra del Fuego, nor even to Ouagadougou."

He laughed, a quiet contented laugh, and added, "But I had great fun trying."

Captain Speed laughed too and said, "But I did get you to Lodwar, didn't I?"

"That you did," Uncle Mark said playing his turn.

"And to Namuluputh too," said Captain Speed. "And to Juba and to Addis Ababa and to all those faraway places."

"That you did," agreed Uncle Mark.

"What was in all those places that you wanted so much to go to?" the Captain asked.

"I haven't the vaguest idea," Uncle Mark confessed .

They were enchanted places with evocative, magical names. Names that created images in his head so powerful they inflamed his soul and haunted him in his sleep.

"They were places I felt I had to travel to," he said to the Captain. "Something within me said that I had to go there; in order to fulfil my mission in life, whatever that was."

Captain Speed made his move and said, "Exactly how I feel about Zanzibar."

It gave him a thrill just to hear the name.

"*Za-n-zi-ba-ri*," he said, rolling his "r" the way he had heard the natives of the island do it.

The very name stirred his old loins, charged his blood with the forgotten energies of youth. It conjured up images of bewitchingly attractive women, nubile beauties, with long, black hair and skin the colour of dry cocoa coconut, dancing in the moonlight while the stars danced with joy.

"*Za-n-zi-ba-ri!*" he could almost smell the cloves drying in the blinding, white sunlight. "*Za-n-zi-ba-ri!*"

He sighed, a regretful, old sigh and moved his piece.

"I have been to Zanzibar," Uncle Mark confessed.

"You have?" the Captain sat up incredulous. "How was it? Tell me how you found it?"

"It was all right," said Uncle Mark.

"All right?" the Captain asked. "Just all right? What did you do there?"

Uncle Mark smiled, a wicked old smile, and Captain Speed asked him, "Were you fulfilled by it?"

Uncle Mark now laughed out loud, a long and happy laugh that left him refreshed.

"You come and live here with me," he said to the Captain. "You come live here with me and, I promise you, we two shall travel to places you never even dreamt of."

"I knew there was something big about you, old man," the Captain nodded quietly.

The tea had sobered him up considerably.

"Be sure I'll be back," he now said resolutely. "As soon as I have collected my pension."

"You do that," Uncle Mark advised. "Even an old soul needs a little sustenance from time to time."

An hour later, Uncle Mark and Mzee Musa escorted the Captain and the horde of *Far Travellers* back to their bus. The passengers were happy and they promised to return. Musa was speechless with gratitude as he wished them all long lives and promised them all free *sambusas* on their next visit.

And on the way back to the teahouse, he stopped to give money to the beggar and the beggar danced about with excitement, totally overwhelmed by the amount of money he had made in one morning.

"Who are they?" he asked of his benefactors.

"They are *Far Travellers*," Uncle Mark told him.

"Where are they from?" he asked.

"From all over," Uncle Mark told him.

"Will they come back again?" he asked hopefully.

"Maybe," Uncle Mark told him.

"They gave me money, uncle," he announced incredulously.

"Then pray for them," Uncle Mark advised. "Pray that they get safely to wherever they are going and come back again some day."

"I'll pray," the beggar promised. "They gave me money."

He walked with the old men back to the teahouse and walked right in, without stopping to wipe his jiggers on the floor by the entrance as Musa had ordered him.

"Give me tea," he ordered. "Give me tea and give me now!"

Musa burst into a torrent of loud swearing, in a language Uncle Mark had never heard him speak before, and which, loosely translated, meant, "Get out of my sight, you uncircumcised, unclean, unbelieving, unrepentant *kafiri!*"

Uncle Mark turned sharply, expecting to see the beggar's head go flying out of the open window.

"*Hau*, old bull," he said to the angry man. "I did not know you could speak Arabic."

Musa did not hear him; he was looking the old beggar up and down and wondering just where on earth he had seen the blatant creature before. Finally, he shook his head, defeated, and Uncle Mark explained to the beggar, as patiently as to an imbecile, that even stray dogs off the street knew that Musa did not give anyone anything.

"I will pay," the beggar promised.

Now Musa gaped. Uncle Mark laughed suddenly and observed, with some satisfaction, that money had not lost its old habit of making people forget who they were and where they were.

369

"I have money now," the beggar said to him. "I can buy you tea now, uncle?"

"Thank you very much," Uncle Mark accepted. "Musa, you heard the man."

Musa swore at him.

The beggar jingled his pocketful of coins and grinned sincerely, then said to Musa, "I can buy you tea too, old man."

Musa was at a loss what to do with him. This was not at all the kind of relationship he wanted from Crossroads and this was turning out to be another mad day, indeed.

"I'll give you tea," he said. "But you will have to pay for *mandazi*."

The beggar was ecstatic. They shook hands over it and Uncle Mark wondered just how long this good feeling would last.

"Have you ever played draughts?" he asked the beggar.

"Draughts?" asked the beggar.

"Sit down; I'll show you," said Uncle Mark.

The beggar obeyed, sitting on the edge of the chair in case he was ordered to vacate it in a hurry.

Uncle Mark whistled happily as he rearranged the pieces on the board.

Chapter Forty-Three

The hills were not the same anymore, Janet had heard it rumoured, but the full extent of their devastation was shocking.

Just as Aids had deprived the valley of its life, the loggers had deprived the hills of their cover, leaving them grotesquely naked and vulnerable to the vagaries of the weather. Where once they had been shrouded in mystery and the promise of romantic adventure, the hills were now plain and bare with nothing to offer to an intrepid heart.

She drove all over the hills, looking for privacy. Wherever they stopped, the car stood out like a burned out stump, an obscene eyesore in the bare rocky surroundings which could be seen for miles around.

Finally, lost for alternatives, she drove to the one place she had resisted returning to all her life. Broker had already made his pilgrimage there, first with Frank and the children, and then many times alone to brood and to pray and to try to turn back the clock.

It was an anti-climactic return for Janet; she knew she should not have come back the minute she set eyes on it. The quiet mountain glade where they had hidden away for hours was now an open, nondescript place, hard and bare and inhospitable. The old brook was a sickly, grey stream and the grass along its banks was coarse and dry from exposure. The ebony tree under which her son was conceived was long gone, murdered in its prime to make wood for the coffins, and in its place sat an impenetrably thorny bush, thick and useless. Even the sunset, when it finally came, was no longer the golden red heart that had warmed their own hearts and fired their minds with passion, but a drab white-hot disc that seared the eyeballs and filled the hearts with dread.

Everything she saw made her want to cry.

"This may be the saddest day of my life," Broker said to her. "But coming home was the best decision I ever made."

"Where did you go?" she finally asked him.

"Everywhere," he told her.

"What did you do?" she asked.

"Everything," he told her and laughed. "Nearly everything."

371

He had nearly sold a visiting French cargo ship to Japanese investors, who thought they were buying a Zanzibari trawler. The deal had come unstuck, however, when the ship was seized by the Ports Authority, for discharging waste into the harbour.

"You should have seen the captain's face when his would-be new masters showed up to bail him out," Broker laughed.

She laughed with him. She had often laughed, though with greater gaiety, when they had come here. It lifted his spirit. But it also saddened him.

"I'm sorry I wasted your time," he said to her. "You deserved greater happiness than I could ever give you."

"I was once happy with you too," she said to him.

"Really happy?"

"Really, really happy."

She stopped suddenly and listened to herself. Was this her or was it someone else speaking? Was this Janet, sitting in this place, speaking like this to the man who had turned her life all upside down and inside out and made a total mockery of it? The man she had vowed would never let set foot in her heart again? Was this really, really her?

It was.

The buzzing in her ears was gone and, it seemed, someone had picked the cotton out of her ears and the rocks out of her head and it was clear and full of light. She was so light-headed she wanted to cry.

On the day of their wedding, Broker had carried her home on the back of a borrowed bicycle, and taken her all over Crossroads, to show her off to the people who had said he would come to nothing, and to spite her father. Along the way, he had stopped the bicycle to announce to utterly astounded people that he had just married the daughter of the Imam, Maalim Juma Maalim, to be his wife for life. Janet had laughed till she thought she would fall off the bicycle; laughed till she cried.

They sat side by side on the bank, their feet dangling in the stream exactly as they had sat many days long ago. Only now the water did not reach up to their feet and there was a solid and visible gap between them, a gap they knew would never close again.

"What happened to your other women?" she asked him.

"Which other women?" he asked her.

"Your other women?" she said.

"My other women?" he smiled warmly. "The ones with whom I squandered wealth and health?"

He had no idea what had happened to most of them. They had decamped the moment they learned he was sick and dying, vanished into the past without leaving a trace of their passing; everyone one of them except Jemina. But he could not tell Janet about Jemina now; that would serve no purpose at all.

"They are all dead now, I suppose," he told her instead. "They too thought Aids was something that happened to other people only."

"And condoms were for fools and cowards?" she asked.

"Something like that," he said laughing.

It saddened and horrified her. It grieved her that death had become such a familiar feature of her people's life that they could laugh at it. And it horrified her to realise that, had Broker stayed in Crossroads, and had he not abandoned her when he did, she too would have been as sick as he was now, if not already dead from the plague. Condoms had not come to Crossroads until long after the people had started dying.

Epilogue

Shortly after the new Mobil petrol station was commissioned, Bakari Ben Broker passed away peacefully in his sleep and was buried next to Janet's grain store.

It was the biggest funeral ever held in Crossroads, after Big George's *Mercedes* funeral. Everyone said so, loudly and with enthusiasm. Some said it with a malevolent laughter in their eyes, but many had tears in their eyes as they marvelled at the marble headstone that Broker had carried in the boot of his car for the purpose.

Uncle Mark and Mzee Musa were there too, looking extremely uncomfortable in old black suits that had, somehow, survived the ruin and despair of Crossroads. The beggar had come with them, followed them there without knowing or caring where they were going but very excited by their strange attire. And finding himself in a place with so many people, he had decided it was business as usual and gone about asking the mourners to give him money. Whereupon Uncle Mark had taken him by the ear, pulled him aside and said to him, "You can't do that here. These people are sad; their friend, and your friend, the Mayor is dead."

The old beggar had nodded solemnly and been on his best behaviour from then on.

Kata and his wives were there too, supporting the devastated Grandmother between them, and not quite certain how to mourn the passing of this peculiar son of Crossroads, who was also their relative; this raging enigma that had come back from the dead, dominated and baffled their lives for a while, then returned to the dead.

Chief Chupa came too, to offer sympathy to Janet and her Grandmother and to confirm that his job was secure, now that the only threat to his unassailable authority as Chief of Crossroads was, indeed, over. The school heads and the church elders came too, and Big Youth brought out a party of schoolboys to dig the grave.

All of the few friends Broker had made in the short time he had been back came too, along with the many people who had hated him, and the multitudes of cynics who would not believe

374

that the man who had brought Mobil's giant Pegasus back to life, and threatened to resurrect Crossroads, was himself now dead.

As the mammoth crowd gathered at the graveyard for the ceremony, Musa insisted on saying a Muslim prayer for the dead man for, though Broker himself did not know it, he was a fellow believer, a staunch Muslim at heart and a good friend. When Musa had finished his prayer, Pastor Bat conducted the burial service. He was decked out in black and white, like an ageing crow, and assisted by a sad, old deacon who himself appeared on the point of death.

"I baptised him when he was born," the Pastor said, of the dead man, forgetting that Broker had come to him a mature rogue and a hardened sinner. "And when he was grown, I confirmed him and when he was ready I married him, and when he was bad I prayed for his deliverance. Now that he is dead, all I can do for him, is to bury him so he may return to meet his Maker. Many people, no doubt, liked and loved the man we have come here to bury today. But there were also those who, for reasons of their own, disliked and hated him. Such is the fate of man. We shall not, therefore, judge the man by his enemies, any more than we shall judge him by his friends. Whatever sins he committed are now a matter between him and his God. Ashes to ashes and dust to dust. May the Almighty God deal with his soul in whatever way He sees fitting."

And the gathering intoned, "Amen."

And it was so done. Another life's journey completed, another chapter closed, another saga concluded.

As the coffin was lowered into its lonely grave, Uncle Mark finally understood Broker's words, regarding the many new ideas and the madness he had injected in Crossroads. True to his devious nature, Broker had not done any of it, not the least of it, for nothing. He had done it all solely for himself; partly to please himself and, partly, in the hope that, if he seemed busy enough, death might forget him for a while.

"The rogue did it to get us here," thought Uncle Mark, with a wry smile. "To gather Crossroads round this grave."

The old rogue had succeeded in all these endeavours, and in a way that not even he could have imagined possible when he had begun.

"He must be happy with himself now," Uncle Mark thought. "Laughing that roguish laugh of his, from wherever he is watching us."

Their communal duty done, the crowd quickly dispersed, some to attend to other burials and others to talk about Broker's burial for the rest of their lives. Big Youth and his gang set about shovelling soil into the grave and Frank took Janet's hand and led her back to the house. Her children followed silently and Pastor Bat fell in step with Janet to wonder loudly what would happen to the orphanage, now that the saviour of Crossroads was dead.

Frank answered for her and told the pastor not to worry.

"Everything is taken care of," he assured. "Broker thought of everything."

"Who will take care of the … things?" asked the Pastor, nervously.

"Janet is in full control," said Frank. "Don't worry about it."

The Pastor sighed and wiped sweat from his forehead. He looked sadder than ever.

"Come in and have some tea," Janet said to him. "I can't thank you enough for what you have done today."

The Pastor perked up then, as he accompanied her to the house.

Uncle Mark and Mzee Musa came up to express their grief. They declined her invitation to tea, said their farewells and went to round up their beggar. They found him gnawing on a chicken bone he had charmed out of the women who were cooking for the mourners. He was entertaining them with tales of how Broker and he had been the best of friends, when Musa took him by the ear, took the bone from his hand and threw it in the bush. Then Uncle Mark wrapped an arm round his shoulders and started him on their hike back to Crossroads.

"*Ni kweli Meya amekwenda kabisa?*" he asked.

"*Ni kweli,*" answered Uncle Mark. "It's true, the Mayor is gone for ever. We'll all miss him."

"Who will buy me tea?" asked the beggar.

"We'll see," Uncle Mark said, patting him gently. "We'll see."

They came to the gate and the man stopped to look back at Broker's burial place. The boys were heaping soil on the grave. Big Youth was dusting the headstone. It was the first burial mound at the homestead.

Uncertainty encircled Mzee Musa's heart, as he recalled what legend said about Crossroads' burial mounds:

Where there was one today, there may be two tomorrow. Two would turn to four and four to eight. They turned into monsters that thrived on human suffering and ate away until they had eaten entire homesteads.

Recalling the legend, Mzee Musa shuddered. Uncle Mark had travelled too long and too far to believe in spirits and things, but he too shivered.

THE END

36473497R00216

Made in the USA
Charleston, SC
07 December 2014